LARKBARROW
A Story of Exmoor

[signature]

Paddy King-Fretts

HALSGROVE

First published in Great Britain in 2007

Copyright © 2007 Paddy King-Fretts

British Library Cataloguing-in-Publication Data
A CIP record for this title is available from the British Library

ISBN 978 1 84114 646 1

HALSGROVE
Halsgrove House
Rylands Farm Industrial Estate, Bagley Green,
Wellington, Somerset TA21 9PZ
Tel: 01823 653777
Fax: 01823 665294
email: sales@halsgrove.com
website: www.halsgrove.com

Printed and bound in Great Britain by CPI, Bath

Front cover illustration
'*Larkbarrow mid-winter*' by Jack Hoar Tel: 01769 572131 e-mail: jackhoar@hotmail.com

Principal Characters

BECKY CARTER. An attractive young countrywoman living with her parents on Exmoor.

SAM HAWKINS. A young farmer and childhood friend of Becky's living near Exford.

MIKE DALEY. A sharp, worldly and quick-witted soldier stationed temporarily in Exford.

DAISY GUNN. A harlot and thief who becomes a close friend of Becky.

ROSE HATTON. A wealthy and beautiful young war widow now living in Dulverton.

EDDIE BRIGHT. A violent and ruthless gang leader from the Plymouth underworld.

Others of note

ERNEST CARTER. Ex-soldier and warden of Larkbarrow, a large farm, set high on Exmoor.

DORIS CARTER. His wife. She and Ernest are Becky's parents.

JACK CARTER. Their son. Away for the duration of the war with the Royal Navy.

DREW HAWKINS. Owner of Hayes Farm, Exford and a life-long friend of Ernest Carter.

BARBARA HAWKINS. His wife. She and Drew are Sam's parents.

COLONEL MILES ASHCROFT. Retired (WWI) who has taken Larkbarrow Farm as his hunting lodge.

PAT STEER. An Exford village girl and friend of Becky and Sam.

MAVIS VELLACOTT. Another village girl and friend of Becky and Sam.

GERRY CHUGG. Friend of Sam.

GREG THORNE. Another of Sam's friends.

MOTHER SUPERIOR OF 'OUR SHEPHERD OF MERCY', ST MARGARET'S CONVENT, TAUNTON.

SISTER BERNADETTE. A lesbian nun.

SISTER MARIA. A cold and brutal bully.

FATHER O'CONNELL. A visiting priest responsible for adoption procedures.

CHIEF SUPERINTENDENT MARK MASON. Head of Plymouth City Police Task Force.

INSPECTOR CHRIS MARTIN. Plymouth City CID.

3

KEN MAELMO, 'KENNY THE SWEDE'. A villain and Eddie Bright's right hand man.

RICKY HATCH. One of Eddie Bright's men.

HESTOR BARCLAY. Rose Hatton's ailing father who lives with her at Duxhams, Dulverton.

CAPTAIN HARRY MAIDSTONE, 17th/21st Lancers. Rose Hatton's cousin.

CAPTAIN 'SPIFFEY' FOXLEY, The Light Dragoons. A friend of Harry Maidstone.

BRIGADIER STAINFORTH, OBE. Senior Medical Officer, British Base Hospital, near Caen, Normandy.

SISTER MILDRED LUSCOMBE. Staff Nurse, Burns Unit, Queen Victoria Hospital, East Grinstead.

DR COHEN. Senior Clinical Psychologist, Musgrove Park Military Hospital, Taunton.

WARRANT OFFICER SANDY HOLMES, R.A.F. Survivor of crashed Wellington bomber.

FLIGHT SERGEANT JIMMY BOND, DFM, R.A.F. Another aircrew survivor.

Prologue

21st August 1943

For the moment LA 986 was holding her own, but only just. Every time he tried to ease his foot on the rudder-bar Flight Lieutenant Tony Boardman felt the Wellington slewing heavily to port, pulling at him like an angry horse. L for Love was crippled. Next to him Chris Amebury, the short, dark-haired Canadian second pilot, was operating the wheel for the tail fin control tabs and Boardman could sense him struggling.

Seconds earlier the crew had decided to stick with the aircraft. He had given them the option of baling out as he always promised he would but no: 'One in, all in,' had been their response and that had been that. Half the cowling had been torn from the port engine and he glanced at the twisted propeller blade, its tip bent and torn by a round from one of the Me.109s. How they had escaped fire he would never know for the outer fuel tank had been holed also and, from under the wing there had been that black, oily smoke.

But Jerry had been good and L for Love had been lucky. Had it not been for the heavy layer of cloud just north of Cherbourg they would have stood no chance. Group H.Q. had predicted that the sky there would be clear of enemy: most activity would be over Pas de Calais so they said. Like hell it was. The pair of fighters must have come up on the prowl from Nantes. And by now the lucky sods would be back down again, grinning away as they reported their kill; most likely sitting back in the sunshine and enjoying a cup of coffee.

"Captain to crew. All right and thanks for that. Your choice but I'm glad...didn't fancy it myself either." He moved automatically as Chris Amebury's flying jacket brushed against his arm. "We'll stay up here 'til we get near the coast...*if we bloody well can*," he thought to himself. "How long d'you reckon, Jimmy? Gimme an ETA."

He waited, imagining the navigator bending over the chart table, squinting through the narrow beam of his navigating lamp. The intercom clicked and he heard Flight Sergeant Jimmy Bond DFM breathing heavily into his mouth-piece. "Twenty-five minutes, skip." The deep voice cleared its throat. "If you can keep her at one eighty...manage that for twenty minutes or so an' you can start to bring her down. Course...er...three two zero. Cloud base should be around fifteen hundred."

"And the top of Dartmoor's about two thousand, eh?" Boardman muttered, catching Bond's laugh. "OK, it'll be tight though. Talk me in as we go, my hands're full. I repeat...course three two zero." Glancing down he reached for the compass ring to change the setting.

"Roger, skipper."

"Oh, and Jimmy, where does that bring us?"

"Just east of Exeter, skip. Said you wanted to stay well clear of the place."

"Christ yes...bloody ack ack nearly had us last week. Dozey buggers...thanks." He paused. "Captain to Radio Ops...anything at all?" Sandy Holmes, the wireless operator, had been with them for nine missions. The tall gangly youth with spectacles had been turned down twice by the medics before the RAF finally accepted him. 'Must've been dead pushed to let *him* in,' Chris Amebury had drawled when Holmes presented himself. But the boy was bright, as the Radio Operator's report had shown. Usually the young Sergeant managed to keep contact with base but not tonight. The long burst from the first 109 that ripped through the fuselage had taken the DF aerial on the roof with it.

"Nothing, skipper. Nothing at all...RT or WT and I'm trying everywhere." The youngster's voice rose as though it was all his fault and he was having to own up about it. "The last contact with base was when Jerry jumped us back there," he offered. "When I told 'em we'd had a good run and gave 'em a fix."

"Hmm...OK, emergency procedure then. Y'know the drill...Jerry knows we're here so everyone else may as well. Just keep plugging away...try anything." Boardman licked his lips. He felt tired, dog tired. They were flying blind and now they were deaf and mute as well, and on one engine at that. It was a mess, and to think that this was almost his last run before his tour was up. That promised spell of leave was within touching distance and then the posting...but now this.

It was going to be Lancasters, they told him, and back to bombing. No more of this sneaky radio eavesdropping stuff over occupied France. Everyone was needed up front. Raids on the Ruhr had increased and just last week they had started to bomb Rome. The Wimpeys had done them well but they were getting old and were being phased out. Their bombing days were numbered and all that was left were either covert missions like this when they went hunting for radio traffic from the maquis or out over the Western Approaches looking for magnetic mines.

He pulled a face and glanced at his co-pilot then raised his fist. They could make it, *would* make it but fuel was getting low. The needles of the port gauges were sitting flat on zero; nothing there. Chris Amebury and Flt Sgt Duckworth, the flight engineer, had fed the fuel, or what was left of it, from the port tanks across to starboard. God alone knew what they had done with it all or where it had gone but the needles on the starboard gauges were now beginning to flicker as well. He tried to throttle back. So far so good: the starboard engine was responding well enough but the revs were too high. Flying like this was thirsty work for the Wellington on her one engine was struggling. They were clawing their way forward rather than flying smoothly.

He licked his lips again then wiped his mouth. The odds were fifty-fifty but she seemed steady enough and he was tempted to go for it. St Mawgan and Newquay were coming up then Chivenor, but St Athan was still within reach and right now he fancied a hot bath and cool, clean sheets. He yawned, opening his mouth wide then shook his head to clear the tiredness.

"Navigator to Captain. Land should be coming up soon, skip. 'Bout five minutes, I reckon. Start bringing her down whenever you like." Boardman eased back the throttle. As soon as the noise died away, the aircraft seemed to relax. Like a runner slowing to a jog, he thought.

"Captain to crew. All right, listen in. I'm going to try for home. Fuel's low and we might have to pancake, but not yet…it's far too wet down there," he joked. "For the moment anyway, everyone stay put…and fingers crossed."

＊

It took them a full fifteen minutes, not five, to reach the coast. But they were out of cloud and into the early morning August sunlight. As soon as he could, Jimmy Bond took a fix on Start Point. They changed course to zero two zero and began the long run up Lyme Bay, keeping themselves well to the east of Exeter's nervous anti-aircraft gunners and crossed the coast above the cliffs. Here they changed course again and turned north to follow the line of the Exe valley.

Less than ten minutes later, Chris Amebury pointed to the gauges. Boardman nodded: it was decision time. The Cornish airfields were behind them: Chivenor and St Athan were equidistant but to reach South Wales meant crossing the Bristol Channel. More water. He paused, his head nodding from side to side as he weighed the options. Suddenly the starboard engine began to splutter.

That was it and Boardman cursed, thinking quickly. They weren't going to make it, weren't going to make anywhere. His body sagged then he took a deep breath and scanned the ground ahead. "Captain to crew. Sorry chaps but we're out of juice…we're going in." Amebury pointed ahead towards the sharply rising land and Boardman nodded. "OK. Get yourselves ready," he ordered. "Move t'your positions then stand by…and good luck."

One by one the crew unplugged their intercoms and moved to the metal cross-frame between the wings where they sat facing aft with their backs against the steel brace. Billy Higgins, the front gunner, his hair dishevelled but grinning away like a terrier emerging from a hole, was the last to join them.

"Straight ahead, look." Amebury pointed. "Exmoor…bare arsed as hell. A goddamned wilderness…but flat. Could be good."

Boardman nodded again, his eyes moving from the instrument panel to the shoulder of high ground in front of them. "We're too bloody high," he muttered. "I'll have to take her round…ease up as well. I'll try running in at one twenty, then drop her down to one ten…then in. Yuh?" He was talking partly to himself, only his eyes and hands moving. As he opened the throttle to begin his turn, the engine rose but then spluttered back again. "*Come on, come on,*" he hissed. "Wheel, Chris…gimme a bit more." Boardman pressed hard on the rudder. "She's coming…*come* on, my beauty." The two pilots stared ahead.

"There look." The second pilot's voice rose. "Beyond that little valley…the long piece of open ground with all those sheep…opposite that farmhouse," he cried. "It's flat…looks wet." Boardman eased back the throttle. Once more the engine coughed then cleared throatily before settling again.

"She's coming." Boardman's eyes were staring straight ahead. "OK…we're going in. Stand by to switch off. Easy now. Down…down. Come on, down you come." Suddenly the ground was rushing towards the cockpit. "Standby," he shouted. "Standby…hang on, hang on. Right…shut down, *now.*"

The scrape of vegetation along the fuselage rose to a long whooshing roar as the Wellington bellied. The aircraft lurched to the right but then bucked before slewing sideways and continuing like that. Boardman watched fascinated: it all seemed to happen in slow motion. He saw sheep everywhere running about panic-stricken and wondered how many they had killed. Suddenly the port wing dipped and she bucked again. He heard a scream from somewhere behind. A low bank appeared from nowhere and his body was hurled forward. His head whipped back and he shut his eyes but they had come to a stop.

For some time there was nothing, just the pinging of hot metal and the bitter tang of cordite and fuel. Then he heard the scream again and his eyes opened. It was one of the four behind him. God knows what had happened to the poor devils when the aircraft bucked like she did, but one of them was hurt and it sounded bad. The scream came again: something about his legs.

Boardman tried to move but a sharp knife stabbed at his neck. He tried again. This time the pain was worse and he winced. Beside him Chris Amebury had slumped forward but they were down. L for Love, the dear old lady who was soon due to be pensioned off, had made it as far as Exmoor. She had brought them back to Blighty.

Part One

HARSH REALITIES

Chapter One

Ernest Carter cupped his hands over the end of the long broom handle. Then, leaning forward slowly, he rested his chin. Even from where he was standing in front of the stable block he could hear her cursing as she struggled to put the ladder against the wall, and he smiled knowingly, as fathers sometimes do.

Becky was ready for more than Larkbarrow: she was ready for life itself. At first the idea of her leaving had upset them for he and Doris would be on their own. But Sam Hawkins had begun to court her. Later that morning he would be in for his midday dinner and Ernest glanced up, shading his eyes. Right now, he was across the valley working in the sheep pens; a hard task at the best of times, let alone today when it promised to be hot.

And Becky was no longer a child. Everyone told him that, even the Colonel. Proud father that he was, Ernest was a man nonetheless and he could see why she stirred men so. Even as he watched she reached up to fiddle under her blouse, then rolled her shoulder to ease the discomfort such confinement brought. For a moment he stared as any man might who came across a young woman attending to herself. But enough! Surprised at himself, and suddenly ashamed, he stood up straight and squared his shoulders.

*

Her task complete, Becky stepped back from the ladder to inspect her neat handiwork. The soft, creamy rose blooms, each shaded in its own lilac pink, were the Colonel's favourites. It had been three years since he had fussed over her while they planted the bare roots, yet she and her father still laughed at how he had been so particular as to what went where and how far from the wall the plants had to be.

The roses, Madame something-or-other, had been brought over from France, from the chateau close to where he had been wounded at the end of the Great War. His gardeners at Court Grange near Porlock had nursed them carefully and the blooms, now spreading themselves across the front of the house, were their offspring. Brushing back a lock of hair, she stepped forward and lifted one to her nose. The rich fragrance, strong in the morning dew, made her gasp and she savoured it again, more slowly this time. It was that very scent, the Colonel told them, which reminded him of the nurse who had cared for him.

Already the early morning sun had risen over Dunkery and she could feel its warmth pressing through the shoulders of her cotton blouse. The low cloud was lifting, as her father said it would and it was going to be a glorious August day, perfect for exercising the Colonel's hunters. He would be coming over after lunch and she listened to the sounds from the stableyard beyond the farmhouse as her father bustled about, whistling cheerfully and occasionally calling out to the horses. Always the perfectionist, he never left anything to chance especially when the Colonel was visiting.

Suddenly she crouched, holding her hand out to the little black cat with the white bib and two white socks. It was hers and she waited patiently. For a moment, the cat wavered undecided with one paw raised and only the tip of her tail twitching. Then she miaowed silently and trotted forward to stand against her friend with her back arched, rubbing herself affectionately.

Two months ago, when her father found the five kittens in their nest in the barn, he had taken three and drowned them. Becky had cried unashamedly, especially when she found the nest deserted. It was not until a month later, when they were carrying hay, that they saw the little cat as she hunted at the edge of the long grass. Behind her, struggling and tumbling in their efforts to keep up, were the two remaining kittens and Becky had been overjoyed.

"*Cum* on then." Becky picked her up and cradled her gently ignoring the cold wet paws.

✳

She should have been happy with the world but the same nagging doubt remained and this morning she felt uneasy. It was Sam. If only he could stay just as a friend, she mused, the same as he had always been. Ever since they had been children at school together she had liked him but now it was different. He and Jack, her elder brother, were good friends and when Sam came up to Larkbarrow she used to sit at the kitchen table listening to their tales when they returned from birds nesting or tickling trout. Sometimes they would allow her to accompany them and it would be Sam who took her hand as she scrambled through gaps in the hedge or hopped across a piece of boggy ground. His hair was for ever a mess and she remembered the short grey jumper with the diamond pattern he used to wear. They were just friends then, but things had changed.

Since his father had rented the grazing on the moorland across the valley, Sam Hawkins had taken to calling at the cottage and her mother had made a habit of asking him in. He was tall and strongly built and his chubby childhood face had ripened, apple-like, into one of rosy ruggedness. What was left of his unruly light brown hair had flattened and receded, giving him the look of one older than his years, an impression enhanced by his soft brown eyes. Sometimes the eyes would dance merrily but mostly they gazed unhurriedly. Like his father, Sam was a gentle, caring man.

At first, she would run out to greet him, even while he was tying his pony to the hitching ring on the shippon wall. Jack was away in the Navy and, for her, Sam sort of took his place. They would chat together in the yard and later in the house, gossiping innocently about village life. Exford seemed miles away but Sam brought it closer with all his news. Hayes Farm where he lived was but a mile the far side and he seemed to know everything that went on.

Then one day, while her mother and father were over at the farm, he had taken her hand. She remembered her surprise and her sudden hot flush but remembered also his brown eyes that were staring back down at her. As he asked her to ride out with him, his thumb kept rubbing across the back of her hand. His voice was softer than usual. "You're twenty now, maid," he reminded her. "P'raps time's come for us to be walking out. Y'can't be stoppin' out y'ere all tucked away 'til you'm an old biddy, y'know."

She had laughed hesitantly but he had kept hold of her hand and asked her to ride with him while he checked the sheep. Her father had been delighted and it was from then that her mother asked him to stop for tea or a meal whenever he was on his rounds. Becky still liked him but had become aware of his feelings and that her parents were encouraging him.

Later this morning he would join them for dinner in the parlour were he would sit crouched over his plate of cold meat and potatoes, clenching his knife and fork tightly and chatting politely with her parents. But eventually her father would rise and signal for her mother to follow. Then she and Sam would be on their own and he would begin again, asking her to stop over in the village with Pat Steer or Mavis Vellacott so she could go up to the Sixpenny Dances in the village hall. It would be the usual performance today; she knew it would and, as she reached out to pick off a deadhead, she wrinkled her nose.

Then, all of a sudden, she stopped and looked round, frowning and cocking her head to hear better. At first she thought it was a vehicle coming down the lane from the Exford road so she craned her neck to see over the bracken at the bottom of the garden. But it was a different sound, bigger and louder and the engine seemed to be stopping and starting.

She looked round at her father's shout but turned back again, this time searching anxiously for the source of the noise. And there it was. Suddenly, from beneath the clouds, she saw the great shape. It was a plane, huge and it was getting lower. It was going to crash, even she could see that. She stood helplessly, quite unable to move. Then her father called again, this time his voice was raised. He was shouting for her urgently and she started to run.

*

The ewe was sitting awkwardly on her rump but Sam Hawkins had firm hold of her. She was propped against his legs and, as he bent forward to examine her feet, he could feel hot, sour breath against his face. From time to time she would grunt heavily or kick out. Eventually he stood, pushed her away with his knees and stretched himself, lifting his cap as he did so. Already it was hot.

Earlier he had seen Becky come into the garden with the ladder. Before that she

13

had been tending the beds and he had watched as she bent this way and that. Every now and then she stopped and straightened, occasionally wiping her brow with her arm. The sight of her, even from this distance, darkened his thoughts. It was the idea of her warm body and her sweat, and how her chest would be rising and falling. He forced himself to work on, catching and turning sheep after sheep until he, too, was hot and breathless. Such thoughts excited him, the more today for they were to meet at noon when, after the long, slow lunch with her parents, they would be alone together. He grinned at nothing in particular, and set his jaw but then he, too, turned and looked up at the sound of the crippled aircraft.

He could see at once that the Wellington was coming down. It was very low, almost skimming the high ground beyond the sheep pens and for a moment he stood watching. It was close now, close enough for him to see the two pilots. Suddenly the engine cut and she seemed to glide down, no more than a few hundred yards from where he was standing. He heard the loud swooshing, grinding of the fuselage as it raced across the marshy ground then a sharp crack as part of a wing broke off.

There were men inside who would need help. As he ran to his pony tied to the hedge, Sam called to the dogs. There might be a fire. He had heard about these things and wondered what he might find. Perhaps he would be in time but he had to hurry. "*Come on…come on*. Hup…hup." He ran beside the pony then jumped across its withers, throwing one leg over the broad back. "*Yaaah*," he shouted. "Gid on…gid on." As the animal gathered pace, he crouched low and hissed encouragement into the flattened ears.

✳

"Gently," Sam gasped. "Steady there…gently…steady now." Carefully he eased the second of the two men to the ground. Sam Hawkins was strong yet even he found the weight of the injured men a burden. They had managed to open the emergency door halfway along the fuselage and he had come across them sitting there unable to jump out. So he had carried them, one at a time, to where a patch of thick heather would give them some cushion from the hard ground. "*Four* more, you say? Cuh…four, be damned."

"Yes," the injured man gasped. He was in pain and his face was contorted. "And the two up front are trapped…can't move, neither of 'em." He sighrd and groaned quietly then looked across to his companion who was sitting hunched forward with his head in his hands. "The skipper told us to get out…said he'd be all right and that help was on its way." Sandy Holmes paused and turned back to his rescuer. "But it's not, is it? I'm the wireless op and I should know. Don't think anybody heard us calling."

"Can't say for sure." Sam stood and turned towards the aircraft then glanced back. Way beyond them down at the bottom of the slope he could see the cart from Larkbarrow. Ernest Carter was urging his horse across the shallow ford where the stream flowed over a series of dark flat rocks. Becky was standing in the cart holding the reins while her father pulled at the horse's head. They too must have seen the plane and would be here soon. "They'm coming...help that is. I'll go an' see they others."

The airman nodded then looked up. "Take care for God's sake...and look out for fire." He watched as Sam hurried back to the aircraft, then lay back and closed his eyes.

✳

Inside the fuselage it was dark. Sam could not see the smoke but the bitter fumes of burning paint, of spilled fuel and the sharp tang of cordite made him catch his breath. He coughed, gulping in the foul air and coughed again. Then he heard a voice. As he wriggled across the floor towards the door, the crewman called out to him. It was his leg, he complained, that and his right arm. Sam saw the long tear in the grey trousers and the deep crimson smudge of blood where the lower half of his right leg was bent strangely.

He jumped out again and stood in the doorway with both arms raised towards him. "Steady there...*woah*...steady." He reached forward and took the man in his arms before drawing him further out. The aiman barely moved.

"It's the skipper, mate...the skipper an' Number Two. They're bad." A sudden whoosh of smoke and flame from the broken wing made Sam stumble. Whatever fuel remained had exploded. "There's not much of that," the man cried. "Bugger all in fact...skip's OK but the Number Two's bad."

"Here, I'll take him." It was Becky. They had left the cart by a dip in the ground and had run forward to help. Sam smiled at her, half in greeting and half in relief.

"Thanks Becks...take the other side and mind that leg. Seems bad." He paused and they looked at one another. He smiled again this time reassuringly. The fear went from her eyes and she returned his smile but he could see she was afraid. "Here...take him...I'm going back inside."

"*No*, Sam. *Don't*...please. *Look*." By now she was supporting the injured man and could only nod at the flames spreading along the wing. "You can't."

"Got to, Becks...got to. There's more still in there." He looked at her father who had hurried to join them. "There's one of they fire extinguisher things, Mr Carter. Come on, quick now."

Sam ran to the door and scrambled in only to reappear moments later. "Here look," he cried pulling on the cord around the neck of the red canister. A jet of foam spewed out. "Over there," he shouted. "Right on it...close as you can." He turned back to the door and heaved himself inside.

It took them almost two hours. The pilot was the easier of the two remaining: his neck and shoulder had been damaged but no more than that. But the second pilot was worse and Sam had been struggling to ease him out of his seat when the sound of voices near the door told him that help had arrived. The Home Guard from Exford and an ambulance from Minehead together with a number of volunteers had reached the site. He was the last to emerge from the wreck and for some time he stood bent forward with his hands on his knees, listening as soldiers were given their orders.

*

Becky and her father had gone. They had left with two of the airmen in the cart and the rescuers who remained were talking amongst themselves. Those in charge had gone also, most likely with the injured men, and he waited to see what needed to be done but nobody seemed to know. It looked like it was over.

He nodded briefly at the short, grey haired Bill Scriven from the village and at one of the soldiers he recognised, then eased his way past those gathered around the injured men to where he had tethered his pony. He was hot and his head ached. His shirt had been torn and there was blood on his hands. He felt too tired to ride so he walked slowly, leading the pony until he came to a spring below the sheep pens where he paused to wash himself.

Once back with the flock, he found his coat and knapsack. He took out the bottle of cold tea which he drank straight down, savouring the cool sweetness which refreshed him. It had been a wild, mad morning with sights and smells he had never dreamed of thrust upon him. He had no idea what he was doing rather he had just leapt at whatever caught his eye. As he sat with his back against the bank he reached out and picked lazily at the last of the foxgloves.

He remembered how the man with the shattered leg had cried out. Most likely he would have to lose it: they would cut it off just below the knee where he had seen it bent almost double. He tried to imagine what a leg would be like with just a raw stump, and he closed his eyes. He pursed his lips then looked across at the sheep who stared back silently save for one or two who stamped angrily at the dogs.

The shout made him start and he sat up. It was one of the soldiers running down the hill towards him. So he was wanted after all. There would be questions, no doubt, lots of them and he sighed wearily: the sheep would have to wait. He rose clumsily and walked over to the hurdles where he wrenched one out of the ground, opening it from the others to let his flock run free.

2.

"I can't thank you enough, Becky m'dear." Colonel Miles Ashcroft rose from behind the mahogany desk. It was almost noon and the sun was flooding into the oak panelled study yet, even so, she could smell the musty odour of damp and old wood ash. She always would; as long as he kept Larkbarrow closed for most of the year there would be no escaping nature's efforts to reclaim the place. And now it was time to shut up once more. The houseguests had departed and tomorrow he would be returning to Porlock, leaving the farmhouse in the care of her father. "They had a marvellous time, y'know. You and your mother really made a fuss of them...spoiled them and they loved it."

"'Twas a real pleasure, sir." Becky Carter looked at him and smiled back at the twinkling eyes. The Colonel, diminutive, dapper and immaculately dressed, had first taken Larkbarrow Farm as his hunting lodge long before the war. He loved the remoteness and would often come out by himself sometimes staying for weeks on end. Occasionally he would bring his invalid wife who they would find sitting in her long wicker chair in the garden, but more often he would be on his own.

Then, a few years ago, he had taken full tenancy, engaging Ernest Carter and his wife as guardians. The Carters lived nearby, in the rough stone cottage on the other side of the track no more than a short walk from the main house. As soon as she left school, Becky joined them and became an additional pair of hands. It seemed obvious and at first she loved working with the horses but she missed her friends and the daily bustle of village life she knew as a schoolgirl.

"Look, I'd like you to take this." As he limped towards her, his deep, gravelly voice seemed to rasp more sharply than ever. "It's just a little something to put by...for a rainy day or something else perhaps. Mmm?" His eyes creased kindly.

"Oh, thankee, sir. Thank you ever so much." She smiled shyly, took the brown envelope and looked away, momentarily confused. "Don't know what to say but 'tis very kind of you."

"Don't even think of it, m'dear. You've earned it, every penny." Ashcroft's eyes moved from her face. Becky Carter had most certainly developed from the awkward little girl he remembered. She was now a fine young woman and he glanced at her admiringly. She had come ready to ride out with her father and was dressed in jodhpurs, the black riding boots he had bought her and an open-necked check shirt. Her appearance and the way she carried herself were powerful.

No wonder young Jamie Wedburn and Harry Oldfield had been unable to take their eyes off her. Much to his amusement, the two young guests had competed for her attention all week, sometimes together but sometimes furtively when one or the other considered a clandestine trip out to the stables might go undetected. There was for sure, in those heavy-lidded eyes an earthiness which would catch any man's attention.

Yet there was also a delightful, almost childlike innocence about her, a purity he cherished. Perhaps that was why he was so fond of her. As she lifted her head and shrugged in embarrassment, the sun caught her mane of dark auburn hair she had allowed to fall free. "And my thanks go with it…really they do." He paused. "Now then, who're you taking out this afternoon?"

"Dastur, sir. I'll be riding him an' leadin' Smokey. Father's taking Fay…the new bay that came up last month."

"Fay, the big mare?" The Colonel looked down and rubbed his chin. "Taking three, eh? Well, yes…yes of course. Dammit, we'll need 'em all. We're staghunting already and there'll be cubbing as well in a couple of weeks."

"Aye, sir. Father thought as much." Becky toyed nervously with her top shirt button. As she waited, she changed weight from one foot to the other, unconsciously allowing her hip to push forward. "That'll be all then, sir?"

"Yes, yes, that's it…oh, Becky." He half turned, raising a finger as if something had all but slipped his mind. "There's just one thing. You ought to know how well your Sam did last week…when that Wellington came down. My word he was splendid." The Colonel straightened himself. "They were talking about it at Area headquarters the other night." Becky waited for him to go on. "In fact all of you were…an' I've told your father so." He shook his head and limped across to the door which he opened and stood aside for her to pass. "He's a good lad, that Sam. You've done yerself well there, m'dear. Mind you, he's damn lucky himself." He caught her smile and nodded.

"Thank you, sir." Miles Ashcroft watched her go, listening as her boots rang out on the flagstones before turning back to his desk. As he crouched to pull up the swivel chair behind him, he cocked an eye appreciatively.

✳

"Colonel reckons the war's going to get worse before 'tis better." Becky had been riding behind her father down the lane but they were now side by side picking their way across the open moor. Beyond them and down to their left the deep, heather-clad Doone Valley fell away steeply. Fay, the young mare her father was riding, shied as a pair of snipe sprung into the air from the piece of damp ground ahead. "Word is that more troops'll be coming afore long."

"*More?*" Becky collected up the bay she was leading. "Heavens…where're they going to put 'em all? Sam says Exford's full up already and they're even camping out on Winsford Hill."

"Aye…an'a right damned nuisance they are an' all." Her father adjusted his cap. "Rushing about as though they own the place. Causin' trouble in the pubs an' all…I dunno."

Becky looked across at him. He too had been a soldier in the Yeomanry and had often told them of the fun they'd had, even when the gun lines had been under fire. And he was still a soldier at heart as his straight back and the neatly clipped moustache reminded the world. "Bet you lot were just as bad," she joked, then laughed out loud when he shook his head. "Go on, Dad. Bet you were…even Corporals like you said you was."

"Oh aye, but us never went breakin' places up, an' going round fighting with villagers an' that. Us were all in tents, proper like, out the way…same as they lot up on Winsford Hill." They rode on in silence, each considering how the war had affected them and wondering what more it might bring. "Colonel said Sam did well t'other day." Becky glanced up sharply. She knew he would mention him. "'Es a good lad an' all…an' a good farmer at that. Same as his Dad."

She said nothing yet felt a sudden tension. Ernest Carter slowed and half stood in the saddle as his horse pulled down to rummage through the bog grass. "You're not turnin' him away are you, maid? Not sayin' no to him?" She saw him looking at her out of the corner of his eye. "'E's a fine young man is Sam an'…and well, Hayes Farm'll be his one day. Not got somebody else in mind, 'ave ye?"

"*No.*" She was surprised at the angry abruptness in her voice and shrugged moodily, looking away as she did so. It was always the same and already she could feel a dark cloud closing over what had been a pleasant day.

"Mother an' I were wondering, that's all, dear. Time's moving on, y'know."

"I *know*…you keep telling me." Now her voice was rising. "Sam's nice…an' good to me. Always has been but…but, I'm not ready for all that talk about marryin' an' that."

"Well, you'm a fine maid, Becks." Her father had turned round and leant towards her with one hand on his horse's rump. "Aye, as fine a maid as I know…look at how they young fellas at Larkbro' took to yer: them young gennelmen as were staying with the Colonel. Even they can see you for what you are." He turned back to pull up his horse. "I dunno, dear…it's just…."

"*Please* father." Becky let him move on ahead then followed him, leading her second horse carefully past a line of low gorse along the edge of the sheep track. "I *do* like Sam. I like him a lot, and Mr Hawkins as well, but I'm not *ready* for that." She caught her breath. "I can't be thinking of it. P'raps when this's all over, when Jack's back home again and we're all together. P'raps then…but don't keep going *on* so. You an' mother's for ever on about it."

"Just don' want to see yer miss a fine chance, that's all. At your age your mother'd bin married a year…and your Aunty Gwen not long after."

"But I'm *not* mother." She was talking to the back of his head but could see he was listening. "In any case it was different then. I don't like all this pushin', Dad. I asked you to stop, didn't I, and now you're on again. Honestly…it bain't right. I'm doing what I can up here for the Colonel and I'm pretty much happy at that"

19

"Aye." Ernest Carter's voice had softened and he lifted his head so she could hear him better. "Well, that's fair enough. I was just wonderin', that's all." He glanced back at her. "A father's got a right to wonder, an' if you'm happy enough then that's that."

They rode on as far as the top of Deer Park where they could see down the valley to where the river emerged from the woods. Becky wanted to ride further. She knew well that their conversation would be relayed to her mother who would bridle at how she had reacted. She wanted somehow to put off getting herself cooped up in the cottage with them, but her father had had enough for the day and they turned for home. As they urged the horses into a trot, the flies that had been pestering their mounts rose in a cloud. One remained stubbornly and she flicked at it, watching grimly as it spiralled to the ground. Good: Becky tossed her head defiantly.

3.

Ernest Carter watched as the sheep ran from the path of the military jeep. Behind it was a larger more cumbersome fifteen-hundredweight lorry and he frowned. The last remnants of the crashed aircraft had been removed more than a month ago. Twice they had come out and asked questions and then a letter arrived for the Colonel telling them that the matter was closed.

He saw the jeep turning down towards them and waited until the lorry followed before leaning his pitchfork carefully against the shippon wall. Hurrying to the water butt, he washed his hands and dried them on the cloth he always kept ready. What it could be he had no idea but they wouldn't be bringing good news, that was for sure.

✳

"Mr Carter?"

"Aye, that's me, sir."

"Lockley's the name. Major Lockley." The tall visitor, dressed in battle dress, saluted nonchalantly and stepped out of the jeep before taking off his leather glove and extending his hand. "Sorry to intrude on you like this but I wonder if we might talk. Inside perhaps?" He cocked an eye towards the cottage. Ernest Carter noticed the polished boots and gaiter straps, the neat creases on the uniform and the silver-topped cane. He could not recognise the shoulder flash but sensed at once that here was no fighting man. A high-up from the staff, maybe, but never a proper soldier.

"Aye…aye of course, sir. Step this way. Here look…'fraid it's a bit of a mess. Us weren't expecting visitors, like."

"No, of course not. But there's three of us, I'm afraid to say…a man from the

War Office and a policeman."

"A *policeman?*"

"Yes, but don't worry," he continued. "Nothing's gone amiss but we have to talk." Ernest waited until the lorry had pulled up and the others had alighted.

"The missus is about but Becky, that's my girl, she's up at the farm. Won't be needing her, I daresay?"

"No." The officer removed his hat, smoothed back his light brown hair and ducked under the low portal. He took in the scene at once, wrinkling his nose at the smell of wood smoke and cooked food. A black and white cat dropped silently from a chair and leapt for the open window. The other two followed behind, quietly muttering their greetings and looking about them. For a moment the room was still and it was not until Doris Carter, thin faced and suspicious, had wiped her hands on her apron and accepted the visitors' hands one at a time, that the table was cleared and chairs pulled up.

Major Lockley pulled at his shirt collar then crossed his arms and looked down. He coughed nervously and began to say something, then stopped and looked at Ernest Carter. "I'm afraid you're not going to like this, Mr Carter, but my instructions this afternoon are to inform you that the War Office has decided to purchase the land around here."

"Oh aye." Ernest Carter leant forward, half frowning. "A good deal of it…or not so much?"

"A very great deal as it happens." Lockley nodded. "And that includes the houses and farms."

"Cuh." Ernest Carter sat back, looked at his wife then at the other two. The short, balding man with his half-moon spectacles and dressed in a flannel suit was searching through his briefcase. The police sergeant lifted his chin to rub and stared mournfully. "Well…daresay us'll be able to manage. Live side by side, like. Us and they together."

"Er, not exactly, I'm afraid." For a moment the Major avoided Ernest's gaze. "You see we're going to be taking over the properties and that means all the buildings…we're going to have to move you. Move you well away from here."

"*No!*" Doris Carter stood suddenly and moved behind her husband placing both hands on his shoulders. "Us can't be moving from here. We've nowhere else to go…us can't."

"Steady, dear." Ernest put up a hand to take hold of hers. "Move *out*, you say." A note of anger had crept into his voice and the policeman looked up. "But you can't go pushing people around like this. Bain't right."

"I'm sorry…very sorry." Lockley looked from one to the other. "It's a most attractive spot up here and I know how you must love it but I'm afraid there's no choice. We've been to see Colonel Ashcroft and we've had orders to see the Little family over at Toms Hill as well. Your neighbours, I believe."

"That's *your* lot, I dare say." Ernest's voice had risen and the man from the War Office started back at his angry look. "Coming round 'ere behind the police and army like this. 'Tis your lot from the Ministry, I'll be bound."

"Steady there, Mister Carter." The police sergeant, round faced and husky voiced, raised his hand. "'Tis nobody's fault…nobody at all. Nobody likes carryin' on like this but the truth is the land's needed. Needed badly for the war."

"And what do they need it for? 'Tis only rough grazin'. Can't grow nuthin up y'ere abouts." Ernest Carter looked from one to the other. "I can tell'e that…can't grow nort up y'ere."

"We need the land for military ranges. I know you're an ex-army man yourself, like the Colonel, and I'm sure you can understand that the army needs ranges. This war's going on for a while yet and we've got to have land for the artillery." Once more the room fell silent. "You'll be taken care of…properly looked after, no question of that." Lockley bent forward. "Believe me, Mister Carter this has not been an easy decision…nor a pleasant one. Nobody likes doing this but the needs of the war have to come first."

"And when'll all this be…and where will us be goin'?" For a moment the fight had gone from him and Ernest looked from one to the other with his eyes raised plaintively.

"In about a month or so." The visitor in civilian clothes checked the file in front of him. "The plan is that we'll be sending you a letter of confirmation outlining the dates and then…."

"And *where* will us be going to, might I ask?"

"Down to Exford. We've found accommodation just across from the green. It's the middle cottage in a row of three."

"Oh, I see…'tis all sorted then," he sneered. "And how's us going to live? Food an' that. Where's the money coming from? Us've got to live, y'know."

"Yes, of course. You'll be on War Benefit and Disturbance Allowance. It's all here." The little man adjusted his glasses and tapped the paperwork in front of him. "We'll be confirming all this in a week or so."

"But there's three of us mind. Four when Jack's home from the Navy."

"Yes." The little man nodded and studied his notes. "Yes, we know that."

"And the animals?"

"All livestock will be purchased by the government. You'll be allowed to take one pet with you."

"*One?*" Ernest Carter's voiced was raised. "Just the one? Us've got two dogs...and they'm good workin' dogs *and* the cat."

"Regulations state one household animal only."

"Don't worry." Major Lockley raised his hand and turned to the civil servant. "We'll see to this," he said quietly. "I'm sure we can arrange for the three animals. Nobody need know."

"But the regulations state quite clearly...here, look...."

"Listen, will you," Lockley advised, one finger still raised. "I'm telling you that we'll find a way round this and that's that...all right?" The little man nodded and lowered his head. Nobody else spoke.

Eventually the Major rose and stamped his feet. "Well now," he said uneasily. "I think that that's about all for now...we'd best be on our way." He nodded to his two companions then turned towards the Carters. Doris was standing behind her husband who was looking down at the table.

"Thank you Mr Carter, and you Mrs Carter." He took a deep breath. "Look...er...I know this has come as a shock, I can see that...and you've been very understanding. But don't do anything just yet, will you...not until you receive official confirmation. And thank you...thank you very much. Please don't move." He motioned them to remain as they were. "We'll see ourselves out."

Ernest Carter took the Major's hand. He could barely look at the man and just nodded. His wife bowed her head and for some time neither moved.

✳

Becky returned from the farm just as the two vehicles went on their way. She could see her mother had been crying. Her father had put more logs into the range and was sitting staring at the flames flickering urgently behind the stove door. Slowly, as if they did not believe what they were saying, they told her. She sat heavily with one hand to her mouth and her eyes wide.

She should have felt distraught like her parents. True she felt saddened at the thought of leaving but she felt a sudden tingle of excitement also. She should not have done, but she couldn't help it. Exford meant her friends Mavis and Pat, Greg Thorne and the others. It meant dances and film shows up in the village hall. There was bustle and life down there, Sam had told her. More and more people were coming to the village – landgirls and soldiers and refugee children. She couldn't visualise life without the horses and the Colonel's garden but she could imagine seeing more of the world, of being somewhere where there was news to discuss and people to laugh with. Exford would be fun.

She rose and filled the kettle, stepping past her father to reach the stove. He didn't move, even when she put her hand on his shoulder to steady herself. Suddenly she felt sorry for him. He looked old and frail, as if the news had really hurt. And her mother, too. This was their home and the only life they knew. Exford, for them, was going to be miserable and they were going to miss the wild open moorland and the freedom around Larkbarrow.

She bent down, kissed his head then crouched beside him. Taking his hands in hers she looked up at the sad face. "Come on, Dad," she whispered. "We'll manage...somehow us'll get by. You'll see...come on, now."

Chapter Two

The two men reached the door together and fell against it laughing and panting. They had run from the main gate where they had been sheltering under the tall beech tree until the heavy shower began to ease. "Bloody rain." Sapper Mike Daley took off his beret, slapped it against his leg and fumbled with the door handle.

"Come on, mate." The other pushed him forward clumsily. "Get in for Chris's sake. I'm too old for this...an' it's still belting down." Inside the room, somewhere in a far corner, a small crystal wireless set was struggling with the Henry Hall Orchestra.

"Red...sails...in the suuuunset," Daley crooned nasally, twirling himself around with an imaginary partner in his arms. "De-dum-didi-da...come on, Smudge. Turn 'er up a bit." He threw himself onto his bed taking care to keep his boots well away from his neatly folded blankets. "Hey, Billy." He half sat, propping himself up on his elbows. "Done me best belt, 'ave yer?"

"Yep, an' that'll be ten fags."

"Let's 'ave a look then...gotta inspect the goods first, ain' I? C'mon then." Daley lay back and closed his eyes, humming quietly in tune to the wireless. Mike Daley, Portsmouth born and bred, had joined the Battery three months ago. Dark, good looking and with black, swept back, wavy hair, it only needed the pencil-thin moustache to provide the Errol Flynn touch and Daley had obliged. He seemed to have been born lucky, landing for himself the plum job of Quartermaster's personal driver.

*

Opening one eye slowly, Daley surveyed the scene. While not exactly the lap of luxury, it was nonetheless preferable to the conditions most of his friends from Pompey were experiencing elsewhere in the world. Along the old woodblock floor, twelve iron beds were arranged, six either side of the main drain that ran down the centre of the building. On each bed was a thin mattress encased in a dirty, off-white cover and on top of these, folded neatly, were three grey army blankets, two army sheets and the regulation pillow. A line of tall, steel-grey metal lockers separated the beds, allowing each occupant exactly the three feet of bed-space he was allowed to call his own. High above and strung haphazardly across the room was a tangle of wires, from which hung an assortment of clothes, socks and undergarments giving the requisitioned stable block the air of an overworked laundry.

Although barely mid-morning, the air was already thick with tobacco smoke. Three men, members of last night's guard, lay asleep, two on their backs and one huddled under his blankets, all three oblivious to the noise and bustle around them. Morning parades over, life for the Transport Section of the Royal Engineers had returned to normal. Those waiting to be called out were relaxing in what had become known as 'A' Block. It was their home: they had arrived in Exford earlier that year and set up their headquarters at Edgecott on the outskirts of the village.

Captain 'Freddie' Bates, Sapper Daley's boss, held his driver in high regard, fiercely protecting him from being taken for duties elsewhere, frequently ordering him out on lone courier duties around the Battery outposts and beyond. Daley, his wits sharpened since the days of standing up for himself in a number of unappealing foster homes, had been quick to capitalise. The 'runs' as Captain Bates called them consisted of visits to ration and fuel depots, Base canteens, NAAFI stores and, above all, the US Army Post Exchange, all tucked comfortably away from prying eyes and all stocked with attractive merchandise for which there was an insatiable demand.

Three years as a bookmaker's clerk had given Daley's already nimble mind a head for figures and a nose for a good deal. It had not taken him long to appreciate that what might be surplus to requirement in one depot was regarded as nothing less than gold dust in another, that what the Brits might go to war over, the Yanks possessed in profusion. All that was needed was discretion, a businesslike mind and the wherewithal to travel from one point of contact to the next. While Daley was the rightful owner of the first two essentials, the good Captain Bates had unwittingly provided the third. Furthermore the local civilian community, while denied many of life's little luxuries, had in abundance such rare commodities as clotted cream, eggs, fresh vegetables, venison, pheasants and salmon, produce from nature's own rich larder.

"Hey, that's spot on, Billy boy." Daley examined the belt brought to him for inspection. "Listen, sunshine…what say you that for a tin of fifty Players Navy you do my boots an' belt for a whole week? Yeah? Haven't time, m'self. Got to be out on the road a bit."

"Oh yeah? So what about that bit of stuff you brought up from Morebath, then? The one up at the dance last week? Time enough fer a bit o' that then."

"She *neeeds* me, Billy boy. Aches fer it, she does…can't live without me, she says. Gotta look after 'er, 'aven't I now. Unfair otherwise, ain't it?" Daley sat up, opened his locker and checked his hair in the tin mirror on the back of the door, turning his head from side to side and patting the black waves into place. "Anyhow, you weren't doing so bad yerself, come to think of it. Diggin' for Victory with that randy little landgirl, if I'm not wrong. Knackered you so she did."

"Yaah…an old cow."

"Now, now, my friend. Be thankful for small mercies…an' 'er two mercies looked big enough for the pair of us." Daley grinned and ruffled the young soldiers hair. "Bet she 'arf murdered you, boyo...bloody loverly, I'll bet. *Anyways.*" He jumped off his bed. "A tin of Players it is, me beauty. An' listen, make down my bed for me will yer. Might be back late tonight. Duty calls." He straightened his tie. "Gotta go an' see Uncle Freddie Bates...see what's lined up and get me orders for the war effort."

"On yer bike, Daley."

"Right on lads." Daley turned at the door. "An' don't wait up, neither." He dodged through, pulling it shut to block the shoe that followed.

*

Arthur Hedlow heard the jeep's horn as soon as it passed through the security gate. Stubbing out his cigarette, he pulled himself slowly to his feet to check then moved as quickly as his ample girth would allow. Lifting the blanket covering the table on which he kept his ledgers, he bent down and unlocked the tin box then struggled to lift out five large cartons of two hundred cigarettes. Breaking one open he placed half on his desk then set about busying himself with the untidy paperwork in front of him.

"Wotcha, Arfur." Mike Daley closed the door behind him. "It's me."

 Arthur Hedlow raised an eyebrow but continued to study the two files, checking one against the other. "Can't be long today," he grunted. "What's it anyway, Daley...what've you got?" Without looking up he shuffled the papers and scowled.

"Clothing coupons and PX vouchers. Said you could use them."

"Pfff." Hedlow shook his balding head. "You're too late, my friend. Nobody's interested now...the whole place's swimming with the things."

"Right then." For a moment Daley hovered, watching him tick at a list of figures. "Right, that's it...I'll be on me way then." He turned and reached for the door.

"Ha-a-ang on, hang on." Hedlow sat back and pulled at his collar. His two beady eyes were now studying Daley from behind his thick spectacles. "How many've you got, anyway?"

"Hundred and ten." Daley turned back.

"That'll be two hundred Lucky Strike." Hedlow's round face was expressionless. "That's all they're worth."

"Oi, you." Daley leaned across the desk. "It was *six* hundred last time...and no messin' neither."

Hedlow shrugged. "Times've changed, Daley. I can let you have two fifty…three hundred at the most and that's with the PX vouchers."

"Look…six it is, Arthur, and yer know damned well it's a good deal. And there'll be more coming."

"Five and that's it. And you're robbin' me, Daley."

"Oh, cor *blimey*…you'll have me in bleedin' tears, you will, Hedlow. Break me heart, an' all." He stood back and wiped his nose. "All right then. Come on, give us a kiss and we'll leave it at that."

Arthur Hedlow nodded. "Right, let's see your hand first." He watched as Daley counted the coupons, leaning forward to see what else might be in the leather wallet. As soon as he had hold of them, Hedlow counted them twice then pushed the cigarettes on the desk across to where Daley was waiting. "Satisfied?" he queried, blowing heavily and nodding at the contraband.

"Oh yeah…bleedin' hysterical." Daley moved quickly, stashing the cigarettes into his canvas courier bag. "Give yerself an 'eart attack one day, you will, Hedlow. I dunno…all this exercise at your age. Be getting cramp in yer fingers next." He grinned raffishly. "'Ere, see me out, will yer…check the coast's clear."

Hedlow stood and checked the compound yard, one hand held up in warning. "OK…on yer way, Daley. Next week, same time? Yes?"

"No problem."

✳

Three hours later and Daley's work was done; all he had to do was to drive back to Exford, park up the jeep and give the Guard Commander two packets of nylons for signing him in late. The day had gone well and he smiled to himself. The idiot on the gate at the American base had never understood that in the British Army rankers were allowed out to drive by themselves. Officer indeed! He had returned the salute as best he could but couldn't help laughing as he did so. And the poor mutt thought he was just being cheerful and smiled back. Oh dear!

The venison and fresh cream he had picked up from Staddon Farm on his way out had gone down a treat with the American Master Chef. And the twenty pairs of nylon stockings, twenty, plus the lipsticks and Max Factor powder puffs they had traded with him would set the village dance alight on Saturday. You wait. Once the girls knew what was about the place…hey presto!

"What are you smiling at, Michael Daley?" Sherry Blake looked up at him. She was lying across the bed half curled up with one arm behind her tight blonde locks. The top sheet had been pulled down far enough to expose her left breast which she was caressing gently with her fingertips. "What's so funny then? Not me, I hope."

"Nuthin' funny about you, darlin'." Daley, sitting on the edge of the bed, bent down and kissed the proffered nipple before continuing to do up his tie. "Nuthin' really…just nice chirpy little thoughts about this an' that."

"Well, go on then." She turned onto her tummy and put a hand on his lap.

He glanced down. "Hey, that's dangerous…a loaded gun down there, y'know." Having finished tidying his collar he started to comb back his hair. "No, it was just a thought. Think about it," he urged. "There's yer old man, Terry…doing his bit on air raid duty down in Tiverton, bless his tiny toes. On parade for King and Country an' all that, while 'ere am I, up 'ere with his missus doing me own bit of duty." He ducked forward to check himself. "An' everyone's as 'appy as pie. Fair enough, don't yer think?"

"Oh, get on or you'll be late." She pushed him off the bed and watched as he did up his trousers before bending forward to examine his face in her dressing-table mirror once more. "You're a right real pansy, you are. D'you know that? Never stop preening yourself an' flashing those long dark eyelashes…quite fancy yerself, don't you now."

"Not me, sweetheart." Daley pulled on his battle dress tunic and returned to the mirror. "It's only what the ladies tell me. Gotta keep meself up to scratch, y'know." He licked a finger and wiped it along both sides of his moustache. "There, look. Can't have nuthin' but the best, can we now? Hey," he turned briefly. "Coming up to the village, Saturday night? Got the Squadron band playing in the hall…all them new Glen Miller numbers." He wiggled his hips and glanced back at her.

"Not sure. Terry might be back."

"Yer *what?*" He pulled a face at himself and turned to look at her, adjusting his cuffs as he did so. "That's dodgy, that is. Wouldn't understand would 'e now? 'Bout you and me, that is…might get all personal like. Know what I mean?" Daley had met Terry Blake once and that was enough; the black-eyebrowed westcountryman was huge and didn't seem to like him.

"Tell you what darling…if you're there, you're there. Right?" He turned to his holdall, opened it and rummaged through the contents before coming up with what he had been looking for. "Here we are look…in loving memory of the good times…an' all that." He rubbed the two pairs of American nylons slowly down his cheek. "Mmmm. Soft as a baby's whatsit, they are. Sheer poetry."

Sherry Blake rolled over to see him better then reached up as he bent down to kiss her. "Save us a bit for next time, sweetheart," he whispered. "Don't go giving it all away to that old man of yours. Can't have you on half rations, can we now?" She waited until she heard the jeep engine fade in the distance then leapt out of bed. It had taken them only half an hour but already she was late for evening shift.

2.

Becky sat stiffly in the wicker chair next to the stove. They should have all been up at Larkbarrow farmhouse but the two removal vans had taken everything that morning and her father had asked the visitors down to the cottage. He had cleared the kitchen table and everybody except her had managed to squeeze themselves around. Seeing this, her mother had told her to leave but her father had said no. She should stay, he decreed and motioned her to the chair. Her mother was always doing things like that and Becky scowled, glaring at her feet and twiddling a lock of hair.

"I'll be here at ten on Monday then." The fair-haired Man-from-the-Ministry as her father described him sat back. He was younger than the one they sent before and much nicer. Earlier the two collies had befriended him when they were up at the stables and he seemed to know something about horses. "Ten should be all right, shouldn't it?"

"Can you manage that, Mrs Carter?" Colonel Ashcroft leaned forward earnestly. "I mean if that's too early then I'm sure we can delay the lorry an hour or two." The room was silent and Becky glanced up angrily. Her mother should have answered him, not just nodded. The Colonel had been really kind and she felt so sorry for him especially when she found him struggling to move the saddle-horses and feed bins on his own. He had been all hot and untidy which made him look older but he had never once complained at having to leave Larkbarrow. He loved it here just as much as they did but all her mother could say was that he was lucky as he had got another home to go to and it was different for him.

"Fine." The Colonel's voice was softer. "And the stock, Carter? Tomorrow afternoon?"

"Aye, sir, us'll have everything ready...such as it is." She heard her father's little laugh.

"Just the two cows?"

"Aye...the little shorthorn's in calf mind. Probably best if us walk them up to the road gently, along with the sheep. 'Twon't be such a long journey in the trailer then."

Becky continued to stare at her feet but her eyes were now wide. Suddenly it really was going to happen and it was horrible. And tomorrow. Then, on Monday, the day after, they too would be leaving and Larkbarrow would be empty. Up to now it had seemed fanciful even when her father had put the

30

wooden packing case in her room. Even when she had helped her mother to pack up the Colonel's things at the farmhouse, it had been as though it might never happen. But no longer. Bracken, the thin brown and white little Ayrshire with the big eyes and her calf together with Heather, the gentle shorthorn, had been sold. They were going to be taken away and they would never see them again. She wriggled her toes then blinked and wiped her eyes hurriedly.

Once she had been looking forward to the move but now the time had come she had this sudden urge to stay. The thought of leaving everything was frightening. Suddenly she realised how much she would miss her bedroom with its little window that never quite shut properly, but from which she could look across the rushy meadow to watch the curlews and snipe nesting. And the ledge with the chipped white paint where she kept her little china things. They would be leaving it all, everything, just as it was; the stables and the woodshed, the gardens up at the house and the old stone linhay with the roof thatched with rushes. Everything, except what they could take with them, was going to be left just as it was and they were talking about the day after tomorrow.

She dare not move or they would see her face but her fists were clenched tight and her legs pushed straight out in front of her. She could feel how her heart was beating. For a while the buzz of voices around the table meant nothing. She sat unmoving and rigid, her mind trying to imagine what Monday was going to be like, then Mr Sanders, the man from the Ministry, spoke. Why his voice caught her attention she never knew but he was talking to her mother. "No, I'm sorry, Mrs Carter…I'm afraid once you've left there'll be no coming back."

"Not even for the garden?" Her mother's voice was raised. "But us'll have to come back, us can't go lifting everything now…not they late teddies an' that. They'm not ready yet. Won't be for weeks." It was a silly question and Becky felt a blush of embarrassment at her mother's stupidity. Of course they couldn't come back. The room was quiet.

"I'm sorry Mrs Carter but once you've left the army're coming in to secure the place."

"Aye, an' they'll be having it all, I s'pose. Just take what they wants and after all our hard work." Becky winced. She could imagine her mother's pinched face turning from one to the other. The tone of her voice had hardened just like it always did when she was angry. "Bain't right, y'know…taking us away from our livelihood…."

"She's right, there, Sanders." Colonel Ashcroft cleared his throat. "Everything like the garden produce, things that can't be taken must be catered for. We'll draw up a list. There shouldn't be much but all these little things are important."

"Yes, of course, Colonel." Sanders nodded sagely and turned to Mrs Carter. "In fact we've started one already." He smiled sympathetically. "We'll put every-

31

thing like that on it...everything that's yours which you're going to have to leave behind and we'll see to the compensation."

"*Full* compensation, mind you." Colonel Ashcroft tapped the table. "These things have a habit of getting lost, y'know." He eased himself on the hard chair. "I'll be watching this."

"It works all right, sir." Sanders assured them. "We've had to do all this down at Okehampton. Exactly the same there and we've had very few complaints. It's never a pleasant business though."

"Quite."

*

"How're they taking it?" With the meeting over the two men walked together.

Ernest Carter glanced at the Colonel then looked away. "Oh...not too bad, sir." Then he sighed. "'Tis hard though...bin a long time up here, so we have. I'll be fine, mind. Hoping to pick up a bit of work at the forge or the stables be'ind the White Horse...Frank Mullins's place." He paused, choosing his words. "'Spose we're just lucky enough not to be living in one o' they big cities where they'm getting bombed night after night. At least we're safe." He shook his head. "Be difficult fer the missus, though. Her's not used to having people round and about the whole time."

Colonel Ashcroft nodded. He had sensed the unhappiness. For once Headquarters had found a man with feeling and Sanders had done a good job but it had been devilishly awkward nonetheless. The Carters had done him proud and it pained him to see such a fine family evicted like this. "The job at Porlock's still there, Carter. Soon as this wretched war's over we'll get you across." They had stopped and were standing on the track outside the farmhouse. Sanders had gone on his way. They were alone and it would be the last time they would be there together. "And the cottage there as well, y'know. You've talked it over together, of course, you and the wife?"

"Aye, sir, an' right grateful we are. Not sure as to how many of us there'll be, mind?" Carter toyed with the front collar stud in his shirt

"Any news of the boy?"

"Jack, sir?" Carter squared his shoulders. "Up at Liverpool. Had a letter a week ago but it didn't say much. Still on the North Atlantic runs, I reckon. Convoys." He laughed thinly. "Can't be much fun."

"That's fer sure." The two men paused, both aware of the merciless toll taken by the war at sea. "And young Becky, what about her? Didn't seem too happy either, poor girl."

"None of us are really." Carter rubbed his chin. "But difficult to say. One moment her's prattlin' on about seein' her friends down in Exford again, next she's all maudlin' about leaving up here. Daresay she'll be fine though...once Monday's been an' gone."

They walked on together until they reached the shooting brake where they shook hands like they always did. Ernest Carter stood back and watched as the uniformed chauffeur opened the door. Miles Ashcroft put a foot inside then turned. "Probably best if I'm out of the way on Monday," he said slowly. "I'll be coming up during the week though. And your place is just up from The Crown, isn't it? One of the cottages there?"

"That's right, sir. The middle one of they three just on from the Post Office. Little white one with a wooden porch over the door. Myrtle Cottage, 'tis called."

"I'll find it." He grinned and touched his cap. "And good luck on Monday." Carter waited until the shooting brake ground on its way then raised his hand in salute.

3.

"What're you doing that for?" Doris Carter stood at the bottom of the stairs holding a pile of blankets in both arms. "No point in doin' that. Not if they're goin' to bomb the place...for Heaven's sake, Becky. Use your sense."

"Father said to tidy up, that's all." Becky, on her hands and knees in front of the stove, sat back on her heels. "Just cleaning out the worst of the ash."

"Don't be so daft, girl. There's plenty more things to be doing an' the lorry's due shortly." Doris Carter turned, looking for somewhere to put the blankets. "And you'll only be getting ash over everything. Leave it...oh *get on*, Becky," she cried, seeing her hesitate. "Leave off that and get on outside. The chickens need to be got up together fer a start." Becky rose, stood and wiped her hands on her dungarees. For a moment her eyes closed then she strode from the room.

✳

She thought of ignoring her mother's remarks and going off to find her father but went instead to the hen run, where she opened the fragile wire gate that almost collapsed in her hands. Her father had been meaning to mend it but it didn't matter now. She hooked it shut behind her then stood carefully on the wet mud that had been paddled flat and was covered in feathers and fat white droppings. One of the hens, old and with a bald neck, approached slowly lifting one foot at a time. It was cawing quietly and peering this way and that to see what was on offer. Becky watched her then shooed her and the others into the hen house before picking up their bowls to wash under the pump.

She had finished and picked the two eggs out of the nesting box when her father's call made her turn. The lorry had arrived an hour ago and she glanced impassively at the two men. Earlier, before her father had asked her to clean out the fire, she had watched them loading. The tools from the woodshed were first, then the three tea chests from the pantry. After that, the furniture appeared from the cottage piece by piece. It was strange seeing it all out in the open like that and she tried to imagine the spaces left behind. It was as though their home was coming apart bit by bit. But it was when her own packing case and leather suitcase were brought out that she turned away unable to watch any longer. She knew she could do nothing about it and that only made it worse.

*

Sam had come with his cart as he said he would and together they loaded the hens then walked from building to building making sure nothing had been forgotten. It was early afternoon already and her mother and father had left. The Colonel had sent his driver for them and she watched as the big, gleaming, wood-panelled car rolled and lurched after the lorry.

Now there was just the two of them and she waited for Sam to load a roll of wire onto the cart. "Just a minute," she whispered, starting towards the farmhouse.

"What're you doing?"

"There's some roses on the wall. I can't leave them."

"Hang on a mo', Becks." Sam tilted back his cap. "D'you think it's right? I mean somebody might come for 'em. The Colonel might send someone up."

"Oh, don't be daft, Sam." As she glanced back, she laughed bitterly. "That's it now…can't yer see. Nobody's coming for nothing. They've all gone. *Look*." She waved her arms at the farm and cottage and shrugged. "They've gone now, *all* of them." Then suddenly she was crying again. She dropped the scissors and bent forward with her face in her hands, sobbing uncontrollably.

"Come on, maid." She felt his arm around her and leant towards him, mumbling into her hands as she tried to tell him something. "Shhh," he soothed. "Come on then, Becks…us'll pick the flowers, then be on our way."

"Oh, I don't know," she muttered, wiping her nose. "I don't know. Why can't they leave us alone, just *leave* us up here out of it all. We were so happy…." She paused then half pushed herself away from him and picked up the scissors, shaking her head and sniffing loudly. "Come on then," she gasped. "Let's see what's what."

They picked what they could but somebody had helped themselves earlier. At last, when there was nothing left, she climbed onto the back of the cart and sat heavily on the sacks Sam had put out for her. She glanced down at the pale, delicate blooms in her hand and lifted them gently to breathe in the fragrance. The scent reminded her of everything, of the farmhouse and their cottage, of the horses and dogs and the great sweep of moorland around them with the open skies above.

She felt Sam's hand on her knee and smiled briefly but without looking up. Then a jolt made her start. He had lifted the reins and was urging his horse to step out. When they got to the crest before dropping down to the road, she stood and looked back, steadying herself with one hand. With the other, the one that was still holding the roses, she swept back her hair then shielded her eyes from the sun. Finally, and until the rooftops had disappeared from view, she stood on tiptoe to see better. Then she sat again and lowered her head, her mouth pressed tightly shut.

Chapter Three

Ernest Carter settled quickly enough. Initially the Steer brothers at the forge could offer him only a day a week when he would help sort the cast shoes and metal, and unload coke sacks from the coal merchant's lorry which then had to be emptied and stored.

More horses than ever were being pressed into service: petrol rationing had seen to that and often there would be a long queue of animals waiting patiently in the road. The owners and handlers would gather by the forge entrance, watching casually as the farriers bent to their task amid the thick oily smoke as they tried the hot shoes for size. The steady clang-ding, clang-ding of the hammers bouncing between metal and anvil or the windy growl of the bellows all but drowned out the buzz of gossip.

But when Frank Mullins at The White Horse stables offered him as much work as he could take, Ernest was happier still. The trouble had been Doris, so much so that he was pleased to get out of the house after breakfast each day. Every time vehicles or horses passed the window she had to rush and see who it was. At first she returned the stares, claiming that those looking into the cottage ought to see that they had been caught prying. But they only stared harder and some waved back or pointed her out to each other, forcing her to tuck herself away in the corner behind the curtains where she was hidden from sight.

She made herself a little space in the shadows and another upstairs so she could watch both up and down the road. Next she complained about being shut away, and then it was the noise, even the staghounds up the road in the kennels. And then it was about Becky idling her time away. Nothing seemed right. Ernest had suspected it might be like that and was glad to be away from it all.

Becky had been fine. For a day or two the poor maid had cried a bit and kept moving her things around the room but no sooner had Pat Steer and Mavis Vellacott called round than she was away. It was almost as though life up at Larkbarrow had been forgotten. The change in the girl made him wonder but if she was happy then she and her mother were less likely to keep on at one another. Ernest counted his small mercies.

*

Becky held on to Mavis and wiped the tears away. Then she bent forward and began giggling again. "Stop it, Pat...oh, Heavens, stop it, you're killing me. Stop." Mavis started to shake with laughter, turning herself towards Becky and burying her head on her shoulder as if she was sobbing her eyes out.

This time Pat Steer stuck out an arm in a Nazi salute but nearly tripped, causing her floppy hat to skew and her thick brown curls to fall and cover her face. Her squat, round figure encased in dungarees that were sizes too big for her, turned and goose-stepped back down the grassy path between the rows of vegetables. She was grinning cheesily from side to side and her eyes, behind her thick spectacles, were wide with excitement. Gladys and Sandra, the two land girls from Peckham began to laugh also, followed shortly by the others and soon, everyone on the Dig for Victory vegetable patch down by the river was laughing helplessly. Then the door behind them opened.

"*Oi.* Come on you lot...there's work to be done and mouths to feed." Mr Warren, grey haired and with his bushy mutton chops reaching down to his hairy nose, stood in the doorway of the wooden shed. "That's enough, young madam...you'll be dancing on stage next." He looked around affectionately. The young women, or girls as he knew them, had been working since eight and it was time for lunch. They had done well and he would get little more out of them. "All right, all right." 'Daddy' Warren smiled at the faces looking back at him. "That'll do for now. Back at two sharp, mind...and not half full of scrumpy neither."

"Coming up the pub?" Gladys, the more heavily built of the two land girls drove her fork into the ground. Mavis Vellacott had introduced Becky to them last week when she began work but she was wary. She had heard her father talking about those girls from London and the soldiers. She hardly knew them and, in any case, they stuck more or less to themselves. And they spoke differently and always laughed at what each other said.

"Too hot, Glad." Pat Steer, now rosy cheeked and sweating from her efforts, fanned her face with her hat. "Phew...oh dear. No thanks. Us'll sit on the bridge. Better there and we'll catch the breeze."

✳

The River Exe that flowed under the bridge was little more than a stream but it began its journey high in the hills beyond Larkbarrow and Becky had learned to stop and peer into the water wondering what it might have seen on its way down from the moors.

They ate their sandwiches leaning against the parapet and watching the world go by. The land girls sat on a wooden bench across the road. Two soldiers were with them. "She's a one, she is," Mavis whispered, nodding towards the others. "That Gladys, there look. A right man eater she is...carrying on like she's never seen a bloke before. Lord know's what they did for themselves up in Peckham or wherever."

"'*Ere...Becky.* Come over 'ere a mo. Someone wants to meet yer." Gladys Strange was beckoning. "Come on...ain't goin' to bite yer. Not now anyways." One of the soldiers guffawed. Sandra, thin and with blonde straggly hair pushed at him but the other man, taller and older, looked round.

Becky froze. "Trust you, Becky Carter." Pat Steer muttered quietly, squinting through her glasses. "Been here five minutes and you've got 'em all hopping about. Always bin the same, you 'ave." She grinned at her friend admiringly. "Don't know how you do it."

"Shush, Pat." Becky could feel herself blushing.

"Come on then." It was Gladys again. "Come on. *Hey…Becky…*says he fancies yer."

Pat laughed. "Go on then," she whispered to Becky. "Go an' have look. They won't eat yer."

"*No,*" she hissed then lifted her head. "Not just now, Glad," she called out. "Honest…not now, thanks." Then she watched horrified as the one who had been looking their way clambered up from the bench.

"What's the matter with you lot, then? Paralysed or summat?" His freckled and sunburned face broke into a toothy grin. "Not going to beat yer to death, y'know." He bent forward and looked closely at Becky. "Aye aye, so who's this then? Eh? New here aren't we? Here…Matt's the name, Matt Bradshawe." Becky glanced at him then looked at his outstretched hand. " 'Ere come on, luv."

Pat's nudge warned her to keep still. "What's it to you, Matt Bradshawe?" she snapped. "She'll tell you her name if she wants to an' that's that. And if I'd known you'd be like you were last Saturday I wouldn't've give you mine neither." Becky looked at her incredulously. "S'all right, love," Pat laughed. "Matt here's not so bad." She nodded at the figure in front of them. "You just behave yourself with my friends, that's all."

"Yes, ma'am." He brought himself up to attention. "See yer Saturday then. Eh? And if I promise to be a good boy then you can take the wraps off your secret weapon here." He grinned at Becky. "How about it, then? Come on, Patsy girl."

"We'll see…and don't you going Patsy-girling me, soldier boy. Come on Glad…Becky." Pat put a hand to her mouth but it was too late.

"Aha…*Becky* then, is it?" Matt Bradshawe quipped. "Right then. Rebecca straight out of the Good Book…along with the fatted calf an' all that." Becky glared. "All right, all right." Bradshawe held up his hands. "Only joking."

*

"That's the army for you. Can't help laughing though, can you?" Pat had her arm through Becky's. "They're fun mind…brought some life to the village. Wouldn't trust them though."

Becky smiled and tossed her head. "What cheek," she laughed. "Goodness, Pat, what blooming cheek."

"I know. They're all like that but it's a good laugh. Treat 'em rough an' they know their place…or some of them."

"I'll say." Becky took hold of her friend's arm and gave a short skip.

2.

"I'm a little bit early, I'm afraid, Mrs Carter."

"Oh, come in, come in, Sam." Doris Carter stood back and held the door for him. She sounded as though he had surprised her but she had been watching him carefully ever since he pulled up across the road and hitched the pony to the rail. She noticed at once the new buff-coloured, checked hacking jacket, the corduroy trousers and the way he had adjusted his cap before straightening his tie. That would have been his mother, she thought. Mrs Hawkins reckoned she knew how to turn herself out and would have made sure her own did the same.

"Oh, Sam. That's kind. You should never have done that. Cuh, what a surprise." She smiled at the sight of the dozen eggs in the basket. "Us misses them now we've lost most of the hens. Here, look. Take a seat, dear, an' I'll give Becky a call. Her'll be down d'rectly. Now then, let me see."

He watched as she fussed with the eggs but turned at the sound of heavy walking shoes clumping slowly down the bare boards of the narrow stairs. It was Becky and he stepped towards her.

"Hullo, Sam." She took his hands briefly but let it fall. "You caught me, I'm afraid…and I was still getting ready. Sorry about that. What time is it?"

"Just gone two." He watched as she hesitated.

"Ah, well…look. Can't be too long this afternoon, Sam. Not today, I'm afraid." She turned to the mirror to check her hair.

"Why on earth not?" her mother queried. "And Sam's come all this way to see you." Becky glared back at her own reflection. "I'm sure he'd be doing other things if he knew you'd be saying that."

"*Mu-ther.*" Becky turned and caught Sam's look. "I'm sorry Sam. It's just that Pat Steer's asked me over after tea and I said I'd like to go. That's all."

"Oh, *really*, Becky…."

"No matter, Mrs Carter." Sam cut in. "Us can go for an hour or so anyhow. Make the most of the sun an' that." Becky sensed his disappointment and felt a moment of guilt, but it couldn't be helped. Besides she had an idea of what was on his mind. His Sunday clothes and the way he was standing there gave him away. He looked uneasy and nervous and she was certain she knew why. "Well," he shrugged self-consciously. "Us best be getting on."

"Stop worrying so, mother." Whatever enthusiasm she might have had for the ride out with Sam had been dashed by her mother's interference. She, Becky, couldn't move in the cottage without her knowing everything about it and offering her advice. Not that she knew any better, she didn't. She just always had to have her say. "I'll thank you to know that I'm old enough to sort meself out."

"Now." She adjusted her headscarf and dabbed at the corner of her mouth, once more glancing briefly into the mirror before stepping outside.

✳

"And it's got everything there," he went on. "Proper little kitchen an' pantry beyond the parlour. One bedroom, two if you count the place what father used as his office." Sam had slowed to let the army lorry pass then flicked the reins. Becky's gaze followed the vehicle and she caught the attention of the soldiers in the back. One called out and she dropped her eyes but smiled bashfully before turning back to Sam. "Plenty of room there is and it'd be quieter than down here with all this lot."

They were trotting past Edgecott and Becky turned to look at more soldiers standing by a jeep parked in the driveway. Still more were further inside and it was the same across the road at the stables. She barely heard Sam and this time she lifted a hand in reply to a wave from one of the men. "So what d'yer reckon then? Eh?" He had raised his voice. "'Tis all there, Becks…if yer want it, that is. Mother an' father'd be more'n pleased. They'd be able to get rid of that land girl then. A right duffer so she is." Becky turned her head and looked back, holding on to her headscarf. "Eh, Becks? What d'yer think?"

"Mmm? Oh, I'll think on it, Sam. Speak to Mum and Dad. But it's not quite so easy you know. I'm working now…out in the big garden along with all they others."

"Don't worry about the gardening, father'll see to that. He'll see Daddy Warren an' arrange for a swap…you an' the land girl. That won't be no problem."

Her spirits fell. Sam was pressing her again and it irritated. It wouldn't be so bad if they were still out at Larkbarrow. Out there, there was no one else to see or talk to and, in spite of his advances towards the end, she used to look forward to his visits when he would bring news of life in Exford. But she was down in the village now and life was going on all around her. There was Pat and Mavis and the others. She could see and do things for herself, hear things in the stores and post office and then make her own way. She was happy where she was.

"Dunno," she murmured, picking at one of her nails before biting it. "We've only just moved, Sam, and I'm still finding things out down here. Only just got unpacked and that."

40

"Hark to they shells," he interrupted, looking up and pointing as the muffled swishing overhead grew louder. Another followed and then a third before the distant crumps told of their journeys' end. "That's Larkbro'," he muttered. "Flattenin' the place."

"And the cottage…our old home," Becky whispered looking up in an attempt to see the next salvo and the one after that as they waffled their way overhead. Suddenly she felt angry and protective. Only seconds before she had been thinking of their home. She tried to visualise what would be happening up there. Smoke and flames bursting out perhaps, tiles and beams would be crashing down where once there had been peace and calm. She thought of the stables and the horses galloping madly about and screaming in panic from the explosions, but there were none, of course, just the sheep. The farmers should have cleared them from the ranges but there were always some left and they, poor things, would be terrified, unable to comprehend what was happening. Some would be killed, flung into the air by the sudden, mad violence while others would be lying injured and in pain, unable to move. "It's awful. I hate it…hate it." She shivered, shaking her head at the thought of the suffering and the destruction raining down on the home she loved.

"Aye, sad reelly." For a while they trotted on, each alone with their thoughts until Sam slowed. "Tell 'e what." Becky watched as they left the road and pulled on to a wide grassy patch under some trees that shaded them from the sun. Nearby the river flowed under a narrow packhorse bridge.

"What're we doing?" she asked.

"This 'yere is where me an' Jack used to come ticklin' trout. Never got much mind." He had jumped down and was holding up a hand to steady her. "Tell 'e what though…if you're not too happy about moving out, you could always come out an' work daily up at the farm. Hayes's not more'n a mile out of the village, just up beyond the church."

"Sa-am." Becky could feel her agitation. He was still holding her hand and had held on to it when she tried to pull back. "Look…I'm not ready yet. Honest, I'm not."

"Not ready fer what, maid?" He still had hold of her fingers.

"All this." She looked up at him and could see he knew what she meant by the concern on his face. "This move and…well, us, Sam." He shrugged and let her hand drop then half turned from her. "'Tis all too soon and what with all this bombing an' shelling an' that, I'm not ready to settle. Not yet anyways."

"Is there summat up…summat wrong, or what?" She could sense he was hurt.

"No," she cried putting a hand on his arm. "No, nothing's wrong, of course not. I like you…like you very much. You know I do and I always have. But it's just that…oh, I dunno. Everything seems so rushed. It's all a bit quick, an' I just dunno where I am."

"Hardly rushing things, is it?" He walked to the edge of the bridge and looked into the water. "I mean it's not as though we've only just met or something."

"I know it's not but we hardly know each other really well, do we? I mean not close, like that. I need time, Sam. Can't we wait a while…wait until Jack's home and everything's settled a bit? All this war an' that…well, can't we?" Somewhere ahead a cow lowed hoarsely, then a magpie chattered in a thicket behind them. Becky waited. "What d'you think?" she murmured.

He turned and she glanced at him hurriedly, fearful that he might be angry or upset. But he was smiling, one of those slow broad smiles of his and she relaxed. "Oh, you're right enough, Becks," he said. "Look, maid…I'm sorry." He took her arms and pulled her gently towards him. "Didn't mean to sound like that. It's just that you being down here gives me all these ideas. You're here now and I don't want to let you go, that's all. But, aye," he nodded thoughtfully. "You're right…we'd best wait awhile and see what's what. But I don't want you getting into no trouble though," he warned, mocking severity. "There's plenty o' mischief down around Exford these days so you take care.."

"*Me?*"

"Yes you, Becks. I'll wait for you but you've got to wait for me as well. Right?" He gave her a little pull towards him. "None of this chasing after they soldier boys nor nuthin'. Not like Mavis Vellacott and they others." He was looking down at her but his smile had gone, just his eyes were moving, searching her face anxiously.

Becky laughed. "Don't look so worried, you big silly. Course I won't. Come on or I'll be late." Without thinking, she stood on tiptoe and kissed him. "Thanks, Sam."

Suddenly she felt free again when only minutes earlier she had been trapped. Her spirits soared. Sam was a dear, dear friend and he had agreed to wait. She was grateful and the thought of the sudden freedom and space he had just given her endeared him to her even more. He was trusting her. As soon as she saw him earlier today she knew that she was going to have to let him know how she felt and it had just sort of come out as they were talking. She hadn't had to begin the difficult conversation and for that she was relieved. And he had accepted it without being hurt or angered or making things difficult and for that she was glad as well.

Once more she was happy and on the way home they chatted easily. Yes, she would come out to Hayes Farm. She would have to anyway to see her father's sheep and she could see more of his parents then. And, yes, she would be going up to the village dances and, yes, of course, funny little Pat Steer would keep those beady eyes of hers on her. They laughed at that and they laughed as they passed the soldiers by the gate at Edgecott, both raising their hands at the three men standing together under the big beech tree.

3.

Ernest Carter knew that autumn was not far off. Even down here in the village he could sense it in the early morning air. There was a freshness and sharpness about the place where, before, the warmth of the previous day had still been present. And autumn meant the Cutcombe sheep fair. When they left Larkbarow, Drew Hawkins had agreed to take in his ewes and lambs for which he would pick out two of the better ones for himself.

He walked steadily up the hill past the hall and then on to the church, stopping briefly to look at the cricket pitch where on Saturday they were going to raise money for the war. Sam would be playing and his mother would be doing the teas. Higher up to his right was Hayes Farm. Leaning further over the gate, he made out the white face of the farmhouse behind the tall hedgerow. Drew Hawkins had asked him to come up. 'See the sheep and stay on fer a bite o' breakfast,' had been the invitation.

He turned back, stretched himself then bent down to pick a leaf from the toe of his polished boot. Straightening himself again, he took out his pocket watch and glanced up at the church clock to double check. Drew would be easy enough, always a pleasure to be with but then there was Barbara. Ernest was not so sure there. As he stepped out, he gave a little chuckle and inclined his head.

✳

"More tea, Ernest?" Barbara Hawkins held up the teapot. "No? Well perhaps some more ham then....or toast? Here look." Ernest held up his hand for his mouth was full. There was no stopping her. She was a fine woman, he could see that, but there was something about her that wasn't quite right. Doris had spotted it and called it her airs and graces. There was talk in the village that she had come from a smart family over Porlock way and there was an aunt up in Cheltenham so they said. But then proper smart people didn't go pushing their way about with all that show. Always dressed up to catch the eye. And the way she spoke, well, it weren't natural. He could never put his finger on it but Doris could: a mite *too* fancy, she said, just a mite.

"Well, look. I've got to dash," she explained. "I've got the flowers to do and then we're meeting up at the cricket pavilion to talk about the tea for Saturday and who'll be collecting the war money." She rose, pulling at her tweed skirt and both men rose with her. "Don't bother with the things dear. Just leave them and I'll deal with them later." Drew Hawkins nodded obediently.

"And it's so good for Sam that Becky's down here, Ernest. He's so much happier and he tells me she's coming up to watch the cricket tomorrow. That'll be nice." Barbara looked away, as she did so her smile faded. "Oh yes," she

43

faltered. "And there's no more of his dark moods either."

"Oh?"

"No, thank goodness. He used to get himself terribly down in the dumps...as though he was pining away." She laughed drily. "So silly really."

"Aye, well, they'm seeing something of each other that's fer sure." Ernest smiled, nodding slowly at the thought. She seemed to be happy enough about their two youngsters walking out. Barbara Hawkins still turned the eye herself, even in the cold weather when she walked through the village with that heavy brown, herring-bone tweed coat of hers and that beret on her head. But now, dressed as she was in her flowery summer frock with the belt at the waist and her fair hair permed and set like it was, she was a fine looking woman, and a handsome one at that.

*

The room fell quiet. Drew Hawkins sat back and lifted his eyebrows then blew heavily. "Tires me out sometimes, she does, Ern'. Forever goin' on about this an' that. Runnin' about keeping up with they Jones's an' that...snappin' away at Sam, telling him to speak proper...cuh, I dunno." Drew was a big man, heavy and slow and it took a lot to upset him. For a moment the two were silent. " All too much sometimes." He paused again. "But her's stopped all that damned nonsense with me.Told her a way back that I am what I am, an' if her don't like it then it's too darned late."

Ernest looked at him then laughed, throwing his head back. Nothing would ever change Drew Hawkins and thank Heavens for that. Barbara was the one who fussed and bothered: more than enough for the pair of them. "Aah, you're safe enough there, Drew. And her wouldn't want you changed for the world. Us can all see that."

"Well, if her does then 'ers not goin' to have any of it", he growled. "'Tis too darned late."

4.

Holding the two plates higher so she could see better, Barbara made her way down the pavilion steps and looked around. Everybody seemed to be there. The collection tins had been rattling and there was a wonderful atmosphere with everybody giving whatever they could. It had rained earlier but the heavy, grey clouds had cleared and the sun was trying to break through. Sam had batted well and they had declared before tea. Once the break was over, Winsford would have to bat.

It was then, just after looking down to make sure that there were no more steps, that she saw the man she hoped might be there. Martin Trumper was a florid,

44

slack-jowled man and, to anybody who was honest, extremely ugly. But Martin Trumper was also extremely rich, in addition to which he was Master of a local pack of staghounds. Beware of such people, her aunt used to warn. They're really nothing more than little fish in little ponds. But it mattered not: to Barbara Hawkins, Martin Trumper was a demi-god, one to whom homage had to be paid.

"Excuse me...whoops, so sorry," she apologised. "Thank you...oh, do excuse me." As she turned this way and that, easing her way through the white flannelled players and spectators, hands reached for the sandwiches on one plate and the buttered scones on the other. "Hello," she cooed. "Lovely to see you...and you, too, Mr Todd. Thank you so much, Wendy...phew, there we are....

"Ha," she gasped. "*Mr* Trumper...caught you at last. Here we are, look...sandwich or scone?" Barbara Hawkins beamed, blushing with excitement.

"Mmm, how very kind of you," the Master took one of each. " Now then, tell me. I do know you, don't I? It's Mrs...er...er...."

"Hawkins, Barbara Hawkins from Hayes Farm, just up the hill behind us."

"Yes, of *course*. Indeed...of course it is. And haven't we seen you out with us from time to time, Mrs Hawkins."

"Oh *Barbara,* please," she gushed. "I'm afraid I can't offer you my hand but do *please* call me Barbara. Everybody does," she lied. Martin Trumper, still chewing, took another sandwich which he raised in greeting to somebody behind her. "We met at the Puppy Show where I was helping Mrs Woolacott with her couple. And they did *so* well," she continued."

Eventually his eyes returned. "Indeed...indeed. Third, I believe." He held a hand to his mouth then raised his head to another greeting from somewhere beyond them. "Look, Mrs...er...Barbara." He smiled briefly. "Look, Barbara, I must be off, really I must or I'll be accused of hogging the sandwiches, or you....*what.*" He leered as he swallowed before inclining his head. "Lovely to see you again. And again, soon I hope." Patting her shoulder, he eased his way past.

Barbara was thrilled. Martin Trumper had indeed recognised her and they, rather *he* was addressing her in that friendly, easy-going manner. So *very* nice. She lifted her eyebrows and took a deep breath. In front of her was the vicar, another *very* charming man who had told her earlier how well Sam was playing. Charles Wardle was a Cambridge man, one could always tell, of course. His sermons were marvellous. She put the plates down and began to take in the scene around the ground. It really was a splendid gathering and her eyes moved from group to group then on and beyond. But suddenly they stopped.

A party of girls from the village were sitting or lying in the long grass between the boundary and the churchyard fence. Becky Carter was there, she noticed her at once, and the Steer girl from the forge. One or two others she recognised also and there were some land girls as well. Beyond them was a group of soldiers from Edgecott. It must have been their lorry in front of the church. Two were pushing each other and several more were lounging about. They all looked so slovenly: even from where she was she could hear the shouts and their coarse laughter. So that's why the girls were there.

Oh dear, her heart sagged. Becky was an attractive girl, she had to admit, with a lovely figure and *the* most beautiful eyes. She was polite, she rode well and she was obviously popular, but that was all. It stopped there. There was simply nothing more to her, nothing of any substance. Her family were, well, very nice but so very ordinary. Ernest was a dear. Colonel Ashcroft, Miles, had told her that and she always found him quite charming, but the mother was an impossible woman. 'Look at the mother and you'll see the child', so the saying went. And Sam was besotted with the girl. Surely, surely he could see beyond those dark, sultry looks. But no, he'd never even thought of looking anywhere else.

One of the girls, Pat Steer so she thought, waved. Obviously they had caught her watching them and for a moment she was flustered, but she raised her hand cheerfully. Two others waved also but not Becky Carter. Perhaps she hadn't seen her.

*

"*Don't.*" Becky pulled Pat's hand down. "Don't go waving like that or she'll have us over for tea with the vicar and they lot."

"An' so what? Don't you like her then? I mean she is Sam's Mum and yer Dad likes her."

"That don't make no odds." Becky frowned. "And anyway she's all hoity toity an' that. Thinks she's ever so grand and goes round talking all smart". She rolled over, pulling Pat with her. "Here, come on, you. What d'yer reckon on they lads then? Over there, look. Seen that fella, Matt, have you?"

"Matt Bradshawe? The one who's eyes were inside yer dungarees the other day? Had the right hots for yer, he did." Pat lifted her glasses and squinted at the group of soldiers, lifting herself up and waving back at one of them. "Bain't there." She turned back and faced Becky then called out to the other girls behind them. "Coming up to the dance tonight, Glad? You and the others, eh? Sandra…you coming? Got a good band on tonight so they say."

Turning back to Becky, she lowered her voice. "You coming up, Becks?" She looked at her enquiringly. "You an' Sam an' the others?" She saw the look of uncertainty on her face. "Come on…never mind about Sam if he don't wanta come. Come on up with us, never know what yer might find."

"Yes, come on." Mavis leant across. "Us'll come by an' pick you up, an' we'll all go on together."

"Yeah, go on." Pat nudged her.

"Come on, Becks."

"Might do." Becky shrugged, looking down as she fiddled with her fingers. Then she brushed at the grass on her blouse. "Why not then? All right," she smiled. What time?"

" 'Bout eight...we'll come by for you then."

Chapter Four

It was still only eight o'clock yet the village hall was packed. Every chair around the walls was taken and groups of revellers stood talking on the edge of the floor. The buzz of chatter and laughter rose higher in an effort to compete with the music under the cloud of cigarette smoke that hung in the air. Tonight, the same as on every second Saturday, the military dance band was playing and the inside of the hall had been decorated with flags and bunting.

Pat Steer stood watching quietly. The next time the couple came round she caught Becky's eye. Only yesterday, after the two of them had returned their forks to the garden shed, Becky had confessed that she was beginning to find Sam's presence oppressive. She felt cornered and irritated by his persistence. Even now she looked miserable, Pat could see it on her face as they danced past.

"C'mon, love." Mavis Vellacott tugged at her sleeve. "Matt's over there with some of they Edgecott lot. Just come up from the pub." Pat turned away slowly, raising her hand sympathetically to Becky who was looking despairingly over her partner's shoulder. The band were good, playing all the new American tunes and the floor was crowded. "They say there's more coming up directly," Mavis shouted. "Reckon there could be trouble...I mean there's too many of them. Packed out, look, and there's Greg Thorne and Archie Chugg with the Dulverton crowd...all standing there black as thunder at their girls with this lot."

"Aye, an' sometimes it's just as well to be out of it all. There look." Pat gave a little skip. "Free as a bird on the wind," she laughed. "That's me...hey, now what?" The music had stopped and Pat, her arm through her friend's, waited as Becky joined them. For a moment Sam stood alone before making his way over to join the Chuggs and Greg Thorne on the far side of the room.

*

"May I have this one, please?" Becky turned at the hand on her shoulder. It was Matt Bradshawe. Beyond him more soldiers had arrived and a group of girls she recognised from Winsford were buying their tickets at the door. Now there was hardly room to move.

"I'm too hot...."

"Aha, no. No excuses, twinkle toes." His arm had slipped around her waist. "Glen Miller waits for no one, not even a pretty face like yours." He nodded towards the band who had begun to play once more. "C'mon, away we go...quick now." She smiled and followed him on to the floor.

Nearer the band she had to lean forward to hear what he was saying but, once past the musicians, he threw her wide then rolled her back into his arms before spinning her away again. He could dance all right and he was fun. She was surprised at the lightness of his touch and laughed gaily at his chatter. As she twirled so her skirts lifted then a shoulder strap slipped and she laughed again, ducking away from his hand as he tried to hitch it up for her. Suddenly he let her go to dance freely by herself while he bent forward jitterbugging and stomping on his own, his blond hair shaking itself into an untidy mess. Two others next to them were doing it also and those watching cheered and clapped.

But at last they were done and the music slowed. "Hey, there," he gasped admiringly. "Wow...I surrender. That was some dancing."

"Great." Becky panted, allowing him to take her arm. "Thanks," she paused, gulping for air. "Mavis Vellacott's been looking for you, y'know."

"Yep, I know," he puffed. "Couldn't see her so I swooped on you instead. Here look." Matt was easing her towards his group of friends when his path was blocked.

" 'Arf a mo, friend." Gerald Chugg was as tall as Bradshawe but broader and his red face behind the dark jowls was angry. "That's my friend's girl you're messin' with. His an' not yours...right. Jest keep yer grubby 'ands off. That's all."

"S'all right, Gerry." Becky lifted a calming hand. "Matt's hands ain't goin' nowhere. Us're just goin' to see some of his friends. Where's Mavis Vellacott? Matt here wants to see her."

Gerald Chugg paused undecided, looking from one to the other. "Ah well. That be fine then. Not too long though, maid, or your Sam'll be wondering what be goin' on."

"*Nuthin's* goin' on, Gerry," she replied tartly. "Matt here's looking for Mavis...not me. I'll be over directly."

"Here, look." Matt put an arm on her shoulder and inched her forward. "A mate of mine, the fella I was talking about. Mike Daley...over there. Hey, Mike." Matt lifted his hand. "'Ere we are, mate. Over 'ere." He waited for his friend to join them. "Mike," he announced. "Meet Becky, Becky Carter."

*

Her second dance with Mike was slower and the music softer. Becky felt his fingers pulling her towards him. As they turned slowly she felt the warmth of his thigh pressing between hers. He bent her forwards in time to the music then pulled her back and into him, their eyes rarely leaving each others. "Fred Astaire an' Ginger Rogers," he whispered. "Magic...*and my heart beats so that I can hardly speak,*" he sang. "*When we're out together dancin' cheek to cheek.*" For a moment her eyes closed, then she felt his cheek against hers. "That's beautiful," he whispered.

She nodded and opened her eyes. "Mm hmm, lovely," she murmured as the music came to an end. "Thank you very much." She tried to pull away from him but he held on to her. "You're stardust," he said. "An' I've never seen anyone like you before…honest. Here." He pulled her towards him. "I want to see you again, just the two of us. On our own. Right? And don't you dare say no. Don't you bleedin' dare."

Becky pulled back and looked at him. Her heart was thumping. She tried to speak, to ask him to let her go but he still had hold of her and she could feel herself warming to him. Suddenly she wanted to throw her arms around his neck and pull him down to smother him with kisses. But she dare not. All she could do was to shrug and smile back at the dark eyes staring her out. "I'll find yer," he asserted. "Matt'll know where you live."

"*No,* she cried. "No, Mike, don't. I mean, I *can't*…honestly. Don't try to find me."

"Find what, eh?" Gerald Chugg and Archie Thorne stood one either side of them. Becky looked round anxiously. Sam was standing with Pat Steer, Freddy Bale and the Wollacott brothers. None of them had noticed. "Time's up, soldier boy. Off yer go an' just leave her alone. Gid on…hop it."

"Stand still, all of you. *Stand still,*" the band leader demanded. "Hey *you,*" he shouted. "*Stand up straight.*" The room stood, every one still wherever they were, while they sang the National Anthem. All that moved were chests and breasts rising and falling breathlessly. But it was over. Even as the drums rolled again and the cymbals crashed, the two Special Constables appeared to see the party-goers on their way.

❉

"Can't do nort about it. Can't force the girl…if that's what her wants then that's all there is to it." Sam Hawkins closed the car door behind him. Outside it was black. Whatever moon there had been was hidden by cloud. He thought he felt a drop of rain and lifted his collar, shrinking back into the warmth of the soft cloth around his neck. "Anyways, 'tis no good raisin' yer fists to they army lot, Gerry. Only makes it worse. Best leave things as they be."

"Aye but don't go taking it lying down, man." Gerald Chugg leant across the passenger seat. "Put up a fight for the girl, Sam…us'll be with 'ee. Her'll think more of yer if yer squares up to they lot. Any case, they'll be gone afore long. Then what? Eh? Think on it."

"Aye." For a moment he stood undecided. Since leaving the hall, a deep gloom of despondency had settled around him. Becky had spurned him: that had been clear and everyone had seen it. The glamour and the fast talk, the uniforms and all those smiling, happy-go-lucky faces had turned her head. They were smart, that lot: they had different things to talk about. They were there together in a crowd and all of them were after the same thing. It was all right for them. They had money and cigarettes and they could play the fool all night long. Then, as far as he could see, they had nothing to do the next day. And they had nothing to lose, neither, no nitterin' and gossipin' about what had gone on, no *face* to lose and no mother and family to come pushing this way and that. No, there was nothing he could do about it, nothing.

"Us'll have to see...see what's what," he replied. "Anyhows, thanks fer the lift." He bent down and took the other's hand. "I'll be all right, Gerry. Don't 'e go worryin', lad. See yer then...bye."

He waited until the dull glow of the shaded headlamps had turned towards Winsford then began walking down the long drive. At the gate looking out down the valley towards the village, he stopped and leant over the top bar, allowing the cool wind to brush his face. Even as he closed his eyes he could see her laughing and her eyes dancing with delight in that pink and green frock of hers as that smart-arse swept her round and round. He had stolen her from him and she was loving it. Sam shook his head. A sudden gust made him duck his head then he lowered it further, resting his forehead on his arms.

2.

"I can't help it, Pat. He's different to all the others. Gentle and...well, not so rough."

"Go on. Smooth as oil, more like." The two stood by the railings opposite the post office. It was three weeks since Becky had first met Mike Daley at the dance. Pat had watched the change come over her. Poor Sam had been beside himself and she had found herself as their go-between. "Honest to God, Becks, he's fun and all that but he's as slippery as an eel. And he's got you hooked. Well, hasn't he?" she asked. "And now you're going with the man. Can't yer see it, Becky? He's just playing you along, having his bit of fun. Doesn't care for toffees. And what about Sam, eh? You're going to have to tell him, y'know...you can't just leave him up at the farm like this."

Becky shrugged. Mike had told her that Sam would understand. Men did, he said. They grew to expect that sort of thing. It was part of the game and they got used to it. Everything would sort itself in the end and there was no need for her to run crying to him, wringing her hands and telling him how sorry she was. "He'll be all right," she muttered.

"*What?*" Pat gasped. "What d'you mean he'll be all *right?* Oh, fer goodness sake, course he won't. Mavis saw him a coupla days back and he looked dreadful. You can't just leave him like that...drop him dead. *Cuh.*" She paused. "An' what on earth d'you think people'll be saying about that...you'll be getting a right name about the place."

"Hmm. Probably got that already. But I can't help it, Pat. Honest, there's nothing to be done and it's not the end of the world, is it? 'Tisn't as though we're to be married or nuthin."

"Oh, fer goodness sake. D'yer Mum and Dad know yet…that you're dropping Sam, I mean?"

"I'm *not* dropping him…I were never his anyway."

"Oh, don't be so daft, Becks. Who ever d'you think you're kidding? Sam…me? Come on, girl. You've dumped him an' that's that…and he knows it." She paused. "Course he does, he could see it for himself that first night up at the hall weeks ago, and again last week. Dancing and making eyes at that Daley all night long you were. We're not blind, y'know. No, Sam's gotta be told straight…and by you. And your Mum an' Dad as well. What's going to happen if Mike Daley comes knocking at the door and asks to see you? Eh? What're they going to be saying then. Crikey…they'll go through the roof, the pair o' them."

Becky looked at Pat then away again. She knew all these things would have to be done but she had yet to muster the courage. And, anyway, Mike said it didn't matter. It had been bad enough facing Sam the other day and telling him she wasn't sure about things and she could never bring herself to face him with this. And her mother and father would go mad. She could never tell them, not straight out. And in any case, they were bound to find out sooner or later and she would just have to see what she could do when the time came. Not now though. For the moment she wasn't going to tell anyone.

"And you're seeing him tonight?"

"Tomorrow, outside the White Horse."

Pat looked at her but her head was turned away. "Oh Becky," she whispered. "Just be careful. You've never been with a man like this before."

"Nor've you."

"I know, and that's why I can see it better than most. Honest, Becks, I'm only saying this 'cos I don't want you to get hurt…or worse…."

"What d'you mean *worse*?" Becky rounded on her. "Worse like what, Pat? You an' the others are all the same. '*Do* this…*do* that…*don't* do this…'. I'm not a kid yer know. I can take care of meself…and Mike Daley, too, for that matter. He's not going to walk all over me, y'know."

"I know, I know." Pat put an arm through hers. "Just take care, love. He's a smashing fella but he's got nuthin' to worry about has he? Not a care in the world. It's just a big laugh for him an' the others. Just take care, that's all." Pat drew Becky towards her and kissed her on the cheek. "Just be careful, I'll see yer tomorrow."

*

Becky parked the bicycle in the dip behind the trees. It was her favourite spot and it had not taken her long to ride out from the village. The water flowing under the narrow bridge was even lower than it was when Sam had driven her there last month. She liked the peace and the sound of water and had suggested it to Mike when they arranged to meet. Last time with Sam it had been warmer and, in spite of cycling out, she was glad of her coat.

She turned at the sound of his voice and laughed as he wobbled clumsily across the grass on his bicycle before coming to a sudden halt under the trees beside her. "How about that then? Smack on." He stood astride the bar and kissed her gently. "Well, here I am, the big bogey man they're all talking about." She smiled ruefully. "Honest, I'm a real danger, y'know. Wait till you see my police record."

"What?"

"Oh aye." He nodded sagely. "Honest. Burglary, riotous behaviour, violence...'specially violence. Plenty of that and pinchin' little old ladies back-sides."

"Stop it, Mike. You had me believing you." Becky blushed suddenly and grinned. "Well, you said you'd like to walk. How about up the river?"

"Blimey, look at it...the Thames at Westminster," he quipped. "All right then, why not?" They rested their bicycles together then he followed her as she skipped from rock to rock across the water. "Like a bleedin' gazelle, you are." He caught her and pulled her towards him. "Gotcha. Where to now?"

"This way." She nodded upstream and led the way, letting him take her hand once more. Suddenly she felt alive, as though she had escaped from a prison. Like some wild bird that had flown from its cage. She remembered the first time he had kissed her, more than a week ago now, and smiled happily at the memory, squeezing his fingers as they walked along the bank, stooping now and then to duck under the low hazel branches. "Ah." She stopped. "Look. We'll have to get over the fence and cross the stream again. The path goes on the other side."

"Why for?" he asked. "Let's sit here, right here on this side. Just where it bends. It almost runs under the bank and we've got the sun as well." For a moment they were silent. Mike sat then half lay back, propping himself on one elbow. Becky took off her coat, laid it down and sat next to him.

53

"Tell me again," she said eventually. "All about that naughty boy in Portsmouth. You only got as far as the home they put you in. Was it really as bad as that?" She glanced at him then got up and rearranged her coat closer before falling back on it to lie beside him. "I bet it wasn't. Go on, tell me everything." She turned onto her tummy and moved even closer.

From time to time she pulled at a long grass, sucked at the juice then lifted her head to spit out the bitter fibres. Nobody had ever talked to her about themselves like that before. She listened enthralled as he told her about how he and the others stole pies from the pannier market and sold them outside the pubs along the harbour front, about how three of them had been chased for pickpocketing, and how they used to catch live rats down at the docks which they sold for sixpence each to the owner of a dog pit. From time to time she laughed out loud, burying her head in her arms and lifting her feet into the air behind her. But then, when he told her how he had spent so long searching in vain for his mother, she was silent and rolled onto her back, wriggling up close and running her fingers down his cheek.

He stopped what he was saying, looked down and stroked her hair, twining it around his fingers. Bending down further, he kissed her gently. She responded but then, as she closed her eyes, she felt one of his hands kneading her breast. She turned and reached out for him but he moved suddenly and was on top of her.

"No Mike," she tried to squirm away from him but he held her. "No," she gasped. "You're squashing me." She tried to wriggle free but his mouth crushed down against hers. She pushed him back. "Stop it," she cried, feeling his hand moving between her legs. "No please, Mike...please." He half rolled off her but still had her pinned with his body. His hand had moved to her face and they lay still. "Why're you looking at me like that?" she asked, blowing her hair from her face.

"Why not?" He laughed quietly and tickled her nose. "Mmm? You're a beautiful woman an' there's no crime in looking."

"*Poof*, enough of that," she chortled. "All that smarm and sweet talk."

"And it's all true," he whispered then bent and kissed her again. Becky lay back once more, feeling his lips on hers before his mouth moved down to her throat and his fingers crept back to her blouse. Her hands went around his head and this time she pulled him down onto her. All of a sudden her breath was coming more quickly, then faster still. She reached out for his shirt and started to pull at it, then for the buckle on his belt. Again he rolled on top of her and this time she rose to meet him feeling him against her as their bodies came together.

3.

Sam watched balefully as the jeep and two army lorries passed him, then crossed the road and opened the garden gate. Twice that week he had tried Myrtle Cottage but Becky had been out. On the first occasion there had been no answer but when he next called her mother had invited him in.

Up to then, he used to feel a surge of excitement every time he ducked through the doorway, even Becky's footsteps on the stairs would thrill him. But no longer; her mother's invitation had seemed strangely out of place. It was as though he was being encouraged to enter an alien and hostile atmosphere, somewhere he no longer had any right to be and where the welcome was false. The one person whose warmth he desired would be cold and distant. If she had any feelings for him at all Becky would have made contact by now.

Pat Steer, when he saw her outside the forge, had behaved strangely, shiftily almost, when he asked if she had seen her and he knew then that Becky was avoiding him. There could be only one reason and that was what he had seen at the dance. For days the memory of her lying back in the soldier's arms as he danced with her had haunted him and her subsequent elusiveness only served to convince. Pat and the other girls knew something they dare not tell him and now, after almost two weeks of silence, he was sure.

*

The speed at which she answered his knock surprised him. Only later did he realise that she must have been watching him as he stood on the far side of the road. "Hullo Sam." The smile was friendly enough but her eyes flitted past him before returning nervously. That was all: no welcome and she came out on to the front step so she could close the door behind her.

"Becky," he nodded. "Thought I'd drop by. It's bin a coupl'a weeks or so now an' I've bin wonderin' how you're keeping. I've brought you these, look." He handed her the flowers he had bought in Dulverton the day before and which he had kept hidden at home.

"I'm fine, Sam. Yes, fine thank you. Oh, and thanks for these," she murmured, taking the flowers. Then she waited, still searching his face.

"I thought perhaps we could talk, Becks. Can I come in...step inside for a minute or so."

She grimaced. "It'd be difficult Sam. Not easy...mother's due back from Dulverton directly and...." With that she backed against the door as if to bar his way.

"It's just that I need to see yer, Becky. I have to talk. Can we walk for a while, then."

Becky folded her arms. Her mind was a jumble of emotions. Her friend of so many years seemed distant and awkward as though he had suddenly become a stranger who had no right to be behaving like this. She would have to tell him yet she felt sorry for the sad look in his eyes and momentarily guilty about what had happened. But it was too late for all that and there was no time for further delay. He had to know now. "Sam listen. I…we can't go on." The words tumbled out and she caught her breath. "I'm sorry but…well…"

"It's him, isn't it?"

"Yes." Their eyes met.

"The soldier…the one at the dance."

"Yes." She saw his eyes half close. "Yes, Sam. It is him an' we're seeing each other. I'm sorry," she whispered. "Sorry, but that's it…that's the way things are. Things're different now."

"Aye," he nodded. "Aye, s'pose they are, aren't they." He looked away, biting his lip then nodded again more slowly. "Yer Mum an' Dad an' that…they know?"

"No, not yet but I'll tell them." She waited, watching him struggle with what she had said. He seemed to stand there for ever but she knew she had to give him time. "They'll be mad at me but they'll have to know." She shrugged and looked at him helplessly. "Everyone'll think I'm mad…or summat like that."

Sam nodded. "Aye," he whispered. "Won't be easy I don't expect." Then he stood back and took a deep breath. "Ah well, Becks, there 'tis…that's it, then." He turned away, his face grim, then he looked round as though he had a sudden idea. "Listen," he said, his voice now eager. "Just s'pose…p'raps if." Then he stopped and shook his head. "No…no matter. I'll be off then."

"Here, Sam. You'd best take these. It don't seem right." She held out the flowers. "Thank you, anyway."

He paused, looking at them. "No, maid. They'm yours now. Best you hang on to them". Then he turned and she stood watching him as far as his pony and trap.

"Bye, Sam." She lifted her hand, hoping he might turn but there was no response. Without a further glance, he turned the trap in the road and drove off, his pony trotting briskly. Her hand fell and suddenly she felt saddened and empty, mean at what she had done. As she went back into the cottage, she looked at the flowers he had given her, wondering what she might do with them.

✳

"You've done *what? What* was that, you said?" Ernest Carter stood, one foot still in the water. His mouth was open and he was staring at her. He had been washing his feet in a metal bowl by the fire. His trousers were rolled up to his

56

knees and the towel he had been holding slipped from his grasp. "Say that again. Go *on...say it again,* I'm tellin'yer." His voice had risen and Becky watched fearfully as his face reddened. Her mother sat staring at the window curtains. As always her face was pinched and one hand was at her cheek as though a tooth was troubling her.

"You've passed over Sam Hawkins...passed him over, just like that. And you've done what? Taken up with one of they soldiers. *Eh? Is that it?*" He stepped from the bowl and walked up to her with his grey-black eyebrows furrowed close together. When he lifted a hand to wipe his mouth, she flinched, thinking he was going to strike her.

"Yes, Dad." She nodded meekly, one hand reaching out to steady herself on the back of a dining chair. "And I thought I ought to tell yer before you heard. We've..."

"Quiet," he cried. "You've said enough, and enough's enough." Suddenly his voice dropped. "So, here you are standing in front of me telling me you've thrown up Sam Hawkins. A fine, upstanding young fella like that with all 'e's got up there up at Hayes Farm...his family an' that. You've thrown all that away to take up with one of that lot. This bleedin' lot...why they're not even real soldiers, none o' them. Idling away their time down here on Exmoor while there's a war to be fought an' that." One hand scratched angrily at his hair. "Not even proper men, none o' them. An' *you, Becky Carter*...my daughter, seen around the village with one of them."

"It's not as if...." Doris Carter started to speak.

"Quiet woman." Becky started at the tone in her father's voice. "Best you leave us be," he said curtly. Go on...find summat out the back and leave me awhile. *"Cuh."* As she hurried out of the room, he returned to his chair and sat heavily."

"Listen to me, father." Becky pleaded. "Listen. You're shoutin' and swearin' as though I've done something terrible. I *haven't*. Honestly, he's nice, ever so nice. Give me a chance. I'll ask him round..."

"No." Ernest Carter turned sharply. "I'm not having none of they lot in my house."

"But you'll never know..."

"And that's the way it's going to be." He slumped back seemingly exhausted. "I've warned you time and again, girl." He paused to wipe his mouth. "Your mother an' I don't want nothing to do with this, an' you've got to stop. Understand?" He turned to her. "You keep away from they lot, I'm tellin' yer straight."

"But Dad..."

"There's no buts about it." He was still glaring angrily but had lowered his voice once more. "I've said my piece and that's it. From now on, you keep well away from them. Away now…..that's enough." He waved her away and sat back, staring silently at the floor.

Even after the silence Becky's voice was surprisingly quiet. "I'm a grown woman, father. As you told me yerself, at my age mother was married. I'm a grown woman and I'll see who I like when I like." She paused as she reached the door. "But don't go worryin', I'll not be bringing him here…wouldn't want to upset you…nor him neither." She paused with the front door open. "But Mike Daley's bin good to me. He's kind…and a fine man."

As the door shut behind her, Ernest Carter raised his head. He looked around at nothing in particular then closed his eyes and sighed deeply.

4.

Daley knew his man. Harry Jessop the barman at the White Horse asked for Lucky Strike and he got them, but the bourbon was something extra. Keep it coming from the American PX and if anything goes wrong then they'll reckon it's one of the yanks that's been greasing his palm. But it didn't go wrong and it wouldn't go wrong. Daley was far too sharp.

The room, up on the second floor at the back, next door to Harry's own room was little more than a bunk but it was enough. In fact it was fine: way out of sight and nobody around. It was just the job. Another bottle of rye and Harry had the coal fire going. It was early November and the guards at the camp were into their winter clothing. The evenings were colder now and that went for the little rooms at the top of the pub, so another bottle of rye it had to be.

"Don't be so bleedin' nervous…jumping about the bed like there's pins in yer pants." Daley brushed the hair from her face. "'Cept you ain't got none on, 'ave yer, eh? Here, relax for Chris's sake, nobody's coming…I got the heavy mob down in the bar."

Becky grinned and turned towards him, throwing one arm around his neck and pulling him towards her naked body. "You're a devil, Mike Daley. A devil with a red forked tail but I love yer all the same. Love yer, love yer, love yer." She kissed him, slowly at first then again and again until their lips met. "You won't be leaving, will yer?" she asked, pulling back and looking at him anxiously. "Not like Matt Bradshawe and they others last week. That was sad."

"Who *me?*" Daley pursed his lips then wiped his moustache. *"Nah,"* he pulled a face. "Never…no chance. Can't do without me here, least that's what Uncle Freddie Bates said. Daley, he said, Daley you're indispensable, just behave yerself. Right, sir, I said. It's a deal an' all." He watched her laughing with her head thrown back then bent and kissed her throat. "So that's it, stardust. This here wilderness of yours has got me for the duration…an' so 'ave you."

"Mmm." Becky rolled towards him again. "Come on, then," she urged. "Love me again, gently this time and slowly." Her hands ran over his chest and up the sides of his face. "Come on," she whispered. "Come on, Mike." In her own time and without taking her eyes from his, she rose and straddled his hips then eased forward until her soft, full breasts brushed against the hairs on his chest. Bending further until her tongue found his she began to move her body effort- lessly and rhythmically in time with his.

❋

Sam had gone early to the carol service to help his father put out the service sheets and prepare the candles at the end of each pew. That afternoon Exford had received its first dusting of snow and by the time the church began to fill it was freezing hard. The Carters arrived just as the lights were put out and the church, save for the candles, was in darkness. It was difficult to see from his seat near the back if they had noticed him.

He waited impatiently for the service to end then, as soon as the vicar had given his blessing and began to walk down the aisle, he moved. Leaving his pew he walked briskly to the door, opened it and moved out into the cold night air before anyone noticed him. He had thought carefully about what he would say, rehearsed it time and again but knew his words were going to fail him, especially if she stopped to listen.

It was going to be difficult to face her yet his mother's constant pressure had forced him into it. Twice they had rowed and on the second occasion he had stormed out of the house, returning only when he knew his parents had retired for the night. His father had tried to intervene but it made matters worse, giving his mother the excuse to tell him to stand on his own two feet.

The dull glow from inside the church enabled him to make out who was bidding farewell to the vicar in the porch. As he waited, he blew on his fingers, shrinking back behind the tall gravestone whenever those hurrying down the path glanced his way. Then suddenly she was there, moving quickly ahead of her parents in an attempt to catch the two Chugg brothers.

"*Becky*," he called quietly, then again. "*Becky*, it's me, *Sam*." She turned, lower- ing her head and shielding her eyes from the light to see better. For a moment she stood motionless, either unaware who it was or undecided at what to do. "'Tis only me, maid. Just hoping to catch yer for a minute." He walked quickly towards her. " Thought you might be here on your own, like. 'Tis not the best place, I know, but I had to see yer…just fer a minute or so."

"Hullo Sam." She stood erect and shivering, both arms wrapped around herself in the cold. "I can't be long, though, and it's freezing. What's up?" She knew of course and wondered how he would broach the subject. "What is it, and why're you jumping out at me in the dark like this?"

"Thought it'd be a good place to catch you, that's all. Here look." He took her arm and they moved into the shadows at the side of the porch. "Just wanted to know, how you'm feeling…how things are, like."

"They're fine, Sam. Everything's fine." She looked away, knowing exactly what was on his mind and sensing he was struggling to continue.

"I was wonderin'," he began hesitantly. "Just wonderin' whether I might come down and see you. Whether we might go for a drink again or p'raps up to one of they film shows in the hall." He paused. "It's just that I'd like to see yer, Becks. I miss seein' yer, miss yer a lot, an' well…."

"Sam listen," she sighed. "It's no good. Really it's not. I'm with somebody now and we're goin' steady. I'm not seeing anyone else. I don't want to and Mike wouldn't want me to neither. Let's just leave things as they are. Don't you think?"

He looked at her. "Aye," he replied eventually. "I thought you might say that but I had to try…just in case like. Owed it to meself…I had to find you and see."

"I'm sorry, Sam, but that's the way it is and it's really best to leave it like that." She caught hold of his hand. "Listen, I've got to go. Mum an' Dad'll be wondering what's up. I'm sorry, really I am." She squeezed his hand. "But we can still be friends, can't we? I mean, I still like yer, Sam. You know that don't you?"

He nodded but said nothing. Only after she had hurried away into the night did he hitch up his collar and walk to where his parents would be waiting in the car.

5.

"So, what's up with you, sunshine?" Mike Daley, beret on the back of his head, stood looking at Sam. He took the cigarette from his mouth, crushed it under his heel then turned to his companions. The three of them, all in their army greatcoats, had come out of the stable block together when the guard at the main gate sent somebody for him. The message was that there was a farmer at the gate asking for him and he had come out with Danny Brown. Dave Allchurch had joined them and the three of them stood together.

"Mike Daley?" Sam asked, nodding expectantly. "Are you Mike Daley?"

"And what if I am?"

"I was wondering if we could talk, just the two of us…you an' me alone?"

"Well, no need to be shy…let's be havin' it here then. Don't worry about my friends. What's on yer mind, eh? Cows ain't got no milk or summat." He turned to his companions and they laughed together.

"Best if we're alone, Daley. 'Tis a bit personal, like, and I'd rather us spoke man to man, that's all."

"Look, mate." Mike Daley walked up to him and the others followed. "I know what's buggin' yer and the answer's *no*. There ain't nuthin' to talk about. Right? It was her decision. I didn't twist her arm nor nuthin. It's a free world an' she's big enough to know her own mind. Anyway, all's fair in love an' war." He paused. "Now then, 'op it. Go on…scram."

Sam looked from one to the other. For a moment his fists, thrust deep into his coat pockets, clenched in anger. He could feel his face flushing but whatever fight there had been in him had gone. Sorrow, not anger, bore down heavily and he turned away.

"An' don't look so bloody miserable neither. Get a grip of yer knickers," Sapper Allchurch jeered after him. "Got it all too easy, you lot. Hiding away down here among all these bits o' skirt."

Sam paused at the laughter and half turned. He had it in mind to say something but turned back and walked on.

Chapter Five

For a while she had to be careful. By now her face was well known due to the fact that her father was working either in the stables behind the White Horse, or across the road at the forge. Furthermore, whenever the weather allowed them to work in the garden, she and the others came and ate their lunch on the bridge. Yet it was this very bustle and the coming and going about the place that made it easier for her to move around. And there was the excitement of it all, too. Once, twice, sometimes three times a week they managed to meet high up on the second floor in the little bunk next to the barman's room.

Sometimes their lovemaking was hurried and urgent, the clothes they tore from each other lying crumpled and scattered untidily about the bed. Then their hot, half naked bodies would writhe together, as they groaned or cried out in their lust before dressing hurriedly and going their separate ways. On other occasions, however, after she had finished work for the day and when the evening stretched for hours in front of them, they lay quietly together, curled in each others arms dozing or listening to the distant babble of voices and laughter far below.

Becky's spirits soared. She bloomed. She laughed and joked, she hummed as she worked and she sang with the music when they danced together. She had found her man with whom life promised so much. Her future looked bright and secure and she began to live as only life can be lived when the spirit within is so high and there's never a care in the world. But she should have taken more care.

She should have taken note of what folks around her could see. Pat Steer told her about Sam's torment yet, instead of showing concern, she appeared indifferent to his plight. Gladys Strange, heavier than ever in her land girl's dark green jersey and baggy breeches, warned her of talk in the bar. And even when Gerald Chugg's bile took her by surprise she shrugged it off, spinning on her heels and tossing her head defiantly. She could have so easily accepted his offer to dance but Corporal Danny Brown from Edgecott was pulling her away. "C'mon, Becky. Why not?" the farmer asked.

"Later, Gerry," she giggled, half slipping as she turned after the soldier. "But only if I'm not too tired, mind."

"Here, girl," he exclaimed. "Enough of that fobbin' me off. You listen to me." Chugg stood in front of her. "No need always to go tiring yerself out with they lot, y'know. There's more round here than just they soldiers."

"Aye, an' most of it's dead from the neck up." Becky pulled away from the hand that was holding hers and stood swaying in front of him. One hand went to her hair. "And you listen to me for once, Gerry Chugg." Her voice was slurred. "If I want to dance with you then I'll come lookin' for you. Right? It so happens that I'm happy enough as I am right now."

"Aye," he replied sourly. "Us can see that. All of us can …see it clear as day an' it stinks."

"Oh, get lost." She went to push past him but he barred her path. "Go on," she remonstrated. "Get out of my way."

Gerald Chugg stood back. He was a big man, far bigger than anyone around him. He had never really liked the Carter girl, not even when his best friend, Sam Hawkins, had taken up with her. He never said anything but it hurt when he saw how she had turned her back on him, dropping him dead like she had. And here she was playing the field for all she was worth in front of them all. "Gid on then, girl," he growled. "Off an' play with they lot…..there's plenty of 'em there."

"And they're better than you lot, Gerry Chugg. All of them an' don't you forget it."

"Aye," he snapped. "And they need their baggage, an' all. Need it bad……on yer way, then."

✳

As January turned to February so the first snowdrops appeared, peeping shyly from their beds deep between the stones in the banks. Others were soon to join them: daffodils, with their tall green stems holding the buds that were waiting to burst into a blaze of yellow and gold, were making their way as were the first grey-green leaves of the foxgloves set in their sturdy rosettes. While in the hedgerows the long trails of honeysuckle were showing the first signs of fresh life.

For a while Becky barely noticed herself. So enthralled was she with Mike Daley and so turbulent had life become at home that her mind was full of scheming and plotting. Twice he took her in his jeep to see the guns firing on Anstey Common. She watched fascinated, with her hands over her ears, as the soldiers ran here and there before guns crashed out, jumping back as they did so. Great gouts of smoke spewed from their barrels as they sent the shells screaming on their way before crashing down on her old home. She had heard them many times before and had tried to get used to the idea but, even now, she listened sadly, often screwing up her eyes in anguish at the deep, growling explosions way out in the distance where she once lived.

Then February passed and March arrived, bringing the savage bite of a sharp east wind that carried with it flurries of snow which tried to push the shoots of spring back into the earth. It was then, all of a sudden early in March, when she was doing her hair and watching the sleet feathering against the windowpane that she realised.

A sudden cold shaft of fear tore through her and she froze, eyes, mouth and face taut and motionless as she stared at herself in the mirror. The eyes that looked back widened with fear. She clutched at her stomach, dropping her comb as she did so then turned in panic as if casting about for help. Her second month had come and gone. Becky felt out behind her, inched her way back and sat on her bed, scarcely aware of what she was doing. Of course, of course. That was why she had been staring so helplessly at the food on her plate. That was why she had been feeling those tiny, elfin tingles of change in her body. Oh, dear God…dear God, no. Her lips moved silently. It could not be so. She *couldn't* be…..she *couldn't*. But she was.

She swallowed, then swallowed again, glancing about fearfully as she tried to remember when it had all begun. It was that week in December, after the middle of the month but before Christmas when she should have taken care. She should have resisted him, sent him on his way explaining why but she hadn't. She had forgotten all about it and their love had been more passionate than ever. And now January and February had come and gone. March was here when she would know for sure, but she knew already. It had to be so. It had to be and she began to count. Hurriedly and panic-stricken she ran over the figures again and again. The child, their child, would be born in September.

✳

Even when Jack came home on leave, her dull, brooding moodiness prevailed. She adored her elder brother. Ever since they were small, when she had ribbons in her hair and white socks on her feet, they had been friends. Although nearly three years older, he and the others played with her nonetheless, listening patiently to her childish prattle and helping her to partake in whatever they were doing. It was Jack who, with Sam, would carry her across the streams or help her over the fences, who would lift her up to see the eggs in the black-bird's nest, or who would make arrows with chickens' feathers for flights that she would put in the bow he had strung. And it was he who would then lead her forward to stand close to the target they had made. She worshipped him and should have been thrilled at his homecoming but she could barely bring herself to smile back at his dancing blue eyes when he picked her up and hugged her while still in his dark blue sailor's uniform.

It was when he went to see Sam that Jack realised how things had changed. His father told him about the rows they had had with his sister and it was Sam who told him, after prompting, how she had turned her back on him and the rest of them. Then his fears grew. On his last day of shore leave they walked out together. He had his arm in hers and when they were clear of the village he begged her to tell him. They had walked up the hill to the church and turned into the cricket ground when he stopped and pulled her towards him, telling her softly what he believed the trouble to be. She could not hold his gaze but dropped her head, shaking it mournfully. Only when he lifted her face and asked her again did the tears come yet still she denied it.

How could she have done so, she now asked herself. How could she have denied the truth to the brother she loved more than anyone else? She could not but she had and, after he had gone, she despised herself for having deceived him and for sending him on his way with his worries soothed by her lies.

✳

"Oh…for mercy's sake." Pat Steer sat back.

"God, Becky…*no*. You can't be…*can't*." Mavis looked at her with both hands to her face. "Tell me it's not true."

"Just can't be." Pat whispered, staring in disbelief.

Becky shook her head. It had been her turn to wash down the tools and lock the garden shed. Mavis and Pat had agreed to help. Becky had asked them and both knew she wanted to talk. Word had come from Edgecott that Mike Daley had become restless. Their meetings, it was said, had become less frequent and they had begun to row. Anything he said or did, so word went, brought on her tears. She had grown cold and no longer wanted to dance, he claimed. Others had noticed it too. Greg Thorne had told them he smelt trouble while Gerry Chugg just laughed, announcing that if there was a problem then it was surely of her own making.

"I wish it weren't," she muttered. "How I wish it weren't but it's three months now." She moved to make way for Mavis to sit on the sacks they put on the wooden bench. The shed was silent; each girl stunned by what had been said. Suddenly, all of them spoke at once.

"Does any one know?" Mavis asked, watching as Becky shook her head.

"Yer Mum and Dad?" Pat took off her glasses and began to clean them. Again Becky shook her head.

"What're you going to do, Becks? You can't stay here, I mean you can't have it here in the village." Mavis took her hand and looked at Pat. "D'you want it? I mean there's places where they can do things."

"*Where?*" Pat asked angrily. She blinked and looked at her friend. "Where to, Mavis? Bain't nuthin' round here. Down Taunton, p'raps or Exeter but *where* for Heaven's sake? An' how's her goin' to get there…and stop there 'till it's over with? An' who's goin' to pay, eh? Costs money y'know. All right if you're rich an' got a car an' that but how's Becks to manage?" Silence again. "No," Pat said thoughtfully, shaking her head. "'Tis no use. Us can't be doin' that…bain't right neither. Carol Walker tried that an' look what happened there." Becky lowered her head.

"Us'll see, maid." Pat replaced her glasses. She squeezed herself down beside

Becky and took her other hand. "But people are goin' to have to know," she murmured. "I mean…three months gone already. Another couple of months an' it'll show."

"I know…I know." Suddenly Becky was sobbing. "I know all of these things. I've been thinking for weeks an' weeks, night an' day. I just don't know what to do." Mavis lifted her hand and kissed it, rubbing it gently but then looked down. She shivered, glowering darkly.

"Tell Mike first. 'E's the father, isn't he, eh?" Pat bent down to see her face and watched her nod. "Right then. See him and tell him straight. You never know…'e might come up with summat. Might knock some sense into him." She paused and looked at Mavis who stared back soulfully. "But listen, love. Sooner the better, right. Don't like to say this but there's been talk. Nobody's said nuthin' about you bein' like you are but people've noticed you an' Mike've more or less split. That you're not seeing him…and people've seen you all down and miserable, like. Well, people do talk an' they know that summat's up…summat's not right."

"Mmm," Becky mumbled, reaching for a handkerchief. Then she looked up. "Yes," she gasped. "I know, I've got to get on with it, haven't I?" She paused again. "Oh dear God," she wailed. "You will help me, Pat, won't you love? You will, won't you?" All three of them stood. Becky and Pat were holding on to each other while Mavis turned away, closing her eyes in bitter frustration. All three knew that Becky's ordeal had only just begun.

2.

It was almost dark when she heard his footsteps on the stairs. Earlier she had found the keys Harry Jessop, the barman, had left behind the cracked flower-pot in the hall. Blackout restrictions had been lifted but she had drawn the curtains all the same. She had considered the fire but could not be bothered as they were unlikely to be there long. Instead she sat on the bed with her coat open and her hands thrust deep into the pockets, rising from time to time to check the setting of her hair in the mirror or the rouge on her cheeks or the evenness of the lipstick that he had given her.

The moment their eyes met his face gave him away. It was wary. He looked bothered about something, as though he was in a hurry and when he nodded he just grunted: there was no hug nor welcoming kiss tonight. Even before she opened her mouth she was in no doubt that he knew. "How long?" he asked.

"Three months."

"Three months since what?"

"Oh, come on Mike. What d'you think? I've missed for three months."

"How the hell am I supposed to know, eh? How do I know it's three months an' not four or five. It could've been any time, since way back when you were running around with that farmer fella an' making eyes at Matt Bradshawe...and that lot. How am I s'posed to know?"

"*Mike*...for mercy's sake what are you *saying*? What's this about Sam and Matt?" She steadied herself on the bed. "What are you suggesting...that it's not you, or something? That you're not the father?"

"Something like that. Yeah...yeah, that's right. How do I know who's it is, eh? How do I know that it's not one of that lot, the ones...."

"*Mike*," Becky leapt from the bed. "How *can* you? How dare you say that? I've never, ever touched another man...*never* and well you know it." She saw his scowl. "Oh yes you do. How can you say that? Come on, Mike." She reached out and clung to him but he pushed her roughly and she half fell back on to the bed.

"Calm yerself, fer Pete's sake...just pipe down an' listen." He stood in front of her with his legs astride and raised a finger threateningly. "Just in case you haven't heard of it let me tell you that there's a whole load of talk in this here dump of yours. An' you know what it is? Know what they're saying? No? Well I'll tell yer, darlin'. I'll tell you what the buzz around here is. It's Becky Carter they're all whisperin' about. Becky Carter the barrack room girl. Good for a quickie, she is. Good fer a leg over."

"*Mike*...."

"I said shut up an' listen, didn't I? That's what the talk is. An' in any case, where've you been these last two months, eh? Where've you been when I've come looking for you? Answer me that. An' when I have found yer you've been as cold as death, cold as a bleedin' grave, that's what. An' you know what that means in my book. Know what that means? It means you've been handing it out...flogging it off to somebody else, that's what."

"*No*, Mike. *No*...I haven't, ever, I promise." Becky's face was in her hands. "No," she groaned. "You know it's not true."

"Oh yes, it is...oh yes, my naughty little mischief maker. You're up the duff an' now you're saying it's me...well, why not one of that other lot? Any one of 'em. There not all bleedin' liars are they? They're not *all* makin' it up. Oh no. You've been around the boys, you have. So don't never go trying to pin that one on *me*." He jabbed at his chest angrily. "Eh? Old as the bloody hills that one is an' you're not catchin' me." He turned and pulled the door open. "Better start thinkin' fast, sweetheart. An' start saving, too." With that he left, pausing only to listen briefly at the door behind him before he ran down the stairs two at a time and out into the evening air.

✳

For two days he brooded, angry at being caught like that and angry at the barrack room jibes. How they knew he would never know. But they always did. He used to mock them himself. As soon as some other poor sod in the billet got caught on a problem they would always know, especially when it was money or a woman, but mainly women. It was then that the jibes and taunting would start.

One more night of it and he cracked. He began by throwing back the jests, laughing at them in turn and giving as good as he got. What did it all matter anyway? It was her problem, not his. There were plenty more little fish like her swimming around and begging for it. Take Sherry Blake for a start or that big raunchy land girl up at the farm where he went for the cream and eggs. Nah, to hell with it all. Sink or swim, she was on her own. *She* took her pants off and *she* begged for it, not him. And as for himself, *we-ell*, nobody could pin it on him, an' anyway Danny an' Dave and 'Bugsy' Hughes would all say they'd bin there as well. Always worked that one did, if it came to it. Just needed yer mates to stand by yer. Fine, end of story so it was, but then he saw old 'Chippy' Wood.

Nobody knew how old Chippy was, but he claimed he was as old as the Quartermaster and that was old. He had never done anything wrong but when they tried to pin a tape on his arm he turned it down. Happy as he was, he told them. Just happy to keep driving and looking after his jeep, to do his guards and to keep his bed space clean. There had never been any trouble, he was never late and always did just about enough. But no promotion, thank you.

They met in the canteen. "Come an' 'ave a word, my son," Chippy Wood tapped him on the chest. "Can read you like a book, I can Daley, and it's a bleedin' 'orror story." He held up a hand, cutting dead the protests before they started. "No, no…none of that, lad. Just come an' 'ave a quiet chat with old Chippy. Yeah?"

✳

"It'll never leave you, my son. They never do, not when it's the likes of you?"

"What're you on about, Chippy? What're you tryin' to tell me, eh?" Daley had an idea what the older soldier wanted to see him about but had no idea what he was going to hear until Chippy spelt it out. At first he denied it, then he tried to laugh it off, then he got angry and tried to walk away but finally he calmed and the two of them sat in a corner of the old stable yard, each with a mug of dinner tea in their hands. "Not sayin' I should marry her for Pete's sake, are yer? Cor blimey, Chippy, if I showed my face even, her folk'd run me out of town. Can yer see me swanning along there and asking her to marry me? Bloody hell, man, they'd skin me alive."

Chippy shrugged. "Up to you, my son. But I've seen it all before…'undreds of times and I'll tell yer what fer nuthin'. Not many can walk away from it like you've been prattlin' on about."

"I can and I will."

"Aah, no. Not you. You're the wrong sort, Daley. Think yerself as tough as nails, an' so yer are…fer most of the time. Sharp as a toothpick an' all. But you've bin banging on about how you don't care, an' what you're going to do, all bleedin' day an' night. And that's the point, my son…it's got to yer. As though you're trying to kid yerself…aren't yer?"

"Aren't I what?"

"Tryin' to fool yerself about walking away from your kid that's on its way. Stands out a mile, sunshine, and I'll tell yer what. Yer can't run from it…yer never will, not now not never. The kid'll be with yer for always, hauntin' yer night an' day."

"Bull shit."

Chippy Wood shook his head. "Only you know the truth, lad, so don't go giving me and the others any more crap." His shoulders jumped suddenly as he laughed to himself. "It's your problem, Daley, m'lad, not ours. So stop fighting yerself an' tryin' to kid the rest of us. It don't work, y'know." The old soldier rose slowly and put a hand on Daley's shoulder. "Think about it, my boy. It won't go away, not when it's yours."

✻

And old Chippy Wood was right. The more he tried to push it out of his mind, to bury it and forget about it, the harder it became. Becky's face, her eyes, her hands as she had taken hold of him and, now, what she had told him was theirs wouldn't go away. It was just as the old soldier had said.

3.

Becky felt surprisingly calm. Why, she had no idea but the three days after Mike Daley had left her had been wretched enough and now, in a few moments, she was about to break the news to her parents. She had set her alarm an hour earlier than usual but woke beforehand and lay quietly with her hands clasped together behind her head. She remembered stretching out hurriedly to turn it off then snuggling back for a few last minutes of warmth as she listened to the birds outside.

She remembered also her feelings in the White Horse after he had stormed out. Not only had he, her one hope of salvation, rounded on her savagely, it was the way he had wriggled by twisting the truth, heaping scorn on the very idea that he should be held responsible, then lacing it all with the accusation that she had been sleeping around. The sheer horror of being abandoned like that together with such brutal humiliation had shattered her. How she got through the night that followed and the day after she had no idea but it was Pat, yesterday, who had brought her to her senses, reminding her that her parents would surely find out, if not through gossip then by what they would soon be able to see with their own eyes. And it was she, her friend had insisted, who must tell them: they must hear the truth from her and nobody else.

At first she had recoiled from the idea, terrified at the thought of such a confrontation. Later, at lunchtime, she had walked with Mavis and Pat and they had persuaded her it was something she was going to have to do. Pat, bless her, had offered to be there but she had turned her down. It was then, from that very moment, the moment she made up her mind to do it herself, that a strange calm had come over her. But why? Her friends were already deserting her, the father of the child she was carrying had turned his back and, right now, as soon as she opened her mouth, she was about to destroy that deep bond with her father she treasured so much. Her predicament was hopeless and there would surely be much more to come. It was as if she had started to slide helplessly down a steep waterfall with all hope of rescue gone.

*

As soon as she heard her parents pulling up their chairs for breakfast, she went down and joined them. Her father looked up. Bidding her a cheery good morning, he passed her the blue and white jug in which her share of the milk remained, before turning back to his toast. Surprisingly her mother smiled also, scraping her chair on the flagstones before she, too, sat with the plate of bacon from the cooker.

Once more the room fell silent. Becky glanced from one to the other. "Mum...Dad...I've something to say. Listen, will you...there's something I have to tell you. I'm...with child." She continued to glance from face to face, waiting fearfully in the icy stillness.

"You're *not*." It was her mother who spoke first, sitting back and glaring in disbelief. Becky watched as she looked at her father. "*Ernest*," she hissed. Then louder "*Ernest*, d'yer *hear* the girl?"

Her father was nodding slowly, but his mouth was clamped shut. Becky watched as his hands clenched tight. "Aye," he muttered eventually, continuing with his mouthful but without looking at her. "And it's that soldier, isn't it? Him, he's the one I'll be bound." He remained staring at his plate.

"Yes," Becky whispered.

"How *can* you?" It was her mother again. Her chair had been pushed back and she was standing with one hand to her face. "And how *dare* you say that. Sitting here at our table as if nothing was amiss then...and then *this*. Why, you stupid, slovenly little fool. You *stu*-pid...."

"Shush." Her father had raised his hand. "Quiet a minute." He turned to Becky.

"*So.*" His face had whitened and his breathing was laboured as though he was struggling to breathe. "And that's *it*, eh? You're with *child*, are you? And you're carrying this *soldier's* child around here in the middle of Exford, are you? And what's more you're sitting down with your parents as if there's nothing amiss…"

"Becky. Have you any…."

"Quiet, I said." Ernest glanced at his wife then back at Becky. "How *dare* you," He growled menacingly. "How dare you come telling us that and after I'd forbidden you and warned you? Eh…eh? How dare you go sleeping about and sullying our name? " He was leaning across the table and about to continue when his wife shouted out.

"*Stop*," she cried. It was more of a shriek and both father and daughter started back. Her hands were raised, demanding silence. "Just stop the pair of you and listen to me." Her eyes moved from one to the other. "*Neither* of you have any idea…you can't have. This is not something that comes and goes. It's a curse visited on the family and it stays for ever…and I'll tell you why." Doris Carter sat carefully on the edge of her chair.

"I'll tell you how I know and it will be something you've never heard before, neither of you, not you Ernest, neither. It's a cross I've bin carryin' all these years." She looked at her husband. "I've never said a word before and neither did my mother and father when you asked for my hand." She nodded at him. "No, never a word was said but such was our family shame that I…*me*…Doris Huxtable as I were then. I was born out of wedlock." Now she turned to Becky.

"And you," she spat. "Let me tell you now what shame you've brought on us. What cruel, cruel shame…and all from this evil, wanton little act of yours. D'you know what that child'll be called?" She nodded towards her daughter. "D'you know? It will forever be that bastard child. Yes…oh, yes it will…that *bastard* child, they'll be saying." Suddenly her head dropped and she was sobbing. "Yes it will, for that was what they all called me."

Becky rose but her father pushed her down. She tried again but he held on to her sleeve. "Stay," he muttered, his face now whiter still. Becky wanted to go to her mother, to throw her arms around her and comfort her but she was too late. Her mother's hands fell away. Although wracked with grief the face that glared back at her was hard and bitter. As she pointed at Becky, her hand shook.

"And it's *you*…*you* who've brought this cruel slur on us all…an' after all that we've striven for…me and yer father…Jack, all of us are now to have our good name smeared for ever by what *you* have gone and done. Lusting and rutting like some farm animal…."

"No, mother…no." Becky was weeping. As she looked from one to another her face was distorted with grief. "I loved him, mother…I did. Truly I loved him."

"Love be damned." It was her mother again. "It was lust. Wanton, whoring lust …and here's the result for us all to see." She pointed dismissively. "You've damned us, Rebecca Carter, damned and sullied our name."

"That's enough." Ernest lifted his hand. *"That's enough,"* he said louder. "There's nort to be gained by shoutin' an' hollerin'. What's done's done…best we stop an' think about what's next."

"Get rid of it." Doris half rose. "And quick, a'fore the whole world talks an' laughs, an' fingers start pointing." Now she stood. "An' if yer can't get rid of it then get yerself away from here…right away, d'yer understand. I'm not having poison spat on my name again. Never again, d'yer hear that…never." The cottage shook as she slammed the door behind her.

Becky slumped back into the chair with her whole body trembling. Her father sighed. Words now seemed meaningless. "Her'll calm," he soothed. "T'was her past come back, all of a sudden, I dare say…ay, her'll calm in time. *But.*" Ernest sighed heavily again. "It'll be hard, maid. Hard as mother said, that's fer sure…down here where all the world will have more'n enough to say about it." Becky nodded, her fingers curling around her father's hand that had stretched out to her. "Us'll manage though," he muttered. "'Twill be hard but daresay us'll manage."

Becky pulled herself forward and fell on his shoulder.

4.

Colonel Miles Ashcroft pulled up at the gate. The hind they had been hunting had given them the slip by clearing the wire fence which bounded the new military training area. By then it had gone two o'clock and hounds were called off for the day.

Behind him the road rose across the open moor towards Alderman's Barrow and the high ground beyond before curling round towards Hawkcombe Head and dropping steeply into Porlock Vale. It was a beautiful ride at any time and now, in the clear light of the early Spring afternoon, he was able to pick out the distant blue outline of Wales across the Bristol Channel. Taking his horse through, he turned and held the gate with the handle of his crop, smiling at the woman behind as she made her way past him.

"Don't be too hard Barbara, my dear." They stood together in the road where both mounts were still sweating freely. In a moment he would have to turn northwards while she, along with several others, would be following the hounds down into Exford. He eased away from the field and their two horses walked side by side to the far verge. "I know it seems a pretty awful black mark right now and tongues're going to wag…for a bit anyway. But life does move on. It'll heal…and the scars'll fade. They always do." Adjusting one of his yellow string gloves, he looked at her out of the corner of his eye. "They're a topping family, y'know. Ernest's been a real rock for me up at Larkbro'. He'll see it through, no fear. And as for Becky, she's a dear, really...and a damn good little worker. Knows her horses, too."

Barbara Hawkins looked down. "I know," she confessed. "I shouldn't have been quite so quick. It didn't mean to sound like that. As you say it's war time." She gave a little laugh. "I suppose these little affairs're going on everywhere...all over the place."

"Oho, indeed they are...oh yes. And they always have done, since before the days of bows and arrows...and not just little country girls like our poor Becky. Hmmph. Goodness, no. High society's just as bad...*worse*...the aristocracy, their lordships, everyone. Royalty even. Call it love or whatever you like but look at our Edward and his Mrs Simpson...all right no child but, my God, what a rum to-do, that was."

Barbara nodded and pulled at her mount who was rubbing it's head up and down Ashcroft's riding boot, forcing his horse to sidestep. "I suppose so. It's just that I'm glad Sam's not involved and well out of it all while the storm's raging like it is. It's all been a bit embarrassing...and painful for the boy as well."

"Mmm, the innocent party. How's he taken it? A bit raw, I'll be bound."

"Yes. I'm afraid we've had a session of his moods again, and rather black ones this time. It's got to Drew as well." She shrugged and looked at him despairingly. "And now at lambing time."

"Well, go as easy as you can," he cautioned. "And try not to think too hard of the girl. Life'll be tough enough without another finger pointing." Colonel Ashcroft smiled warmly and reached out to put a hand on her horse's withers. "Look, I'll have to be on my way. We've some folk coming in this evening but, listen Barbara, thank you so much for your company today." His eyes were twinkling. "It's always a pleasure to see you, m'dear and on a chilly afternoon like this it's bin a tonic." Then he paused, pulling on his chin. "Next Saturday perhaps?" He glanced at her. "How about that? They're meeting at Winsford Hill and I'll be staying at the Crown."

"That'd be lovely, Colonel." Her heart jumped for the invitation to ride together had come from him. "Yes, of course," she stammered. "I'll be there."

"Grand...well." Colonel Ashcroft raised his silk top hat. "My thanks again for your company...and a safe journey home. Bye now."

"Good day, Colonel." Barbara Hawkins turned down the road and kicked on, rising to her horse's trot as she hurried to catch the last of the riders.

As soon as she had fallen in with the Colonel earlier, the subject had come up and she had grasped the opportunity to vent her feelings. She told him how

Becky Carter's predicament had given her the chance to let Sam know how she felt and there had been no excuse for him to defend the girl.

What she failed to mention was that her views had driven her son from the house and that Drew had told her she had gone too far. The boy, he said, was torn between shame at being jilted and his fondness for the girl. Her husband had got up from the table to follow him out; as he did so he turned and pronounced that, in his opinion, it was by no means the end of the story. She had risen also and asked him to explain himself but he had merely waved her away and gone out after their son.

Even so she had said too much to the Colonel and was cross with herself for having spoken out so harshly against the girl. He had heard, of course, and had his own strong views about Becky Carter and her family which were so different to hers. He may or may not have thought less of her for her outburst but she, Barbara, had not been able to conceal her satisfaction at how events had unfolded. Sam, whatever his views, had been spared further entanglement. Barbara Hawkins pushed her hat down and pressed on.

5.

Jack Carter shook his head. His leave had been cut short due to the convoy receiving orders to sail earlier than expected but he had managed to get down for a long weekend. The atmosphere in the cottage had been grim, worse than he feared and he had not helped by telling his parents that it was not the work of the devil as they had been proclaiming. He tried to explain that the horrors of war had thrown thousands of young people together and that these things happened. Perhaps not in Exford, he told them, but up and down the country such events were not rare and were having to be accepted.

But that had only made it worse and he was accused of having no morals himself, of belittling the matter in the way common folk might find themselves but which those who feared God never would. It was his sister, he had been reminded, his very own sister, who had brought shame and disgrace on the family. At that he had rounded on them, accusing them of thinking only of themselves and their name rather than of Becky and her forthcoming plight. Even when his mother told him of her own beginnings he found it difficult to be patient.

That evening he and Becky had walked to the forge where, by lantern light, Pat Steer had been raking and setting the fire for her father. The three of them had talked and it was then that he told them of a shipmate whose girlfriend had died after trying to get rid of the child she was carrying. It had been a terrible end, he heard, and it was then that he begged Becky to keep hold of hers. It was asking a great deal of her but no one could think of an alternative and the next morning he and his sister had faced their parents with the decision.

His mother had protested but he reminded her coldly that if her own mother had risked what she was now urging Becky to do then she, his mother, would

not be with them. The silence which followed had been painful – anger, bitterness and a feeling of helplessness all swirling around the parlour together but
the shouting had stopped: it had to for there was no other course to be taken.

＊

He had heard of Sam's loneliness and walked up to see him at Hayes. He found
his friend napping by the kitchen fire, sitting huddled in an old army greatcoat
with a rug over his knees in the armchair they had brought down for the
lambing. He was unshaven and bleary-eyed but pulled himself up and took his
hand in both his own, grinning with real pleasure and apologising for his state.
They had been lambing for two weeks, he explained. There was still another
week to go and then the work would really begin. Jack nodded. He remembered his boyhood at Larkbro' when his own father used to catnap whenever
he could throughout the time the young lambs arrived, exhausting himself in
his bid to save every one.

He helped Sam with the kettle and fetched milk from the dairy before they sat
at the table together. Sam was still hunched in his coat but now he scratched
himself and yawned in a bid to wake up while Jack sat quietly, leaning back
and watching. "I'll never blame yer sister for everything," he announced. "Not
entirely, like…can't, can I? Always takes two but 'tis always the girl gets left wi'
the problem."

"But you've taken it bad I can see that."

"Aye, daresay." Sam nodded slowly.

"Feel cheated, don't you?" Sam nodded again and for a moment the two were
silent. "Cheated and trapped, eh?" Jack confirmed.

"Aye, that's it." Sam sighed and glanced up. "Yer feel right second best fer
being passed over like that. 'Tis as though the whole world knows you've had
yer nose rubbed in it by another man. Rubbed hard and then, soon as the
story's out, they're all there given you a damn good kickin' as well with all
their talking. It's as if the…the child what's coming has shown them all how far
the swine went with her…what 'e did to her an' when 'e did it. An' 'tis all there
fer the whole world to see and there's no escaping." He filled his cheeks and
blew heavily then shook his head. "Bloody trapped, I be. Trapped among all
the talk…an' all this 'ere." He waved his arm at the room. "Aye an' out there,
look." He half rose and waved again at the yard outside and the buildings
beyond. "Bloody trapped, I am."

Jack nodded. He thought Sam would feel this way and now he could see it.
"Get away then, lad. Aye…get away from it all. Look." He leant forward and
nodded enthusiastically. "Seriously, Sam. Get away and join up. Come with me
or join the army. Like thousands…there's always room for more," he joked.
"Honest, think on it. Your mind's as black as hell for all this. You're workin' yer

guts out for sod all and you're letting yerself get driven half mad by the gossip an' that…all they lot." He waved towards the village.

"*Pah.*" Sam shook his head. "Gotta hang on here. Father'd never manage on his own."

"Course he would. There's more'n more land girls now. Honest…plenty o' farms where the younger folks've gone off to the war. The Dales at Chibbet, there you are…Freddie's gone. And the Ridds up to Burley. They're all managing. Think on it, man. Bain't no good sitting here getting yerself beaten down like this."

Sam looked at him. "D'yer reckon?"

"Go in and ask 'em. I did. Castle Street in Taunton…or down to Wyvern Barracks in Exeter. Can't do no harm in findin' out." He watched as Sam took it in, nodding slowly. "You've got to get away," he urged. "Yer need summat different in life, summat that'll get you back on your feet. Think on it." He reached out and patted his friend's hand. "No good stopping here like this."

Chapter Six

Suddenly the whole world knew and for Becky it was grim. The attention she attracted made her feel as though she was deformed or that her belly, although she was not yet five months, had become gross and distended. The furtive glances as she walked by were bad enough but it was the look of rebuttal or disdain on the faces of those she chanced upon that hurt most. A great finger was pointing down at her and some hidden voice was crying out, "*There* she is. *There* look...just look at her."

At first she thought she was imagining it all having listened to her mother complaining about how she and her father were being shunned. Her father denied it, claiming that the farriers and stable lads had little time for such nonsense. Initially one or two had mentioned it to him more out of sympathy than for any other reason, however hands still patted his shoulder and life in the Carter household was included in the conversations at the stables along with everything else.

But Doris lost her job. Early in the New Year a reference from the Colonel had secured her a little part-time work as a cleaner at The Crown. Then at Easter, when Becky was about four months, the manager called her in and told her that he was economising and that her job had to go. She knew exactly why and, a week later, her suspicions were confirmed when she heard that a woman from Winsford had been taken on. Soon after she was refused service in the village stores. The manager's wife ignored her until she was the last then simply locked the till. After that she rarely left home where she would sit for hours, brooding bitterly.

Becky had no escape. Daddy Warren at the garden saw her plight and asked her to come earlier in the day to help him prepare, then later to close the shed when the day's work was done. Pat and Mavis stood by her as did the land girls. It was the thin Sandra Bates with the straggly hair who told them she had never seen such a fuss. It happened in Peckham all the time, she affirmed. Well, not all the time but often enough to make no odds. But *here*? Had they never seen a girl like this before? They needed to sort themselves out, she said. A few nights in the shelters with the bombs raining down and the sirens wailing would soon wake them up. But, for all their support and sympathy, there *was* no escape.

Even the short walk home was an ordeal. Twice she saw Sam, once with his pony and trap and once with Greg Thorne. They saw her as well, said something quickly to each other then turned and raised their hands. Recognition but no more. The soldiers were everywhere, no matter how she tried to avoid them. She never saw Mike but then she hardly dared look, keeping her head down to avoid the leers and the digs. Soldiers always did that. She remembered laughing and holding her ears when one of them showed her how they whistled at girls, but now they were even worse.

Women talking together would see her coming and hurry on their way. People would slide behind their doors and shut them quietly as she approached. Others coming towards her would catch hold of their children and cross the road busying themselves with their shopping baskets or handbags. Even outside the church there would be a sudden silence when those in the porch would stand aside and nod before looking away and letting the Carters through.

She was shunned and she was shamed yet Molly Haycroft, Ted's wife and a month further on than her, was feted and cosseted wherever she went. Women, young and old, gathered around to praise her good fortune and to admire her condition. Bright eyed with excitement they would ask her about her child-to-be, chatter gaily about her family and finish by wishing her well, calling out and waving cheerfully as they went on their way.

But for Becky it was different. The child she was carrying had no such approval. There were no encouraging smiles and the love and affection given so freely else-where was not for her. Her child had been condemned and for that she blamed herself. She tried to imagine how it would be when the child grew up and under-stood what the world was saying. Would it, like her own mother, be forced to go through life avoided by those around her? Would the dreadful tag of the 'bastard child' remain with it like the curse its grandmother warned about?

As the days wore on her torment deepened. She could no longer remain alone in the cottage with her mother and she could barely face the staring eyes and the backs that turned away. There was no escape for her yet it was springtime and the world had woken from the long winter night.

Suddenly, as if by magic the swallows and martins re-appeared. The last time she had seen them was at Larkbarrow and the sight of them darting and wheel-ing above the green brought memories flooding back. Her heart ached for the peace and solitude of the high moors. Once the fluting, bubbling cry of a curlew passing overhead called down, urging her to come up and join them. She missed the trill of the larks that filled the sky above her old home, the harsh croak of the ravens as they went about their business and the sight of little Exmoor horn ewes leading their lambs through the sedge and the bog moss.

By now she could even see her child. Taking the small mirror from the wall above the washbasin, she placed it on the floor against the wall where it looked up at her. Then, after taking off her clothes, she would stand in front of it and run her hands gently across her belly and back again. The hard bump was there. She could feel it and see it then, turning sideways, she could see it more clearly still. Turning back once more, she would stare down at herself wondering at these changes, how her shape of the smooth, round whiteness above the soft hairs was moulding and swelling as a new life grew with slow assuredness.

For Becky there was no way out; it was her mother who broke the spell.

✳

"It's not exactly a welcoming place." Hilary Dalton, heavy-bodied and fleshy and with her dark blue, wide-brimmed hat half covering her face, looked out of the bus window. "They don't show much sympathy to these young women I'm afraid, and they work them hard as well. But I told them that you're happy for them to do whatever they must. Yes?" She had her handbag clasped between both hands in her lap.

"Of course...and it's no bad thing." Doris Carter adjusted her scarf. Her cold was better but her eyes were still running, giving her face a more pinched than usual look. "It won't harm the girl to get her hands dirty. If she'd had a decent job in the first place then all this might never have happened."

"Hmm. Usual story." The two women swayed together as the bus turned onto the main Taunton road. Doris had known Hilary for years. Still a spinster and now a Catholic social worker in Minehead, she had helped young women in the past and it was to her that Doris had turned. Becky knew nothing of it. Cooped up with her wayward daughter, Doris's anger and frustration had grown until she had written to Hilary. Soon afterwards, she went to see her in her neat, whitewashed cottage with the bow windows below the chemist's shop in Dulverton. It could be arranged, Hilary told her, but it would mean a trip to the convent and an interview with the Mother Superior.

"Oh she'll be working all right." As she spoke, Hilary Dalton glanced at her. "No fear of that. The Sisters here are mainly Irish and they know a day's work, that's fer sure. The order's known as Our Shepherd of Mercy and there's plenty of chasing about the place. Oh yes." She gave a satisfied chuckle. "They've got the laundry contract for the hospital and the prison down at Paddlefields. St Margaret's, that's what it's called, is what's known as one of those Magdalene laundries. And if there's time left in the day they get them making things for the Navy, holdalls or something. There's not much sitting around down there."

"Won't hurt." Doris Carter peered past her friend. They were now in the outskirts of the town and either side of them there were lines of redbrick houses set back from the road behind their own hedges. "Nice here," she nodded.

"Yes, and not long now. We'll be dropped at the end of Springfield Road...just over the crest. Then it's only five minutes or so."

✻

The Mother Superior looked a plump, maternal figure. Almost too kindly, Doris thought until she heard her speak about her charges. "And we do *not* tolerate casual behaviour," she advised, tapping her blotting pad. "These young woman have erred enough. They've fallen from grace and they're here to find their way back to Our Lord." The eyes that looked out from behind the heavy, owl-like spectacles glittered defiantly. She sat up, tidying her white collar over her black habit then clasped her hands. "From Godliness and cleanliness comes purity…eventually, that is," she added. "But before we reach that stage the self-discipline has to be instilled and the…your daughter will need all the encouragement we can give her."

Doris nodded. She and Hilary were sitting on two hard-backed chairs in front of the Mother Superior's leather-tooled desk. It was a large, spartan room with its bare wooden floor, its ice-blue walls and a high ceiling that gave off a slight echo as they spoke. Doris Carter shifted her position. What she was hearing now was what she hoped to hear. Becky needed to see the error of her ways and, if that required discipline, then so be it.

"Now then." The Mother Superior took a small red file from one of the top drawers of her desk. "The question of payment." She looked at Hilary Dalton. "Do I understand that the family circumstances are limited? Mmm?" She frowned. "We cannot achieve what we do here on thin air alone, you understand."

"That's so, Reverend Mother." Hilary Dalton opened her handbag. "We've brought what we can…here." She handed over a buff envelope. "The balance will be forthcoming."

"Then you'll let Father Reilly have it, yes?" Her soft brogue seemed to emphasise the point she was making.

"Yes, madam."

"Grand…so." She put the envelope in the file, closed it and replaced it into the drawer which she locked. "We'll take the child as soon as you're ready, Mrs Carter. The sooner the better…for you at home, of course. The sooner she's away from the shame and disgrace she's brought upon you all the better, but for us too. We need to get some work out of the girl and the sooner we get her here then the sooner her purification can begin. It'll take time, y'know, and it'll not be easy. But with the help of Our Lord," she paused briefly. "With His help, she'll be returned to the fold cleansed of her sins."

"And the child? The baby?" Doris cleared her throat. "Do we…I mean…" She glanced at Hilary Dalton.

"As you wish." The Mother Superior looked back over her spectacles. "But we strongly advise that the best thing is for the child to be given a new life…and that's better for the mother, too. We have a well-tried system here. You can discuss it with Father O'Connell, our visiting priest. Once you have given your consent we deal with the girl…and that's the end of the matter."

"Me?"

"Oh yes, Mrs Carter. It's far better to discuss these things with the family rather than with the child herself. On these occasions, emotion clouds all reasoning and common sense. The young mothers have no idea what they're planning to do with themselves and if we were to let them have their way they'd all be straight home again and bringing their troubles along with them."

"Yes, I see. Well I'm sure that's best. In that case…."

The Mother Superior held up her hand. "We can deal with this later but with *you*, you understand, not the girl. There's *no* need for her to become involved…and it's better that she does not. In fact I forbid you to mention the subject. Should she ever hear about this discussion of ours then I'll have to reconsider our offer of help. We can see to it all when the time comes, as it surely will. And now." Her tone changed. "While we're discussing the matter, the parents who adopt the children, the foster parents, they pay for our services…a contribution to our charities." She paused. "And this, of course, can go to offset our admission charges to *you*." She leaned forward and peered sharply. "Am I clear, Mrs Carter?"

"Yes, of course, madam," Doris nodded.

"Good…fine. I'm sure that'll be best for all concerned. And now." She looked from one to the other. "We discourage visits while they're here. The young women have got quite enough on their minds and we like them to reflect quietly on what's taken place…and, indeed how they're going to face the future. Distractions of family and friends are rarely helpful under such circumstances. They're best left to us." Doris nodded again.

"Then I'll bid you good day." The Mother Superior rose, still matronly and surprisingly petite for the power and authority she exuded. "I must away now but you can rest assured that here at St Margaret's the salvation of your daughter is dear to our hearts and we'll do whatever is necessary to save her soul." She raised her right hand. "Now…may the Lord go with you." Doris Carter nodded in reply and smiled. For the first time in months she felt cheered.

On their way back to the bus stop she slipped her arm through Hilary Dalton's. As they walked together they chatted and laughed happily.

2.

Mike Daley looked at the sergeant major behind the desk. He thought he had heard correctly but he had to make sure. "*Me* sir? Why me and what's the place called?"

"It's you Daley because the Squadron Commander has selected you. You along with all the others…six in all. Right? That's why. And it's the Tracked Vehicle Driving School. Near Bordon, up north of your Portsmouth."

"Right, sir and…er, then what?"

"An Assault Regiment…not sure which one yet. On leaving here you'll become a regular, the conscription papers should be here tomorrow. A regular soldier you'll be, Daley, m'lad, and driving a flail tank or an armoured dozer. Right up the sharp end so you'll be…frightening the living daylights out of our friend Mr Hitler an' his chums."

Squadron Sergeant Major Boyd was in a good mood. Wounded in both arms at Dunkirk he had managed to stay in the service but had been given an administrative post far away from the action; and Exford was about as far as one could get. Those around him here had no idea of what it was all about but now things were changing, and changing fast. Men everywhere were being dug out of their dark little corners and prepared for whatever was coming. Rumours were rife but the feeling was that something, somewhere was in the wind and it was big, very big.

"Holidays are over, Daley. No more of this cushy little backwater for you. Mr Churchill's decided that Exford's not going to be bombed flat and he's told us that he needs you for something else. Here look." He held up the posting order from Brigade HQ. "Now then," he frowned impatiently. "Anything else?"

"Yes sir…when? Any idea when this'll be?

"A week tomorrow." S.S.M. Boyd glanced at the piece of paper in his hand. "That's next Tuesday. Early breakfast for all of yer, then outside the block and ready to move by 0800 hours. Clear?"

"Sir." Daley came to attention, turned to his right and left the office.

✳

For a time he was panic-stricken. It was not meant to be like this. Several men had gone already and word was that the unit was soon to be closed down. Postings were in the air and he had hoped for another driver's job or something with a Postal and Courier unit. But this…a bleeding Assault Regiment and driving an obstacle clearing vehicle that was armoured. Blimey! Just as the S.S.M. said, this was a job right up at the sharp end and that meant Jerry…Germans all over the place and nasty, unfriendly ones who wouldn't take kindly him and his tank.

He thought of going sick but the M.O. was a tough one. He thought of doing a runner but there were Military Police all over the place. He thought of trying to buy his way out but who was going to buy this little number? No, it looked as though he was going to have to go along with it like all the others. Chippy Wood had gone last week and Daley sat on his bed. For once the barrack room was empty and he leant forward with his elbows on his knees. Chippy Wood…yes, of course. Chippy Wood and what he'd said that day.

And that was why he kept thinking about her. Chippy warned him he would. Never get it out of yer mind, he'd said. And he was right. It had been almost three months since he'd seen her but he had not forgotten. She was still there in his mind, as clear as day. She and the child, their child, just as Chippy said. And now he was going to be posted. Where to, God only knew but he was hardly likely to see her again. She and the child would be gone forever. He had to see her.

*

"You deserve nothing, Mike Daley, nothing at all." Pat had brought Mavis with her. She knew instinctively what he had in mind and the three of them stood together on the bridge. "If you knew what a mess you've made of her life…what a miserable, rotten time she's had, you'd just creep away from here with your tail between your legs.

"I know." His head had dropped. "I ain't come here looking for bouquets nor begging favours neither." He glanced from one to the other. "An' I'm off in a week so I can't be no trouble, can I? I just want to see her, that's all. Just the once."

"But not on your own." Mavis had her hands on her hips. "Only a week to go or not, I wouldn't trust you as far as I could throw yer. *If* she agrees, and only *if* then we'll be there with her." She saw his frown. "Oh yes. Don't think we're going to leave her alone with you or any of your lot."

"Unless she wants to, that is?"

"We'll see about that, Michael Daley." It was Pat. "But don't you dare to start laying down the law. If you want to see her then you'll do as we say…when and how. Right?"

Daley nodded.

"We've had enough of you struttin' an' swaggerin' about the place. You haven't exactly made yerself popular round here, you lot, an' we're pretty much fed up with you." He nodded again. "All right." Pat Steer had lowered her voice. "I'll see what she has to say…but don't go banking on nuthin," she added. "We'll let you know…we'll leave a letter at the camp gate, like last time. But listen." Pat rounded on him. "Just, fer once in yer life, keep that big mouth of yours shut. There're ears everywhere here an' if Becky even sniffs that anyone else knows about this you can say goodbye to her now."

*

It seemed silly to have the hood up on such a warm April evening but Becky had insisted and the three of them rode out together in Pat's father's trap. Mike Daley was there waiting, and Becky saw at once that it was the same spot where they first met, even under the same tree.

Pat told him to get into the trap. She and Mavis remained outside within earshot but unable to hear what was being said. He wanted to take her hand but knew she would not have accepted him so they sat opposite each other talking quietly. "I'm glad of that," he said in reply to her answer.

"But it's nothing to you, Mike, you told me that. It's my baby and I'm going to keep hold of it," she replied. "Don't you remember when you were only too quick to deny it were anything to do with you? Didn't wan't to know, did yer? An' how you didn't half slate me, accusin' me of sleepin' around…remember all that?" Her look held his. "You've no idea how all that cruel talk hurt, have yer, eh? Couldn't give a damn, could yer?"

He stared. He was caught, cold, and his words and his bravado had been thrown back at him. "Yes," he muttered, now looking away. "Yes…I do. I remember it all. I panicked, Becks. Panicked and ran. 'Twas dreadful…a right terrible thing to do. Right bad…but…." He paused. "Look, I've come back, y'know. Haven't I? I couldn't leave you, Becks…couldn't leave you an' the child."

"And pretty damned horrid it were, too," she went on. "An' my God it hurt. Left me with nowhere to go, an' no one to help." She paused. "But then times have moved on…things *have* changed. Bit different now isn't it? But I'm keeping hold of my baby no matter what, an' that's that."

"Yeah, sure…sure." He hesitated, glancing down at his fingers. "But some don't want to…don't want to know even." He paused again. "So where'll you be having it?" His voice was barely above a whisper. "Here, at home?"

"No," she sighed. "It'd be hopeless here, the whole world's against me and life at home's impossible. "No," she shrugged. "They're sending me to Taunton…to a convent. I'll have it there."

For a moment he was silent. A hand had gone slowly to his mouth. "Oh, cor blimey," he groaned. "I might've guessed it. They're dumps, dreadful places and they nuns…jeez, they're awful."

"So I hear."

"Isn't there nowhere else? I mean there're people who take you in an' things…look after yer, like. Ain't there nowhere else…can't see yer in one of them places."

"Where, for God's sake?" She waited, still looking at him. "Go on then, where the hell can I go around here? It's a bit late fer you to start worryin' about things like that."

He looked away, now lost for words. She and the others would have thought about all that already and he felt a sudden surge of anger at himself for having sounded so foolish. He shook his head then rubbed his eyes with his hands.

"But…but they'll try to take it from you. They always do in them places. Soon as it's there they'll want to bundle it away."

"*Never.*" Becky glared at him. "They'll never do that. I'd never let them…I'd die first. I've lost everything, Mike, everything I ever had and they'll never, ever take my child from me."

He looked at her, trying to speak but was unable to. She watched him studying her face, saw his head shake slowly, then more slowly and slower still. "Say that again," he murmured. "Go on, Becks, tell me again…tell me you'll never let them take the child."

"That's what I said, didn't I?" She looked at him with her jaw set.

He swallowed hard. She could see that what she said had hurt. Suddenly the Mike Daley she knew and who once she had loved was lost for words. "Look…can I ask one favour?" he whispered eventually. "One thing, that's all I ask…." He faltered. "No, I *beg* you, Becks, beg you with all my heart."

"Go on." She could feel herself softening. "What d'you want now? Said enough already, haven't you?" she laughed drily. "There's nothing more to say."

Slowly, as he began to speak, his hand reached out. At first she started and tried to pull back but then allowed him to hold on to her. "Listen, Becks. I know, I know I've been a bleedin' nightmare, honest I do. But it's this." He pursed his lips, thinking carefully. "If you hold on to your…to our child then I'll come back for you. I promise you, promise you faithfully…that's if you want me to. I swear to God I'll be back. I will, Becks…honest to God."

She could barely see his eyes in the gloom of the trap but she felt his grip tighten as if he was pressing home his point. So he *did* care, or did he? Was there something there after all? Had his feelings been turned by the child she was carrying and what she had just said or was this the same sweet talk she had heard so often before? She dare not believe what she had been hoping. Yet she was tempted there and then to take his hand in hers, then to hold his face and smother him with kisses. Her love was still there, she could feel it but she dare not believe he felt the same for her. It had to be too late.

 She glanced down and paused, her mind tumbling wildly, then she looked at him again and nodded. It was a slow, thoughtful nod. "All right," she whispered hoarsely. "I'm going to keep the child whatever…and if you want to come back, then we'll see."

3.

Becky stood and watched while her mother pulled the bell. She could hear it ringing somewhere inside and looked up, taking care not to fall back down the flight of steps they had just climbed. The two doors were enormous but they were dusty and the dark blue paint had begun to peel. Only the brass name-plate was clean, having been polished until it shone, leaving the smokey-grey stains of polish rubbed into the plain wooden surround.

The bus journey had been difficult and they had barely spoken to one another. She had sat on one side while her mother took the far seat across the aisle where she spent most of the journey staring out of the window. Becky knew her cold had gone yet her eyes still looked red and watery and her face, under the same russet-brown scarf, was haggard and grim.

At the moment she felt more depressed than afraid as to what might lie ahead. For weeks they had been arguing as to where the baby should be born yet her mother had insisted on it being here in Taunton at St Margaret's. She had tried to accept it and two weeks ago told them she agreed with their decision, but it made no difference. Her mother had remained unmoved and her presence was now silent and uncomfortable. Whatever affection Becky had ever felt for her had gone, which only went to make the parting from her father more difficult. When he caught hold of her as she was about to climb on to the bus outside The Crown, his voice faltered and she watched his eyes fill with tears. It had been dreadfully hard, yet even now that sharp pang of sadness had dulled. It had been replaced by a deep gloom that bore down on her as the bus rolled and swayed on its way.

❋

They both watched intently at the sound of keys rattling against the far side of the doors. One then swung wide, revealing an elderly nun and Becky picked up her small leather suitcase. It was her father's and she had secured her few belongings by tying the case with string.

Later she remembered how, as they had alighted from the bus at the end of Springfield Road, the conductor had stood on the step, forcing her to squeeze past him. He had stared at her figure and grinned knowingly. Even if he could not see her condition he had guessed and, as they walked the short distance to the convent, she felt every eye of those they passed staring suspiciously. By now she was anxious to get inside the building and she smiled at the nun. But there was nothing in return: the elderly woman merely peeped round from behind the door, waiting impatiently.

"Follow me." They both started as the heavy door closed with a crash that echoed around the gloomy hall and up the tall flight of stairs. Inside it was darker than she expected and far cooler. Muttering "This way" and raising one hand like a guide, the nun turned and limped awkwardly across the black and white tiles towards the bottom of the staircase with her head bowed.

Becky caught her breath, noticing at once the strong smell of polish and boiled food. It reminded her of the corridor at school but here, instead of the accompanying laughter and chatter, there was nothing. Somewhere in the distance she could hear muffled voices then a door shut loudly. Further away a large, deep bell was tolling. The pale green walls were bare save for a black and gold crucifix set against the far wall high above the wooden banisters. As she followed the others across the hallway, their footfalls rang out loudly. She had never been inside such a large or forbidding building before and she gazed about fearfully, changing her suitcase from one hand to the other.

*

"The child is in good hands." Sister Agnes regarded her mother patronisingly. "Our nursing staff are first class...and, as I told you earlier, we will have her spiritual and moral well-being uppermost in our minds." As she spoke, she raised her head in order to make her next point. "Of course, not being of the Faith and having fallen from the path of true righteousness presents its own problems, y'know. You must understand that but we're lucky in that Father O'Connell who is a devout and most compassionate man, will take all this into consideration. She need have no fear...we will look after her." For the first time Sister Agnes smiled. "Just as our dear Lord, the Good Shepherd, would wish. Now then." The nun rose briskly. "I'll leave you to say your own farewells."

Becky watched as the tall, colourless woman who had conducted the interview took her mother's hand. It had been a strange, somewhat disturbing exchange between the two of them in which her own presence had been ignored entirely. They had discussed her in the third person as if she had not been there. Even when considering her health and the belongings she had brought with her, she had not been consulted. It was as if she had been of no consequence whatsoever, nothing more than some inanimate object of supreme indifference. Her mother, she noticed, had from the beginning acceded readily to everything that had been suggested, nodding hurriedly and compliantly without once considering what she, her daughter and the subject of the interview, might be thinking.

"And you'll remain here."

"Yes," Becky nodded meekly.

"Yes, *Sister Agnes,* my child. I should not have occasion again to remind you that we are in the house of the Lord where His servants are recognised as such." Becky's eyes dropped away from the cold look but she glanced up again as the sister turned back to her mother. The nun's former pleasant demeanour was at once restored. "So, Mrs Carter...I'll bid you good day and trust you will have a safe journey home."

They were alone and Becky stood quietly, watching her mother as she gathered her things. All of a sudden she realised that the last link with home was about to be severed. As soon as her mother left she would be on her own when everything she knew and held dear to her would have disappeared as well, leaving her alone and friendless in this forbidding place. "Mother," she whispered then hesitated for a moment before throwing her arms around her in a sudden panic. "Mother, I'm going to miss you…I'm going to miss you all, and I'm afraid."

"Don't be so silly." Her mother drew back. "You heard what Sister Agnes said and how they'll be seeing to you."

"I know…yes, I know." Becky held on to her. "But there's summat creepy here. It's not like home. It's different and these people…the nuns…they're, they're cold and they look at you all fearsome, like."

"Oh, don't be so stupid. Becky." Her mother stood back, adjusting her scarf which Becky had pushed aside when she caught hold of her. "Look, it's too late for all this now. You should've minded yerself months back, afore all this started and saved yer father an' me all this trouble." She turned to pull on her tweed jacket then shrugged it into place. "'Tis no good worryin' now. What's done's done an' you'll have to see it through.

"Mother…."

"What?"

She paused, uncertain as to how to say it then changed her mind. "Oh, it's…it's nothing. It doesn't matter," she sighed then stepped forward and drew her mother to her once more, brushing her cheek with her own. "You must go now," she whispered. "Or you'll be late…I'll be all right. Say hello to father for me…you will, won't you." She held her tightly, letting go only when she turned for the door. "Bye, bye, mother."

"Bye, Becky." Her mother squeezed her arm. "You'll be fine…and it's fer the best, y'know. It's fer yer own good, m'dear." Then she turned and left the room.

Becky followed her, in two minds whether to catch up with her and take hold of her again but it would do no good and she stood looking over the rails on the landing as her mother descended the two flights of stairs. She remained there, standing quite still, listening to her every footfall ringing out until the front door closed loudly. Then she returned to the day room.

It was then, just as she was walking towards the half-window that looked out over the courtyard that she felt a flutter. She stopped, looked down and clutched at her stomach where she felt it again. Her child had moved. For the first time the new life she was bearing had stirred. She reached out hurriedly for a chair and sat where her mother had been a few minutes earlier, then felt her stomach again but there was nothing more.

In that moment and in its own unconscious way, her child had spoken to her reminding her of its presence and asking not to be forgotten. Becky looked down again but turned at the sound of footsteps and stood hurriedly as another nun came into the room.

"Rebecca Carter?"

"Yes, sister."

"Pick up your case and come with me."

4.

She sat on her bed more depressed and exhausted than she could remember yet she had been in St Margaret's for less than two days. Momentarily her eyes closed in sheer resignation then, shaking her head slowly as if in disbelief, she sighed and reached up to where the boney, white hands of Sister Maria had taken hold of her hair. But there was nothing left: the rich, dark locks that had been there since childhood, had been shorn off, leaving the back of her neck cold and exposed. But it was her fingers that made her wince. Even as she touched what was left of her hair, the cuts smarted.

It was sewing the canvas holdalls that had made them so. Throughout the afternoon she and several others had sat together in the sewing room forcing the thick needles through the heavy, unyielding material. Her hands were too soft and had been made more so by the hot water in the laundry where they had worked all morning. She had asked for a thimble but the nun had just laughed. Gradually, as she tried to work the needle, the skin had worn away until the tips and sides of her fingers were raw and bleeding. She had tried to save herself by wrapping a scrap of canvas around the cut but it had barely helped and once, when her fingers slipped, the eye of the needle had been forced deep under the nail. Even now, it hurt.

*

Freda Wright came and sat by her side. The older woman, her fair hair already greying but her face still kindly, slept in the bed next to her. She had been in the convent for years since losing her own child at birth. On the first night, she had said little but earlier today they had worked together in the laundry. Becky shuddered. She had already come to loathe the steaming place where their sweat ran freely, yet it was there that she was destined to work until her child was born.

The sight and the stench of the bundles of dirty linen from the hospital sickened her. Often the nurses simply bundled up the sheets and bedding, leaving the blood, the excrement and the other dreadful things all together in a congealed and foul smelling mess. Sometimes it had all been there so long it had hardened into a crust and it had been her job to scrape the worst away with a blunt kitchen knife. After that she had no option other than to rinse off what she could with her bare hands before committing the linen to the vat. The heat and steam in the laundry made it worse and twice she had staggered away, retching and gagging at the sheer awfulness of it all. On the second occasion she almost fainted and had clung to the door frame for support. But the supervising nun caught hold of her and pushed her back, shouting at her and slapping her about the head. And there were four months more of this.

"You'll get used to it." Freda had been stripping down the bed behind the dormitory door and held the sheets bundled together in her hands. Becky flinched at the sight. "Don't worry," she laughed, nudging her playfully. "They're Megan's...I've just stripped her bed."

"Who?" Becky looked up puzzled.

"Megan Davis...over by the door there. She's due tomorrow and they've moved her to the nursery."

"She's the little dark one...with the shaved head?" Becky queried. "Why did they do that to her...take off all her hair, I mean?"

"Because she fought with the priest when they made her sign the papers...the adoption papers. Fought like hell she did but they got her in the end."

Becky stared horrified. Nobody had said anything to her about this but she had heard talk earlier of the children being adopted. She had thought no more of it, believing it was only the ones who didn't want their child. "You mean they take them away from you...even if you don't want them to?"

"Sure. Didn't they tell you that?" Freda looked at her, her eyes scanning her face. "No?" She queried. "Oh yes...before you come in they tell the families, your people, that it's better that way...better for mother and child, they say. Then the priest gets you to sign. Consent, they call it. And as soon as you've done that, that's the end of it."

"*Why?*" Becky was staring back in disbelief. "Why in God's name did she sign? Even if they put a pen in my hand and forced it across the paper, I'd never sign to that...never. I won't, Freda."

"Hmm, don't bet on it. They're used to the screaming an' yelling. Fighting the devil, they call it and they're happy enough to beat it out of you. Lock you away and starve you if needs be. All in the name of *Our dear Lord*," she added. "Fighting the curse of the devil gets them all going."

Becky caressed her stomach where, last night, her child had moved again. She shook her head. "No," she whispered. "Not mine, Freda...I'll never let them...never." She felt the older woman's arm go round her. "Why're they like it, these people? Why all this shouting and beating and taking the children away."

"God knows," Freda shrugged. "Or I expect He does. As far as they're concerned you're nothing less than an evil sinner who's going to pay dearly. You're a nothing, you're rubbish...and especially you. Not being a Catholic makes you worse still. You're a heretic who they're going to force into godliness come what may. Honestly, that's how they see you." She grimaced and pulled Becky towards her. "But anyway, listen. You're due your medical tomorrow, yes?" Becky nodded. "Don't fight them, d'you hear?"

"What d'you mean?"

"Oh it's nothing really. They just poke you around for a while and have their bit of fun. Get you to get up on the delivery bed and put your feet into the stirrups. An examination they call it but it's nothing really. Just gives that nurse, that fat-faced Sister Bernadette her little thrill...peeping and feeling an' that."

"For Heaven's sake."

"Listen." Freda cautioned. "Nothing's going to happen, all right. It'll not hurt or anything like that so don't make a fuss of it, d'you hear? They'll only beat you."

"*What?*"

"Of course. You're a pretty wee girl and that Bernadette'll take a shine to you, that's fer sure. Her fingers'll be everywhere. I'm telling you now just to warn you but don't go fighting mad and make a scene or they'll knock you about. Shut your eyes...grit your teeth, anything you like but no heroics. And it's nothing, nothing at all. Promise." Freda hugged her. "C'mon now."

✳

She waited in the dispensary just as Sister Bernadette had told her to do. Freda warned her again, wagging a finger in her face and she had agreed not to make a fuss although the very idea made her stomach churn like it did in the laundry. Even as she washed herself in a basin of hot water they had given her rather than the ice-cold water from the tap room they used in the mornings, she cringed at what they might do. But now, as she stood, nervous and vulnerable and with her arms hugging herself tight, it was the sounds from next door that took her mind. Since she came in she had heard everything, every cry and every word as Megan Davis had her baby.

As soon as she had come into the nursery wing from across the main hall, she heard the cries and listened incredulously. Megan was crying out, sometimes shouting in agony then gasping in great lungfuls of air and groaning as she thrust away. Two nuns, or it sounded like two, were telling her to hold on and to push and push again, one of them encouraging her in a shrill voice.

It seemed to go on and on yet suddenly it was over and she heard the thin, high-pitched wail of the baby. The infant, helpless and confused by its new world, was crying for reassurance. Becky stood stunned, with her fists to her mouth and filled with a sudden desire to rush next door to see for herself. She started for the door but stopped and listened again. Something had happened. Megan was calling out but now her voice was raised above those of the others.

She listened horrified as the young mother pleaded for her child. Sister Bernadette was arguing with her, the other nun also; all three were talking at once. Then a door shut. Someone had left and the room fell silent before she heard Megan's sobs. Again she had a sudden urge to go and see for herself, this time to help, but there was somebody still in there with her. Whoever it was, was talking quietly and trying to soothe her. But of the child there was no sound. It had gone, of that she was certain.

Now she knew that she was to lose her child. Freda had been right. As soon as they were delivered, the babies were taken, to be returned only at feeding time until they went for good, bundled away to their new lives never to be seen again by those who had borne them. "Oh no they won't." Her lips barely moved but as she looked down at her stomach she shook her head. "I'll not let them take you...no matter what," she vowed. "You're mine, my dearest. They're never, ever going to have you."

Chapter Seven

Daisy Gunn was a harlot and a thief. She never knew her parents, having been brought up by an elderly aunt in Burnthouse Lane. She was tiny, just eighteen and the first thing Becky noticed was the deep red gash above her mouth on what was an otherwise beautiful face. The doctors had tried to tidy her harelip, she explained, but they had only made it worse and had decided to leave it as it was. She had been brought to St Margaret's from Exeter's County Jail when they found she was three months pregnant. That was a year ago and the baby, a boy, had died three days after its birth, some time before Becky came in.

Why she was still there nobody seemed to know but Daisy suspected her records were lost when the prison was bombed. Whatever the reason, Becky was delighted. She had found a friend and when they moved her into Megan Davis's bed space she was happier still. Daisy was as cheerful as her name suggested in spite of the fact that most of the nuns had taken a dislike to her, condemning her for her evil ways and punishing her cruelly whenever they found an excuse. Her face, Sister Francesca pronounced, had been marked by the devil when he slept with her mother. But Daisy was used to such taunts and when she rounded on her tormentor telling her that it took one to know one, they shaved her head and locked her away in the windowless cellar underneath the pantry.

*

"Kept me down there for a month or more," Daisy chuckled. It was their turn for dining room duties and she and Becky were clearing away after the midday meal. "They let me out to do the very worst of the chores...scrubbin' the swill bins an' that, cleaning the drains an' so on, then locked me away for the night."

"Weren't you afeared...down there all alone?" Becky carried through a pile of dirty plates from the nuns' table.

"Not at all." Daisy eased up to her at the deep metal sink. She lifted the plug then scrubbed vigorously as the tepid water drained away. "They could never keep me in," she grinned impishly. "The locks here're easy...no problem. Stupid cows left me alone to do the dirty work...wouldn't come near when I were in the swill area or drains, nor the scullery even. An' here look." She nodded at the array of kitchen tools and implements. "Got everything you'd want to work the locks...pieces o'wire, there, see. Knives an' spikey things. Learned my trade years ago, when you were still at school. But 'twas me downfall in the end," she went on. "Got picked up inside the shop when the others did a runner, didn't I? Got nicked fair 'n square. Never said nuthin though an' my fingers still know their business, even now...watch." She flicked the water from her hands and wiggled her fingers in front of Becky's nose. "There...see."

Becky flinched, looking at her in amazement. "So you let yourself out...out of where they locked you downstairs? But why didn't you run away, clear off out of here and go back to Exeter?" Daisy shrugged. "I would've done," Becky continued. "I'd 've been off soon as...well, as soon as I could after the baby."

"Dare say you would." Daisy turned and leant against the sink then bent forward to check that they were on their own. "But it's not so easy. Not if you're like me."

"But you just told me it was. Easy as pie, you said, an' once out of here there's no prison wall or anything like that. Honestly, Daisy. I'd go fer it...get away from this beastly place."

"Phhhew." Daisy blew heavily and looked down. "No," she sighed. "You don't get it. You're different you are, Becky. You're a lovely girl, everyone says that. You've a home to go to, an' a mum an' dad. An' a man waitin' for yer...but me...." She paused. "Just look at me." Her head was bowed. "I've nowhere to go, no home. I'm a criminal now...an' a thief, an' I'm as ugly as sin. Oh, yes." She looked up at Becky. "Who's goin' to have me, eh, with my ugly mug? Nobody looks twice. Soon as they see this 'ere, look." She twitched her lips. "They jump back in fright...don't wanta know. All 'cept the poor mutts who've gotta pay fer it. An' then what 'appens?" she quizzed, patting stomach. "The poor little mite goes and dies on me."

Becky stood there, suddenly confused, then turned and pulled the girl towards her. "Oh, I'm sorry," she whispered. "I'm ever so sorry, Daisy. Didn't think, did I? Just opened my big mouth."

"Oh, it's nuthin." Daisy had her head on Becky's shoulder. "Don't worry yerself. One day I'll be away, when I'm ready, like. But right now I'm better off where I am. I can do what I like, see. Nowhere here's safe from Daisy Gunn. Learned to go quietly when I were a kid. Walk near the walls, down the sides of the stairs. I can tell yer where every board here creaks, how every door opens."

Becky hugged her, half out of shame and sympathy but also in admiration, as if to congratulate her for stealing one over their tormentors. "What'd I give to do that," she whispered. "Oh, what fun it'd be...just to be able to *do* it an' then look at 'em all straight in the face. Just imagine...knowing what you can do and they'd never even know."

Daisy nodded. "Aye, summat like that. Sort of evens it all out, don' it. Makes it not so bad here...better than bein' on the game, I can tell yer, an' better'n being locked away an' that."

"*I'd* go though." Becky grimaced. "I hate it here...really *hate* it. All this beatin' an' shouting...all these prayers an' bells ringing, an' the bowing and scrapin'. I hate it, Daisy. I can't stand it."

94

"Well, you'll be away. Soon as they've taken the child you'll be out the door."

Becky stiffened. "No Daisy. I'm not going out of here without my child. It's coming with me. I'll do it somehow. This lot're not having my baby."

Daisy stood back. "Creep off wiv it, will yer?" She watched as Becky nodded, looking her up and down slowly. "That's what's on yer mind, is it?"

"Somehow…I'll do it somehow." She paused. "Perhaps…perhaps you'll…."

"Look, don't say nuthin." Daisy cut in, turning back to the dishes. "Don't go sayin' nuthin to anyone about what us've just said?" She looked at Becky then placed the dish on the draining board. "Let's see…let's have a think. 'Spec there's a way somehow."

2.

Sam could not settle his mind. For weeks after Becky had gone his mother had kept on telling him how fortunate he was to be out of it all. At first, while the wound was still raw he tried to convince himself she was right. Perhaps it was all something that was never going to work. Even if Mike Daley had not come along and she had remained faithful then, sooner or later, somebody else would have taken her fancy. And, by then, they might have been married when it would have been too late. Gerry Chugg and Greg Thorne said the same.

They all said the same yet his emotions ran deeper than that. He had known her since she was that shy little schoolgirl and then watched with growing awareness as she blossomed into the young woman she had become. His affection spanned all those years not just these last few months when it had all gone so horribly wrong. The Becky he knew was not the one they said she had become. Underneath it all she must still be the same as his memories cherished; she had to be. What had happened had been a dreadful mistake.

＊

But Daley, the man in her life, had come and gone. In fact most of them had gone and Sam, like everybody, knew that something was happening. Everywhere soldiers were on the move. The Guards had gone from Winsford as had the Paratroopers from Winsford Hill. More and more guns were being fired on the ranges. Tanks were training above Molland with more on the beaches at Saunton. Convoys everywhere were blocking the roads and the Americans at Morebath had begun to move south.

It made him restless. He felt useless and out of it. Everyone was on the move except him. It was as though he was shirking, hiding away and for that he despised himself. He began to envy those preparing to go off to war and felt ashamed to be sitting safely at home. His guilt, and Jack's advice, played on his mind until he was desperate to become involved.

Without telling his parents he took the bus into Taunton where he found the Recruiting Office in Castle Street. They were pleased enough to see him, and the sailor behind the desk asked him to fill in a questionnaire. An officer saw him next, inviting him into his office and questioning him further. It seemed to be going well yet it came to nothing. The moment he said he was working at Hayes, the officer closed the book. Farming, he was told, was a Reserved Occupation and for him there would be no call to arms.

Sam pleaded. He told him about the others he knew and lied that his father could manage but they would have none of it. Miners and farmers were wanted at home. He would have to go back to Exford and forget about it. Let others do the worrying. Fuel and food were vital, the very life blood the nation depended upon and that was where he was to play his part.

It was a cruel rejection and for days his misery deepened. Everywhere he looked he saw the posters crying out for able-bodied men yet he had been turned away, told to go home to till the land and tend the sheep. It sounded like the easy way out, nobody would believe he had tried and been turned away. Jack might, but not the others and certainly not the soldiers. He remembered their taunts at the gate and he had to try again.

✱

"Hayes Farm…Hayes Farm. Ah, here we are. Yes, Hayes Farm, Exford. Mr and Mrs Drew Hawkins. Occupation…farmer, one son…Samuel." The elderly Captain with a white moustache and monocle looked up. His office, just inside the main gate at Wyvern Barracks was bigger than the one in Taunton. There were more maps on the wall, more charts and Sam's spirits rose. "Exford's in Somerset," he announced. "Shouldn't be coming here…Exeter's for Devon …you're Taunton."

"I've been, sir"

"Oh? So what's the problem?" The Captain pulled on his moustache. "What's brought you here?"

Sam took a deep breath. "Turned me down, sir…told me I couldn't leave the farm." He leaned forward. "But I want to go, sir, honest I do. Bain't right stuck away along with land girls an' old men. Plenty of others've gone and it hasn't made no odds."

Captain Brasher looked at the census papers and pulled a face. The great build up was over. Units everywhere were up to full war establishment. Reserve units were coming up to strength and the training depots were full to overflowing with reinforcements. And his orders had been clear: nobody from the farms or the mines was to be enlisted, nobody at all. The Atlantic convoys were still struggling to get through and the country needed every morsel of food it could grow and every sack of coal. Farmers and farm hands were not to be taken on, they were needed at home.

He sighed and shook his head. "I'm afraid my hands are tied," he said sadly. "Look, here we are in black and white." He held up the papers. "There's a complete block...really there is and they're right, y'know." He looked up mournfully. "I'm sorry, lad, very sorry but I'm going to have to say no." He saw Sam's look. "It's tough, I know, especially for youngsters like yourself but we've all got to go where we're needed most."

Sam nodded. It was the same again. Nobody, it seemed, had any interest in him. "Right," he muttered rising unsteadily. "If that's it then, I'd best be getting' back." He nodded again. "Sorry fer wastin' yer time."

Captain Brasher smiled sympathetically. "We *do* need you, y'know. We need you all so don't let it get you down too much." All of a sudden his face brightened. "And anyway, many of the youngsters coming through here'd give their eye teeth for a steady life on the farm like yours. I'd make the most of it...think yourself lucky to be out of it all."

Almost at the door, Sam checked himself. That was just what the others would think...that he was lucky to be staying at home and missing it all and that he had chosen it that way. "Aye, dare say they would," he replied. "But 'tweren't my way of seeing it though. Not my way at all."

3.

They had been on board the landing craft for three days. Last night they had been warned that they would be sailing but the weather had worsened and it had been postponed. They had simply changed moorings and moved further down Southampton Water. Now the wind had backed and dropped yet the flat-bottomed vessel still skewed awkwardly as it rolled side-on to the incoming tide. Daley, like everyone else, had been sick. Two of them had been so bad that when the claxon went calling them to quarters they had not moved.

*

Everybody seemed to be there for the briefing, crammed tight into the mess hall that reeked of vomit and sweat. Peering about him through the stinging haze of tobacco smoke, he could see infantrymen of the Dorsets and the Hampshires and the tank commanders of the Sherwood Rangers. Artillerymen and engineers were wedged in between them while, just in front of where he was standing, the flail tank drivers of the Westminster Dragoons were grouped together.

They were due to sail tonight and he, like everyone else packed around him, sensed a nervous tension in the air. Somehow they knew that this time it was for real. Some wore their berets, others their tin hats. Many carried their rifles or had pistols buckled into their holsters. Some sat awkwardly, others perched or leant back wherever they could, many were left standing.

What had been a low burble of chatter, broken by the odd shout of laughter or cough, suddenly ceased. L/Cpl Mike Daley nudged his driver, Terry Winter, and nodded towards the dais where a major he had never seen before raised his hand for silence. Somebody cleared his throat, somebody else sneezed but an expectant hush fell on those gathered for the briefing. Save for the endless rising and falling away as the landing craft pitched and rolled, everybody in the room was now quite still.

Ten minutes later they knew. It was on…Operation Overlord was underway and now they were going through their final orders.

"Our beach is here…between Le Hamel and Les Roquettes, here." As he pointed to the map, the tall major with dark, curly hair raised his voice. "That's you, the Hampshires, on the right and here…what we've called Point Fifty-four…here on the left. That's the Dorsets' objective." Silence once more as the places were picked out again. "Everyone got that? Right, now let's run through it one last time from the beginning." Daley watched as their own squadron leader took the stand.

"Here we go, mate." Sapper Winter nudged his friend. "It's us…we're on."

Round and balding and with his row of ribbons clearly visible, Major 'Sammy' Cole lifted his chin and tugged at his collar. He coughed quietly. "First off and straight in behind the leading infantry companies will be the Westminster Dragoons…you've got to get those flail tanks of yours going straight away. O.K.? We need clear lanes from the water's edge right up to the dunes and fast…here and…here." He paused, waiting for those taking notes.

"Then the dozer tanks of One Six Two Regiment." Mike Daley closed his eyes. "Make sure you tuck yourselves right in behind the flails. Keep right up their backsides and keep going until they hit the soft stuff where the dunes begin…then you take over. Don't wait for orders just get on with it. Jerry will be on to us by then and we've got to get the traffic moving up through the dunes."

Terry Winter blew slowly and looked up at the ceiling. "Jeez," he muttered. "That all?"

"You'll have infantry up in front giving what covering fire they can but any vehicle movement in front of you'll be Jerry. We'll have nobody out there…you'll be the furthest in, so don't hang about."

"Bloody charming." Mike Daley had his hand to his mouth and was looking around him. Thirty, forty, maybe fifty heads were nodding. Some were writing, others leant back nonchalantly. One was sitting on the floor and leaning back against the wall, asleep and oblivious to the drama around him. "Beat that will yer?" Mike Daley nudged his driver.

Major Cole coughed again and waved his hand at the smoke. "We'll get a troop of Shermans up to each of you as soon as we can but we can't do much until the dunes are breached. Second and third waves of dozer tanks should form up and wait beyond the high water mark in the assembly area…here, ready to take over from any casualties."

"That's you, Terry, my boy." Mike Daley whispered out of the corner of his mouth. "Catch yerself a quick one an' a return trip to Blighty."

"Don't bank on it matey. Jerry's all over the place, Panzers an' all…plus all that stuff they've got on the beaches. You're in it too, pal…up t'yer neck."

Daley's mouth was dry. He glanced at the faces around him. They all looked so calm and self assured yet he bet they weren't. He bet their stomachs were churning and flapping like old Harry, just like his own. "Ah well, this time tomorrow we'll all be there, won't we? Buckets and spades in the sand, eh?" As he spoke he reached for his wallet and took out the photograph. It was worn, creased and curling at the edges where he had cut it out. Becky was leaning back against the gate and smiling shyly. He rubbed his thumb gently across her face and smiled back before looking up sharply.

The dining hall had gone very quiet. All eyes were on the senior doctor who had taken the stand and was giving instructions about collecting and burying the dead and getting the wounded back to the Dressing Stations.

4.

"Well, goodness me, what a surprise." Barbara Hawkins put a hand to her hair. She could feel herself blushing as she smiled with pleasure. "How simply lovely to see you, Colonel…do, please come in. I'm afraid everything's a dreadful mess…it's all been a bit of a rush this morning," she added bashfully.

"No, no." Miles Ashcroft raised a hand apologetically. "Most unreasonable of me to descend on you unannounced like this but I was passing and…well, just wanted to make sure you've heard the news…I'm sure you have?"

"The invasion? Yes, it's wonderful isn't it…absolutely marvellous." She hesitated. "We heard it on the wireless about an hour ago. What d'you think? D'you s'pose everything's going to be all right?"

"Can't tell." He sighed and shook his head. "Not yet anyway. It's impossible to know for certain. We've just got to be patient and see what they say. It might be days yet…weeks, perhaps, before we know how things are going."

Barbara nodded and looked at him. "Drew's up at the church right now. We're having a service tomorrow, a sort of thanksgiving I think. The vicar called earlier wanting to know what the village would like. Drew's a warden but he's gone up to pass word on to the bell ringers as well."

Miles Ashcroft nodded. Porlock were doing the same later as were Selworthy and Luccombe. "That's wonderful," he smiled kindly. "Anyway there's nothing any of us can do about it except try not to worry too much. We've got a service ourselves later this afternoon but I felt I had to get out or I'd go mad worrying about what's going on out there." He looked at her and laughed. "So I'm off to have a look at the river. The weather's been awful and there's quite a bit of water coming down."

"What a lovely idea but look, do please come in, just for a moment. It's so miserable out here." She opened the kitchen door, standing back to let him in. "A quick cuppa, perhaps?"

"No, my dear, really. It's very sweet of you but I've got Simpson waiting outside with the Humber." He went in nonetheless, smiling warmly as he usually did, his face creased affectionately into its wrinkles. "My goodness it's warmer in here," he joked, rubbing his hands together. "But tell me, how're things? How's the boy?" he asked quietly.

"Sam?" Barbara turned back from the stove, looked at him and pulled a face. "*Ohh*, I don't know," she sighed. "Did I tell you he went into Taunton and tried to join up?" She saw his surprise. "Yes, first the navy then he tried the army at Exeter but they wouldn't have him."

Ashcroft pulled a face. "Reserved Occupation, I daresay and all that goes with it. Mmm?" He nodded sagely. "It's very hard on the youngsters like Sam who're keen to do their bit, but we've got to have them here, I'm afraid. Can't have them all rushing off." He paused, laughing lightly. "But he's all right otherwise...about young Becky Carter, I mean?"

"Oh goodness yes. All that's way behind him. Seems to have quite forgotten her...hasn't mentioned it for weeks." Ashcroft glanced at her. "As soon as this weather gives us a break we'll be starting the hay...then there's the shearing, of course, so there's plenty to be thinking about."

"I'm glad." Colonel Ashcroft stroked his chin. "A shame though, Barbara. They might've done well for each other...but there we are. And I see that most of the unit up at Edgecott are on their way. Looks like they're closing the place down."

"Can't say I'm sorry."

"No, but they weren't a bad lot, y'know. And several of them'll be out there on the beaches right now...an' fighting for their very lives, I'll be bound."

"Goodness...yes, I suppose they will."

He looked at her again. "That's war for you, m'dear. Peace and quiet one minute then all hell breaks loose. No doubt we'll know soon enough how they're getting on. Anyway, look, I must be on my way." He pushed himself away from the table and stamped out the creases in his trousers. "I'll make sure we give you proper warning next time, none of these nasty surprises."

"No it was lovely," she gushed. "Just let me know and you can stay for a bite"

"That'd be wonderful."

"Promise?"

"Absolutely…couldn't be nicer." He took her hand. "Bye, my dear. You're looking as lovely as ever." He patted her hand. "My regards to the menfolk."

✳

It was a silly argument and began in the yard where Sam had been sharpening the long rows of teeth on the mower blades. His mother had just brought in one of the hunters and thought it looked lame. She called out to him but he ignored her for it was drizzling and he wanted to get the job done. She called again, louder, and he threw down the file knowing well she had seen what he was doing.

"Don't be like that, dear. Look, I think Larkspur's gone short in his near fore…can you trot him while I check." Sam lifted his cap and scratched his head in an unconscious demonstration of frustration. "Sam don't *do* that," she frowned. "There's absolutely no need to behave like that."

"Not as though I haven't got enough to be doing, mother." He could feel his anger rising. "Can't us see to the horses later…can't you let me finish here first?"

"What on earth's the *matter* with you?" Barbara Hawkins led the horse towards him. "Honestly, you've been like this for days now…scowling and brooding. What's the matter…not still sulking about joining up are you?" She watched as he shook his head. "Well what is it then, for Heaven's sake?" He shrugged and looked away. "Oh do *answer* me, Sam. *Something's* getting at you…it's not, not still that Carter girl is it? You're not still pining for her…are you?"

"I'm not pining, mother." His voice had hardened defensively. "You're always tryin' to make a laugh out of me an' Becky, so you are. Always tryin' to rubbish it, like yer did in front of father."

"Oh, don't be so silly. It was hardly a romance, was it? Nothing more than a little light fancy, and if she decided to walk away from you and get herself tangled up with those soldiers…well that's her affair." Barbara looked up at her son. "And look what happened…look at it. For goodness sake, get her out of your mind, Sam…forget it. If she's going to behave like that she's not worth remembering."

"Oh yes she is." The words grated out. Sam could feel himself smarting at yet

101

another dismissal of his affection for Becky. "An' don't you ever go sayin' *that*. Not to me." Suddenly he was standing over her and pointing as he spoke. "Becky Carter's done wrong. I'm not denyin' that and nor's anyone else…like all they lot who've got nort better to do than go rubbishin' her name. And that's you an' all, mother…you'm the worst of the lot." He saw her step back. "Never give over, you don't. The way you go on an' on, anyone'd thought Becky had killed or murdered the way you and they others carry on. She's a fine girl for all of that's took place…a loverly maid who's bin welcome here ever since her were a child."

"*Sam.*"

"Aye," he cried. "Aye, it *is* Sam and Sam's had enough of it…enough from you and all they lot." He waved a hand behind him. "If I have feelings fer Becky Carter then that's my affair. *Right?* Mine and no one else's." He glared at his mother and turned away.

"Sam…Sam, wait a minute." Barbara caught hold of his arm but he pushed her hand away. "Sam wait…listen." He pushed her away again and stormed away through the stables leaving his mother with one hand to her head.

✳

"Bad is it, lad?" Ernest Carter wiped his hands and studied the face of the figure standing astride his cycle outside the forge. The soldier pushed back his beret and watched as others gathered round.

"Can't be sure." Corporal Phillips took off his glasses. The elderly soldier was one of the few remaining at Edgecott. Most had moved on already and the remainder were due to go in a few days. "But word is that five, five or six of the lads've been hit…one or two were bad but that's all we know."

"Any idea who 'tis? Any names?" The question from behind Ernest sounded anxious.

"No, none…not yet. Difficult to get any sense just now. Captain Barker's keeping on trying. All he's been told is that the fightin's hard an' that several of the lads're down. That's it." The corporal looked around and shrugged nervously.

"Well, let us know when you can, buiy." Ernest Carter patted the man's shoulder. "Good or bad news, whatever 'tis, let us know. Us'll be thinking of 'em…that's fer sure."

5.

Nobody had had any sleep for the last seventy-two hours, in fact most had barely been off their feet. It showed and as Mike Daley looked around the group gathered in the ruins of the farmhouse he could see the looks of sheer fatigue. Some had the remnants of black camouflage cream etched on their faces, others had pieces of foliage threaded through their clothing and equipment. Several had waded ashore three days ago and had remained wet, soaked through first by the seawater and now the rain, their heavy, salty clothes still unable to dry out.

Breaching the dunes had gone well and for a moment it had all seemed too easy but they had been lucky. It was only when he and the other tank dozers had been pulled into a narrow dip in the dunes for refuelling that he had seen how others had fared. In less than a hundred yards from them six or eight vehicles had been destroyed three of which were still burning fiercely. Most of the traffic was either grinding its way slowly inland or waiting patiently in long queues stretching back to the beach waiting for their turn to move up through the gaps.

But it was the steady trickle backwards that caught their attention. Some of the wounded were walking or limping slowly with their white bandages showing starkly against their khaki uniforms. Many, however, were brought back on stretchers, a few in ambulances. Some were being carried and several, the majority, driven. They watched as the drivers inched their way carefully over the rough ground while those sitting with the casualties did what they could to ease the jolts. The doctors had been right.

✳

Their respite had not lasted long. They pushed on and now, about three hundred yards ahead of them and running across their front on the near edge of a thick wood, lay a deep drainage ditch. It was well hidden from view by a screen of tall bullrushes and it was not until you got right up to it that you could see how wide it was and how deep. One of the Sherman tanks had tipped forward into it while a second had been knocked out as it was searching for a crossing point.

The ditch had to be filled in so that both wheeled and tracked vehicles could cross. It was a job for the dozer tanks. Men of the Dorsets had waded across earlier and were clearing the woods on the far side but the fight was still in progress. As they sat quietly they could hear the sound of small arms fire, some of the rounds cracking and whining overhead. Shells were landing close to their farmhouse and one, closer than most, sent showers of plaster and dust raining down.

"What d'you think, Corporal Daley?"

"We'll start on the left, sir." Daley glanced up at the officer from the Dragoons. Lieutenant Smythe looked ridiculously young with his short, fair hair parted in the middle like that. Most of those around him were, many scarcely more than boys; he had seen earlier that he was one of the oldest there. "I'll get my first pair o' dozers working over there, just this side of that thick hedge. Then I'll take the next approach, a bit further this way."

"It's pretty exposed there, y'know…you'll be more or less out in the open."

Daley shrugged. "Gotta be done, sir." He smiled ruefully. "Can't see any other way. Soon as we've got these two crossings open and can get some heavy stuff across then we'll go for the next two. Here, look…and over there by that barn or whatever."

"And covering fire?" Edwin Smythe looked at the gunner sergeant.

"On the far bank as back as far as the wood, sir, but that's it. The Dorsets're working their way through there and we can't risk lifting the barrage any further."

"How long before you're ready?"

"Give us ten minutes, sir…any time after that."

Lt Smythe looked at his watch. "Right…three-fifteen then?" He looked round the group then waggled his pencil at the tank commander. "Billy, get your Shermans up to just behind the leading edge…just behind where we are now…there, look." He pointed towards the orchard beyond the farmyard. "And then, when the dozers go in, come forward and give 'em covering fire. Right?" He looked around again. "It *shouldn't* take long," he stressed. "If the infantry have cleared the wood and if you chaps can get your skates on," he nodded towards Daley. "Then we should be across. And we need to be," he added. "We've got to press on."

Daley rose with the others then ran, half crouching, to where the rest of his troop were waiting.

✳

Even when standing in the low turret of his command tank it was difficult to see. "Wheel left, Terry." He had the mouthpiece right up to his mouth and was adjusting his earphones. "I wanna see what the other two're up to. Over there…that piece of open ground."

"Roger." Corporal Daley hung on as the big machine swung round, its tracks throwing up great chunks of earth and its engine now a clattering roar. His promotion had come last night when they learned that their sergeant and another corporal had been killed on the beach.

"Half left, half left," he barked. "Get in under those trees and hold it there."

"Under the trees…roger." As soon as the engine slowed he could hear the crackle of small arms fire. Some of it sounded only inches above them and he crouched lower automatically. He could see the two heavy dozers working side by side less than a hundred yards away, shovelling great mounds of soil into the breach. It all looked so leisurely yet he knew that those inside would be working feverishly. He watched as one of them crossed the obstacle they had just filled, almost digging itself into the far side as it bulldozed an exit. Then the second one followed and he flicked his radio switch.

"Hullo Able One, this is Three. Well done, sunshine…looks good. Couldn't've done better myself. We're on our way…keep an eye on us and be prepared to take over."

"Roger." Suddenly a huge mound of earth and debris erupted in front of him, followed immediately by a hot blast. He could smell the cordite…German cordite and all of it aimed at him. "Swing her round, Terry, and let's get on with it," he called.

Glancing over his shoulder he could see the Shermans and infantry moving up to cover him. 'Ringside seats,' he thought as his dozer drove hard towards the drain. "OK, now…blade down and shovel like hell." He watched fascinated as the mound of earth in front of them grew rapidly. "Slow…slow…and in she goes. Right," he shouted, turning to look behind him. "Back up, fast and then the same again."

*

The first shell struck the front of the tank as he was turning back once more. He heard little. There was just a great red flash and he felt the tank shudder as his head was punched hard by something solid. But it was Terry in the driver's seat that worried him. The tank was on fire. He could see the flames and black smoke pouring from where his driver was sitting. Unclipping his harness, he struggled out of the turret then slid down the front of the tank towards the flames. The force of the second shell exploding lifted him into the air and he felt himself tumbling slowly. First he saw the sky then both his legs above him. As he put an arm out to steady himself so his body slammed into the ground.

He was on fire. The flames were all over him and he tried to rise but his left arm was useless. He tried to roll and half turned, rolling onto his own flames like a dog begins to roll. He scrabbled at the heat on his face and screamed out as the pain knifed into him. Blood from somewhere was flooding into his eyes and he could smell the burning meat. It was sizzling and he was roasting and he screamed out again. Then he saw a face.

"Roll 'im…roll 'im," somebody was shouting. "Here, my coat…over his head. Get the flames…there." The voices were fading. "Here, quick…quick." He heard somebody calling again but they were getting further away. One by one they seemed to be leaving him until there was silence…and peace. Peace at last.

*

"No, can't be." Pat Steer looked at the soldier in horror. "Mike...Mike Daley? No, I can't believe it." She covered her face and leaned against Mavis. The two girls, along with others had heard word from Edgecott and had gone up to see. The base was almost empty and strangely quiet yet they were told to wait at the gate. Somebody would go and find out

"Looks like it, love." The soldier nodded. "Came through this morning...he and four others."

"*Dead*...all of them dead...*killed?*" Mavis looked at him, frowning in sheer disbelief."

The soldier nodded again. "Aye, 'fraid so...that's what they're saying. The lads were hit pretty hard and several others're hurt bad as well." He paused. "Better get word to his girl. You know, the one he...."

"Yes, yes." It was Pat again. Her face was white. "Yes, we'll tell her. Oh God, poor Becky." She turned to the others. "She loved him y'know, loved him in spite of everything." Then her face screwed up in grief. "Oh, dear God...poor soul." She buried her face once more and clung to Mavis as she began to weep.

Chapter Eight

"An' that Olive Burton said to me 'What's yer daughter going to do now he's gone,' she said." Doris Carter shook her head angrily. As she reached up to tidy the strands of grey hair that had come loose when she took off her hat, her face looked furrowed and angry rather than its usual paper grey. "Didn't know what to say...nothing I could say, was there?"

Ernest closed his eyes and waited while she took the hairpins from her mouth and tidied herself. "Everyone's heard the news...everyone 'cept me that is," she went on. "'Spose that's meant to be our fault as well." She swung round and looked at him. "Didn't you hear nuthin, not down the forge or at the stables? Everyone else has."

The wet, miserable summer had continued into the weekend and Ernest had been unable to get into the garden. Yes, he had heard. Everybody had; all yesterday there had been only one topic of conversation but nothing was certain. There were rumours everywhere, almost as bad as being back on the gun lines when they heard that the front had broken "We don't know fer sure yet, dear. Nothing's fer certain yet and 'tis all talk." He pulled himself out of his chair and went to rake the fire. "Even the lads at Edgecott have only heard. That Corporal Marsh, the one what does the post, even he's seen nort and they posties're always the first to know. But that's what they're *saying*."

"Well everyone seems to know and you're the one fer saying that news like that always gets there first. Must be summat in it all."

"Aye," he sighed. "Summat's there and 'tis a terrible shame whatever...young lads like that...cuh."

"An' that man of Becky's one of them." Doris had moved into the kitchen. "Olive Burton couldn't rub that in hard enough." She paused, bending forward to put on her apron. "Can't say it's not justice though."

"*Hey*, that's enough o' that." Ernest, still stiff from sitting in his chair, caught his foot and stumbled on his way towards the kitchen door and stood supporting himself on the dining table. "Us never...*ever*, says ort like that. *Never*...d'yer hear, no matter what. Just imagine if it were our Jack. I mean he's never been in trouble but 'spose he were to be lost like that. What then, eh? Nuthin's certain yet but if '*tis* true...if 'tis, then the lad's given his all...given everything."

"And left his mark." Doris turned to him wiping her hands on her apron. "'Tis all too easy to forget isn't it. When summat like this happens everyone's all forgive and forget but look at the mess 'es gone and left. Eh? This war'll be over one day, but our Becky an' her problems won't, will they? Coupla months time she'll be back an' all that there talk'll start again. Oh aye, mark my words." She caught her breath. "That Mike Daley an' they lot'll be heroes…all forgiven, but not our Becky. Oh no…tongues will be waggin'…damnin' her and damnin' us." Doris brushed past him and went to set the table. "If it weren't for St Margaret's seein' to the girl us'd be in a right old state. I've had it all before, Ernest Carter, when I were a child, an' it's not summat that goes away, I can tell yer."

"But there won't be anything…a babe, I mean. Will there? They're taking it away."

Doris glanced back at him. Her husband had talked before about his daughter keeping her baby. They had argued, several times, and she knew of his desire that what he claimed belonged to the family remained with them. "An' that's a good job an' all," she snapped. "I've said my piece an' that's the end of it…I'm not hearing no more. You keep on an' on about it. Can't understand, can you? Can't see it that us could never live here like this, not all of us together with a bastard child like that."

"Still bain't right," he muttered, grimacing to himself. It had taken him time to calm after Becky told them. First came the fire of rage which burned for weeks before eventually subsiding into a mound of smouldering embers. It was not until Becky left home that the ashes finally cooled and the last wisps of smoke faded from sight. Then he began to miss her. His companions at work consoled him, making light of what had happened and assuring him that bygones would be bygones no matter what. In the end, they told him, nobody would know any different and the child would grow up to lead a happy life among friends.

But now, all of a sudden, it was different. The child's father had died a soldier's death and for that his name would be revered rather than despised. Things would change and Becky would be forgiven for loving a man who had given his life in battle. There was something tragic and honourable about it. Somehow the terrible news had cleared away the shame and tarnish. His daughter's child, their grandchild, would be able to talk with pride about the father it never knew. All it would hear would be admiration and gratitude for the father who had gone off to the war, rather than cruel jibes about the ne'er-do-well who had slunk away.

To his mind it was no longer right that Becky should lose her child. They should be kept together, made welcome and looked after. The village should rejoice that the child of one of those who left to fight for them had come to take his place. Ernest knew in his heart that what had been decided was wrong but he was helpless. It was the church, as far as he knew, that had determined what was to become of the child and if the church had decreed that, then who was he to protest. There was nothing to be done about it. The decision had been made and, in any case, he had no idea where to begin.

He longed to see his daughter, to forgive her and let her know that she would be welcome home. But he could not, for those at the convent had forbidden any such visits. All he could do was to wonder. He was helpless and then, on top of everything else, he knew how her mother felt. While she was like this, it would have been impossible for Becky to bring the child home.

"Coming fer yer dinner, Ernest?" Doris was holding his plate above the pie-dish. He must have missed her setting up the table behind him and bringing the food through. Even the bread had been cut and spread with dripping.

"Aye," he drawled turning slowly back from the window. "*Cuh*, dear me," he spluttered apologetically. "Dreamin' again, I were...miles away."

✳

Sam heard the news at lunch when his parents returned from church. He had been due to go with them but his father had decided to leave shearing until the weather improved and had asked him to move the sheep. It was a long, fiddly job and he had ridden out with the dogs as soon as breakfast was over.

Drew and Barbara heard together. Gwen Steer told them just before they went in to Morning Service. Later, after the sermon, the vicar had said prayers for those that had given their lives and for the wounded, as well as for those who were still fighting on. No names had been mentioned but they heard again afterwards and the news was that Mike Daley's name was among those believed to be lost.

 Barbara seemed indifferent and had not mentioned it as they drove back to the farm but Drew was saddened. He did not know the man but, as far as he could tell, he had been a typical youngster who had courted and won Becky Carter's heart. Couldn't blame him for that however hard it was on Sam and when he heard of her plight well, that was the way of the world and Drew had been among the first to console her father.

✳

"Aye, seems that way." Drew saw the look on his son's face. "Don't know what the maid'll have to say," he continued. "Daresay Ern' an' Doris'll be telling her directly. But the babe's to be adopted, isn't it?"

"So they say." Sam stood stock still by the car. His mother had hurried inside and his father had broken the news as soon as they were alone. Drew had been wondering how he might take it and could see that the news had shocked him.

"You all right, buiy?" His father took his arm. "Bit of a shock, I dare say. News like that always takes yer breath away."

"Yes." Sam cleared his throat. "Mike Daley, an' all they say. An' several more, eh?"

"Aye." His father paused. "Here, c'mon, lad...looks like yer seen a ghost. Not that bad is it. Sad an' that fer sure but didn't 'spect to see you quite so bad as that."

"Yes…well I'm not sure." Sam had a hand first to his head then to the back of his neck and turned away frowning, his mind racing. Becky, he knew, would be heartbroken. Even when she and Mike Daley had parted she never looked at another man. But now he was gone and in two months or so…three perhaps, she would be home again. Pat Steer had told him about the child being adopted so she would be on her own. How would she be, he wondered. There would be changes, of that there was no doubt, but would she still be the girl he remembered after all this, or would she have hardened and become bitter? And what about her family, and her child and all their friends in the village? And what about him, Sam Carter? What would she make of him?

The more the thought about it the more complicated it became. He had to clear his head and think it through. "I'll be fine, Dad. Just need a minute or two that's all. I'll be in directly…tell mother not to wait with dinner. I won't be long."

2.

Becky wiped away the sweat. The laundry rooms were as hot as ever and now the hospital at Musgrove Park was open as well. More and more dirty linen, so much of it heavily dirtied, was arriving every day. They had heard about the new military hospital and listened to the nuns talking about how it was filling with the war wounded.

She was almost seven months and Daisy had warned her that the long hours in the steamy heat would take their toll. Twice that morning she had had to find somewhere to sit but Sister Theresa had shouted at her, on the second occasion pulling her to her feet and screaming in her face above the noise before standing back and slapping her. The force of the blow made Becky sink to her knees but the nun had pulled her up by her hair and glared at her from behind her spectacles with her pointed nose inches from her face, before pushing her back to her place at the vat.

Daisy had been there. She had wrung out a corner of a freshly laundered sheet and wiped the blood from her nose but now Becky felt faint again. She found herself swaying and held on to the wooden surround with both hands. Only when she heard her name called and turned did her head clear. Somebody was beckoning; she was wanted.

＊

"Pat…Mavis, oh, dear Lord." The three huddled together in the interview room. "Oh my God, how wonderful to see you…how wonderful." Becky kissed first one then the other then both of them for a second time. "Oh…my goodness me. How *are* you and what're you doing here? How's home and how's everyone…and how're mother an' father, an' the others?" She paused, momentarily lost for words. "Oh, this is marvellous…it's so *lovely* to see you."

She hugged them again then hesitated. "And what news...anything of Mike and the others...I'd love to...."

"Listen, Becky, we can't stay long." Pat pulled herself away. "The nun told us five minutes and then we'd have to leave."

"Sister Francesca?" Becky looked at her then bent to wipe her face with the corner of her dress. "Old grim face, eh? Oh but she's not too bad, reelly...better'n most."

"What in God's name have they done t'you?" Mavis was running her fingers through Becky's hair. "Look at it...they've butchered it. And look at yer face, Becks. You look so tired, you're exhausted. What the hell're they doing down here. And yer nose...bin bleedin' look. What've you bin doing to yerself?"

"Oh, nothing much," she shrugged. "Reelly, it's not...just the way things are in here. But don't worry, I'm fine, honest I am...I'll get by." She smiled bravely. "Only a coupla months, eh? Then back home again."

"Becks, listen." It was Pat again. Becky saw the look on her face and her smile faded.

"What is it?" Becky glanced from one to the other. "You look all worried. What is it, Pat? What's up? Nothing's wrong is there?"

Pat just stared back then glanced hurriedly at Mavis who put one arm round Becky's shoulder. "Yes," she whispered, nodding in reply to the question. "Fraid so, love...it's Mike."

"What...what's happened?" A hand went to her face. "Tell me, Pat. Quick."

"Well...they say, they say he's been killed...killed in France. Nothing certain yet, nothing at all but Mavis an' I thought we'd come an' let you know what we heard...what they're saying."

Becky went to say something but her mouth closed; then her head dropped. For a while they were silent. Mavis reached for a chair and helped Becky to sit. Then she crouched in front of her. "You all right, love?" She watched as Becky nodded then saw her face as she looked up at them.

"But he promised to come back," she whispered. "He promised me and, y'know what, I believed him. I was sure he would and that somehow we'd make a go of it. Just the two of us an' the babe." She shrugged and suddenly gave a little laugh. "Y'know what...he was all I ever had...and all I wanted." She looked from one to the other again then pulled a sad face as if she was holding back her tears. "But there we are...not to be, is it?"

"Becks listen. We don't know fer *sure*...don't forget." Pat crouched beside her also and stroked her face. "Nobody yet knows for certain, love, but they said we'd best come to warn you."

"No...he's gone all right." Becky sounded quite composed. "I know he has. Soon as yer said it I knew. They don't make mistakes like that do they?" She shrugged. "Not fair reelly, is it?" Her face looked anguished. "Don't reelly need it, do I? Not now." Again the three were silent.

"We'll all be there when you're back home." Mavis took her hands and shook them gently. "It'll be hard but we'll all be there to look after yer. Honest, Becks, everyone's asked to be remembered. Said how they're all longing to see yer."

Becky nodded and lowered her head again. She wanted so hard to cry, to release the grief and heartache she felt. Instead a wave of tiredness swept over her. Suddenly she felt feeble and ready to drop. Then her baby moved, forcing her to draw in her breath and to ease herself on the chair.

"Thanks," she whispered, smiling kindly. "I'll be fine. The girls in here're great. Reelly they are, they're lovely and they've seen all this sort of thing...they'll know how I'll be feeling. Thanks love." She reached forward and drew Mavis towards her. "Thanks...an' you Pat." She held up her other hand and took hold of her friend's also, the two of them twining their fingers together.

The sound of footsteps made them look up. "That's long enough, I'm afraid. You'll have to be on your way." Sister Francesca was standing by the open door. "We've chapel in a minute, Becky, and there's work to be done before lunch." For once there was a smile.

Everybody stood. Pat and Mavis watched as Becky walked towards the door. "Bye Becks." Mavis raised a hand. "Not long now." Becky said nothing, just walked on and past Sister Francesca, leaving her two friends where they were. The nun smiled again and signalled for them to follow her.

*

Becky had been right: the others understood. Only once did she weep and that was when she was alone with Freda. It wasn't for the man she had lost neither was it for her own grief. Rather it was in hope, after what the older woman said. Freda Wright, too, had lost the man she loved and had known the darkness of despair. When she told Becky she pulled up her sleeves and shown her the deep scars on her wrists where she had tried to escape from it all.

But Freda had failed and now, years later, she was glad she had. Even here in St Margaret's life brought its joy, she told her. It was she, Freda, who assured Becky that after every stormy night there dawns another day, and it was then that her tears came. For days the words played on her troubled mind. Slowly, as the weeks passed by and the date of her confinement drew near, the agonies eased. Step by step, she felt able to face the world again. As her confidence

112

returned she began to look ahead to the new life she was determined to have. A life with her child, their child.

3.

In all probability Father Michael O'Connell visited St Margaret's more frequently than was necessary. Appointed to the post of visiting priest in order to oversee religious affairs, he called in as often as he did simply because he found the experience gratifying.

He was a tall, muscular and swarthy man whose appearance gave lie to his forty years, so the sisters flattered him when they dined together. He knew that, once inside and taken on his rounds, his masculinity exuded an intimidating power. Everywhere he went, either with the Mother Superior or an accompanying nun, his rich baritone voice, of which he was justly proud, heralded his presence. The nuns, and he would always acknowledge their presence, stepped aside submissively, fawning on him and blessing him as they bade him good day. Those working there, the young women who had fallen from the path of righteousness or who had yet to see the true light, greeted his presence with due regard. And that, he considered, was exactly as it should be.

Healthy and vigorous, and with what might have been a handsome face save for his arrogant hautiness, Father O'Connell had always been a tactile man. It was an expression of sympathy he used to good effect, but it was also a token of affection designed to encourage those who sought closer fellowship with their priest. Such a gesture sent out many signals, the very touch itself offering a myriad of options to those persuaded to respond. There were many who did, not least the ones for whom the very idea of male company was considered a sin. And there were others whose bodies had known man already and who, incarcerated as they were, craved closer attention.

As he sat waiting in the interview room he smiled to himself, raising an eyebrow appreciatively and smoothing back his neatly cut black hair where the steam from the laundry was still damp. Sister Maria had pointed out the girl he was due to see. He had noticed at once the fullness of her body where the thin, damp working frock had clung to the curves. As he watched her, she had glanced up and their eyes had met. They were large, sultry eyes. The face was full and the mouth sensuous. Even with her hair cropped so short he could see the earthy beauty as she stood there looking back at him, sweat-soaked and her chest heaving with exertion.

That she had lain in sin already he had no doubt. How she had done so and how that young body of hers would have received her man was still exercising his mind when he turned at the knock on the door. "Come in, come in," he replied, standing hurriedly and adjusting his habit. "Aha, Sister Maria. I thought it would be you...we're ready, are we not?"

"Ah, bless you father and to be sure we are. But in Heaven's name look at you,

you're so hot. 'Tis the heat of the laundry, is it not?" Sister Maria, her fleshy, red face smiling obsequiously behind her thick glasses, looked at him pityingly. Her small, piggy eyes with their ginger eyelashes wandered admiringly over his features. "And your poor face looks so flushed...and you're perspiring so. Here...allow me." He closed his eyes while her handkerchief dabbed at his face. "There," she cooed. "That's better."

He nodded, feeling where her hand had been. The great brute of woman revolted him. Forever flattering and toadying, she possessed a cruel, violent streak nonetheless. Her presence was feared rather than accepted around the corridors but that was not necessarily a bad thing. One disciplinarian like that, Father O'Connell surmised, had its advantages.

"Tell me," he commanded, reaching out for the file she was holding. "This young woman, is she likely to object...to make a fuss?"

"Rebecca Carter? No, she'll be no problem. But she's a determined little minx to be sure and she's inclined to mix with the wrong company. Daisy Gunn...you remember her?" Father O'Connell nodded. "Aye, her and there're others."

"And if she does? Surely her family have given their consent, yes?" He opened the file then nodded, answering his own question. "Yes, here we are...uh huh. Full agreement, I see here, signed by her mother. And the foster parents?"

"The Mother Superior's interviewed them, father. A fine couple, very well established and of the Faith, the Lord be praised. And they've paid, too. Handsomely...see here, look." Sister Maria inched towards him then stood on tiptoe and pointed towards the bottom of the page before drawing back respectfully. "And there's to be a substantial donation also, so we believe."

"Grand. That all looks quite straightforward then. Now, you're going to be here and who else?" Father O'Connell enjoyed nothing more than a battle of wills with a young woman desperate to keep hold of her child. The deeper and more agonising the grief and the harder the fight, the more thoroughly the soul was cleansed. Redemption through pain as demonstrated by Our Lord made for purity of mind and body: Sister Maria would see to that. And, were battle to be joined, then any Holy Sisters present would witness the struggle and the triumph of good over evil. Word of his prowess would spread.

"Sister Bernadette, Father. She asked if she could be present. She has kindly feelings towards the girl and, well, we thought that it might be helpful." Michael O'Connell inclined his head, unconsciously wrinkling his nose. He knew the nun well and of her ways with other women. As for the girl herself, he had detected a brooding sullenness in her look, a spirit of defiance that would have to be forced out of her, crushed if needs be. That was his duty and the thought of the coming battle of wills with this wanton young woman aroused him. He could feel his manliness: his blood began to surge again and his heart to beat faster.

114

"Right. You'll be with her, in the chair just here. And I'll have no nonsense from the girl, mind you, Sister. Should she put up a fight and her spirit break…and it may come to that, then I'll see to her alone afterwards. A troubled soul needs to be calmed, you understand. So, there we are…away and fetch them in."

*

"*Every* child belongs to Our Lord." Father O'Connell leaned forward. They had tried to persuade her and now she was arguing. She was indeed stubborn and his patience was wearing thin. "Only those joined in Holy Matrimony and who have vowed before God to consider their duty reverently, discreetly and advisedly, may lay claim to their offspring. Those whom the mystery of Holy Matrimony has made one, only *they* may bear the lawful fruit of procreation. The child that you bear is *not* yours and never shall be so. It is…."

"It *is* mine." Becky cried defiantly. "Look, here it is," she held her stomach. "It's mine, nobody else's. God has given it to me."

"Don't you *dare* speak to Father like that." Sister Maria grabbed her hair from behind, forcing her head back and was now leaning over her. "Don't you dare *ever, ever* to make a claim against Our Dear Lord…never." Becky blinked at the spittle from the nun's mouth, then closed her eyes as her head was shaken roughly from side to side. "You have sinned against man, against God Himself and against His Holy word. The seed you bear is of evil creation…d'you understand…*evil* and there is no way the Lord would ever give such a union His blessing."

Father O'Connell raised a finger to steady her then waited until the girl in the chair had recovered her composure. "There's no point at all in arguing against what is written." He lifted his hands as if to emphasise the futility of her protests. "You can read it for yourself or we can read it to you…either way. Holy Matrimony, as Saint Paul told us, is the sole prerequisite for procreation in the eyes of God. It is not a matter to be taken lightly or wantonly, to satisfy man's carnal lusts like a brute beast as you have done. The issue, now carried by you, is God's by His divine right and it is my duty, as His most humble servant, to save the soul. I hope I have made myself clear?"

"But it's *mine*." Becky's voice was thin: she could feel her tears coming. "Whatever happened it was the will of God that I should have this child and I'm goin' to keep hold of it. I am…I am, you know."

"*Quiet.*" The blow from behind rocked her and Becky put a hand to her face. "Don't you *dare* speak like that. "D'you hear, girl. Father O'Connell's not here to waste his precious time listening to such blather. You heard what he said…you're a beast and a brute and your child has been created through mortal sin." The second blow came from the other side. "Father's here to do his duty to what is God's and in the name of the Lord God Himself…to grant salvation to a poor lost soul."

"Listen Becky." Sister Bernadette had come forward and crouched in front of her, lightly and easily like a young athlete might. She was younger than the other nuns, handsome in a masculine sort of way and she spoke softly. As she reached up to stroke her face, she smiled compassionately. "It's for the best, you know. The best for all of you, really it is. You couldn't give the child the life it so richly deserves. It would be impossible, you wouldn't know how." She paused and took hold of her hands as if to comfort her. "Listen…the poor wee mite would forever be living in the shadow of its parents' shame. And that's a fact. It's not fair, not fair at all…far better to give the child a fresh start, in a loving family and a Christian home. Think of the child…and its life ahead. Can't you see?"

"I don't know…just don't know." By now Becky's head was in her hands. "I just want my baby, my own child. Nobody could love it like I love it now. It's mine…it will always be my baby whatever happens."

"But it's *not*. Those born outside Holy Matrimony belong to God and it's our duty to see the best for it." Father O'Connell sat back and glanced at Sister Maria impatiently. "It's vexing having to go over this ground again and again. You understand what I'm saying, don't you?" He glowered at Becky and waited while she nodded despairingly. "We're only trying to make it *easy* for you," he continued. "It is my duty, as Sister Bernadette has said, to do what's best. Either we can do it like this when you agree quietly and in a civilised manner to what your family have already decided upon or…and I hope it never comes to this, we will have no option but to take the child when it's born. Recover it for its own salvation."

"You *can't*." Becky looked up horrified. Her eyes, wet with tears and red rimmed, were opened wide. "You can't do that," she whispered, looking around. "You can't."

"Oh yes we can." Sister Maria moved clumsily from behind the chair. "You'll be having the child here, just like all the others and after the birth you'll be in no position to do *anything*…anything at all. We, the nursing sisters that is, we'll be looking after you and once the child's delivered you will be in no position to argue. You'll barely be able to stand on your feet, let alone move from the bed or keep hold of the child should we decide otherwise."

"Come on, Becky." Sister Bernadette whispered, lifting her hand to brush away her tears. "It's for the best, dear…'specially for the little one. Let's make it easy…mmm?" Becky lowered her head once more, now sobbing helplessly. Her head was shaking from side to side and she was mumbling to herself.

Michael O'Connell, his chin resting on his hands, watched satisfied. The girl had put up a fight but she was broken, as she had to be. He checked the file nonchalantly, noticing the details of the foster parents and the donation they had promised once the child was theirs. "Here." He pushed the papers forwards to Sister Bernadette.

"Come on, Becky, you know this is best…best for everybody." Becky looked up. For a moment there was a look of wild defiance. Her eyes moved from one to the other, but all three stared back impassively. It was useless. She was cornered, defeated and her shoulders slumped. Slowly she reached for the pen, pausing briefly at where Sister Bernadette was pointing then signed. Moments later her world collapsed.

∗

"Shhh, don't worry." Daisy cradled her head against her breast, rocking her gently. "Yer always feel like that after," she murmured. "Always feel as though you've just thrown a new life away. They all do."

"He was awful," Becky sobbed. "Took hold of me like he did when the others'd gone."

"Aye, a right lecherous old sod an' all." Daisy sat up. "Should've warned yer about that but we knew you'd come to no 'arm. An' anyway…you'd enough worries."

"And to think I trusted him." Becky shook her head in disbelief. "When he took hold of me I thought he was being kind, comforting me. I lent against him, I did. Put me arms around him and held on to him."

"Aye."

"Then he began feeling me, putting his hands all over me…then took my hand and put it on himself." Becky shook her head again. "And I just did it," she wailed. "I felt helpless…I thought of trying to fight him off but he's so big an' strong…what could I 'ave done? An' to think that's what he wanted and after all that he'd said about God…an' what's sinful an' that."

"Listen." Daisy pulled her around. "He's gone now…finished, amen. So stop yer worryin', eh? Nobody's dead an' nobody's hurt." She pulled Becky into her. "An' so *what* if 'es had his dirty bit o' fun…sod 'im fer a start. But now, listen, will yer. Yer want yer baby, right?" Becky nodded. "Well, all right…why not then?" Becky looked up in amazement.

"An' why not?" Daisy continued. "Eh? I'm not sayin' nuthin, not yet, anyway. But just you trust Daisy Gunn. Just trust me." She put a finger to her lips. "Don't say nuthin an' stop getting' all dreary an' glum, like that. Bain't over, y'know, an' it's your turn next. Truly." Daisy lifted her face and kissed her. "Come on, Becks. Give us a smile…an' a big one at that."

4.

Brigadier Stainforth had seen it all before, yet it hurt now just as much as it did then. The thin, tired face under the mass of snow white, curly hair shook sadly.

As a young medical officer at Passchendaele when the British had finally broken through in November nineteen-seventeen, then again six months later on the Somme when the German offensive so nearly broke back, he had seen more than enough. And yet here he was, more than twenty-five years on and Senior Medical Officer, and nothing had changed.

The base hospital had been set up in the grounds of the old chateau at St Croix-sur-Mer, half way between Caen and Bayeaux. It was the German resistance at Caen that had confounded the figures and casualties were now much higher than expected. The hospital was full, even as they evacuated those fit enough to travel home through Arromanches so every bed they had was re-filled. And they were all so young. Gerald, his son, gunnery officer on the destroyer HMS Quantock was older than most and he was but a boy. The brigadier rubbed his eyes and looked at the charts on the wall of his office, a dark and pokey affair set just off the chateau's main entrance.

They would be coming for him soon when he would have to go and make the decisions. Even though it was the responsibility of his surgeons, he insisted that the final word on who was to stay and who was to be evacuated was to remain his. They could recommend, indeed they could insist but the final decision was his. Compassion had to be tempered by the harsh realities where a nod either way could spell life or death. The worst cases, the very worst who were either too weak to be moved or whose chances of survival were negligible were held back, the beds on the hospital ships going to those who would survive or at least whose chances were better.

 How do you tell a lad with multi-limb trauma whose body had been blown apart; or another with defunctioning colostomy, where the bowels had been scooped out by a shell splinter as it howled through the air? Or a man whose face had been torn from the front of his skull yet the holes left exposed still gurgled grotesquely as he fought for life? How do you tell them that it would be better if they stayed awhile longer? And how do you listen impassively as those whose life is ebbing away, cry like a child for their mothers? Somehow it was always their mothers. It was never easy but now, at the age of fifty-one, it seemed harder than ever.

*

"Both legs, sir. One below the knee and one above. We tried to save the left knee but there was too much damage. Infection, too…we couldn't take the risk"

"Right," Brigadier Stainforth nodded. "And what's this here?" He pointed at the surgeon's notes.

"Yes, I was coming to that. Traumatic castration, I'm afraid. The anti-personnel mine, one of those jumping-jack devils, did its worst. The blast caught him…scrotum and penis gone, ripped off. Lost a lot of blood and we had to go up into the stomach after several pieces of shrapnel. We found further infection there as well."

"What are you recommending?"

"I think he'd better stay. The septic shock's pretty bad. Infection got in and the blood's full of muck. We'll keep on trying, of course, but...well..." Major Charles Cranford, tall and good looking but now grey with fatigue, pulled a face. "Very slim, I'm afraid, sir. Harry Bateman and I both feel there's little chance."

"All right, get them to move him into 'M' Ward. We'll watch him but the lad's in one hell of a mess, isn't he?" As they walked to the next bed, Stainforth muttered something to himself and closed his eyes as if in a moment of prayer. "And what've we got here?"

"An interesting case here, sir." The surgeon looked at his notes. "We thought we'd lost him...twice as it happened." Cranford looked up and grinned. "A tough egg." He paused to check his facts. "Took a shell splinter in the left temporal area of the cranium...just above the ear. A lateral splinter that exposed the dura but failed to breach it, thank God. That was straightforward enough but then there were the burns. They're bad...second and third degree. The left side of his head...right on the temporal wound which didn't help, then part of his face and half the shoulder. Oh yes," he added. "Fractured tib and fib just for good measure."

The brigadier pulled on his nose thoughtfully. "So how do we stand right now?"

"Better than a couple of days ago. Much better in fact. One of the young surgeons up at the dressing station did a remarkable job on him. An Aussie...chap by the name of Walker. Stabilised him. Took a couple of weeks mind you before they got him down here but then adult pneumonia set in ...the shock simply tore him to pieces and one of his lungs filled. We thought he was a goner but here we are...and against all odds."

"And his chances...what d'you reckon?"

"*Phewww.*" Charles Cranford blew quietly and closed his eyes. "Until yester-day lunchtime I reckon he wasn't going to make it. In fact we'd earmarked him for 'M' Ward when one of the sisters, Molly Brack, noticed a change."

"And now?"

"I reckon he's worth the chance. If he can keep going like he is then he's not a bad bet."

"East Grinstead then? From what you're saying it's the burns"

"Reckon so, sir. The   hospital carrier 'Duke of Lancaster's' due out after midnight for Portsmouth. We're doing a run down to her just after ten and we could get him on her."

"And what's his name?"

"Daley, sir. Corporal Daley from One Six Two Regiment, Royal Engineers. Did a good job apparently and they're putting him up for something. He drew the enemy's fire away from his men, so they say, but then caught most of this while trying to get his driver out when the tank brewed up."

"Good for him." Brigadier Stainforth sighed heavily and passed the notes back to his surgeon. "When the hell's all this bloody madness going to stop, Charlie? Mmm? Haven't they all had enough, for Christ's sake? All right, get him back tonight...so...who've we got next?"

Chapter Nine

Mike Daley and Brad Proctor sat next to each other in the saline baths. They had done this every day for a week, both enjoying the attentions of the petite, blonde nursing sister who oversaw their treatment.

Proctor, a tall, rangy and very talkative Canadian from Alberta, refused to believe that Mildred Luscombe wore anything at all underneath her white nursing coat and told her so. Daley, half submerged in order to allow the solution to cover his neck, agreed and they demanded confirmation, arguing that she was safe because they shared but one good pair of eyes between them. Mildred Luscombe refused, attending to their naked and tortured bodies with a lofty detachment – and an indefatigable sense of humour.

Almost a year earlier, Sergeant Bradley Proctor of 'A' Squadron, the 6th Canadian Armoured Regiment had been organising the re-fuelling of his Sherman tanks whilst training on Salisbury Plain. When the petrol bowser caught fire it exploded. In the ensuing inferno, four men died and six were burned badly, two of them, including Proctor, almost beyond recognition. One of these two, Le Quesne a French Canadian, died soon after but Proctor survived, first at Queen Alexandra's Military Hospital in Aldershot then later at Queen Victoria's in East Grinstead. It was here that Archibald McIndoe, the New Zealander from Dunedin, now head of the burns unit and known affectionately by everyone simply as 'the Boss', began the painstaking business of reconstructing the face and hands that had been consumed by flames.

By the time Mike Daley reached the burns unit, Proctor's rebuilding programme was underway. The once handsome face which a careless match had transformed into a battered red turnip with grinning teeth, was almost human again; rather it was a plastic imitation of how it might once have looked. The two men were in the same ward and their friendship grew, interrupted only when Mike Daley was moved to Rehabilitation.

However, each day he would hobble out of his hut on his crutches and along the concrete paths that ran between the lawns and rose beds to the baths where he would meet up with his journeyman. Here they would lie grotesquely with most of their burns exposed and Daley with his plastered leg held high in the air. Afterwards they would sit together when Mike listened to the husky croak that emerged from underneath the swathe of bandages. Subject matter ranged widely ending, inevitably, with a discourse on the intricacies of the female anatomy and the potential it offered; a topic enlivened by the presence of Mrs Hagglesby, their ancient and humourless char lady.

*

Brad Proctor was a bachelor yet he, too, had left a woman with his child. They

were now half a world away in the small cowboy town of Wainwright somewhere out on the Canadian prairie. The boy, Ted, was seven according to Brad
and, as the charred photograph showed, he was a tall, gangly child with a
serious face and a shock of blond hair. Today, as usual, the two talked as they
lay together.

"You're quite dreadful, the pair of you." Mildred Luscombe checked the rope
hoist holding Mike Daley's right leg. She listened as they talked, her advice or
comments often being sought. Sometimes, when discussion turned to their
past escapades, she gave her opinions freely, well able to handle the ensuing
banter. "Honestly, it's no wonder all our young women are warned to keep
away from military uniforms. And in any case I couldn't ever imagine anyone
in their right mind wanting to go near either of you."

"But you have to be asked first, sweetheart." Proctor's heavily bandaged face
and head pointed itself roughly in her direction. "And that means you'd be
safe enough, doesn't it," he hissed. "It's only the pretty ones who've got
anything to worry about and they love it...love it...all of them." His throat
rattled at the attempted laugh and he gasped involuntarily.

"Well thank you very much, you. We're not exactly Douglas Fairbanks
ourselves, are we?" she chided before pausing to kneel beside him. "Here,
come on, Romeo, let's see to that left shoulder of yours." Sister Luscombe took
gentle hold of the Canadian. "Here," she whispered. "Just lower yourself a
bit...steady...there we are. Anyway, enough of that cheek and listen to me. The
Boss wants to see you after this," she continued. "He's pleased enough so far,
very pleased in fact but he wants to see what they can do about your
eyes...eyelids and eyebrows in particular. It'll mean full exposure, I'm
afraid....all dressings off in the decontamination tent for the inspection. But, all
being well and if he's happy, they'll be taking you in tomorrow for the op...and
I reckon you're ready."

For a moment there was silence. "Aw, Jesus...not again," he muttered. "You'll
be there, will you, babe? In with the Boss, I mean?"

"Yes," she replied briskly, hiding her sympathy. She and the others knew only
too well what agonies were suffered as the dressings were removed for inspection and then later when they were replaced with fresh ones. "And Sister
Dennis has said you can come over after two this afternoon, Mike. All right?
Brad'll be ready then...all parcelled up neat and tidy with his bottom
powdered." Daley turned towards her and nodded. What plaster and light
bandaging remained on his face covered his badly damaged left eye and ear.

It had taken two operations to rebuild the base of his face and a further three
for McIndoe and his team to reconstruct the features. The indentation where
the shell splinter had done its work above his left ear had been transformed
into undulating purple-pink skin that had once been covered with hair. The ear
itself looked little more than putty and the deep burns on the left side of his

face would remain forever as unwanted souvenirs: that apart Mike Daley was as handsome as he was likely to get, even his pencil-thin moustache had survived together with three-quarters of his wavy, black hair.

"And when are you leaving, Mike?" Sister Luscombe, her attention still with Brad Proctor, glanced back at him.

"End of September," he grunted trying to sit up. "Sending me out on re-hab…down to Taunton, of all places."

"I know. Musgrove Park…one of those new ones down in Somerset," she remarked. "And isn't that where your young lady's having the baby?"

"Near there. A little place called Exford, tucked away in the hills an' miles from anywhere."

"How lovely…you'll be able to see her then. They get you up and out and about as soon as they can, down there." She stood and dried her hands. "What's it going to be, I wonder," she mused. "The little one, I mean. Next couple of weeks, isn't it?" Sister Luscombe paused. "Well, you're going to have to be a little patient; it's going to be a while yet before you can go crashing around and misbehaving again."

"Just be sure to get there, pal." Proctor's head rose as he tried in vain to look at Daley with what was left of his remaining eye. "She'll be needing you…and so will the kid, too."

"No worry." The bath water around Daley was draining away. "I'll be there, mate…weekend pass in my pocket, an' all. It's only an hour by bus."

"But don't expect them to have the flags waving for you." Proctor tried to laugh. "Nobody down there's going to be pinning any medals on you, pal…not her folks any hows, not after you've bin firing live rounds at their little girl. Tread carefully, my son…if you can, that is."

"*Huh*, some chance." Mildred Luscombe held out her hands to Mike Daley who took hold of them and eased his naked body into a sitting position. "But Brad's right, you know. Whatever you do, don't go barging in and claiming ownership. *If* she wants to see you again, and it's a big *if*, mind, then you just take your time." She adjusted her gloves. "Becky…that's her, isn't it? Becky's got the child remember and that's going to be coming first in her life from now on, long before you." She paused, holding him steady and patting his skin with a towel. "And everything's going to be different at home, too. Oh, goodness me, yes," she chuckled. "Her Mum and Dad for a start. Just as Brad said, they're not going to be exactly thrilled to bits to see our wounded hero coming up the garden path."

Mike Daley looked down and nodded. It was going to be hard, hard all right

123

seeing the state he was in, but he would have his back pay and there were those he knew who might help. And then there was Becky, if she would have him. Life didn't look too bad: it could be worse, a lot worse. Take poor old Brad for instance.

2.

Becky had been moved in with the quiet, red-headed woman where they shared the dimly lit bedroom in the maternity wing. The delivery room was next door.

The view from their first floor window across the forecourt to the gardens was a busy one and showed the world as it was. Whenever she had time, Becky would stand between their beds watching people walk past the gates at the end of the drive. The convent looked so open and friendly from there but it wasn't. It was locked and barred from the inside, all coming and going dependent upon chains and keys. She gazed longingly. Whenever somebody approached or a car arrived, crunching its way slowly across the gravel, she would duck back from view but continue to watch with only her eyes and nose above the sill.

Although Mary Coward had been in St Margaret's for over six weeks, Becky hardly knew her. She had been sleeping in a dormitory on a different floor and worked in the laundry annex, away from most of the others. She was older than Becky and came from Bridgwater where her father was a chemist. The father of her baby, she claimed, was a master at the local grammar school who wanted nothing to do with the child and who had denied everything. Rather than face up to the life-long stigma, her parents had forced her into adoption. To Becky, Mary was a quiet, sad soul who said little as they cleaned the corridors and brasswork together.

When her time came, Mary's pains began a little after midnight and her waters broke soon after dawn, just as the sun rose high enough to shine through their little window. It was then that they moved her and Becky was not to see her again. But that was four days ago and now the foster parents were coming for the child, exactly as Daisy and Freda told her they would.

*

As soon as she heard the commotion from the room across the passage, Becky knew what was happening. It was a dreadful noise and she hurried from her bedroom covering her ears in horror but the pleading and crying continued to echo throughout the annex. Immediately afterwards, Mary was moved to a room far away on the third floor at the back of the building where her cries could continue unnoticed. Becky despaired: she, too, had signed away her child and now knew for certain that there could be no escape. It was later, long after the lights had been dowsed, that Daisy stole into her room.

Becky gasped at the sight of the figure in the doorway but a finger raised in warning kept her silent. She said that she had come to see how she was but she spoke in riddles, warning her about something as if she knew things might change. She sounded confident and assured but Becky remained far from convinced, believing her presence was no more than a generous attempt to bolster her spirits. "I'm saying nowt," Daisy whispered, once Becky had got over her surprise. "Nowt at all 'cept to tell you not to jitter an' moan so. Just let *them* see you're reelly afear'd an' that yer dyin' of worry. Right?"

Becky pulled a blanket from her bed and the two girls sat huddled together underneath. "Get yerself into your mind that the baby's going to go, that they're goin' to take it…right? Just like poor Mary's. Tell yerself you'll never be seein' it again then make yer wailin' an' blubberin' sound fer real. An' you're good enough at that," she joked, taking her hand. "Just trust me, like I've told yer to."

But for Becky the dread and worry continued. She remained distraught at the idea of some grim figure cloaked in its long black habit reaching out to take hold of her child as it lay at her breast. The helpless mite, so warm and secure against her beating heart would lie still in the cold, claw-like hands, uncomprehending about what was happening. The hazy eyes would stare about vacantly and confused while a tiny pink hand might stretch out to seek reassurance. But the child would be taken.

It was made worse for her the following afternoon when she watched as a car pulled into the forecourt. Two people, a man and woman and both smartly dressed, got out and walked to the side door. Even from where she was she could hear the bell ringing and, now standing on tiptoe, looked on as they were let inside. Half an hour later they reappeared. Becky heard them talking noisily as they bade farewell at the door then stood and watched once more, taking care to stand well back from the window.

This time the woman, still in her navy blue overcoat and a yellow patterned headscarf was carrying the child. Becky couldn't actually see it but knew it was there by the way the woman walked and how she cradled the bundle in her arms. Her husband, or whoever he was, had a hand on her shoulder and, as they walked, so they laughed and joked happily. Mary Coward's child was being taken away. In a moment it would be gone, having been taken from the arms of its mother whose love it would never know.

3.

Pat Steer waited until he got out of the trap and walked over to join her before the two of them made their way towards the village stores. Sam was looking happier than she had seen him for months: even as he was securing the pony to the rail he looked back at her and grinned. But outside the shop he stopped and checked himself, lifting his hat as he thought about what she had just said. "Aye, 'spose so," he said thoughtfully. "Must be any day now. Knew it was soon, like."

"Well, end of September was what her said an' here we are, look…Michaelmas on Sunday. She'll want to be seeing you, Sam. I mean things 'ave changed for 'er an' she'll be missing the baby summat dreadful."

125

"'Spose 'er will." For a moment he looked down as though he was studying his feet then he glanced up at her again. "D'you reckon she will though, Pat? I mean, after all that's gone on d'yer think she'll take kindly to me?"

"Course 'er will." Pat Steer took his arm. "She'll need you, Sam, need all of us fer that matter. It's bin hard enough with all that's gone on but there's still those around 'ere who'll be turning up their noses and walking past."

"But she won't have the child, will she, so it's not as though anyone can see anything."

"Doesn't matter. There's enough of them on their high horses to let her know they've not forgotten. No, t'will be up to us...me...you, Mavis an' Garth an' that. Us've all got to make her feel welcome. It's over and done with, eh? 'Tis time to be moving on."

"Gerry Chugg's got no time for her. Said the other day that once a ewe's broken out of the field...once she's a breaker then she's always a breaker."

"*Poof*". Pat tossed her head. "That Gerry Chugg's all mouth. Don't go payin' no attention to him. If he feels like that then 'e's just about the only one of us what does." She paused then nodded towards the stores. "Coming in?"

"Can't stop, maid. Dinner's on an' father's ploughin' today...they two fields above the combe. But listen." Sam hesitated. "Ern' an' Doris Carter've asked me down. Just fer a cuppa tea, Ern said. What d'yer reckon?"

"*Go* then. Go on." Pat Steer pushed at him with her basket. "Bain't nort to worry about there, yer girt fool. They've always been fond of you an' I daresay they'll be asking you again once Becks's home."

"Aye." Sam watched as she crossed the road. What she had just said settled the matter and he would go but his mother would be furious about it if she knew. Luckily he had not told Pat that she, his mother, out of all those with harsh things to say about Becky, had been quite the worst. And it had hurt. As soon as he mentioned that he was looking forward to seeing her home again, she had banged the table. What was it she said? A soldier's moll, and nothing but a common little grubber? Twice they had argued and on the second occasion his father had stood square to her and told her to mind her tongue. She had been livid and he had been forced to leave them to it. Becky had been a fool, they all knew that, but she had paid the price, losing first her man and then her child. Pat Steer had cheered him and, in any case, he was going to make his own mind up about it all.

✳

"Not sayin' it's goin' to be easy for the maid, dear, but if Sam, here, and all their friends're thinking like that...well, 'tis fortunate enough." Ernest Carter poured some hot tea from his cup into his saucer and supped noisily. He had been delighted to see Sam the other day and had asked him to stop by, and here he was, dressed up in jacket and tie and doing them proud. "Us don't know fer sure but the end of the month is what her said, so us'll have to see."

"It'll be tryin' for her, Mr Carter, no doubt about that." Sam moved himself uncomfortably. It had not been quite as easy as he expected. Becky's father had welcomed him warmly but her mother had been as awkward as ever. Now that Becky was due home any day, her mother really had to try to forgive. The soldier, Daley, had gone and gone for ever, and now there would be no child.

"An' that serves her right." Doris put down her cup and wagged a finger at both of them. "Not sayin' I'm goin' to make it hard for the girl but she's got to realise what she's done."

"Aye," Sam nodded thoughtfully. "Aye, Mrs Carter, I'm sure you're right. Becky's a loverly maid and she'll be knowin' what she's been and done all right. No doubt she'll not be findin' it easy, knowin' what folks'll be sayin'." He scratched nervously at the back of his head. "But she's got her friends to look after her."

"Oh aye," Ernest nodded. "Us just needs for folks to bide their time an' not go too hard on the maid."

"Well, they'll all be doing just as they please an' there's nort we can do about *that*…nor Becky neither." Doris held up the plate of scones. "'Tis a nice gesture, Sam, an' we're grateful enough for you stopping by. Aye, that's right." Doris glanced at her husband. "She's a lucky girl, that's fer sure. Anyways, dear." Now she turned back to Sam. "You're more than welcome here…any time. You know that. Becky'll be more than pleased to see you, same as we'll be."

Sam looked across at them. "Just be glad to see her back safe and sound, that's all." He sat back and smiled broadly at the thought.

4.

Every light was out. The building had gone to sleep and the hall clock had just struck eleven when Becky saw the door of her room open. It was Daisy again, moving like the ghost she had been two nights ago. Becky half sat and watched as the silent shadow slid past the door, then she moved over hurriedly to make room in the bed.

Daisy took her hand. "Now listen," she whispered, so close that Becky felt the hot breath in her ear. "It's always three days at least before they take the babes away. Told yer so, didn't I? 'Tis harder for the mothers when they keep hold of them like that an' they'd do it sooner if they could. But they can't, see. They've got to give the babe time to pick up…get a bit of strength an' that for itself, so I'll not be coming for yer on the first night after."

"*Coming* fer me, Daisy? What d'yer mean? Jesus, what's on yer mind?"

127

"*You*, stupid." Becky felt her giggling silently. "You're going to get out...aye, you an' yer babe."

"But how...."

"Shhh," she hissed, putting a hand to Becky's mouth. "Just shut up an' listen to me, will yer. Me an' Freda's goin' to get yer out, as I said...on the second night after. Us haven't said a word, haven't dared to before in case yer let summat out. Now then, come the second night an' you'll be all cleaned up an' settled by then...strong enough to make it away." Becky sat there shaking her head in disbelief then suddenly clutched at her friend. So *that* was it: *that* was what she had been hinting at all this time.

"Now then." Daisy took her hand. "I'll be in to see yer the night after the birth, just like now but you'll be in the room across the way there," she pointed vaguely past the door. "Across there where they put Mary after she'd had hers. Us'll have to be quiet, mind. That Sister Maria's further down the way. Guards the place like an old dragon, 'er does, but not to worry."

Daisy put an arm around her friend. "So you'll be away, my love. Away out of the gate and off down the road afore the cock crows twice, as they say. I'll be bringing you yer things, see...but now, hush, not a peep to anyone...an' watch that tongue of yours. I'm away now."

She slipped out of the bed and bent down to kiss her. "Remember just keep believin' yer goin' to *lose* it, an' they think you'll know nuthin'. We'll miss yer, Becks, dear. Miss yer bad, we will, but there we are. They deserve it, this bleedin' lot. Deserve it fer lockin' me away like they did." She kissed her again and squeezed her hand affectionately.

Becky watched and listened but there was not a sound as Daisy Gunn slipped back into the night. She just sat there, exactly as she was and seemingly for hours, before falling back to lie staring at the ceiling. Even then her heart was beating with excitement.

✳

Lunch was over and it was just after she had pulled herself up the stairs by the rail, stopping at the top to catch her breath, that Becky felt the first pain. At first she thought it was nothing but then, when she was lying on her bed before her afternoon chores, she felt them again, and again soon afterwards. She struggled to sit up, suddenly panicking about what to do and what was going to happen. When they came once more, this time more fiercely like a sudden cramp, she made her way as fast as she could to the laundry room.

Freda saw her first, half doubled up and holding on to the doorway, crying out to make herself heard above the noise. Sister Bernadette took her back to her room then left her. A while later, when the pains were coming more frequently, she returned having changed into a voluminous white gown. The midwife, came soon afterwards.

Mrs Trant, small and busy, with neatly permed brown hair and piercing blue eyes, smiled kindly before taking her hand, telling her what to expect and calming her. The two of them took her into the delivery room where Sister Bernadette changed her clothes and washed her. Becky remembered what the other girls had said about the sister and what she, herself, had thought of it all but she cared not a bit, only glad that at last she had found someone gentle and friendly.

*

"That's right...that's right...keep pushing." Mrs Trant was bending forward between Becky's raised and parted legs. "It's coming nicely...and again, now. That's right...I can see the head and it's fine...a wee mop of curly black hair." She looked up. "Water ready, Sister. Not too hot, mind. Get the bowl ready...over there, look."

"That's grand, dear." Sister Bernadette looked up and nodded obediently at Mrs Trant, wiping the sweat from Becky's brow. "Do as she says and I'll be back in a second...come on, keep pushing." Becky was half sitting, propped on her elbows. Her head was thrown back and the veins on her neck stood out. As she gasped and pushed, so her hands, with her knuckles white, clutched at the rubber sheet.

"Nearly there," Mrs Trant called out. Now she was standing, watching intently and easing back the flesh to make way for the head. "Push now...harder." Becky's head was turning from side to side. Her eyes were closed and her screams and grunts came through her clenched teeth. "Legs, sister...hold back her left leg...it's coming...here we are...yes, once more...*there* we are, we're there. Wonderful...clever girl, Becky." Mrs Trant paused, then leaned over the bed towards Becky and smiled happily. "Well done, well done...you've a lovely wee girl and she's as pretty as a picture."

Mrs Trant moved quickly, wiping the baby's mouth then cutting and tying the cord. Becky lay back exhausted. She was panting for air, smiling weakly and licking the sweat from her lips. Sister Bernadette was wiping her brow and Becky's eyes remained closed as she felt the cool freshness of the damp towel caressing her skin. Slowly, as if she could hardly believe it, her hands moved across her stomach but there was nothing there, nothing at all. Her body was as she remembered it all those months ago.

The thin, plaintive cry made her look up and she tried to sit in order to see better. Sister Bernadette held her head and she watched fascinated as her daughter was washed. The tiny arms and legs wind-milled feebly in protest and her face was screwing itself up in a mighty effort to protest even more loudly at what she thought about it all.

Chapter Ten

The gale that had been blowing for the last twenty-four hours finally died at around midday. Then came the rain but, by early evening, that too had passed, allowing the day to be closed by a cloudless sunset. It was still bright, even now, making the lengthening shadows look darker yet, once again, the countryside looked washed and fresh.

Becky had fed her baby. She sat rocking the child against her shoulder, humming quietly and with the child's head against her cheek until Sister Deirdre came for her. As usual she cried, not because Daisy had told her to, but because she missed the infant's warm softness, the baby smell and the sound of the tiny lips smacking together as she savoured the last remnants of her feed. Yesterday, as soon as she had been fed, they took her and locked her in the nursery, leaving Becky alone and pining, desperate to mother her or simply to sit by her as she lay asleep in the wicker crib. But tomorrow would soon be upon them and the child was due to go.

All evening Becky agonised as to whether or not Daisy would be true to her word. It had to be tonight. But what if there was an accident or she had been sent away on some task or other? What if the nuns moved the baby to a new room further away which Daisy did not know about? There was only tonight's feed at around eleven o'clock, then the two in the morning and, finally, one at midday. After that would come the slow crunch of wheels on the gravel, the ringing of the doorbell and the sound of voices raised in cheerful anticipation.

Tormented with worry, she moved the bowl from her bedside chair and sat. She bit her nails and brushed angrily through her cropped hair. She rose and paced up and down, turning sharply at some sudden thought or distant noise. She lay on her bed and shut her eyes trying to nap but tossed endlessly, frightened by the thoughts tumbling through her mind. That same deep chill of fear and uncertainty had returned. At eleven, as soon as she heard the footsteps and the rattle of keys, she was up by the door, standing ready to scoop the child from the sister's arms.

Less than an hour later the nun returned to wait in the doorway with her cold, white hands outstretched. Becky's anguish and her lonely vigil continued.

*

But Daisy did not let her down. She came as she promised and waited quietly while Becky dressed herself with the clothes she had brought. Then, beckoning her to follow, she crept silently ahead and down the moonlit passage, stopping only to point towards Sister Maria's door where she raised a finger in warning. When they reached the nursery, there was no rattle of keys because she had brought along just the one she needed.

Becky waited, shivering with excitement, as Daisy slipped into the room then followed her, pausing briefly as she locked the door behind them. "In case she cries," she breathed. Ducking low in order to see better in what little light there was, they inched their way forward once more, one slow step at a time. Becky took her hand, feeling in front of her with her feet and stopping when they came to the crib.

She stared transfixed. Only the dark outline of her head was visible above the covers but there, underneath, her child lay asleep. For a moment she was undecided. "Come on," Daisy whispered, nudging her. "Here, a piece of blanket. Take her up…wrap her and hold her to yer breast. Cuddle 'er close and stand quite still…see if her'll feed…better that way, an' quieter too." Twice the baby cried out, once as she was lifted from the warmth of her bed and once again, grumbling this time, as she settled in her mother's arms.

For what seemed like ages, they waited, listening then it was Daisy who moved first, leading the way back past Becky's room and across the landing. The stairs were hard for Becky who, with the child in her arms, found it difficult to see where her guide wanted her to step. The shadow that moved in the dining room was Freda who had been waiting for them with a coat and a dark grey shawl she had found in the main hall. Becky stood watching as they whispered together. One of them, she suspected it was Daisy, had unscrewed the lock on the window and it had been raised just enough to squeeze through. Again it was difficult, especially with the child, but they made it at last.

When she turned to say farewell Becky stumbled, finding Daisy almost on top of her. After passing out the baby, she, too, had scrambled out, to bid farewell. They said nothing, just held on to each other until Daisy pushed her away, warning her to stay clear of the gravel. "Go on, love…go now. Yer need every minute, every second you've got afore the bells start ringing. Go on…bless yer Becks, bless yer, darlin'".

Becky started out but turned to look back. She could barely see for her tears yet her heart was beating hard with excitement. At last, at long last she was free, both she and her baby…and they were going home.

✳

She knew she was on the right road for Freda had told her which way to go, but what she was going to do next she had no idea. After an hour she heard the first birds. Behind her, way out to the east beyond Taunton, the sky was getting brighter and overhead, one by one, the stars were fading as the light grew. She could see cattle and sheep in the fields then, suddenly, as though some great veil had been swept from the landscape, it was morning.

The child got heavier, waking and complaining as Becky changed arms again and again. Twice she stopped, first by the roadside where she adjusted her shoe, then again, a while later, when she felt pains in her stomach. It was there, as she leant up against the gate, that she heard the vehicle. Shrinking back from the road, she forced her way into some brambles and watched fearfully as the old steam milk lorry rattled past.

Another hill and the first rays of sunlight were touching the treetops on the crest across the valley. By now her heel was raw and the pain was forcing her to limp. It was slowing her yet she had to press on. In spite of the dawn chill her mouth had dried. She found a brook that ran under the road where she knelt and scooped handfuls until her thirst was slaked. For a time she was refreshed but then her discomfort returned. It got worse. Her head ached and, as her mind began to spin, she began to stagger and weave about. Now, afraid they would fall and more weary than she knew possible, she looked for somewhere to stop but the banks on both sides of the lane rose steeply.

Then she heard another vehicle. She could tell it was a tractor and that it was coming up behind her. Once more she looked around for somewhere to hide but there was no cover, anywhere. She panicked and broke into a run with her child, swinging from side to side as she went, but the vehicle was catching her. It was hopeless. She slowed, came to a halt and looked round despairingly.

At first, pressed back as flat as she could make herself, she thought it was not going to stop but the driver slowed and pulled up beyond her when the sudden silence made her feel more vulnerable than ever. Her heart sank as she watched him leave his seat and lower himself slowly to the ground. She had been caught and they would surely send her back to St Margaret's.

"'Ere," the voice commanded. "'Tis early enough fer to be out walkin' abroad wi' a babe in arms like this." The man bent forward. He was staring suspiciously and approached her cautiously. "What's all this, then?" Before he came up to her, George Denner stopped to take a better look. Becky was relieved to see a smile. "Summats wrong, that's fer sure. Should never be out this time o'the mornin'," he announced. "What's a maid like you be doin' out an' about like this, eh?" He peered at the child. "Cuh, my dear soul and with a little mite like that, an' all."

She had no idea what to say and lowered her head. "I had to," she whispered. For a moment the two of them stood in silence. "I'm tryin' to make my way home."

"Tryin' to get home?" George Denner scratched his head. "Oh aye," he said slowly. "Oh aye. Now then...I've a mind that you're from that there convent place." Short and red-faced and with greying-brown hair poking out from under his cap, the farmer nodded as if he knew the answer. Then he craned forward to see more clearly. "Aye, that's it...that's where you'm from. Back down the road there, I'll be bound."

Becky leant back against the trailer. Nodding slowly she put a hand to her face. She wanted to weep but was too exhausted. "*Well then.*" The sudden change in

132

his voice startled her. "If that be the case then you've bin an' found the right man," he announced. "Can't abide they lot back there, an' nor can Mrs Denner neither." He put a hand on her shoulder. "Don't 'e worry, maid...you'm safe enough. Safe as can be."

She stared. "I had to leave," she explained, fearing she had not heard him correctly. "I had to, they were going to take my baby and I just had to get out before I lost her."

"Aye, I don't doubt it," he growled. "Don't doubt it at all. What you need now, m'dear, is summat t' eat...and then a good rest. Eh? Well then," George Denner rubbed his hands together. "Mrs Denner'll be more'n pleased to see yer, 'er will. Come on...up in the trailer, alongside they sacks an' that, an' us'll be home shortly. No," he muttered to himself as he took her arm. "Us can't abide they lot in that there place, an' the further you're away from there the better.

"There, then." He waited while she sat then stood on tiptoe to peer once more at the baby. Becky lifted the child and smiled warily. "*Cuh*...missus'll go all dappy when she sees that littl'un. Us've had five of our own but they've all flown now." He paused. "Cuh, 'er'll go right proper dappy."

✳

Becky stayed at Drake's Farm for almost a week. After three days she reckoned she was well enough to press on but Mabel Denner would have none of it. Becky would leave when she and her little maid were ready and not before.

Both came to the bus to see them away. After turning back to wave until she could see them no longer, Becky settled down in her seat. Exford, the driver told her, would be an hour at the most and she leant her head against the window.

2.

Group Captain 'Freddie' Bowen glanced up at the man across the desk. He still looked weak and the medical reports in front of him stated that more physio-therapy was required, especially around the shoulders and neck. And then there must be time allowed for the wound to settle and for the man to adjust to his new world where, for the rest of his life, people were going to stare in horror at the face confronting them. On top of all that, and once he had been medically discharged, there would be the re-settlement course.

"It's going to have to be a couple of months at least, Corporal Daley," he said kindly, noticing the anxious look. "There's still quite a bit to be done. Musgrove Park will work on your shoulder and neck but the main wound looks fine." He searched through the notes. "Yes...here we are. It's cleaned up nicely and they're very pleased. How does that sound?"

"Could be worse, sir." Mike Daley grinned ruefully. "Just want to get out and get on with me life."

The Group Captain nodded. As Military Commandant at East Grinstead it was up to him to see every man away from the hospital. But he had to be careful, satisfying himself that recent events had not left too many scars on his patients' minds, scars that were likely to break open should the next critical step back to normality be too much. Sometimes it was difficult to decide. Daley looked ready, yet even now there was something in the paperwork that suggested there might still be a problem. As far as they knew, there was no family, neither was there a home for him to go to. The Group Captain had to be sure .

*

"But this girl...and a baby as well, eh?" Freddie Bowen raised an eyebrow beneath which his eyes twinkled merrily. He had heard it so many times before; usually it was nothing more than faint hope, imagination even. "Spoils of war, eh?" he quipped. "Or something more? Are you really keen to get in touch again?" He watched him carefully. "Mmm. All right...tried writing yet?"

"Yes sir. No luck though," he shrugged.

"When was that?"

"Must've been about three weeks back, sir. Mrs Luscombe reckons it may've bin caught up in all that lot from 'ere what went missing when the train was derailed...up Croydon way."

"Uh huh." Bowen sounded speculative. He hesitated, lifting his chin and rubbing it thoughtfully. "Could be no bad thing, y'know. In the long run," he added quietly.

"Why's that, sir?"

"Well...if what you're telling me's true then you've both been through the mill one way or another. She'll be feeling pretty raw I daresay and to write and let her know that you're on the way for a second helping so to speak...that could put the cat among the pigeons." Daley looked at him. "You really want to save the relationship, I take it?"

He nodded, searching the Group Captain's face.

"Well, my advice would be not to push things too hard before you actually see her again. Things might be a bit strained anyway and, if that's the case, you want to start on an equal footing. Letting the family know you're on the warpath only gives them time to think about it...and bolt the door perhaps." He smiled and sat up, pulling at his belt.

"Why not wait until you're on one of your exeats down there? Get a weekend pass then go along and see for yourself. There're certain advantages, y'know. I mean you're in a bit of a mess yourself...not quite as she remembers you. But it could help. Maybe they'll think you're not such a bad lad after all. You've won your spurs, sort of thing."

Daley raised an eyebrow. "Never thought of it like that," he grinned. The old man certainly knew the score. "Bin wonderin' what its goin' to be like...Becky seeing me all like this, I mean."

"You just can't tell." The Group Captain sighed, inclined his head and shuffled the papers in front of him. "Sometimes you chaps leave here in one hell of a mess, far worse than you, and the girl...the wife or whatever, picks up just where they left off, as if nothing's happened. Other times...no. The poor lad's ditched an' that's that. I just can't tell you which way it's going to go," he mused. "When it does go like that it's very sad and that's one of the reasons I recommend you go and see for yourself...face the music. You'll know soon enough and there'll be no time for shilly-shallying about."

Daley pulled a wry face. He knew, they all knew, it had to come to that sooner or later. "Thanks, sir...I'll give it a go, anyway." He smiled gratefully.

"Well, you've done well, my lad. Not only here...you've been good fun here, but out there where it all went arse over tit." Daley grinned at his language. "Mind you, that's not for me to say, it's for others," he went on. "And they've done just that...and all the way up the line as well." He saw Daley frown.

"Here look." The Group Captain opened a drawer and took out a small, white cardboard case. "Seen one of these before?"

"No sir." Daley peered forward.

"MID...Mentioned in Dispatches. It's yours...your award and a damn good show too. It came through yesterday, in the post as they do. But they don't give 'em away, y'know...it didn't actually 'come up with the rations' like they say." Freddie Bowen laughed at the thought. "And from what they tell me yours was a good 'un...well earned. So, well done, my boy. Better ask Matron to get it sewn on."

"Blimey, sir."

"Yes, well, there we are. The Boss normally does the presentation but he's away today and asked me to do it on his behalf." Bowen cracked his knuckles. "But he has asked to see you in the morning before your transport gets here. You're away when...the ten twenty-five up to town, isn't it?"

"Yes sir. Gets into Taunton just after four."

"Grand...grand." The Group Captain rose. "So one chapter closes and another opens, eh? Life's never dull…not here anyway."

"Summing like that, sir." Daley rose also. He took the Group Captain's hand and they left the room together, the officer holding the door and ushering him through.

3.

While one of the whippers-in rode off to fetch the pack, the tufters waited patiently with the huntsman. Thus far the season had been indifferent. Autumn staghunting had not gone well but today the wise old hounds had managed to put up a fine stag. He had not wanted to leave the covert at all and it was not until the huntsman had dismounted and forced him from where he was lying up that he eventually got underway. Even then he took time out to turn and lower his antlers at a couple of tufters who had ventured too close to his heels. But then he broke into a steady canter and cleared the wire fence at the edge of the plantation.

As he waited, the huntsman spoke softly to his few trusty hounds who had done their job so well. One came up to talk, getting close to his horse as it stood mouthing its bit and throwing up its head impatiently. Another bayed and feathered his stern affectionately, while a third yawned as if he was tired of waiting. But they knew exactly what was coming and were quite happy to wait quietly by the side of the track that ran through the heather.

Behind them and further up the slope, the field were waiting also. As soon as the pack arrived from the farm where they had been kennelled, they would be laid on to the line and the hunt would be on. Earlier there had been a distinct chill in the air but now the sun was trying to break through. High overhead a buzzard mewed plaintively, wheeling gracefully in great, slow arcs above its territory. In the wood below them, a pigeon suddenly clapped away while further down still, somewhere along the riverbank, a magpie rattled angrily at having its morning disturbed. Scent, today, would be good.

＊

Colonel Ashcroft led the way. Today he was riding Fay, his favourite, and he allowed the reins to slacken as the mare picked her way carefully through the bracken. He had first seen the young woman on her dappled grey just after the meet but had been unable to get up to her. Now, waiting and watching like everybody else, she was standing apart from the rest of the field and he took the opportunity. He had known the family for years and had helped her father with their recent move. "Hullo Rose…isn't it a marvellous morning." Miles Ashcroft raised his top hat and smiled warmly. "So glad you could make it. Couldn't have picked a better day if you'd tried."

"Morning, Miles." Rosemary Hatton inclined her head in acknowledgement. The slight figure in tweed jacket and buff breeches was superbly mounted as usual and dressed to match. Even from this distance the Colonel noticed her fine features. Rosie Barclay, as she once was, had always been beautiful, ever since she was a child at Roedean when he had first met her parents. Jamie Hatton, the young R.A.F pilot had eventually won her but it had not lasted, the second of three ME 109's over Ashford had seen to that during the very last week of the Battle of Britain. Her broad smile from under her bowler showed her surprise and delight. "I *thought* you'd be out...how lovely to see you."

"Well, here we are." Ashcroft replaced his hat. "Now, m'dear, look. I've brought some very good friends over to meet you." He turned. "Barbara, here's Rosemary...Rosemary Hatton...Barbara Hawkins." He waved his hand to effect the introduction. "And somewhere," he turned further and bent down to look behind. "Ah, yes....there you are, Sam." Miles Ashcroft pulled back to allow Barbara and Sam forward. "Rose used to hunt here before the war," he announced. "Couldn't leave Exmoor alone, could you. But that was, goodness me, years ago now." Rosemary Hatton nodded, replacing her glove. "Now she's back again but doesn't know many folk. Hardly anyone."

Barbara's bay twisted and turned. He was a young horse, fired up with excitement and already sweating freely. Scolding him noisily, she turned away to give herself more room to bring him under control. "Now look, Rose. *Sam* here's your man." Ashcroft put a hand on his shoulder. "Want to know anything about this part of the moor then he's the fella to follow. Is that not right?" Sam nodded, smiling bashfully and raising his eyebrows in surprise at the sudden accolade.

"Thank goodness for that." Rose Hatton's eyes lit up. "I haven't a *clue*. Really I haven't and I could never bring myself to go round asking everyone where this and that is...I'd feel awful." She laughed lightly, covering her mouth with one hand. Colonel Ashcroft backed away then turned to rejoin Barbara.

*

Rose studied the strong face under the tweed cap that had been watching her. He was a big man but the horse, a dark bay with a thin, uneven blaze, deep chested and strong bodied, was carrying him easily. He had a natural seat and he sat calmly. Horse and rider, she could see, were in harmony. "*Would* you mind if I stick with you from time to time?"

"That's no problem...but I'll not be up there with the greyhounds." Sam smiled self-consciously. "Bit of a plodder in a way." He paused. "So you're new, then?"

"Yes, very. Only a couple of months, in fact. Daddy's bought a place in Dulverton...a place called Duxhams, up at the back on the top road."

"Oh aye, up past the doctor's place."

"That's it. And what about yourself...Exford isn't it? I'm sure Miles mentioned it the other day. He told me he thought you'd be out and that he wanted us to meet."

"Aye, born an' bred. Dad's a farmer. Up by the church."

"How lovely."

"*Lovely?*"

"Gosh yes. I simply love it down here. It's so, so different to London and Kent…there it's all push, push, push and I'd just had enough of it. Really." She lifted a hand despairingly and let it fall then shrugged as if she might have said too much. "After Jamie was killed, that's my husband, I couldn't wait to get away." She pulled a wry face. "Even so it's taken us more than three years."

"Aye," Sam nodded. "Colonel told us about that…I'm sorry." Suddenly, as he looked at her, his feeling of guilt returned. How was it that all these people had been affected by the war while he, try as he might, was not allowed even to offer himself? She must be wondering what he was doing here, out hunting like this and enjoying himself while her husband and so many others had been lost or hurt. "I tried to join," he blurted. "Tried but they wouldn't let me. Told me I had to stop home and help run the farm."

"That's all right." She could sense his awkwardness, as though he was ashamed of what he'd said. "We couldn't have done without you all…the farmers, I mean. Honestly." Her voice had softened. "Don't worry though…about Jamie being killed and you being here. It's just one of those things."

The field was beginning to stir. Hounds had arrived and they watched as the huntsman led them forward to the line the stag had taken half an hour earlier. "S'pose so." Sam collected up his reins. "So you're on yer own then…just you an yer father, like?"

"That's it. Just the two of us." She turned her horse alongside his. "But he's getting rather frail now. Over eighty would you believe and I'm helping look after him. He should have been at the meet today but wasn't feeling too good. Luckily we've a very good nurse so he's at home with her."

"Shhh." Sam held up his hand. "Hark…there, listen. They'm on to him." Everywhere around them horses heads were up, their ears were pricked and their bodies tense. In the distance a hound whimpered, then another. Then the horn blew. Another hound gave tongue then another, then several more and suddenly the valley beneath them was filled with the sound of hound music. One or two riders began to move off while, further ahead, some of the field had already broken into a canter.

Rose Hatton turned and looked at him expectantly. "You go on," he told her.

"Keep up with they lot…I'll make my own way behind, fer a bit anyway until they start droppin' back. I'll see 'e directly."

"You sure?"

"Aye…gid on," he cried, waving her on. "Or you'll lose them else. I'll be right be'ind." As he checked his girth, he frowned. What a young woman like that was going to do with herself down here, he had no idea. There weren't many of her sort about with that kind of money and those that were, like the Colonel, were old enough to be her father. But that was her problem. Becky would be back soon, any day now according to Pat Steer, and he couldn't be wasting his time nursemaiding ladies from the smart set about the place. She'd have to take her chance with the rest of them.

Once satisfied, he kicked on, rising in the saddle as his horse broke into a steady canter.

4.

For a moment she sat there, her eyes taking in all the familiar surroundings. It was lunchtime and there was little sign of life: her mother and father would be at home as well. Suddenly she felt afraid and looked down as her baby stirred in her arms. Did the child, she wondered, know that something was up? Could she sense her mother's jangling nerves and feel her heart beating as it was?

"Exford, dear." The driver turned and looked at her. "This's as far as we go."

"Thank you." Becky struggled to her feet. Holding her child high so she could see better, she inched her way forward down the aisle. Almost as soon as she had alighted the bus pulled away and turned, leaving her on her own. It was all so strangely quiet. Even from where she stood, she could see the cottage door and smoke drifting up from the chimney.

Part Two

NO PLACE LIKE HOME

Chapter Eleven

The leaves seemed to lie patiently on the mat waiting for somebody to open the front door. Whenever that happened, a handful would lift themselves and blow skittishly into the parlour. As the doormat itself was still wet, Ernest Carter shook it thoroughly rather than beating it against the cottage wall. Replacing it carefully, he stood straight and stretched, forcing his hands into the small of his back. It was the sound of the catch on the garden gate that made him turn before screwing up his eyes and putting a hand to his face in the bright sunlight.

"Hullo, Dad…it's me." Ernest bent forward to see better. He blinked and stared then started towards her but stopped. "I know," she continued, forcing a smile. "There's two of us, I'm afraid. I've brought her home with me."

"*Well*, I'll be…." He caught himself, unable to continue. "I thought…but mother said…." He took another step, rising to peer at the bundle in her arms.

"Yes, I know, but I wouldn't let them take her from me." Becky paused. "She's mine, Dad, all mine and I weren't never goin' to let her be given away…I couldn't."

"*Cuh*…my dear soul." He looked closely at the sleeping face then up at his daughter, then back again at the child in her arms. "And she's a little girl, you say?"

"Yes. I've called her Maud…Maudie and she's just over two weeks now."

" Cuh." He bit his lip, seemingly lost for words. "'Ere," he said anxiously, glancing first down the street then across to the village green. "Best to come on inside, dear." Turning back to her he studied her face. "An' you'm lookin' right worn out, maid, tired as can be. C'mon now." He put a hand on her shoulder then pulled her in to him, hugging her close. "Mother's inside and we've bin expecting you…but I don't right know what 'er's goin' to say. I mean 'tis come as a bit of a surprise…."

"I don't doubt, Dad, but I couldn't let you know." She adjusted the baby in her arms. The child gave a sudden cry and Ernest moved hastily towards the door.

"C'mon, dear…c'mon on inside."

✳

"Dear God alive." Doris Carter stood frozen. "What the *devil* have you got there, fer mercy's sake?" Now she started in horror with her eyes wide and both hands up to her ears. "Why…what…Becky? What on *earth* have yer bin an' gone an' done? What have yer done?"

Becky saw her mother's anger at once. No sooner had she recovered her surprise than the tirade began. It would be impossible, she stated, quite impossible. They had nothing here for a small baby, no crib, no clothes, no nappies, no pram, nothing. And, anyway, where was the child going to sleep? And what about the noise, and the Verney's dogs next door, the two that barked all the time? And, if all that was not enough, everybody knew that the child was going to be adopted. Nobody was expecting it so what would they all be thinking now?

"But *I* never knew," Becky cried. "Nobody told *me*, mother, that you an' they nuns, they terrible, terrible women, had plans to take her from me. She's my own baby...my very own...*ours.*" Her head was shaking in disbelief. "They were going to force me to give her up and they said that 'twas you that had asked for it. *You*, mother...yes *you.*" She saw her mother's shocked look: her face had fallen. "Oh aye," she said quietly. "I can see it now, see it written all over you...yer wanted none of this, did yer? But I was never goin' to let them...*never.* I'd rather die."

Becky stood defiant, still in her coat and rocking the child in her arms, her eyes moving from one to the other. The baby stirred and she kissed it gently. But suddenly she was tired. It was just as she expected. Her father, bless him, had taken her in but her mother was the same as ever and, as she listened, so the well of energy of hope and expectation that had buoyed her drained from her body.

"I must sit," she muttered, trying to close her mind to the acrimony. Holding the child in one arm, she pulled a chair away from the table then sat and slumped forward to rest her elbow before lowering her head wearily. "So please, mother. No more of it," she demanded looking up anxiously and suddenly alarmed at the silence. "I'm sorry," she murmured, pausing before glancing at her father. "Dad, I'm terrible thirsty...haven't had anything for hours," she pleaded. "D'you think I might have a drink? Water'll do...just a glass'll be enough."

Both her mother and father watched as she drank it down before gasping and wiping her mouth. "Thanks," she whispered, easing the weight of the baby. The child started to whimper so she lifted her into a higher and more comfortable position then took a deep breath. "All right." This time she looked at them. "I'll be goin' then." Her voice sounded calm. "I'll not stop where we're not welcome. I'll...."

"But you...,"

"Don't worry, father." Becky cut him short. "I'll find somewhere. As I were sayin' I'll be off directly but I need to change her. Is there anywhere I can...p'raps the wash house, mother? I can clean her there, can't I? I haven't got anything but if you've got an old towel, have yer? Summat I can cut up to make a nappy or two?" She saw her mother's look. "It's all I'll need, mother, honest it is. If yer can spare one, that is. I'll clean her and feed her then be on me way."

"And that's quite enough o' that." It was her father again, but louder this time. "I want no more o' that talk…you'm here, maid and here you'm stopping."

"An' how d'you think us'is goin' to manage, eh?" Doris Carter had her hands on her hips. "Us've got nothing. No clothes, *nothing,* just as I said. And what'll folks be saying, eh?" She opened her arms in a questioning shrug. "Well…come on then?"

 "Damn them." Ernest had turned to go and find some linen but now stopped with one foot on the stairs. "Listen," he cried, turning and raising a finger. "There're plenty of decent folks about…they're not all monsters, y'know. Oh aye, there'll be talk all right just like there's always bin talk, but that'll be that. Our Becky's home with her babe and that's where she's stopping…an' not you," he pointed. "Nor me, nor anyone's going to turn her away."

"But…."

"An' there's no buts about it. That little mite…little Maudie's…ours. She's our own flesh an' blood, an' now's up to us to look after her. We can never consider showing her and her mother the door. She's as welcome 'ere as anyone else. Now then…." He continued on his way.

"I'm sorry, Mum." Becky looked at her. "I didn't think you'd be happy but there was nort else I could do."

"Well, 'tis done now." Doris paused. "And what did the nuns have to say? The Reverend Mother an' that? 'Spect they had summat to say."

"Don't know." Becky's head, now shaking slowly, was in her hand once more. "I don't know," she muttered feeling her tears coming. "I didn't say anything, didn't ask them or anything, I just ran away…ran away in the night. I took Maudie and ran before they took her away. Oh God," she sobbed. "I'd nowhere else to go, mother, nowhere…I just thought I'd…we'd be safe here and that you'd look after us." Doris was silent. "She's got no father, poor little thing. Mike's gone so there's nobody…nobody at all except you and father."

"Well, what's done's done." Her mother went into the wash house. "'Tis too cold out 'ere so we'll see to 'er in the kitchen…'ere on the side, look. I'll put the kettle on and we'll see what's to be done."

"Aye, us'll see, that's fer sure." It was Ernest. Becky looked up at the direction of her father's voice as he clomped steadily down the stairs. "There's a towel or two here, look. Can cut they up fer a start an' I'll get over to the stables an' see what else us can find from they others." Once more he caught his wife's look. "Listen, dear." His voice was stern but had softened. "Bain't no use at all, carryin' on like that. 'Tis no good shoutin' an' that. Folks in the village'll know afore dark what's up and who's here. Best thing we can do is to get as comfy as us can…see what us can beg an' borrow fer a while." He lifted a cautionary hand. "There'll be talk fer a day or two an' then summat else'll come along. You wait."

Doris was not convinced but already the shock was wearing off. "C'mon then, Becky." She had put on her apron and was standing by the draining board. "Let's clean her up. Lord alone knows what'll be happening next. C'mon, girl." She held out her arms impatiently, watching as Ernest helped his daughter from her chair and took her face in both his hands.

2.

At first, when Pat came with the news, Sam was stunned. He was alone in the shippon and they sat talking. Pat could see his feelings were mixed. For weeks they had spoken about Becky's homecoming and how she would be able to start afresh. The land girls had even suggested a party in Daddy Warren's shed, but nobody had bargained for the baby.

Now it was different; it was as though Becky had brought her past back to haunt her and there would be those in Exford who would enjoy having their say. But the father, a soldier, had been killed in the fighting. His name and those of the others had been spoken of in awe. To all of them in Exford they were heroes already. Little Maudie would grow up believing the father she never knew was her mother's rightful husband and that she was their lawful child. Time would confuse the issue: Maudie's friends would know no different. They would grow up together unaware of the truth, knowing nothing about the strange ways of the war when different people from all over were thrown together. She would make her own way among the new generation, leaving only the old to mutter. But what about Becky, and now Sam?

"Don't see it makes no odds." Sam was leaning against one of the oak uprights in the old stonewalled cowshed. What Pat had just told him made him pause and think, but only momentarily. "'Tisn't as though she'd never bin with the man…we all know that. I mean if she'd come back without the child it would-n't have been any different, would it…we'd all know she'd bin an' had his child. Us all know that."

"But she *has* got the child, Sam." Pat Steer was finding it hard to believe he was taking it so calmly. All year Sam Hawkins had been cut to the quick and they had worried for him. "As long as you're sure it makes no odds then that's fine but you wouldn't want to go seeing her again and coming away all upset because of the baby."

"Can't wait to see the maid." He smiled and pushed himself away from the beam. "Bain't no good me worryin' about what's happened. She's back an' that's the main thing." He bent down to pick up the tools he had been working with. "An' now she's on her own 'tis up to us. Becky'll always be the same Becky to me, child or no. I'll get along down there directly."

※

146

"They'll be back in an hour or so." Doris Carter beamed kindly at Sam. And to think the boy had taken the trouble to get himself cleaned up like he had and found time to get away from work. As soon as she saw him coming up the path she had opened the door and stood there, taking off her pinafore as if to show she was expecting him to come in. The kettle had been simmering on the range so tea only took a few minutes.

At first she was glad that Becky and her father had gone to Dulverton for it would be easier to find out what he knew and how he felt about things if he was on his own. "Don't 'spect you've the time now, Sam, but she'll be ever so pleased to know you've called."

"Thought I'd just drop by," he lied, trying hard to disguise his disappointment. "Daresay things'll be hard fer a while."

"Nothing we can't see to, that's fer sure." Doris Carter leaned back in her chair and folded her arms. She was still smiling warmly, looking at him with her head on one side. Somehow, watching him come up the path and stand in the doorway had taken her mind back to Larkbarrow when he would come in after doing the sheep and wait for Becky. Ernest would love to see him but she knew he couldn't stay.

"I expect you know she's brought the baby with her?" Doris was searching his face. "Wasn't what we were expecting mind. Gave us quite a surprise."

"Aye, daresay." Sam frowned. "Must be hard seein' that the father's gone...killed over in France like. Sad reelly...he were quite a man...an' to go like that." He pulled a mournful face.

"Well." Doris drew herself up. "'Tis harder in some ways but now she can start again afresh, that's if she's a mind to."

"Oh, I'm sure of it." Sam put down his cup. "Can't see Becky not makin' a good go of it."

"But she'll need a man in her life and that won't be so easy now. Not with somebody else's baby like that."

"Dunno." Sam looked at her and nodded assuredly. "I dunno, Mrs Carter. Your Becky's a special sort. There'll be plenty of young men who'd be glad of her hand, I've no doubt." Her look embarrassed him and he glanced away, uneasy at what he had started to say.

"Well, that's nice to know, dear, and especially from a young man like yerself. I mean to say you've known Becky longer than most and me an' Ernest have always minded the time when you an' her were walking out." Now she, too, paused. "But daresay you'll be thinkin' o' other things now," she murmured.

147

"Can't say that, Mrs Carter." He shifted uneasily in his chair. "Can't never be sayin' that." He wanted to go on, to tell her to stop worrying and that he, Sam, would be only too happy to catch her eye once again. He had missed her dreadfully. Even after the stories of her pregnancy were out he had longed to tell her that he forgave her, and when her man had gone he wanted to take hold of her again. But, by that time, she too had gone. He had written twice but heard nothing. It was Pat who told him that they would have made certain his letters never got to her. He had wanted to go and see her but both she and Mavis said it would never be allowed. "Best thing is that she's back home safe an' sound. 'Tis wunnerful news."

He rose uneasily realising that she wanted to go on talking and listening to his views but he had said enough already, too much probably. "Best be on my way then, ma'am." He waited with one hand on the back of his chair as she stood. "P'raps say to Becks that I called. If yer don't mind that is."

"She'll be more than pleased, dear, and so will her father. Drop by again, will you? She'd love to see you, y'know." Doris Carter hurried ahead to open the door for him. "You do know that Sam, don't you? Becky'd be ever so pleased to see yer, if you've a mind to."

"I'll be back, Mrs Carter." He took her hand, looking almost straight down onto the top of her grey head. She had to step back to see him and saw that his face had broken into one of his a grins. "Just as long as she don't go away no more. Aye," he added confidently. "'T'will be good to see her again."

✳

Barbara Hawkins inclined her head. The two men were still drying out in the kitchen and she had been half listening to their banter while trying to get lunch. Now they were discussing Becky's return and the arrival of her child. It was Drew that had seen Ernest at the forge earlier when he had told him his news, apparently overjoyed that he was a grandfather. Sam laughed, telling his father how he had called in at Myrtle Cottage. "Good job the maid's back 'ome," he replied.

"And to think what a stupid little fool she's been." Barbara's voice was raised so they could hear. "Well, she'll be paying for it dearly now, that's for certain." Drew checked himself but looked up at his son who was staring down at his hands. Sam's face was flushed and his father could see the anger by the way his knuckles had whitened. "I can't think why on earth she's brought that man's child back with her."

"'Cos it's hers, mother." Sam's head was raised but he was looking out of the window.

"Well, we all know *that* for Heaven's sake but I would have thought it better for everyone if she'd had it...what do they call it...adopted. At least then she'd be able to look the world in the eye."

"I don't see it that way at all." Sam walked in and pushed his chair round to face the stove. As he looked at his mother, his chin jutted defiantly. "Everyone knows what's bin about…in fact there's several that reckon 'er's done the best thing."

"Oh for *goodness* sake, Sam. Be your age. That's what they say, of course they do, but that's not what they think." She rounded on the table, pointing with a wooden spoon. "And I'd be very grateful if you'd stand back from it all. It's a fearful muddle and I don't want you getting caught up in it…you were far too close before."

Drew put a hand on his son's arm. "'Tis all right, father," he assured him. "But there's summat you best know, the pair o' yer, an' that's this." He paused, drawing in a deep breath. "I've a mind to see Becky and just as soon as I like. What's done's done. I've known the lass since she were a child an' I'm not turning my back on her now."

"Well don't get in-*volved*, that's all." Barbara sounded agitated. "There's nothing there that can be swept under the carpet. She's a mess and I wouldn't want our name linked with it all."

"I'll be doin' what I'm minded to, mother, an' if Becky Carter were to hold out 'er hand then I'd catch 'old…an' that's my business."

"Don't *speak* to me like that." Barbara came up to the table. "You'll do what I say as far as this's concerned. *You* might not have a care in the world but I do. Becky Carter's sullied her name and I don't want ours mixed up with it."

"Oh fer cryin' out loud." Sam's chair scraped as he pushed it back. "Stop treatin' me like a child, will yer." His father rose as well and Sam saw his face. "'Tis all right, Dad. 'Tis just that mother goes on an' on about who's right an' who's wrong. I'll tell 'e what." He raised a finger angrily. "I bet if her name were Rose Hatton an' there were a child there. I'll bet there wouldn't be none of this talk about keepin' away then. Oh no." He was breathing heavily. "Be pushin' me right forrard, I'll be bound. Oh aye, and it bain't no good looking at me like that, mother. If I've a mind to see Becky Carter, then I'll see her."

He stopped, suddenly confused then wiped the spittle from his mouth. "Daresay it's best if I leave yer to yer own dinner." He muttered, taking up his cap and leaving the kitchen.

3.

Mike Daley sat on the medical couch stripped to the waist with his head bowed, moving it obediently from left to right as the two doctors examined him. In spite of being told he would have to stay on for a further two weeks, the letter from Eddie Bright had encouraged him.

Almost as soon as he arrived at Musgrove Park three weeks ago he had been advised to look to his future. For him, they said judgementally, Army life was over. The Medical Board which sat every Thursday to make such decisions had not taken long over their deliberations. His left eye would recover partial sight in due course but his left ear had lost most of its hearing. The facial and upper body burns on their own were enough to see him out of the service and then there was the head wound. As the Lieutenant Colonel had said with a wry smile, it was chapter and verse.

Eddie Bright was a player, of that there was no doubt. They had first met in Southsea years ago when Mike was little more than a boy. There had been a bit of trouble and he, Mike, had been up before the beaks but it was in the Yorke Street Community Centre that Eddie sent for him. The big, crinkley-haired Cuban with the full lips and half-closed eyes had heard about him, so he said. He had heard that he knew a thing or two and could handle a car so he had taken him on for a trial. The job that came later only lasted a year but Mike had seen how Eddie handled himself in the clubs around Old Pompey's Gunwharf Road and Armoury Lane.

Eddie had almost got away with his next robbery when the copper's narks fingered him. Almost but not quite and he was already in custody when one of the two who had squealed was found in the harbour. Eddie went down for a year and it would have been longer but for the lack of evidence. Mike saw him again once or twice, even did a bit of driving for him when he was home on leave. Eddie had said to keep in touch and he had. In his last letter, written a month ago from East Grinstead, Mike had asked him if he might be able to help.

The postmark, after Eddie's next letter had been forwarded, said Plymouth and, in it, Eddie Bright told him he was looking for a good hand behind the wheel. Would he, Eddie wanted to know, be interested. Mike replied by return and Eddie had written back last Monday, telling him he would hold the job open for him.

"Ooof," Mike gasped. "I felt that one a bit...yes, just there." The doctor stood back, lifted Mike's chin and glanced from one shoulder blade to the other.

"There's still a little way to go, Corporal Daley...sorry, Mister Daley now," he quipped. "Look, I'm pretty sure we can get a bit more movement out of the left shoulder and I'd like to do what I can before you're away. It won't be long...just a couple of weeks or so."

"OK Doc." Mike rolled his shoulders. "But the rest's all in order...yeah?"

"Fine." The diminutive Dr Dennis Hurst smiled encouragingly. "Difficult to know whether you've been lucky or unlucky. You've taken a pasting that's for sure, but my goodness," he shook his head. "Another inch here or there and we'd be looking at a very different story."

"Well, there we go…fortune favours the brave, so they say. Eh?" Daley grinned mischievously. "Yeah, they might give you all that crap about favourin' the brave an' all that, but I was shittin' meself all the way through. Bloody right I was, an' I'm well out of it, I reckon."

＊

Mike Daley had taken to Bill Clarke as soon as they met. The tall, balding gunner in the next bed had lost his left leg on a mine just north of Falaise. After field surgery and repatriation, followed by two months at Roehampton where they fitted his artificial limb, he, too, had been sent to Musgrove Park. Bill, with his long miserable face, sounded all gloom and doom but, underneath there lay a lot of common sense and a generous portion of wicked, black humour. "I dunno, Mike," he drawled. "Sounds dead dodgy to me…this guy Eddie what-sisname. Fer Chris'ake man, he's done time and there's a record there as long as yer arm. Wha' d'ya doing?" Bill Clarke looked across at him and rolled his eyes. "Sounds as though you want that hole in yer head looked at."

"Listen mate." Daley leaned towards his neighbour. "It's the devil yer know, right. I mean you've got yer Dad and yer brothers up in Henley on the gas board, right, an' a nice cushy number lined up. Well, bully fer you, pal. If it were me it'd drive me right up the bleedin' wall."

"Yeah, all right, but take yer time, Mike. This war's going to be over soon enough by the looks of things an' there'll be plenty of jobs coming along. Puttin' the country back together again fer a start. Why rush into it…an' with that nasty bit o' work Eddie whatever? Eh? Come on, man…it's bleedin' madness."

Daley shrugged. The letters had come and gone. A job was there and, in any case, Eddie was a good mate. He was smart and fun and he, Mike Daley, wanted out of hospital and back into the action. "Why not?" he shrugged. "Gotta go fer it, 'aven't I…what else is there, eh? Flogging shirts in Denholm's…or basket weaving up in Bridgewater. Fer Christ's sake, come on, Bill, give us a break."

"Hmmph." Bill Clarke scratched his nose. "All right by me, tosh. Just never say I didn't warn you, that's all." For a moment the two men were silent.

"Ah, c'mon yer miserable old sod." It was Mike Daley who spoke first. "Any more of this crap an' we'll be dead before we get out of the place. C'mon…get that 'orrible wooden peg leg of yours going and we'll get down to the canteen. It's scrumpy on me an' we'll see if that fat old hag behind the bar still reckons you're God's gift." Daley hauled his companion off his bed and held him while he struggled with the buckles of his false leg. "She's all yours, pal, I can tell yer. Nobody else wants to touch it."

4.

Inspector Chris Startin sat back and looked at the wall map. He looked at it daily, sometimes for hours on end and sometimes long into the night when he would be on his own, supported only by endless cups of thick, sweet, plastic-tasting tea from his two thermoses. Organised crime in Plymouth, so the Chief had told him, was getting worse. Statistics showed that, year in year out, it ebbed and flowed dependant occasionally upon the bombing and port activities.

But the bombing had stopped way back and what was left of Millbay and Devonport had always fairly crawled with unpleasant people. The trouble was that the docks and harbour were the hub of city life where thousands of good honest folk lived and worked. Yet among them, like maggots enjoying themselves in the depths of an old carcass, the criminal fraternity thrived.

Short, slim and neat, and with his grey, receding hair swept back, Chris Startin was a Plymouth man and knew the extent of the task confronting him. Always short of manpower and equipment, and with never enough time to finish the job, he was lucky to keep things as they were. But they weren't as they were. They were getting worse and the Chief was not happy. Chris Startin sighed. Adjusting his spotted bow tie he got out of his chair and went to study the street plan more closely.

It was intelligence, or the lack of it, that was always the key. In the months after the blitz it had been good and it had kept coming. People had enough trouble to contend with and could do without criminals as next door neighbours. But that clean-out was three years ago and most of his sources had gone. At first the slowdown of information was gradual as though a windpipe was being squeezed and the passage of air was getting ever more difficult. Then, since the invasion back in June, it had virtually dried up all together. And when that happened it meant only one thing – somebody, somewhere was squeezing very hard indeed. Somebody down there with big, strong hands was having his way and it didn't need the Chief to tell him.

*

Eddie Bright nodded and pushed the letter across the desk. "He's a good breeze, 'e is…got a brain between his ears an' all. Look at his writing." Ken Maelmo, Eddie's right hand man picked it up, turned it casually then let it drop. "Educated somewhere. Christ knows where," Eddie went on, his body shaking with mirth. "Mike Daley educated…spare me. But he is, I tell yer. Sharp as they come, even wiv 'arf his head blown off."

"He'll need to be." Maelmo toyed with Mike's letter. The tall, skeletal Swede, with his pale, gaunt face almost devoid of hair, sucked at the hole in his molar. "He's no time for learning and we need him to drive fast and clean…yah?"

"Yah," Eddie mimicked. "He's all right, is Mike. Got a mind like a camera too, so he has. Worked up in Pompey with me and he had the patch sussed in days…hours even. Never took a wrong turn, never did nuthin' to catch the eye…an' kept his mouth zipped tight. He's all right."

Strangely enough the worst of the bombing had fallen to the east of the docks and further north. The city centre around the Guildhall had been flattened as had much of the housing around Victoria Park. In places, Union Street had been hit hard but not hard enough to prevent life returning to the rubble. A favourite haunt of sailors, marines and Saturday night revellers for as long as anyone could remember, life in Union Street and its near neighbours had picked itself up. Whatever young men of any age wanted on a night out was there to be had, for a price.

Eddie Bright had heard about Plymouth for years and, as soon as he was able, he had taken the trouble to see for himself. The more he saw and the more he heard, the more he liked the veritable rabbit warren of old cobbled streets either side of Union Street. First he had taken the 'Blue Rose', next the 'Naked Angel' and then his favourite the 'Legs Eleven'. Young men needed girls so he bought a pitch in Phoenix Street or rather he gunned and knifed his way into ownership. Older men, with money to burn, liked to gamble and drink peacefully long into the night. Then there were those who needed Eddie's strong arm to look after them. Others, not so clever, got to feel the strength of his arm whether they liked it or not.

It had taken him three years but now he was comfortable, comfortable yet impatient for more. The trouble was the bigger his patch became, the more difficult it was to hang on to what he called his own. Eddie Bright's half-closed eyes were never still, neither was the mind behind them. Out there somewhere there was always somebody who had to be seen to, or a place where a calling card had to be left. Or somebody who had forgotten to return a favour and who needed a little reminder.

✳

"Who is she, anyway?" Eddie Bright rubbed his eyes and glanced at his watch. He was late already but Kenny the Swede wanted him to deal with her first.

"Up London way. About twenty-five, I reckon. Says she's nineteen…not a bad looker neither. Jeannie, she calls herself. Trouble is she keeps forgetting what she's earned. Can't keep count of all her boyfriends. Needs to be helped a little…yah?" Maelmo's face was contemptuous. "She needs to learn, Eddie. If not then more of our girls think that to forget is clever and then we…you, lose money. And that's big money…we haf twenty-eight girls now."

"Uh huh." Eddie wiped his mouth. "They've got her here?"

"Yah…I told them to be ready."

"OK." Eddie waved a hand and watched the Swede go to the door. Once upon a time there were three bedrooms in the second floor above the Blue Rose. One, the one they were in, was Eddie Bright's office, the second he kept spare and the third he used as a meeting room. It took the Swede only seconds.

She had been a looker once but age and the game had taken its toll. More like thirty-five than twenty, Jeannie stared sullenly, her dark eyes closing only briefly as her arms were twisted up behind her back. Two men were holding her and a third stood closely behind. Kenny the Swede moved back to his chair.

"You can't count, darling, can you, eh?" Eddie's voice was soft. "See, we've been watching you. Three nights, forty punters at two pounds a trip…that's eighty. Eighty whole luverly pounds for Eddie and what do we get? Huh?" He nodded slowly and paused, then suddenly he leapt to his feet, erupting into a blaze of fury.

"*Twenty*," he snarled, smashing his fist down viciously onto the table. His brown, heavily pockmarked face was contorted, now purple and grotesque. "*Twenty sodding, miserable, bleedin', 'orrible pounds.*" He yelled, inches from her face. The girl was staring back transfixed, wide-eyed and rabbit-like, shaking her head.

Almost at once he sat again, pulling in his chair without taking his eyes from hers. Unnervingly his voice had returned once more to a soft, chilling whisper. "And where's the rest, might I ask? Eh?" He pulled on his lips thoughtfully. "We have a nasty little thief here, don't we now? Eh? Don't we?"

The girl swallowed. "No," she pleaded. "No, honest, Eddie. I forgot, honest I did. Couldn't remember."

The cutting motion of Eddie's hand in front of her face silenced her. She had just time to see him nod when the gag was thrown over her head from behind then pulled down and across her mouth, the sudden force jerking her back savagely as it was tightened. She tried to call out and tried to twist free but she was trapped, held rigid by the men on either side. Quickly, as if well rehearsed, her cardigan and blouse were pulled up behind her as far as her neck, exposing her back and the pale-grey straps of her bra.

"No blood." Eddie Bright nodded and looked on nonchalantly as the two men, one on either side, pulled hard on her wrists, stretching her arms wide in order to hold her still. The third, now in his shirtsleeves, lifted the thickly plaited stock whip high behind him then lashed it forward and into the soft flesh. The girl exploded, jumping and twisting in the vice-like grip, her face puce and distorted and her eyes screwed tight in agony as she leapt desperately to free herself. The second made her fling her head back, exposing her throat, then forwards again as she bucked like an animal trying to throw off the pain. This time the muffled screams were louder. Then came the third then the fourth and the fifth, the sixth, seventh and the eighth. Then Eddie held up his hand.

For minutes the room, save for the choked moaning and the sobs from behind the gag, was silent. Those holding her never moved, keeping her arms stretched wide so she could not fall but with their eyes on their boss. They were breathing heavily and waiting for her cries to subside. Eddie cleared his throat. "Look at me," he commanded. The eyes that looked back stared wildly in terror.

"That," Eddie whispered, wagging a finger admonishingly. "That was nothing more than a quiet, little warning. *Never* cross Eddie Bright, my dear. *Never*…you understand?" He waited until she nodded again. "You're going to be a good girl now, Jeannie, aren't you?" She nodded again. "The boys like you lots, all of them. So go back out there, my sweetheart, and give them lots of fun. Yeah? But don't forget nothing again, my love. Nothing…right?" He paused. "Hey, that's good."

Slapping the table he rose briskly. Grinning widely he nodded some silent command at the two men holding the girl. As they turned to take her from the room he leant forward to examine the deep, purple-red wheals where the whip had done its work on the soft, white flesh. Smiling appreciatively at no one in particular, he paused before checking his watch, then clattered hurriedly down the stairs and out of his club. Now he *was* late, very late.

Chapter Twelve

For a moment the two were silent. They had left the village and climbed up to Chibbet Post before turning out towards Winsford Hill. Sam clicked at the pony and shook the reins, then glanced back at Becky who sat swaying to the movement of the trap with the rug pulled over her knees. Although her face was half hidden by her red and orange scarf, he could see she was lost in thought, staring almost trance-like at the beech hedge that ran alongside the road. It was a bright, clear afternoon where one could see for miles yet the wind had a November chill about it as though the weather was considering a change.

The last six weeks or so had turned out better than he expected. For a start the atmosphere in Myrtle Cottage had eased. Becky's father had been sympathetic from the start but her mother had taken her time before accepting the new situation. Eventually she had mellowed and now, much to his surprise, she seemed pleased for him to call on them and see Becky. She had even offered to look after Maudie, allowing the two of them to ride out and spend a few hours together.

Sam looked back at her again, wanting to smile affectionately but her mind remained elsewhere. As he watched, she wiped a tear from her eye and sniffed as though she was crying silently but he knew she wasn't: rather he was confident that her mind now was made up. A little while earlier, before she sat, she had stood beside him with one hand on his shoulder as they trotted along.

*

Becky's mind had indeed been drifting. For her, Mike Daley was still there. Those hard black eyes of his were still glittering as he stormed from the room in the White Horse that evening, but so too were the gentle, soft eyes that used to study her face as they lay together, and the eyes that laughed wickedly as they walked hand in hand in the heather with their fingers entwined. The arms that used to hold her close were still outstretched and beckoning, just as they used to do. Even now, she could see him standing with his head on one side, stroking his thin moustache and frowning yet somehow keeping an eyebrow cocked as he listened to the music. And there were times when she could still feel the warmth of his breath on her throat as they caressed. The memory made her move involuntarily and she lifted a hand to touch that very spot.

For weeks after she had come home, Sam had meant nothing more to her than a friendly face who kept calling on her with his cap in his hand and a kind word. She had seen the affection in his eyes and in the way his body moved when he hastened to help her, such as when she was pulling out a chair or opening a door with Maudie in her arms. Sometimes it had been difficult to concentrate on what he was saying, hard to avoid his eye and keep from him the irritation she felt at this attention. But that was some time ago. October had passed and now, half way through November, there were the first mutterings of Christmas. The staghounds were hunting hinds again. The leaves had gone, swept on their way by the autumn winds, and the blue-grey smoke from the cottage fires hung heavily in the outside air before being snatched away by a sudden gust.

He never told her what his family felt about his visits, but she guessed. She heard that from Pat Steer who told her also that he, Sam, still adored her and had long since forgiven her for what had happened. Eventually, and initially she thought it was through boredom, she began to look forward to their outings and, as the nights drew in, to his evening visits. He must, she suspected, cherish her company if he was able to find the time he did.

Now, as she grew used to him being back in her life, she began to feel more secure when they were together. However, she was never quite sure whether she was seeing him as her guardian against those who remained ill-disposed towards her, or whether it was something deeper. But she knew how fortunate she was and realised how much she needed his support. Gradually, although slowly at first, she began to listen to his chatter, accepting what he was saying about their future and nodding in silent agreement. Yet still she remained uncertain.

Then, only last week, Pat's voice had risen in anger at her prevarication when she had scolded her for not seeing what the hand of Sam Hawkins would mean. She had been right, for yesterday when Sam called briefly on his way back from the kennels where he had taken a carcass, they had talked and laughed almost as though they had been back at Larkbarrow. Then today, just a few moments ago, she found herself asking him about Hayes Farm and it had been just as they were climbing the open road onto Winsford Hill that he turned and asked her, face to face, about their future together. She had begun to reply but had stopped, unable to find the right words.

Such uncertainty made her feel ashamed so she slid herself along the bench until she was closer to him, turning up her collar and looking around before tucking her hands back under the rug. "You know." She still hesitated, finding her words difficult. "I *have* been thinking, about all these things you've been saying."

"Oh aye." Sam flicked the reins, glancing down briefly before staring at the road ahead.

"Well, I have," she continued. "But d'you think that, perhaps, if we waited a while." Now she paused, undecided. "I mean everything's been so rushed and there's things like…well, yer family, y'know. Bain't easy, Sam…yer mother, I mean. P'raps if we were to wait until all this war's over an' Jack's home again. I'd like fer him to be here afore we did anything."

He looked down at her as though to check on what she had said. The pony had slowed to a walk and he relaxed his hold on the reins, letting them go loose. "You serious?" The words came as though he did not believe her. Becky shrugged, suddenly nervous at the huge step she had just taken but then calmed again: it was something she had rehearsed many times in her mind.

"It's bin hard, Sam, I have to tell yer that. Not bin easy with all that's gone on and…well," she paused again. "Mike's bin there." Her words came quickly. "I've tried to forget and move on but 'e's bin there in my mind. I can see him in Maudie, every day an' it's bin difficult to forget."

"I've seen that, maid." His voice had softened. "But it'd never make no odds to me."

"It's so silly really, 'cos he's gone now an' that's that, isn't it? It's just that I've needed this time to, well, to tell meself that, an' to try to see …well, about not being on my own, like."

"Aye."

She stared down at her hands clenched together under the rug and watched it move as her thumbs rubbed anxiously together. "What I'm tryin' to say." She shifted herself and laughed nervously before suddenly breaking off again. "Well, if you *mean* what you've bin sayin…about us…then, yes. If yer do mean it and if we can wait then I reckon…well, yes."

"And you'd be happy?"

She paused and frowned, uncertain what happiness would mean. It would be difficult to love anyone as she had loved before and that was surely where true happiness lay. But she would have him by her side, Sam, gentle and kind as he had always been. She would have a home, as would Maudie, and they would have their friends. All that, added together, might not make for such happiness as she had heard when true love was spoken about but she would be out of this dark, miserable closet. And there would be happiness of a kind, of course there would. Life would, once more, be for living. "Yes," she nodded eagerly and looked at him, smiling as she took her arm from under the rug and slipped it through his. "I reckon."

✳

Gerry Chugg stood with one foot on the bottom bar and leant over the gate. He and Greg Thorne had come up to Hayes to collect the rams that were due to be put in with the ewes in less than a week. Their own four had been summering with Sam's and now duty was calling them. The animals had been loaded and Greg had gone into the village. He and Sam stood waiting together.

"You'm not serious?" Gerry Chugg pushed at a stone in the gateway with his foot.

"Aye." Sam nodded then bent to pick at a stalk of dead grass. Suddenly, with a gust stronger than the others, it began to drizzle. Both men turned their backs to the wind and lifted their collars. "Aye, serious enough all right."

"Thought you'd be sayin' summat like that." Gerry Chugg shook his head. "And the word's about, too. *We-ll.*" The young farmer raised his eyebrows in surprise and blew long and hard. "For what it's worth, my friend, her's not your sort...no sir." He glanced at Sam out of the corner of his eye. "She's a right rover, she is. Got a rovin' eye...always had, like with they soldiers and I can't see her stuck away up 'ere at Hayes Farm...year in year out, minding yer shirts an' that, an' cookin' yer dinner. She's a breaker, is Becky Carter...an' her'll be breakin' out again, I reckon."

"Yer can't say that."

"Oh aye, can't I now." Chugg chuckled but it was bitter and cynical. "An' I tell 'e what, my son. She's still got her head in the air. D'yer know that? Gave Greg a right eyeful o' spite t'other day then lifted her head an' walked straight past 'im."

"Aye, so I've bin hearing." Sam could feel his own anger rising. "Pat an' Mavis told me an' all. The maid went to them cryin' her eyes out. Bain't right, y'know, Gerry. Folks keepin' on and on like they are. There's no end to it all. An' they Thorne buiys won't let her go...keep on and on, sniggerin' and that. Oh aye," he had seen Gerry Chugg's look. "I heard about that, outside the stores weren't it? Just won't let times move on."

"Well, I'm only telling yer, Sam. You'd be looking a right fool taking on that Becky an' someone else's spawn."

"Hey, c'mon, Gerry. No need to go draggin' it all down like that." Sam stood and faced him. "That bain't right, an' yer know it."

"An' that's just what it is, Sam...as right as right can be. That's exactly what it is an' trouble is yer can't see it, man. 'Tis right down there." He nodded towards the ground. "An' can't get no lower'n that...and that's fer what most of Exford reckons."

"Well, that bain't right...not for the girl and not on me, neither."

"Aye, an' that's why I'm here standing in front of yer an' telling yer, Sam. Somebody's got to say it...an' say it to yer face, like. Nobody wants fer you get caught up like this, buiy...none of us."

Sam shook his head angrily, turned as to walk away then turned back sharply. "Good job you're my friend, Gerry...an' a damned good job an' all. Talk like that makes me go mad...right daft it does." He felt himself yet again angrily defending his corner, just as he had done so often in the kitchen and parlour up in the house. It was that same bitter feeling of wrath and pain. "Well, it so happens that you're too darned late, all of yer. I've asked her ter come back and she's said she would, just soon as Jack's back home again."

"You're mazed, man." Gerry Chugg pushed himself away from the gate. "You want ter think on it hard, Sam. There's yer whole life in front of yer here, y'know. Tell me, where an' how are you goin' ter take on a woman like that, eh? *Marry* her? *What,* with somebody else's child draggin along be'ind? *Cuh*...vicar'll not be touchin it, I can tell yer that. And yer family...jeez, Sam, think on it, man. What're they all goin' to be saying? You'm building up summat fer yerself that'll not be easy ter change and once it's up, it's up."

"We'll see." Sam had turned back to the gate and was leaning into the drizzle. "Becky an' I've talked and talked for long enough." He nodded at his own words and looked down at the ground. "Us know what folks are sayin and us know where we're goin'. Becky's given me her word." He looked back at Gerry. "The maid's given me her word, Gerry, and that's good enough fer me."

2.

Sam brooded for days but what they were saying made no odds. It seemed as though the whole village still had something to say but he let it ride. He sensed his mother had heard what he was about and there was an occasion when she began to talk about it but he stared her down, rising from the table like the anger that welled up inside, and the matter had been dropped. What Gerry Chugg said last week still rankled but his mind was set. The Chuggs and the Thornes, and anybody else who was minded to, could have their say but he was not going to change.

Strangely enough out in the hunting field where usually the gossip was stronger than anywhere else, he had not heard so much. Perhaps he had missed the winks and nods, or perhaps they had all had their say and found better things to talk about. But it was here at Hayes that he found the peace he sought and he longed for the day when Becky would be there to share it with him rather than being trapped down in the village where she still had to face the cold and hostile looks.

✳

Barbara Hawkins had been surprised to see the car easing its way cautiously into the yard and was even more amazed when she recognised the driver peering carefully over the wheel as she steered the sleek, black machine. By the time she had opened the front door to greet her, Rose Hatton was on her way to the porch, grinning mischievously at having arrived unannounced.

She had been to Winsford, she explained apologetically, turning to let Barbara take her grey wool coat. Only one of the people she had driven over to see was at home, so she had decided to come on to Hayes. She was not going to stay,

she proclaimed, but walked across the kitchen to stand by the stove nonetheless, rubbing her hands and chatting cheerfully. She had heard so much about
them from Miles Ashcroft that she had to come and see for herself, and to
discover where her new hunting companion could be found. In fact she had
come hoping to see him today and to call on his expertise, but first she broke
the news about Edwina Ashcroft.

"I told him I'd be seeing you and would tell you," she said. "He's so upset,
poor dear."

"And is this for good?" Although she had known him for so many years,
Barbara Hawkins had hardly ever met his wife. Ever since the Colonel had
married her, the woman had remained a distant mystery, appearing in their
conversation only from time to time when he would apologise for her absence
or explain briefly why she was unable to be with them. "I know Rosemount
House and very often once they're in there, y'know, the patients tend to stay."
Barbara looked at her guest expectantly.

"I just don't know." Rose shrugged and let her arms fall against her finely cut
tweed jacket that was being admired. "Daddy's asked him to come over to
Duxhams and we'll know more then. I just hope he can cope, poor
darling...he's so sweet."

"Lovely." Barbara held up the teapot but Rose shook her head, lifting a hand
to decline yet remaining silent. "We all think the world of him here but surely
he's got help over there, hasn't he?"

"Heavens, yes." Rose laughed. "But it's not the same is it." For a moment she
hesitated. "But then, I suppose he'll find things easier in a way. I mean it was
getting hopeless with her in the wheel chair and they were starting to change
the house around so she could move about...poor thing."

"Dreadful." Barbara shook her head thoughtfully trying to imagine him stumbling around behind the heavy wheel chair as it stuck in some dark corner, then
struggling to lift the front wheels and all the while apologising to the helpless
invalid. The thought hurt and she changed the subject. "But look, it...sorry, it
is Mrs Hatton, isn't it?"

"Oh Heavens, how awful." Rose put a hand to her mouth then onto Barbara's
arm. "Goodness, I'm sorry." She laughed, blushing at the same time. "It's
Rose...please, please...and may I call you Barbara?"

"Of course." Barbara Hawkins looked down shyly but felt a warm glow of
gratification nonetheless. "Now then," she stammered. "What I was going to
say was, is that you've come to see Sam, haven't you? About the hunting, yes?"
Rose nodded. "Well, he's out on the farm and I'll give him a call if you want."

"Goodness no. Really, I'll go and find him myself.

"Well, it's an awful mess," Barbara laughed. "And you'll need your boots…he's up in the top field, up behind the stables…over there, look." She took her visitor's arm and pointed through the window. "It'll be dreadfully mucky. They're up there pulling swedes, would you believe. It's the most God forsaken job and I expect Drew's left him to it but Sam's there all right. He hates it and you'll give him a lovely surprise." Barbara walked with her towards the door. "Come back afterwards and I'll have a cup of tea ready."

✳

For some reason she felt excited. Even after she climbed over the gate and dropped into the field where the long leaves of the roots soon soaked her slacks, Rose felt her heart beating faster than it should. And why not, she asked herself. Here, if anywhere, was a man she imagined all men of the moor to be like. She had watched him in the hunting field, she had caught sight of him in Dulverton from time to time and had even heard word of his broken love affair.

As soon as the dogs growled, Sam saw her coming. He stood, scratching at the back of his shoulder and waiting patiently with the bill hook hanging loosely in his other hand. The task of pulling the bulky, deeply rooted swedes from the ground then topping their leaves and throwing them onto the cart was as hard as it was dirty. He picked a handful of dark green leaves he had cut already and wiped his hands then flicked them dry before wiping them again on his breeches. It had been hot work and he could feel the sweat cooling already so, now he had stopped, he pulled a sack from the cart and threw it across his shoulders, watching his visitor as she stooped down to greet the dogs.

"Hi there." Even from this distance her voice faded on the wind. He raised a hand in reply and frowned, wondering what it was that brought her here, dressed like she was. "I had to come and dig you out," she explained, laughing cheerfully at his look. He hesitated before taking her hand but did so when she held it out waiting for his touch, noticing at once how fragile and white it looked. "Don't worry," she laughed getting out a handkerchief. "Mud's mud, that's all."

"Sorry about all this." Sam waved at the sight around him. "Don't get visits up this way, not usually anyway." He listened as she explained that she had called in to see them in order to seek his help at home.

"It's about the horses," she explained. "And I'm not happy with two of them. Can't seem to get comfy with them…trouble is I don't know why," she laughed. "It sounds ridiculous, doesn't it, but before I go splashing out I need a second opinion, somebody to tell me where things're wrong. And that's where you come in." Rose raised her eyes questioningly. "Would you…d'you think you could manage to come over and have a look?"

Sam shifted his weight. "Not sure you'm asking the right man." He was confused at what she was saying yet at the same time he was inquisitive. He knew the house for he had passed it many times and had always wondered what it was like. And then there was the woman herself. What was she doing coming out here like this and asking such a damn fool question? A sudden thought crossed his mind but he dismissed it immediately. That would be daft, impossible. "Not sure what I'd be looking for," he muttered. "But since you've asked, don't suppose I could do no harm."

"Oh, *would* you? Would you really?" She tried to clap but her hands were tucked away in the sleeves of her coat. "Oh Sam, that'd be marvellous. Come and have some lunch or something." She was looking at him gratefully but her eyes strayed from his, taking in the breadth of his shoulders under the hessian sack, his strong bare arms and the way he was standing there so casually, holding the hook. There was a power there, deep and brooding yet, at the same time, his presence was reassuring. She wondered who the girl had been and what had happened between them. As a hand went to sweep back his hair so their eyes met again. "That'd be wonderful," she murmured, now holding his gaze once more. "Look, it sounds crazy but I've got to go. I only just wanted to ask you that…you probably think I'm mad coming all the way out here but I thought, as I was passing then why not."

Sam took her hand again then watched her go, calling back one of the dogs that started to follow her through the roots. He bent to his task once more, pulling and cutting before standing to load them onto the cart. She had reached the gate and was about to climb over when she turned and looked back. He had stopped to watch her and started, suddenly flustered at being caught like that, but he returned her wave then continued to watch as she climbed over and stepped down the other side.

It was that look she gave him when he said he would go and see her that remained with him. Why she had come out to see him, he still could not imagine, even when the thought he cast aside earlier returned. As he bent and pulled at the roots, so he laughed out aloud at the idea. Come on, man, that would be madness, sheer madness. But what other reason was there for her to come all the way out across the fields to ask him like that? He stood once more, stretching hard to ease the stiffness in his back then stopped and leant against the cart. Only when the wind cut through his waistcoat and into the chill damp of his shirt did he stand up straight and stamp life back into his limbs. Rose Hatton indeed: the very idea made him laugh again.

3.

Even as the Colonel turned to speak to his chauffeur, the front door of the house behind him opened. It was Clements, Hestor Barclay's man, who had come to greet him and he looked pleased to be doing so. Miles Ashcroft's face crinkled into the smile he saved for those he knew best. "Clements, my good man. How are you? Come to make sure I don't get lost, eh?"

"Of course, sir. And very good it is to see you again, too." The portly, bewhiskered butler with the huge nose, inclined his head. He was standing rigid with his thumbs pressed down the seams of his trousers like the old soldier he was. "Mr Barclay's waiting...and much looking forward to your company, sir. Now then." Clements was about to lead the way but stopped and turned. "Don't worry about your man, sir, I'll see to him directly. He'll be more than welcome to join us in the kitchen."

"Grand." Ashcroft raised a hand in thanks. "But listen. Before we get inside, how is the master? Mmm? Miss Rose told me he's not bin keeping so well."

"Bearing up, sir, bearing up." For a moment the butler looked serious. "A little frail perhaps but then the move took its toll on all of us."

"Mmm, quite." Ashcroft shook his head, still mystified at why Hestor Barclay, late of Coutts Bank, Boodle's and Scammells, his country house near Dorking, had decided to up sticks and abandon everything dear to him. Well, he, too, had done that of course and he shrugged to himself. But Hestor was different and had been ever since the two of them met before the Great War. It had been at a shooting weekend at Gresham Park way back in nineteen-ten. He, Miles, had been twenty-five at the time and on leave from his regiment in the Curragh while Hestor, a mere blade at three years his junior, was still up at Oxford.

Hestor Barclay had always been the brilliant young madcap to whom the whole world seemed to beckon. But, come the war and he had put aside the promising city career, surprising family and friends alike by joining the Navy, seeing action at Gallipoli where his ship was torpedoed. Hours in and out of the water broke the body but the spirit had survived although the whole wretched business had caused him to be invalided out and it was then that he married Sarah de Courcy. Their first child died but then came Rosamund Sarah who chose to make her arrival just as the bells of victory were ringing out on that wonderful November evening. But there were to be no more. Rose, as she became known, was their only child and when Sarah died a few years later she was all that her father had left.

Life for young Rose Barclay could have been easy but Hestor never allowed it to be. Although the floorboards at Scammells creaked under the weight of house parties, dances and Christmas balls, her father kept the lid firmly on excessive extravaganza, until the Season when Rose came out. Miles Ashcroft remembered the ball at the Savoy after the palace presentation when the three hundred guests danced till dawn. A young pilot, Douggie Hatton, was there that night and the young couple never looked back.

They were married just before Douggie and his squadron went to France, leaving Rose at Scammells. When France fell he came back to Manston and flew from there, but seeing less and less of his young bride as the battle overhead raged. The end came during the second week in September, the same day as Miles went down to stay at Scammells, arriving only hours after the despatch rider bearing the news had left. It had been Clements who met him then, whispering the sad tidings as he was shown in. Rose, as they all remembered, had been the strong one, holding up her father while he came to terms with another family loss.

*

"God alone knows, Miles." Hestor Barclay, paler and fleshier than Ashcroft could remember, smiled sympathetically and examined the bottom of his glass. Talk had been about the families and Edwina Ashcroft, in particular when Miles explained the situation. "We're all getting pretty pathetic, my friend," Barclay grimaced. "Look at me, doddering about with this godforsaken arthritis business. I tell you what…the grim reaper's going to have us all before the bloody Hun. You wait."

Miles Ashcroft looked on as his friend inched his way towards the bell rope. He pulled at it hesitantly, almost stumbling, then stood and watched the door with his head cocked like an old dog waiting for somebody to come in. "Ah, there you are," he announced, sounding surprised at the sight of his butler. But then he half turned as though struck with a sudden idea. "You'll be staying for a bite, of course, Miles? *Yes?* Right then." Once more he forced himself round. "Ask Mrs Down to see to it, will you, Clements. She'll be able to manage all right, won't she?"

"Of course, sir. There won't be a problem." The butler rose on his toes. "Might I suggest about twenty minutes then? Time for one more perhaps?" Without waiting for an answer he collected the glasses then left, returning a few minutes later.

*

"Now, come on then, Hestor, what about your new life down here?" Ashcroft waited for his host to join him at the window seat where they sat together. "You going to manage, all right? It's a bit different to Surrey, y'know." He watched his friend as he eased himself down painfully. "And what about Rose…it's a very different kettle of fish for her? Wonderful having her down here with us…she's a breath of fresh air, but…well, I have me doubts she'll stick it."

Hestor Barclay sighed, leaning back until his head rested against the windowpane. His eyes were closed. "She's changed, Miles, changed more than you'd give credit for…like one of those damned chameleon things." He lifted his head and pulled on his collar. "After Douggie went it was the same old life, for a while anyway. I thought she was trying to hide from it all. Seemed to be going mad…y'know, the gay young widow and all that." Ashcroft nodded. "A bit tricky actually," he went on. "Almost as though she couldn't give a damn about it all but then *poof*," he lifted a hand. "Oh, I dunno, it all changed."

"In what way?"

165

"Turned her back on it all, on everything. Yes, seriously." He pushed himself away from the window to see better, grunting with exertion as he did so. "Almost as though she'd seen the great light on the road an' all that sort of thing…a big finger wagging down at her from out the clouds. The partying stopped, then the young men were shown the door…one after another. I didn't give it much thought at first; just sat there wondering what the hell was coming next."

"Well?"

"Then she started talking about here, Exmoor. We'd been down often enough…Sarah used to bring her down when she was tiny then I brought her hunting and we'd come again in the summer when I used to take that stretch on the Barle…up above Landacre. Remember? I knew she loved the place but not *that* much, for Heaven's sake. To be honest I got a bit windy and talked to a chum about it, a shrink up in town. He reckoned it was escapism, or something like that; gave me a whole load of that psycho mumbo-jumbo. I asked him if it would last and he said we'd have to wait and see. *Huh*…fat lot of good *that* was, but it's been some time now."

"Mmm." Ashcroft crossed his legs. "Well, if that's what she's after…escaping, then she's come to the right place. I mean it's a glorious spot down here but there ain't much around for a girl like Rose. No life, no youngsters…nothing much. There're a few families tucked away here and there but all their young're away. There's the odd farmer about but no one to take her in hand, to look after her."

"Well, she's changed, that I can tell you." Hestor Barclay shook his head mournfully. "An' we've been through all that business about nobody being here time an' again, 'til I was blue in the face. What can I do, eh?" He laughed suddenly. "Over four years now since Douggie was killed and three at least since she decided to get out of it all." He shrugged again. "What can a father do, for God's sake?" He shifted himself again and glanced out of the window. "To be honest, dear boy, I'd run out of puff meself by then. A year of her carrying on like that and I was waving the white flag. Then this goddamned arthritis or whatever it is came on so I thought, why not?"

"All very well while she's got you around." It was Ashcroft's turn to laugh. "But, you know, life moves on and what then? Nothing much here."

"God alone knows." Barclay was pulling himself slowly to his feet. "We've talked about that as well….an' that's driven me up the bloody wall, too. Says she's perfectly, perfectly happy where she is." He looked at Ashcroft as though he still could not believe it. "In love with the place, so she tells me. What? Loves it here, loves the people, the countryfolk…farmers, people here in Dulverton. Happy as a lark, honestly. God knows." He half turned. "Come on…let's have a spot of lunch and ease the mind."

"So it's pretty well permanent then?" Ashcroft stood also and bent down to pat the cushions. "I mean it's not some prolonged 'let's get away from it all' before she changes her mind or something?"

"Seems to be." Hestor Barclay turned and put a hand on his friend's shoulder. "But she'll make her way all right. Don't you worry, old bean…let's not worry ourselves about that. Somebody's out there somewhere, but he'll have to be one hell of a chap to take her on. Indeed he will, by God."

Ashcroft stopped but held out his arm, supporting his friend as he moved around the sofa. Both then glanced up as Clements came in and opened the door through to the dining room.

4.

"Let me try and guess." Dr Cohen sat back smiling broadly. He took off his gold rimmed spectacles and waited with that confident, reassuring look that his patients liked to see. Mike Daley shrugged and grinned bashfully. "I'll bet you that it was the kids who were the worst. Not the little ones," he added hurriedly. "But the ones coming home from school who were just loafing around and bored to tears."

"Spot on." Daley nodded thoughtfully. "Little sods. Could've rung their bleedin' necks.

"And then…the young men?"

"Ye-es." Here he had to think a bit. "Some of them let their eyes pop out on stalks, but it was the little kids, the real nippers, that hurt most…seeing 'em jump back as though they'd seen Old Nick."

Sammy Cohen, the small, neat and universally respected senior clinical psychologist at Musgrove Park nodded. It was nearly always the same and Daley had been no exception. To present yourself to the world with half your head and most of your facial features burned purple-pink, then watch the shock and the horrified looks was an experience to challenge the most confident. Daley had done well, very well, but Cohen could see the signs of strain.

"They're the two types that cause the most upset." He leaned forward to catch Daley's attention. Children, especially the older ones…the ones that gave you a hard time, can be very cruel without realising the impact they're making. And as for the young men, well…they see you as they imagine themselves to be under similar circumstances. The shock you saw in them was as if they were looking at themselves in a mirror. But don't worry," he urged. "Everything you've told me is quite natural and very common…sometimes we can predict how our fellow human beings are going to react, especially when they come face to face with the unexpected."

"Face to face with the demons o' hell, more elike." Daley shrugged. "Just got

167

to live with it, haven't I?"

"Yes, for sure you have but there're a number of points. First, and you'll be out on the streets again tomorrow, you now know what to expect. Sadly that's the way it's always going to be. What we've got to do now is to get the ball back over the net and here it's a case of you showing the world that you're positive about it all…that you're not creeping about all tucked up and ashamed about what's happened and how you look. You see, there're two ways you can go. Either like that…hiding away from the world…and yourself come to that, or else toughening it out and getting on top of it. And it's *that*, that second approach we need to have."

Cohen's eyes were watching his patient's face. "And you know what? The best tool of all is the simplest one…and it's one that you, you Mike Daley, possess in abundance." Cohen grinned impishly. "*We* call it a motivating impulse…*you* call it a smile. Yes, that's right, a simple little, old fashioned smile…it works wonders. Very difficult, I know when you're feeling down or upset, but you've got to make every effort to do just that and you'll see what I mean. A smile and a handshake or a pat on the back or a joke from you and you ease the tension. It disarms them, calms the shock and creates a pleasant and positive atmosphere. People'll smile back, you wait…they'll see you're OK. Whether they do so through sympathy or relief, it doesn't matter. For in that brief moment you've won them over. They'll feel able to have a quick look at you just to check on what they've seen and then get on with it whatever it is…filling the car for you, getting that packet of rice down from the top shelf, whatever."

"Didn't feel much like it this afternoon I have to say."

"Of course not but we reckoned you'd be able to take it so we sent you out unprepared. In that way you could see for yourself what it *might* be like, *could* be like…and what we're going to be building on. Let's see now." Cohen checked the documents in front of him. "What've we got, two weeks?"

"Yep." Mike Daley stirred. "An' I'll be out of here like a jack rabbit."

"I'll bet…so what're your plans?" Cohen looked at him. "Home or what?"

"No, I've had a bit o' luck actually." It was Daley's turn to lean forward. "An old mate of mine down in Plymouth's got me fixed up…driving an' that."

"Great…and you re-qualified last week, I see here. Out on the circuit at Trull?"

"Uh huh. Not so easy as I thought, though." He pulled a wry face. "One and half eyes take a bit of coordinating." Cohen nodded. The Vehicle Driving and Maintenance report had said as much but here, too, he had done well. "Question of getting used to it, that's all: the vehicles ain't changed much."

"And what about home life?" Cohen played down the question but they needed to know where the patients they had just released were going to end up and who would be waiting for them. "Anybody around?"

"Got to find her first." Daley smiled awkwardly and for a moment he looked down. "Last year, when I was up on Exmoor, before all this." He pointed at his face. "There was a girl there and we saw quite a bit of one another before I was posted away."

"Still there, I hope." Cohen sat back allowing the patient to talk. "A local lass? Not an evacuee or something?"

"No, no. Nothing like that. Born there, and then...well, just before I left she told me that she was...."

"With child, perhaps?" Cohen said it for him, watching as Daley nodded. "Well, these things happen. Not always most popular with the family but it's all happened before." He paused. "So you're going back to see her, mm? To pick up the traces." He paused once more. "D'you think she'll be keen to see you again?"

"What with all this?" Daley waved at his face again.

"Well there's that, of course, but how did you leave it, I wonder? Sometimes these things get a bit fraught and the fur can fly."

"No, she's fine," Daley nodded cheerfully. "She said she'd give it a go just before I left on my posting. See...she'll have the baby by now. Be about a couple of months or so, I reckon."

"That's splendid." Cohen closed the file and looked at him. "Sounds as though things are pretty good then. All being well you'll pick up your new family and then away down to Plymouth."

"Yep, that's the plan anyway."

"Grand...grand." Cohen was thoughtful. He'd heard it all before. They always sounded so confident, as if they were clinging to some wonderful dream. As if the dreadful run of bad luck had turned and life was suddenly going to become sweetness and light again. But who was he to dampen such hopes: in any case it could all work out, just as the patient was hoping. He nodded slowly to himself then looked up. "*Right* then. Well, we've got just these two weeks left to let you have a look at the wide world out there, and let the big, bad world get a glimpse of you...and then see what you all make of each other. How does that sound?"

"Bloody marvellous." Mike Daley got to his feet. "And any more from they kids an' I'll 'ave 'em. I will...scare the little buggers 'alf witless." He paused. "Thanks, doc." He took Cohen's hand. "Yeah, thanks a million for every-thing...it's been great."

169

Chapter Thirteen

"*Boo!*" The heavy, squat figure bending down behind the reception desk gave a startled cry and looked up. The sudden voice had made her jump. Their eyes met and Mike Daley watched as her face froze in horror. "Don't worry love." He smiled and put out a calming hand. "The other half got bitten off...honest."

"Oh, my dear soul." Edna Gowan, bespectacled and matronly, gasped in surprise. "Whatever d'you make me jump like that for," she muttered, smiling self-consciously but her eyes were still taking in the burns. They began from where the hairline should have been on the left side of his face, went down and across the eye that winked out from behind the puffed and wrinkled skin, before dropping down to the corner of his mouth and disappearing under his chin. The hair on that side of his head together with most of his left ear was missing. It was, she thought, as if somebody had painted one side of his face with purple paint. The other side was fine.

"Don't worry yourself, sweetheart. If looks could kill they'd 'ave strung me up months ago."

"Oh dear, I'm so sorry." Edna Gowan blushed in confusion. "I just didn't think. It's just that I, well, I hadn't...."

"Shhhh." Mike Daley put a finger to his lips. "Not a word...don't mention it, honest."

"You're up in number twelve, aren't you?" The new receptionist at the White Horse hurriedly busied herself with the register. "Two nights, yes?"

"That's it, darling. An' don't bother to knock when you come an' tuck me in. Yeah?" Daley grinned raffishly.

"Now there's a thought." Edna's body shook with mirth at the idea. "Off out, are you?" she asked, glancing at his grey mackintosh and the brown trilby in his hand. "Dinner's from half seven...until nine," she blurted, stretching up and back to reach for his room key. "Just you on your own, isn't it?" She looked at him again but the shock had gone from her face. "Be all right, will you?" she asked kindly.

"No problem," he replied adjusting his hat. "Me bag's up in the room...just off out to see some friends."

"That's nice. There'll be afternoon tea in the lounge from...well, any time now till half-four."

"Lovely job." Mike Daley picked up his brown paper parcel and winked. As he turned for the door, he sensed her eyes following him. No doubt she, like everybody else he met these days, would be wondering who he was and what had happened.

*

Myrtle Cottage looked much the same as he remembered. He had met her father before, briefly a couple of times, but not her mother. Becky had warned him about her and he had kept his distance, catching sight of her only once as far as he could remember, when she was standing staring at him from across the green with one of her cronies. He knocked again, ignoring the slight movement from behind the curtain and waited until the door opened quietly.

For a second or two Ernest Carter had no idea who it was. "Mr Carter?" Daley looked at him quizzically. "Yes? My name's Daley, sir. Mike Daley. Remember?" He held out his hand. "I've come to see you...and Becky...that's if she's around."

"*Daley*...Mike *Daley*...the *soldier*." Ernest stared aghast, looking him up and down. He took the hand limply but he was taking in the man as a whole and barely noticed the burns. "Why, we thought...I mean, we'd heard you'd been killed...*dead*. You and several others. Word came back that you'd...."

"It was close." Daley stood still, his coat over one arm and the parcel in his hand. "Damned close, it was. Shook me up a bit but it could've bin worse." He shrugged and pulled a long face, then hesitated. "But look, sir, I've come back to see Becky and...the baby, if I can. That's if everything's all right."

"Who is it, dear?" Daley could see the figure emerging from the gloom and watched as she stopped then staggered and steadied herself as she shrank back from him. "It's you?" she whispered. "*You*, the soldier. What're you doin' here. I thought...I thought...and why've you.... "

"'Tis all right, dear." Ernest turned. " 'E's come back...back from France an' not like we'd heard. Well then, look." He turned back again. "You'd best come inside fer a minute."

"*No*." Doris Carter came closer. "No, he's not comin' in here." Now there was anger in the voice. One hand was still raised in caution and her head was shaking vigorously. "No, that wouldn't be right."

"Don't be so daft, woman." Ernest waved her aside, dismissing her remark. "Can't do else other than to ask him to step inside fer a minute." He turned back to Daley. "You'm all right, are you? Hurt pretty bad, I see...come on, come on in." He held the door wide.

"I'll not stay long, ma'am." Daley ducked under the doorway, noticing how she avoided his eyes. "'Tis Becky an' the babe, I've come to call on really, but

171

I've brought you these, look. Bain't much, just a bit of sugar an' butter from the hospital kitchen...sort of spare rations the cook gave me," he addded. "Here." He held out the parcel but Doris stood motionless. "Here we are, then." Mike put the parcel on the table. He could sense the shock and suspicion still in the air. Her father seemed to have more or less accepted him but her mother looked as though the evil ghost from the past had suddenly come back to haunt them. "Any chance?" he queried. "If she's around, that is. Or perhaps later?"

"I'll tell her you called." Ernest appeared to have recovered his composure. "Her'll be shocked, mind. Same as us but more so, I dare say."

"She'll not want...not want to see yer." Doris Carter was shaking her head.

"'Tis for *her* to decide, Doris. Becky'll make up her own mind," Ernest cut in. He was trying to recover and to assert himself. "Best I can do is to tell the maid that you've...well, that you're here an' alive...an' well. An' then us'll have ter see what her makes of it."

"And the baby?" Mike glanced at Doris then back to Ernest. "Is it...he...she? Is it all right?"

"Aye, the babe's fine. A little girl so she is. Maudie so Becky's called her." Ernest paused, watching the soldier mouthing her name. "Best t'let Becky decide what's to be done. She'll be back d'rectly...you'll be stopping here, in the village fer a while, I dare say?"

"Just round the corner...in the pub, the White Horse. Just for a coupla nights." He could still feel the tension and was trying to work out if it was simply because they had not expected to see him again or because he, the father of their daughter's child, had been brazen enough to barge in on them like this. "Well, look." He smiled from one to the other, trying to sound cheerful. "Seeing she's not about, I'll be off just now. But p'raps you'd tell her I'll be across the way an' that...well, I'd love to see her again, her an' the littlun." He held out his hand but Doris shrank back again. Ernest took it but he, too, was speechless and the two men simply eyed one another. Mike Daley opened the door, then turned and nodded again. As it shut behind him, he heard the woman's voice rise in anger.

∗

Becky had been in a hurry so she never knew why it was that she called in at the newsagents next door to the forge. Had she not done so then she might have missed him altogether. As it was she saw him when she looked up, just after she had pulled the door behind her and was standing on the step adjusting her scarf. He had passed the village stores and was coming her way.

At first she gave him no more than a casual glance but then she looked again and watched as the slim figure in the open mackintosh gave a little jump before kicking out at a stone on the pavement. The rim of his hat was shielding his face but when he rolled his shoulders just like he used to do her heart missed a beat. It was him. She felt sure it was but she knew it couldn't be. It was impossible. Then, as she looked closer, she could feel her heart beginning to race madly. He half turned, looking back at where he had just come from then he turned again and she caught her breath. Now she knew for certain.

"*Mike,*" she gasped, stepping down and onto the pavement. He was no more than fifty yards away and she started to run before stopping suddenly, uncertain at what he might do. "Mike...oh, Mike," she whispered to herself and started towards him again. One hand was outstretched and as she walked so her pace quickened. "Mike," she called, catching his eye as he looked up.

Her eyes, already wide and disbelieving suddenly grew wider, for now she could see his face more clearly. "No," she muttered. "Oh God, no, Mike...it can't be." She ran until she was close enough to touch him then stopped again, one hand still outstretched.

"Hi." Mike Daley stopped. He had it in mind to turn his head away from her but already it was too late. He could see the horror on her face. "Hi, Becks." He didn't smile but stood there waiting to see how she would react. "Sorry about this." He tried to sound casual but he was watching her closely. "Not too pretty, I'm afraid."

"Oh, dear God," she whispered. "You're alive...but, Mike, look at you." Both hands were over her mouth and her eyes were searching his face. "What've they done t'you?" she muttered. "Oh, dear God what's happened? We all thought...I mean, we'd heard you'd been killed."

"I know...I know." He smiled reassuringly. He wanted to pick her up in his arms but he dare not. Her face was a mad tangle of emotions. She was staring in shock and there was a hint of revulsion. Her eyebrows were raised high in horror. She was hurt and she was grieving for him, peeping out at him from over her fingers like a child saying its prayers. "Your Mum and Dad told me. They said you'd all heard I'd copped it. But no, here I am." He opened his arms. "Topped and tailed a bit, but more or less the same old me. And you, Becks?" he queried. "You've a little girl, I hear." He watched as she nodded. "*Our* little girl," he murmured."

Her hands were still at her face but she nodded. "Yes...so they told you that too, did they?" At last her hands fell away and she paused before the words came tumbling out. "She's ours, Mike, you're her father." Her eyes never left his. "And she's like you, y'know. I've called her Maudie. Don't know why," she shrugged, giving a little laugh. "She's got dark eyes and a mop of black hair...just like yours."

"Becks listen." Again he wanted to catch hold of her. "I'd love to see her. Honest, I would an' love to see you, too. Just to talk...to see how you are an' what you've bin up to. I'm staying here." He pointed past her. "Same old place," he grinned. "Perhaps I could call by yer parents later...come and see the babe. Just a peep," he added hurriedly. "Wouldn't want to break in, like. Reckon yer Mum and Dad're a bit shocked as well. Can't blame 'em. An' yer Mum's none too pleased to see me...can't blame her fer that, neither."

"I don't know." Becky shrugged, stepping back uncertainly. "It's all...it's just all such a shock, seeing you like this...and all this, look." She stared at his forehead. "Poor you...oh, you poor thing," she whispered. "Honestly, Mike, it's just so hard to believe that you're here...alive and talking like this."

"Look." Now he took her by her shoulders. "Don't say nuthin just now, love. Honest...get yerself back home and I'll come round later. If yer don't want to see me then that's fine but I'd love to see my little girl...love to. Can I, just fer a minute or so? It'd mean everything to me, Becks."

"Yes," she nodded. "Yes, of course." One hand went to her head. "Goodness, I'm still so...so confused."

"I know," he soothed. "I know."

"Say about six then." Becky looked at him. "I'll have fed her by then and, well...you'll be able to see her before I put her down."

"And yer Mum?"

"I'll tell her." Becky looked at him. "Don't worry. I'll tell her she's yours as well and she'll have to step aside."

Mike nodded and patted her shoulder. "OK," he whispered. "I'll be there."

∗

It was dark when he returned to the cottage and a wind was blowing yet, even as he entered, he could sense the resentment. The atmosphere was tense and he knew there had been harsh words. Her father was civil enough, making room for him but her mother was cold and withdrawn, taking herself off to the kitchen as soon as he bade her good evening. His parcel lay unopened on the table where he had left it earlier. Nobody had even noticed it. He tried to imagine what it must have been like in here and what had been said when Becky returned after meeting him outside the forge.

She was standing with her back to the stove holding the child and rocking her in her arms. When he moved towards her she held the infant up, presenting her to him as he pressed down the corner of the shawl to see her face. As he gazed at his daughter in the soft lamplight, Becky watched him closely, studying his wrinkled flesh and the hairless scalp. Only when he looked up was she able to see him properly. He was smiling but there were tears also, from one eye which he wiped but not the other that was half-hidden behind the swollen skin.

He did not stay long but asked if he could come back and see the child again in the morning. Becky looked at her father who nodded, saying it would be fine but her mother remained silent, staring coldly from the gloom of the other room. He bade them good night and let himself out, turning last of all to smile at Becky who had their child's face pressed up against her cheek.

2.

Becky lay listening to the sounds of the night. Sometimes, throughout the long hours of darkness, a floorboard creaked. At other times she would hear mutterings or growling snores from her parents' room next door, or she would hold her breath and listen as Maudie sighed or whimpered in the crib beside her. Dawn, she knew, was not far off when the cocks from two houses away would end the night watch. But right now, in that chill hour before daylight, she lay staring up into the blackness where she could see the outline of his face.

Time and again she had caught him looking at her. Sometimes he had been smiling as he had smiled at his daughter when she held her out to him. Or like he did when he turned to her in the street after she called out to him, when the naked wound, raw and bleeding in her dream like a side of beef, had come into sight and he apologised for the way he looked. And when he put his hands on her shoulders and begged her to come and see him so they could talk, just the two of them. His voice that had called down to her from the darkness was the same as it always was, like his smile, and his fingers when she looked down at his hands when he had caught hold of her.

But then came the other faces. They seemed to crowd around and stare down at her as she lay there. She saw her father's anxious looks and her mother's hostility. She heard the shouts and taunts of Gerry Chugg and listened to Pat Steer's and Mavis Vellacott's voices of alarm, echoing back and forth in the night. And suddenly there had been Sam. He had just stood there, looking quietly on until Mike had come and stood between them, blocking him from sight and taking his place. Fingers, long and accusing, were stabbing and pointing, brows were furrowed and tongues were wagging behind shielding hands. Then, for a brief moment, she saw Sam again. This time he was standing in the yard at Hayes. He was smiling and beckoning but so too was Mike. One of them faded. She couldn't remember who and she worried herself trying to decide which one it was.

Suddenly, she started, twitching nervously and jumping in her sleep. Next door her father had stirred. She could hear him through the wall, moving about and talking quietly and her mother's muffled replies.

✳

The morning had gone quickly. It was time to say goodbye and Becky looked at him knowing her face was expressionless. Even as he had been speaking she had watched as his eyes searched hers, looking for that small hint of enthusiasm but there had been none. Everything he said had sounded too easy. "I can't see it, Mike." She shook her head sadly. "Honestly, all this about a car and a job…and life in Plymouth. We're still at war, for God's sake. Look at us all, we've got nothing and look at you…you've been hurt bad and have only just come out of hospital. And you expect me to just jump sticks like this, and follow you off somewhere…into the blue…and with Maudie?"

He got up from his bed and walked to the second of the two chairs by the wooden table next to the window. The curtain he had pulled earlier had caught and he tidied it before sitting beside her. The table, like the room itself, was bare. Becky had come to talk as she said she would and he had met her in the front hall. This time the receptionist had smiled and they had chatted briefly when he enquired about Harry Blake, the barman. He had gone, she explained, one of many changes since the soldiers left in the summer. That had made him laugh but now he felt flat. The room was soulless and depressing. His arrival at Myrtle Cottage had been an ordeal and now Becky was being evasive.

"But give me a chance," he pleaded, leaning across the table. "Honest Becks, he wouldn't have written to me if he'd got nothing to offer. You'll like him," he urged. "Eddie Bright's a good bloke an' if he says there's something there then there is. Why'd he write to me?" he appealed. "Must've dozens of others down there but he wrote to me, didn't 'e?" He tried to take her hand but she pulled back. "Let me go an' see."

Becky shook her head. "I dunno, Mike." She looked up and shrugged, laughing emptily at her own indecision. "I mean it's a lot, isn't it? Maudie's just settling and everyone's getting used to me being back." She shrugged again. "Just to leave here like that…it's daft…*I can't.*" She noticed the wide chalk stripe in the grey suit he had made in Taunton. That and his dark blue shirt and matching tie suited him. "No, it's crazy," she whispered trying not to sound too unkind.

"Look." This time he took hold of her hand and held it. She looked down but made no attempt to draw back. "Just give me a chance, right? I'm getting a car an' I'm off next week. I was going to buy one with my back pay but Eddie's promised to get me one. It's part of the job. An' I'll be back by Christmas. Yes?" He shook her hand. "Come on, love, trust me."

"What're yer going to do…over Christmas? D'you have anywhere?"

It was his turn to shrug and he laughed. "Haven't thought, really, but up here I s'pose. See Maudie if I can…if you'll let me. I'll wanta bring her something. And you, of course…Christmas stockings, eh?" He pursed his lip. "How about that, then? Christmas here in Exford and then away."

Becky looked down at her hand still in his. "I'll see," she whispered. "I can't be

176

saying nuthin' fer certain. Not now anyways. And look." She pulled her hand away. "I must be going, it's late fer Maudie." Suddenly and before she could move, he reached out and took her face in his hands.

"I'd not forgotten yer, Becks," he whispered, drawing her closer. "Here." She closed her eyes as he bent forward and remained still as he kissed her lips. It was a gentle, lingering kiss and she wanted to respond but forced herself to freeze.

"Thanks," she whispered as he drew back. "I'll come and see you off tomorrow. OK? I'll be here just before the bus gets in at one." She rose quickly and picked up her coat, frightened that if she stayed she would be unable to resist him. She could sense that he craved for her affection and half of her was telling her to stay but she had to get away. "I'll go," she said. "No, don't come down. No," she cried as he rose. "Let me go on my own. I'll see you tomorrow."

3.

Sam heard the next morning. The letter from the War Office telling them that the army would be relinquishing the use of the land around Larkbarrow had come earlier that week and he had gone up to see how the grazing had been affected. As he passed Myrtle Cottage he stopped by the gate and whistled cheerily but there had been no reply so he rode on, vowing to stop on his way back.

The old farmhouse was in a dreadful state, something he noticed from as far back as the wire fence surrounding the farm and cottage. They had tied red signs about the danger of unexploded shells along the wire but he could see where the live rounds had landed. Most had thrown up the turf, leaving deep, round scars of bare soil but some had struck the buildings, shattering the roofs and knocking away great chunks of masonry. The place had a forlorn emptiness about it: it was difficult to imagine how life had once been and almost impossible to recall the peace and gentleness of the old homestead which they had all loved. It was as if some great vandal had delighted in smashing and breaking everything in sight.

The sheep pens were still there, tucked into the corner of the hedgerow, exactly as he had left them and further on up the hill he could make out where the plane had come down. It didn't take him long to check. The old pastures, he could tell, had suffered from not being grazed but there was little to be done and nothing for the sheep until the first flush of grass next spring. As he rode away, he slowed for a moment and looked back, his eyes searching in vain. Any nostalgia he might have expected to find had gone. Larkbarrow, to him, felt desolate. The place was broken and cold, something else touched by the cruel hand of war.

※

He had been preparing himself to tell them about their old home, worrying how best he might describe what had happened without sounding too depressed. The old couple, he knew, would be saddened by his report but, in the event, the subject had not even been mentioned. Doris came to meet him at the door but looked grave. Neither Becky nor the baby was there and it was when he saw Ernest that he knew something was wrong.

"Becky's soldier's back." Doris made the announcement as he was taking off his coat. For a moment he stood undecided with his back towards her, half in and half out of the sleeve.

"But he's *dead.*" Sam's struggled on but his face was impassive. As he tidied himself so his eyes remained on the floor. "Well, he can't be, can he," he added, suddenly realising the truth. "But back, you say? Back from the wars or what?"

"Back from France and badly smashed up but alive and well, more or less all right." Ernest Carter sat heavily in his chair by the stove and waved Sam towards one at the table. "Came up Friday night, from the hospital in Taunton. Came to see Becky and the babe."

"Oh aye." Sam sat and pulled on his chin. "And Becky…what's her got to say about it, then? After 'e dropped her like that."

"Struck dumb like the rest of us." It was Ernest again. "Didn't know what t'say but she's bin across to see him. Staying at the White Horse he was, but 'e's away back to Taunton right now." He pulled out his watch. "Bus leaves d'rectly an' she's gone to see him off."

"I don't like it one bit." Doris was sorting cutlery by the kitchen door. "Came in here like he owned the place…said he wanted to see this an' that. Quite upset me he did and that's on top of all he's done."

"Now that's not fair." Ernest sat up. "I know how you feel about him, dear, but 'e's bin a proper gennelman 'yere in the house, an' us can't fault him fer that."

"Well, I don't like it all the same. He's nuthin but trouble is that Mike Daley…all talk an' trouble. Can't you see it…*you* can Sam, dear, can't you. Oh, I wish you'd tell her," she sighed. "Have a word with her, Sam. Before she goes and does something silly again."

"Like what, Mrs Carter?" Sam shifted uneasily. He knew what she was implying and already he had an uncomfortable feeling about how things might develop. "There bain't much I can do. Not reely. Becky knows her own mind and, well, this Mike Daley's the father of her child after all."

"Well she's got to be told." Doris Carter watched as her husband got out of the chair. "Either you or Ernest's got to be firm with her."

"Bain't as easy as that, y'know." Ernest had gone over to the window. "Fer a start, he's the father...just as Sam's said. Us dunno what they've bin talkin' about but I daresay its no different to what any other father an' mother might 'ave bin sayin'." He paused and hitched up his trousers. "Then there's the maid herself. Once anyone starts tellin' her then away she goes... 'Why can't people leave me alone', an' all that."

"Because she gets herself into such a dreadful mess, that's why." Doris Carter folded her arms. "I'd tell her meself but she only gets mad and then the baby gets upset...poor little soul. No, she must be told."

"Hey up, bus coming." Ernest was looking out of the window. "And there's the pair o' them together, look." The three in the room crowded together where Ernest had pulled the curtain back. As they watched the bus turning, Doris stood on tiptoe to see better.

✳

Mike knew he had not won her word. It would take more than their discussions and he suspected she really had begun to feel settled at home. All he could do was to ask her to have faith in him and not make up her mind one way or the other until he came back.

Becky had seen the sadness in his face as he cradled Maudie in the bedroom, just before they left the room. Earlier she had watched as he lay the little girl on her back on the bed and tickled her chin before opening and shutting his mouth in front of her like a fish. As soon as she smiled, he had turned to look up at her and they had both laughed in delight. Suddenly and for a brief moment they were together again.

Without thinking she had sat beside them and put a hand up to his burn, all her instincts urging her to soothe the pain she knew must still be there. He had caught hold of her hand, turned it over and kissed it gently, all the while watching her eyes. In spite of that she had forced herself to remain aloof but, even as they were leaving the hotel, she knew she was going to miss him and would be counting the days until his return.

"Middle of the week," he replied. As they were walking towards the bus, Becky had asked him about his visit to Plymouth. "Take a train, then stop off down there with Eddie until Sunday, then back into the Musgrove."

"I thought all that was over now...all that hospital business."

"Just a week or two more then I'll be away down to Plymouth again...see Eddie an' that, then up here...*to submit my official report...in duplicate.*" She laughed gaily at the pompous voice and let their bodies touch as they made their way down the street. She knew he wanted to carry the baby and she wanted to let him then slip her arm through his as they walked along but it would never do, not here in Exford. "Here we are then." Mike turned to her.

"Bye then," she whispered, as he took her hand.

*

Standing in the cottage, the three looked on huddled close together. They saw him take her hand and bend forward for a quick kiss before patting her shoulder and getting onto the bus. And they watched again as she stood waving until the bus had climbed the hill and gone on past the church, holding her hand high until it was lost from sight.

Suddenly Sam felt angry with himself and embarrassed at having been caught prying like that with her parents. It seemed mean and he was ashamed. He knew he had to leave before she got back to the cottage but he knew also that he would meet her on his way out. He took his leave as quickly as he could, still feeling guilty and was untying his pony when she came abreast of him. Neither knew if she was going to walk on but both knew what was going through each other's minds.

"Hullo, Sam." Becky slowed rather than stopped in case he chose to hurry on. Had he done so she would have been able to continue on her way rather than been left standing in the road.

"Hi Becky." He had already checked his girth but stopped and came across to her, leading his pony. For a moment they looked at one another. "Mike Daley's back, I hear," he offered, finding the words difficult. "Mother an' father told me when I dropped by. I was up at Larkbarrow earlier an' thought I'd call in, like."

"Yes, that's right...he gave me, gave us all a dreadful turn. But he's gone now...I've just seen him off." She waved in the direction of the bus stop.

"Oh aye." Sam stood undecided at what to say next. He was desperate to know more, to know how they had got on and what had been said but he dare not ask. Had he mentioned anything she would have turned and made for her door just a few yards away and the moment would have been lost. "Coming back, is he? He'll be visitin' again, I dare say?"

Becky shrugged. "Says he might. Talking about a job down Plymouth way, but says he might look back. To see Maudie...his daughter." She blushed suddenly but held her up as if to confirm what she had just said.

Sam nodded. He had it in mind that much more had been said between the two of them. It would have been, of course, for her parents told him that she had gone over to see him at the hotel. The mere thought of them together in his room like that cut deeply. For a moment, just as he was collecting the reins and preparing to mount, their eyes met again. He could see there had been more but he had no idea what. It was simply that she had the look about her of a child that had been asked what she'd been up to but who had declined to say.

For her part, Becky could see he was suspicious, but she stood there waiting as he got up and turned his pony for home. "Bye then, Sam." She bent herself back to lift a hand in a wave.

He watched as her hand dropped and she half turned, pausing awkwardly. Suddenly he didn't want her to go. He wanted her to walk over to him, to put her hand on his knee and look up at him. He wanted her to tell him that everything really had changed and that she was staying...staying with him. But she didn't of course and, by now, her back was turned. "Bye, Becky." He cleared his throat and braved a smile lest she turned round, but she didn't. "Be seein' yer soon, daresay," he said quietly but only in hope.

4.

It was a stroke, only a mild one but a stroke nonetheless and the next few days would be critical. Dr Stuart McKinney had given his verdict a little over an hour ago. They had met the doctor almost as soon as they moved in and her father had immediately taken to the brusque Irishman. At first, Rose had been wary but the more her father needed his attention, the more she came to like him. "Call me," he had demanded, taking hold of her hand in the doorway. "Any sudden change, don't hesitate now, just give me a ring or send your man."

Rose got up from the window seat, paced the room then turned and sat again, all the time fiddling with her pearls. Minutes earlier she had lit up a cigarette from the larger of the two silver boxes on the sideboard. It was something she rarely did and she detested the bitter taste, stubbing it out angrily and cursing herself. Mrs Harper was off until five so that meant no tea unless she got it herself but she didn't know where anything was. And Clements had gone to find the District Nurse. With luck she would be able to come up with the name of someone who might be able to live in. That her father required nursing was now obvious. She had discussed it with the doctor who had advised her to find a downstairs room for him. Stairs, he declared, were now too much.

She would be able to cope with so much but there was everything else as well. Once more she got up, this time walking through to the telephone in the hall but she hesitated, turning back suddenly and rubbing the back of her neck while trying to clear her mind. The new feed bins for the stables were due to arrive after lunch and she had to see Jenkins about the leak in the potting shed roof. Bridge, this evening, would have to go and that meant excusing herself again. What the Smythes would think, she had no idea. She sat again, this time covering her face with her hands in despair. Only then did she realise how much she was shaking: it was the shock of listening to the doctor when he told her how seriously ill her father was. This time, when she got up, she went straight to the telephone.

"Hullo, operator...this is Dulverton four eight nine. Yes, that's right. Can you

181

get me an Exford number, please…Exford three one six. Hayes Farm…yes, that's it…thank you." The phone seemed to ring for ages but it was Barbara who answered eventually. Even as they started to speak, Rose knew that Sam's mother sensed something was amiss, and it was when she was asked outright that she burst into tears.

✳

Sam had not really wanted to drive over to Dulverton. Gerry Chugg had called earlier and the conversation they'd had only served to depress him further. The worst part about it was that what he had said about Becky had an element of truth in it. If what Sam had told him was right, Gerry declared, and she was considering taking up with that fellow Daley again, then he really was better off out of it all.

But he had seen how anxious his mother had been, and when she told him about old Mr Barclay he had filled the Austin with one of the three cans of petrol they kept hidden in the calf shed. He left straight after lunch, arriving to find that Rose had been waiting for him. He could see she had been crying again and he tried to cheer her suggesting that, as he was over anyway, it might be a good time to see about the horses.

✳

As soon as she led the big gelding out of his box he could see he was wrong for her. "Too big," he said, running his hand over the withers. "Nigh on seventeen hands, I reckon."

"Just under…sixteen two, in fact." Rose was holding him by his head collar and had been watching as Sam stood back and looked at them both, comparing them, before coming forward to check the animal's legs.

"Aye, and pretty much a handful, I'll be bound," he muttered, standing back once more. "Fifteen two's more your size an' my advice would be to find something with a bit more body…deeper chest an' stronger legs, that's what you need on Exmoor. Stamina or *go* is what you're after down here with the staghounds. I thought as much the other day when I see'd you out at Simonsbath." He walked up to her again. "But now, seein' you here together standing like this, 'tis plain as day." The second horse, the grey, was the same. Both were fine animals better suited to up-country conditions rather than the hills and rough going of the moors.

Afterwards he helped her with the feed bins, lifting them one corner at a time while she pushed planks underneath to keep them off the floor. It was easy enough for him but he could see she was flushed. Yet the work seemed to have calmed her, brought back the smile that had been missing earlier when she told him about her father. He couldn't stay on, even for the tea she offered, as he needed to be back before dark.

182

"Thank you so much, Sam." She turned to pick up her jacket and it was then that he noticed her neat figure beneath her yellow cardigan. She was tiny, he thought, more like a girl, but trim and all of a woman at that. "Sorry I was such a drip when you arrived but…well, everything seemed to come at once. You've been absolutely marvellous."

"Hardly," he laughed. "Nice to get off the farm fer a bit. Been on my mind to get over here, since we spoke about the horses the other day." He glanced round then back at her, nodding appreciatively.

"Well, you're very kind," she continued. "And I heard that things were…well, your mother said that you had plenty of other things on your mind just now."

"BBC Home Service…that's her." She detected the hard tone in his voice. "Never can stop telling the world about everything and everyone," he added bitterly. "Cuh…mothers."

"Don't be too hard. I'm sure she only said it to help me. Sort of equal misery for all, in that if you were miserable then I'd feel better." She laughed at the idea. "And I was being really pathetic when I rang her."

Sam nodded. "Just one of them days, I s'pose. But yep," he raised his eyebrows and sighed heavily. "Not sure what's up at the moment. Just have to wait an' see."

"Don't worry." Her hand was on his arm. Suddenly he looked vulnerable. She had no idea who the woman was. Barbara had not elaborated, simply mentioned that he, too, was in a quandary and that it had happened before. "I'm sure things'll turn out," she said quietly. "She watched as he pulled a face. "Don't be too upset."

Sam looked down at her. Nobody had spoken to him like that before. All through the business with Becky and the baby, and Mike Daley, voices had been raised in anger or concern. Advice had been offered and accusations levelled but there had been nothing like this. She was soft: she sounded as though she really understood and cared, even now with all her own troubles to worry about. "No," he cried, sounding more confident than he felt. "I'll be fine…just knocks one back a bit, that's all." They had reached his car and it was the rueful smile he gave when he turned that took her by surprise.

She appreciated later that it had been no more than a brave front on his part yet when he turned to go like that she suddenly realised how lonely she was going to be. He would be driving off back to his family and the farm and everything else that filled his life while she would be left here on her own. His presence had given her confidence. His quiet strength had been good company and there was something about him which made her feel able to confide. In his own rugged way he was a handsome man. But he was also quiet and sensitive, someone who could do without the angst and worry of a tangled and messy love affair. It all showed in his eyes: either they smiled kindly or they looked hurt and sad.

But then, if he, too, was going to be on his own, perhaps he would learn to enjoy her company. Perhaps he needed someone like her who understood; she might be able to bring a smile back into his life. It would be nice to see him happy, and to see those eyes smiling again, to see him throwing his head back and laughing. And how would she feel, she wondered, if she was with him? Suppose they were happy in each other's company?

"You'll come again, won't you?" she asked, looking at him anxiously. "You were tremendous this afternoon and, well, it'd be lovely to see you."

The car door was still ajar and Sam looked up at her from the driving seat. "Aye," he muttered, glancing away for a moment as if he was thinking. "If that's what you'd like then, well, 'tis more than fine with me." As he pulled away, he held up a hand to wave only to find that she had caught hold of it. They were able to smile briefly as she walked beside him and before she was forced to let go.

Chapter Fourteen

Almost immediately they met, Mike Daley became wary of Kenny the Swede. For a start the man was ugly and most of his hair had come out. Tall and thin, with his eyes sunk deep into their sockets and hidden further by a permanent scowl, the man looked like walking death. His handshake was cold and he said little. Daley sensed at once that Eddie Bright's man resented his presence and the fact that he and Eddie had known each other for years. The Swede, he decided, would have to be watched.

The journey from Taunton had been uneventful and it was only when he changed at Plymouth Central, taking the spur line into Millbay, that he saw the full extent of the bomb damage around the docks. Everywhere were deep scars and gaps in the long rows of terraced houses where the bombs had simply selected somebody's home and obliterated it, leaving the neighbours unscathed. Sometimes one half of a building had survived and he could see the outline of the old stairways going diagonally from floor to floor, passing each wall of a different colour. Occasionally a small, black fireplace stuck out pathetically where it had once heated the room, but the room had vanished along with the occupants. What it must have been like in the middle of an air raid when the air was full of screeching whistles and shattering explosions, when flames and smoke gushed from stricken buildings, when debris flew and when anyone who couldn't find shelter ran about screaming in terror, it was difficult to imagine.

Mercifully, although the air still reeked of charcoal and damp brick dust, the bombs had long since gone. Those who lived and worked in the docklands were somehow managing to carry on in spite of the devastation around them. Much of the rubble and been cleared away and, as they walked past the docks, Daley saw that the wharfs were once more full of warships and merchantmen. Stray dogs and litter were everywhere. The Swede walked fast, hunched and loose-limbed, lifting a shoulder to slide around those he came across on the pavement rather than stepping aside to make way. The collar on his coat was pulled up, almost meeting the rim of his hat.

Although a chill December breeze was coming straight off The Sound, the walk warmed him and he had to stop to change his suitcases over. Once or twice, as they turned up Mary Street, Daley noticed a hand lifted towards the tall figure or a nod of recognition. The two women working the cobbled entrance to George Place moved quickly out of their way. The Swede, so it appeared, had made his mark.

After the first floor, the stairs above the Blue Rose were bare. Mike noticed at once that, while the Swede moved effortlessly and silently on his rubber soles, his own footsteps rang out noisily on the boards. At the top, his guide opened one of the three brown-painted doors and motioned him to go in. The moment he did so the door closed behind him.

Inside it was strangely quiet. Although owning a musty smell, the room was far too high above the beery stench of the ground floor for that or the noise of the bar to reach them. He dropped his cases and took off his coat then stood gently massaging the burn on his cheek which had begun to itch. The room, he could see, was once a bedroom but the view from the window showed little more than the houses on the other side of the street.

He walked across to see better but barely had time to notice one of the girls in the street approaching a sailor when the door opened. He turned quickly, momentarily disappointed at not witnessing the deal clinched. It was the Swede again. Mr Bright, he announced looking past him, would see him now.

✳

The meeting lasted longer than either of them expected but then Eddie Bright had taken his time. "Ricky Hatch here'll show you my spread." He nodded towards the heavily built young man with the American-style crew cut. The object of Eddie's attention was standing with his feet apart and his arms folded. The face, immobile save for the jaw that was chewing, stared back sullenly. Probably a bone-head, Mike thought: loyal but stupid, just like the team back in Portsmouth. He looked again, his nose twitching at the cheap and ill-fitting pale grey suit.

"First you get to know my boundaries…in here." Eddie Bright tapped his head. "Then you get to know the patch…every street and every turning point. Every goddamned inch of the turf. Right? 'Cos when you drive, Mike, you'll be driving fast and with your eyes shut if it's dark. There'll be no 'Sorry, Eddie, wrong turning," he mimicked nasally. "Yeah?"

"No problem."

"Then you take in my houses…all of them, starting with the Angel down Moir Street. You'll see where an' how to park, which way the doors go, where the lights are…everything. Front an' back, yeah? Ricky'll show you." Daley ignored the brute. "That'll take a day or two, then you'll learn who we've got out there…who the neighbours are, where there's a welcome an' where there ain't no welcome." Eddie Bright paused to pick up his Havana and flick away the ash. He then sat back and studied him. "Three days, that's all."

"And the car, Eddie? I'll need to work on the motor."

Eddie shook his head, lifting his chin and exhaling slowly. "Steady, boy," he wheezed. "There's more yet. Get my street plan first…get a look at the girls an' the guys that run 'em…get to know my eyes out there, the lookouts. Yeah? Then there's the law…where they live, who they are…the beats. All that, Mike. It's all gotta go in there." The fingers holding the cigar pointed at him. "And

186

when you're doing it, cover up that ugly looking bonce of yours...you an' Kenny're a right pair of nightmares between you. Get a balaclava...or a good, big hat. People don't forget a face that's just scared the living shit out of 'em. An' walk with a limp, put a pad in one of your shoes. Cover yourself...you don't want no one to recognise you." He paused to draw heavily on his cigar. "But the car?" Eddie coughed and turned to the Swede. "What about it?"

"Mason's garage, North Road. Jacko's our man."

"And?" Mike sounded impatient.

"Ford Pilot...V8...one of the best. We haf tickled her up a bit and she's fitted with a crash bar behind the front fender...steel girder. Yah. She's big enough for three in the back, four at a push when we're doin' business."

"Jeez." Mike whistled, glancing back at Eddie. "That's big. Stick out like a bulldog's whatsits, won't it? I mean they're not two-a-penny, y'know, not up Pompey way anyroads."

"But they're nice." Eddie drew on his cigar again and slid a finger behind his shirt collar. The man whose mother had come from a sugar plantation on the outskirts of Cuba's Marianao district had prospered and prospered well. The white man's war as he called it was no business of his, except when they wanted to amuse themselves in between beating each other to death. And amuse themselves they did, on the playgrounds Eddie Bright provided.

Silk ties and shirts, hand stitched suits, heavy gold rings and his beloved Havanas were Eddie's way of enjoying himself. All that and little white girls. Eddie Bright had never forgotten the story of what the three Londoners had done to his mother when she was just sixteen and on the game in Stepney. They had savaged her mercilessly and apparently he had been the result. The white girls that paced the beats on Eddie's turf were his pay back for the past: it was their turn. They were there to be used until they were broken and worn when they would be discarded like a pair of old shoes.

Way back Eddie had told him this and the other means by which the big, mean half-caste fed his bitter resentment. Why he took it out on helpless white women when it was their menfolk he detested so much, Daley never asked. His own upbringing had taught him that there were certain things in life about which it was better to know nothing. He smiled. His new boss was having a good war, and he saw no reason to do anything other than exactly as he was told.

"I'll give yer a week, Mike." Eddie lifted a finger. "After that I'll need yer firing on all eight cylinders out there. Get to know the patch an' thy neighbours well, my son...but none of this loving 'em crap like the Good Book tells us to. Know the oppo, my boy, an' learn to handle the cars. "Yeah? Oh, and here." Eddie Bright lunged forward, picked a brown envelope off the desk then shuffled further forward in his chair to pass it across. "Summat to help yer feel at home, my son. Good ter see yer, man." Eddie held out a hand.

Kenny the Swede remained slouched against the wall with his hands thrust deep into his trouser pockets. Only his eyes moved as Mike left the room followed closely by his new-found friend, Ricky Hatch. He lifted his eyebrows, took a deep breath and blew slowly. Whether he liked it or not he was in with Eddie now, and here he would be staying - whether he liked it or not. Getting away from the man and his friends, he suspected, might be a touch difficult.

*

There were two rear view mirrors in the big Ford Pilot, one to see what was happening outside and one to see what was happening inside. Mike never turned round to look but kept close watch in the mirror least his attention was needed. Tonight, as his eyes moved between the mirror and the darkness in the street outside, he listened casually to the struggles and the muffled shrieks from behind the sliding glass partition. Sometimes, like tonight, the moans and cries were serious and they took his mind back to the worst of those burns at East Grinstead. Right now they were coming from the overweight and balding manager of the Naked Angel who Ricky Hatch had invited to join them and to whom he and the Swede were now devoting their energies. The whole car shook.

He grimaced, not at what was going on behind him but because twice this week already, when they had conducted similar meetings, it had been his lot to clean up the mess the following morning. On the first occasion it had been the damp patch on the back seat which had stunk of urine and worse but, on the second, there had been blood, and lots of it. On the floor, right underneath his driver's seat, were the remains of three fingernails the Swede had eased from their last visitor.

But it was a job and Eddie was a good boss. It would be Christmas soon and Eddie wanted him to work right through the New Year. Plymouth, he said, would be jumping. The war had moved on to Belgium and they'd sunk the Tirpitz. There was a buzz in the air and they were going to have to hurry, he claimed, or it would all be over. And when it was, Eddie told them, life would become far more difficult.

*

Becky would have to wait. He had tried not to think of her and at first it had been difficult but then work had begun in earnest and there had been big Anna, the squeezy blonde with the body who did the drinks in Leg's Eleven. It was Eddie's favourite bar and whenever Mike was inside with his boss it had been she who had made all the running. All the same he wanted Becky. In spite of the fact that she might be a drag on his freedom, he wanted her to be there ready for him. But it was little Maudie he missed most. He had it in mind to

188

get up to Exford when time allowed and he would, but it would be a couple of months or so and they would have to wait.

*

The glass partition behind him slid back. "The Hoe." It was Kenny the Swede but the man beside him was still struggling and the Swede had to raise his voice. "Get us right down to the bathing pools on the front...*Madeira Road. Yah?*" Mike nodded and slipped the big car into gear then waited for Kenny to join him in the front. The driver on his own with three in the back at this time of night would only raise eyebrows.

"All be coming back home again, will we Kenny?" Mike gunned the engine gently and pulled out, turning into Phoenix Street then out and onto the wider Citadel Road. Although he and the mechanics at Mason's had opened the apertures as far as they dared, the narrow strips of light from the shielded headlamps barely shone to the ground.

"Yah." The Swede nodded slowly. "But first haf to show him what the bottom of a pool is like...then on to the City Hospital. We leave him there, this time."

"Oh aye. Bad is he?" Once on the open road the big engine growled hungrily.

"No, not really." Kenny reached out and clutched the dashboard. "Hell, man...slow *down*. Hey...*hey*, slow, for Jaysus Christ's sake."

 Daley slowed as bidden, quietly satisfied at his passenger's discomfort. He didn't care for the Swede anyway but he wanted him to see how a car should be driven. He wanted to show him that he knew the car and the roads like he did, and that he could handle them both in the dark. Eddie's right hand man might not like him, and he didn't, but he needed to get the message that the best drivers, those like Mike Daley, were hard to come by.

2.

It was sometime after Christmas that Sam made up his mind about Becky. He had seen her several times since the family Carol Service but it was there, when she had come in with her father and the child and had sat in the pew a few rows in front of them, that he realised she had been left on her own. He had spoken to her briefly after the service when there had been mince pies and mulled cider in the village hall and, even then, she had hinted at despairing over Mike Daley's continued absence.

January had been cold, on occasions too cold for snow, but towards the end of the month the blizzard swept in from the north-east out beyond Dunkery Beacon. His father had seen it coming. Before it struck he had spoken about the flocks of fieldfares and redwings in the fields below the roots and signs of where foxes or badgers had tried to get at the hens. Hunting had stopped. The snow had drifted across most gateways and the ground from where it had been blown clear, was bone hard. Deer had come in from the moors and onto the roots.

Eventually the weather changed but only after they had used most of the hay in the Dutch barn. Today Sam had wanted to help his father open the last of the root clamps but had gone down to the forge instead, taking the two farm horses and his mother's hunter to be re-shod. It was crowded and he had time on his hands so he decided to call in on Myrtle Cottage.

Doris had welcomed him warmly, chiding him for not coming sooner, before chattering away about the rationing and the weather. But it had not been long before she claimed she had to go out, leaving him and Becky to talk and with instructions for her daughter to get their dinner. Sam, she insisted, must stay also. Becky had seemed quiet at first but appeared more relaxed after she had changed Maudie, leaving her visitor to slice the carrots and potatoes that were to go in with the rabbit.

*

Talk turned to themselves and when he mentioned Mike Daley he thought she might find it difficult to continue but it was she who had done so. It had been almost four months, she told him, since he had left and there had been only the one letter and a parcel of knitted woollens for the baby. "Sometimes I wonder if I'll ever see him again," she mused. "All the talk about coming back at Christmas an' that. A load of old rot that was." She smiled self-consciously at Sam and shrugged. "Sometimes I reckon I've bin a right sucker. Waiting fer this an' hoping fer that...I dunno."

"Hardly your fault, maid." Sam wiped his wet hands on his breeches. "Daresay he's gone off an' found work an'...."

"And another girl, mm?" Becky looked up. She was chopping an onion and wiped her eye with her sleeve. What she had just said was more of a statement than a question.

"D'yer reckon?" Sam sat beside her. "Thought he was s'posed to be over the moon with you an' Maudie."

"*Poof.*" This time she sighed heavily. "Precious little moon these last four months," she observed drily. "All talk, I reckon...all blooming talk. Back with his friends and the bright lights an'...well, there we are. I've bin a right stupid fool. You should hear mother carryin' on."

"So what d'yer reckon then?" Sam caught his breath. "Still fond of him are yer, I mean like you were?"

She laughed bitterly. "And a right bloody idiot I were at that," she exclaimed.

190

Cuh...made a right scene of it all, didn't I just."

Sam wanted to agree with her. He had it in mind to tell her that he and every-body else had told her so but it would have done no good. She was hurt, he could see that. In spite of the brave words, she had been cut to the quick and the tears were there behind the remorse. One harsh word or a remark that might be taken wrongly would break her. Slowly, in case she wanted to draw back, he put his hand on hers. She froze but let it stay. "That's over, Becks," he whispered, bending down to look into her face. "Honest to God, it's finished...an' you're nobody's fool."

He watched as she nodded, then picked up her hand and held it in both of his. "Mustn't get like that, maid...can't have yer all maudlin' about what's done." He paused, trying to pick his words, sensing that she knew what he was going to say. "I'm here, y'know," he added, rubbing her hands gently. "Maybe I'm no man about town nor nuthin but, well...us've known each other fer years now."

She looked down and away, startled as if it was the first time he had said anything like this. But it wasn't. She had heard it before, many times, but not since Mike Daley had come and gone before Christmas, when word was out that she had rejected Sam Carter once more. And she had, of course, yet here he was again. In spite of everything, he must still think highly of her. His concern and the way he stood by her made her feel guilty and ashamed of turning her back on this decent and compassionate man.

"I know," she whispered unable to find words for what she wanted to say. "You've bin very good to me, Sam. I never deserved all this. Honest." She looked at him. "Reelly," she stressed. "I've never deserved nuthin' like this."

"Well." Sam hesitated. "Maybe us can try agin. See if us can't put it all be'ind, an' look to what's ahead."

"Yes," she murmured. "P'raps we can." She so wanted not to upset him but there, lingering deep down, was the longing to see the father of her child again, the one whose promises she had so innocently and naively clung on to. "I'll try, reelly I will." She looked at him and smiled affectionately, her eyes searching his. "I *will* try...it just takes time, that's all."

"I know," he soothed. "So long as you're happy, then I'm happy too." He squeezed her hand, then stood and pulled her to her feet. "Every time I'm here with you, maid, I'm happy as can be. Honest." He lifted her face and kissed her softly. She tried to respond but it was difficult.

✳

The letter from Plymouth came the following Monday. When it arrived, it was lost in the middle of a bundle of back-mail that had been tied together with string and kept in the Dulverton sorting office until the postmen could get through. Her father had come down earlier but had left the bundle to open when he returned.

Becky read it once, then again immediately, sitting at the table and scarcely able to take in what it said. It was only when her mother started down the stairs that she looked up in panic and thrust the letter down her blouse. She excused herself, ran upstairs and read it again, this time by the window in her room, holding it with both hands to stop the paper shaking. Her heart was thumping and her mouth moving, mouthing the words silently as she read it yet again.

He was fine, he said. The job was brilliant and he had a car. Plymouth was a wonderful place. Although it had been bombed badly, the blackout had been partly lifted and there was dancing on the Hoe every Sunday afternoon. His pay was good and he had found somewhere for them to live. The folks he was with were fun and he knew she would like them. He would be coming up for her the last weekend of the month. He would book in at the White Horse and she should come to see him late on Friday 26th March when they would make a plan. She should, he told her, be ready to leave but best not to say a word to anyone, not yet anyway.

Becky shut her eyes and lowered her head, pressing the letter against her breast. She clenched her fists and shook with excitement. He was *coming*...coming for her at last. It was *wonderful, wonderful* news. And so soon, too. The twenty-sixth was little more than a week away but then the letter had been held up in the post. Yes, my love, she whispered to herself. Oh yes, she would be ready. Oh, dear God, oh yes, she would be ready.

3.

Rose sat at her father's bedside. The last few days had been terrible and they had all been expecting another stroke. But when Dr McKinney came he pronounced himself puzzled, suggesting that Hestor Barclay should go into hospital for some tests. Hestor Barclay refused. He had been quite all right until the weekend and, in any case, Harry, his sister's boy, was coming with that chum of his for a couple of day's hunting.

Harry Maidstone of the 17th/21st Lancers was the son Hestor Barclay never had. Tall, uncommonly slim and with fair, wavy hair, Harry had been wounded at Caen while serving with Montgomery's headquarters. As soon as his left leg had been repaired, he was posted to Bovington as an instructor where the bracing air and regular beagling completed what the doctors had begun. His uncle had doted on him ever since he was knee high, but a close relationship had been forged from the time they went down to Sherborne for Harry's first term. It was Hestor's old school. Much later, after Harry had joined his regiment, his uncle announced that whenever he was allowed to escape, Duxhams was to be his hunting lodge.

Captain Harry Maidstone was due to arrive sometime late Tuesday afternoon and Hestor Barclay was damned if he was going to miss the fun. The house party was to go ahead. Rose was delighted for she, too, adored her cousin. Although several years older she had gone to his final speech day at Sherborne and attended his commissioning parade a year later. It had been she who had driven her father to see Harry in hospital, and it was there that they met Harry's great friend 'Spiffy' Foxley of The Light Dragoons.

The two had been at Sandhurst together where they boxed and played rugger for their college. In between, and whenever meagre funds permitted, they and others disappeared to sample whatever the less reputable side of London life had to offer. If Harry Maidstone was tall, Spiffy Foxley was short. Where one was slim and blond, the other was stout and dark, and where Harry tended to drawl languidly, Spiffy made a noise. The week ahead, Rose predicted, would be a lively affair and she sympathised with her father's refusal to be absent.

＊

Rose glanced around the oval dining table. In spite of them dressing for dinner it was a casual affair. Miles Ashcroft had joined them the night before so he could hunt with them and Spiffy had brought his girl friend, making the party just six in all.

She had put her father at the far end with Harry on one side and Annabel Smith-Wise the other. She, Rose thought, was a funny little thing with a pretty face under a mass of fair curls, who certainly knew how to ride. Spiffy thought the world of her and Harry had intimated quietly that wedding bells might not be far away. Be that as it may, she had separated them for this part of the evening, putting Spiffy across the table and opposite Miles. And she had separated them later as well. However the young lovers might anticipate spending the night was none of her business, but Mrs Crowcombe had put the two men together in the twin bedded spare room on the second floor. Any reorganisation would be up to them.

She had warned Annabel that they were not going to leave the men to sit it out when Clements announced coffee. There were only the two of them and she refused point blank to be shunted off to wait demurely in the drawing room for the gods to reappear and honour them with their presence. And, in any case, she liked a glass of port herself and had, over the years, developed a penchant for her father's Dominican cheroots.

The day had gone well with the stag running hard across Anstey Common before turning north to Willingford and then on to Landacre. They had been expecting a long chase out over the Forest but the deer had doubled back into the Barle valley where they killed just below Tarr Steps. Talk at the table had been about news of the war, then of the hunt and who had done what. Now, with the port circulating, conversation turned to the future.

"You're missed, you know." Harry made the announcement exactly as the room fell silent. He had just bitten into his cigar and was still removing the debris from his mouth. "Honestly, Rose...you both are. You, sir, as well." He nodded across to her father. "You may as well know that I've been sent on a mission this evening," he joked. "Jamie Upton and the Blackfords...*and* the Incletons, they all told me to find out what was going on down here and when they might expect to see you again."

"Too bloody late." Hestor Barclay studied his port. "I'm dug in now and damned if I'm going to move again. If they want to see me then they can come and have a look...get themselves down here before I turn me toes up."

"We're here to stay," Rose added, glancing at Harry. "It's totally different to Surrey...*totally*, and I love it."

"But there's nobody here." Spiffy Foxley leant back, looking around the table with one arm over the back of his chair. "Take today for instance...the staghounds met at Dulverton. Right? And you can't get a more central meet than that. And look at the field. Who's there, for God's sake? Forty...fifty?" His eyes lingered on Rose. Her full-length, scarlet silk dress suited her black hair and, holding her cheroot like she did gave her something of a wild, bohemian look. She was, he considered, wasted by tucking herself away down here.

"Well, there's a war on, don't forget." Miles Ashcroft leant forward. He had been listening quietly, occasionally fiddling with his bow tie. "Not many young about, just now. Travelling around the country's none too easy either, and money's tight as hell." He pulled a gloomy face. "We manage to get by though, have our bit of fun...it's just a question of hanging on until the damned thing's over and done with. Ah well." He sipped his brandy thoughtfully. "We're over the Rhine now, two weeks ago in fact, and news from the Far East's good so, pray God it won't be long."

"But even when it is, even when everyone's home and things're, well, the same as before, it's still going to be pretty damned quiet down here." Harry turned to Rose. "There's nothing much to get excited about, apart from the hunting and fishing."

"Doesn't worry me a bit...really it doesn't." Rose grinned, shaking her head. "All that we were talking about earlier's now in the past. It's gone, Harry...honestly. Since Douggie went a sort of line has been drawn...."

"Not hiding away from it all?" It was Harry again.

"No, not at all." She shook her head vigorously. "It was a bit difficult at first, course it was. A little strange but then I suddenly woke up and realised there was more to life...didn't I, daddy?"

"I'll second that." Hestor Barclay looked up quickly as though her question had just woken him. "Yes, you certainly did, m'dear. Hadn't been for you we'd still be back at Scammell's wondering what to do with ourselves."

"But what about *people?*" Spiffy Foxley looked anxious. "I mean, you've got to have people about...chums, an' that sort of thing."

"They're here." Rose could feel the conversation moving towards her own situation. She thought she had got used to it but it still rankled no matter how well intentioned it was. Everybody seemed hell bent on pairing her off again. "There're some wonderful people around...local people who're not dashing about the place all the time."

"Like that farmer chappie we met this morning...what's his name?"

"Sam? Sam Hawkins?"

"Yes, he's the one. Well, Lord, all right, but you can do a bit better than *him.* I mean, he's a nice enough fellow an' all that but pretty limited. I mean...take him away from his farm...his sheep an' all that and he'd be lost...couldn't cope."

Miles Ashcroft looked from one to the other. Rose, he noticed, had stiffened. It was Barbara Hawkins who had told him that she had come out to Hayes to see Sam. He had thought nothing of it but now he wasn't so sure and that tilt at Sam had hit home. Why, he wondered. Something there, perhaps? Stranger things had happened. Her father, he could see, was oblivious to the fact. Happy enough with his port and cheroot, Hestor Barclay was listening keenly as the young parried with one another.

"Don't be such a snob, Spiffy." Annabel had joined them. "Honestly, what's wrong with the man? I thought he was charming. *Very* sweet...and he was beautifully mounted."

"No, it's nothing to do with being snobbish."

"It jolly well is."

"No...look, hang on." He held up a hand. "Don't get on at me like that. It's just that Rose needs good company. She needs, well, the same sort...."

"A well bred *chap*, you mean. Public school and all that."

"Sam Hawkins's a fine young fella." Miles Ashcroft's deep, drawl silenced the table. "Lovely parents....I've known his mother since she was in white socks. And there's damned near five hundred acres of farm behind him as well...an' that's big for down here." Even as he spoke he could see Rose relaxing. He thought he might even have caught the hint of a smile. If there was anything there it was difficult to tell but the conversation had gone far enough and she was being boxed in.

195

It was not their fault, they couldn't see it. They couldn't understand why she had run from everything that was now being demonstrated around the table. But run she had, and it didn't look as though she was going to run back. He pulled on his chin thoughtfully. Perhaps young Sam might be right for her after all. And why not? But then he was caught up in this other business over Becky Carter that he had heard about. And she, poor girl, was in one hell of a pickle with this child of hers.

"Right, away you go, girls. Lead on." It was Hestor Barclay. Dinner, he had decided, was over. "And you young fellas as well. Off yer go. Clements'll want to clear away." Miles Ashcroft's eyes followed the young. Rose had recovered but he doubted that she had forgotten what had been said. He had seen her smart, one of them had touched a nerve. Sam Hawkins was a very good lad but he wouldn't have had a hope in here this evening with this lot. He would have been way, way out of his depth, wouldn't have got inside the door even. But the man had something about him, my goodness he had. And this was Exmoor, and Rose looked set to stay.

"C'mon, lad." Hestor Barclay put his hand on Ashcroft's shoulder. "Reckon they know it all, that lot. Eh?"

"And we were just as bad…well you were." Miles Ashcroft grinned and led the way through.

4.

Sam had no idea about Becky's letter from Plymouth but he very soon sensed that something had changed. As usual, when he was down in the village, he called in at the cottage. He knew she was there because he had seen her walking home when he was waiting at Bawden's garage. He knocked as he always did; he wouldn't have done anything else. But then he opened the door and called out.

Becky was ironing. At first he thought she was concentrating on what she was doing but she barely looked up, even when he had ducked inside and shut the door behind him. And even after she'd finished one piece and was reaching for another she avoided him. It had certainly been a quiet welcome but perhaps that was something to do with the ironing. He tried again, asking about Maudie but she was still non-committal. Eventually he stopped, deciding to give her a chance to say something. But she didn't, even when she swung the basket of ironing onto her hip and glanced at him on her way through to the kitchen.

"What's up, Becks? Summat's wrong this morning, isn't there?"

"No, nuthin'… I'm fine." The answer came too quickly and it was glib, discouraging any reply. Something was wrong and Sam waited but, again, she had nothing to say.

196

"Hey…c'mon," he urged. "Not tellin' me that something's not gone amiss. C'mon, Becks." He walked towards her but stopped when she moved away. "Hey, what is it?" he demanded.

"Nothing, Sam. Nothing at all. I just don't feel like talking much today, that's all."

"Well, thanks fer that." He watched as she shrugged at his reply. "Well, all right then but don't 'spect me ter keep dropping by if that's how yer goin' ter feel about it."

"Well don't then." The words had slipped out easily. She knew she shouldn't have spoken like that but it was too late."

"What the bloody hell's the matter with you then? Eh? What've I done to get all this from yer?" Sam's voice had risen. "Summat's up, that's fer sure. That Daley fella again is it? Eh? Bin knocking at the door sniffin' again has he?" He paused, now angry. "Oh aye, that's it then, isn't it? That fella's bin back…a right smart arse, he is."

"Smart arse yerself, Sam Hawkins." Now Becky's voice was raised. "If yer have to know he hasn't bin back…an' if yer have ter know 'e's a good man is Mike Daley…..an' a brave one at that."

"'Ere…I'm not stopping here just to take this." Sam picked up his cap and went to the door. He half opened it and then turned. "If that man Daley's be'ind all this." He was pointing at her. "Then good luck to yer, that's what I say. But don't expect me to stop by an'pick up the pieces when 'e's made a mess of yer next time. 'E's done it once an' he'll do it again. Mark my words."

"I'll mark nuthin…not from you and not from anyone. I'll…." But the door had slammed shut and she watched through the window as he strode purposefully on his way.

Chapter Fifteen

Becky turned away suddenly but Mike caught hold of her arm before she could reach the door and pulled her back to him. "Take your time, Becks." For a moment the two stood there, she staring wide-eyed at the carpet in front of her, he searching her face anxiously. "Nothing daft now," he murmured, taking her into his arms. She nodded, leaning away from him and still avoiding his eyes. "Just go back an' say you've been seeing some friends...then wait till they've gone up for the night. Right?" He paused, still watching her face. "C'mon love, we're going to be fine...think about it, think of us. We're going to be together...for always...you an' me an' Maudie. An' there'll be more, all of us together. Mister and Missus Daley...eh? How's about that, then? An' all in a place of our own."

"Really? D'you mean that?"

"Course...what d'yer think I'm here for. Eh?"

"That'd be nice...yes...be luverly." She smiled, opening her eyes at the thought, her imagination caught briefly by what had been said. But then she nodded sombrely. "Yes, it would...but it's just that...oh, it seems so cruel and hard, running out on 'em like this. They've bin good to me, Mike. Not like they nuns at Taunton. That were different, this is mum an' dad an' it just seems I'm cheatin' them, that's all."

"Shhh, *look*. It's not as though you're going fer good, nor nuthin. It's just easier this way an' there won't be any arguing nor shoutin'. An' it's better this way for them an' all. You'll be *back*, course yer will. Give it a coupla months or summat...say June or the summer, like, an' yer can come up and say hello." He kissed her on the top of her head. "Off yer go," he whispered. "Soon as everything's quiet get back here. I'll be waiting downstairs, in the lobby. I'll put you an' Maudie in the car then go an' get your cases...simple."

"All right." Becky squeezed his hand, then stood on tiptoe and kissed him gently. "See you later."

*

Mike Daley had arrived earlier than he said and remained in his room until after dark when he had gone down and waited for Becky. The hallway of the White Horse had been busy until around nine when she had come, just as it was getting dark. Earlier it had been raining and a wind had got up. As she came through the door, a strong gust blew at her, swirling her coat and making her grab hurriedly at her headscarf.

He saw at once that she was uneasy and they talked in urgent whispers. It wasn't that she didn't want to go, she told him later with her arms around his neck. It was the wrench of leaving home just as she was getting settled. They sat on the bed together, he with an arm around her shoulders encouraging her with stories of Plymouth and who they would meet.

Becky asked him about a cot for Maudie, and a pram and where she might find baby clothes and nappies, and if he was happy about finding the money. She was worried about the journey, she told him, and whether the child would settle in a strange house. Maudie was barely six months old and had never left home before. She should have been alerted by the way he answered her and by his touchiness at her questions. But she wasn't. She merely nodded in reply to whatever answers he gave.

It was only then, when she went to the door to leave his room that she realised exactly what she was doing. Up to that moment she had been too excited and nervous to think clearly. Thoughts on leaving Myrtle Cottage with her parents asleep upstairs as she crept away like a sneak thief, weighed heavily. She kept imagining their faces when they woke to find her and Maudie gone, imagining first their grief then their bitterness when they realised that she had left them without saying farewell. And she could imagine their faces as they stood reading what she had said. Her letter, which she was going to leave on the table, would only make it worse and she knew it. She had written that she had gone with the man she loved, Maudie's father. She had gone because they needed each other and their child needed them both. There was not enough room in the cottage for all of them, she explained, and she had to start afresh. She realised that they, her parents, would never understand but they would have to believe her when she said that she loved them both, and would get in touch to let them know that she and her baby were well.

There had been tears in the bedroom but he had calmed her and helped her to think carefully before she returned to the cottage, where she would collect her child and wait for the night to settle. She gave him one final glance at the door, searching his face for the encouragement she needed. He smiled reassuringly, telling her to go on before catching hold of her arm like he did.

An hour later and it was done. He paid for his room, telling the girl that he would be leaving early next morning then waited for her. As soon as she and the child were in the car, he collected her cases from where she had left them and they were away while the village slept. Somewhere in the distance a dog barked but dawn was still a long way off.

2.

"Here we are, girl...The Ritz." Mike's feet came to a halt at the top of the narrow stairs in front of her and he lowered her cases. Then he turned. Becky and Maudie were three of four stairs behind and he had to look down and back into the gloom of the stairwell. "Not much, love," he warned, turning back and fiddling with the keys. "But we'll get it right d'rectly." Becky followed him into the room, her senses alive and alert to what her new home had to offer. Maudie was heavy. She could feel her mother's tension and struggled in her arms grizzling. "There we are look...a bit sparse, but not too bad."

Number 27B Adelaide Street was cold, as cold as the sharp sea breeze that caught them when they walked across the road from where Mike parked the car. The place was damp, Becky could smell it, and what lights that worked were dim as she tried them one at a time. The kitchen was soulless. Someone had tried to clean the stone sink but the plug had gone and she could tell by the marks in the cupboard underneath that the drain leaked. There was hardly any coal in the hessian sack by the little black range but the coalman would be coming tomorrow, Mike assured her. He always came early and left the sack for 27B in the basement, three stories below. Becky lifted the catch to the oven and saw the rust. The ash can was full but there was no kindling for the fire, just a few old newspapers. She prodded disconsolately with the toe of her shoe at the bare linoleum by the sink, where the pattern had worn away.

Still in her long, shell-grey coat, she turned slowly. There was nowhere for the baby to go and the whimpers were getting louder. There was little to see from the bedroom window and only a cold tap in the washroom. The toilet, he explained, was shared with the dock worker and his family on the next floor down, and the saucepan on the boards behind the door was to catch the drip, but somebody was coming to fix it. She could see by the way the plaster had come away from the watermark on the ceiling that it had been like that for sometime.

Becky sat on the bed, shushing the child and rocking her gently. Suddenly, in that short time, her hopes had crashed. Everything she saw was either broken or old or different. She had never been in a building this size, let alone lived above the ground and already she felt trapped. Spending what little money she had saved on having her hair done in Dulverton two days ago now seemed madness. Even as she ran her hand through the waves, it felt untidy where her head had lolled against the back of the car seat. And there was Maudie. Tongue-tied and with her tired mind racing and stumbling, Becky stared down at her shoes.

"A bit bare, I know." Mike tried to grin cheerfully but the smile faded. "What's up, then? We're here, ain't we?"

"But there's nothing, Mike." She shook her head despondently. "Nothing for Maudie. Where'm I going to put her? Mmm?" Now their eyes met. "Where's she going to sleep?" Becky sat the baby in her lap. "And it's cold...freezing. Where's...where's the food and everything? There's nothing here."

" 'Ere, hang on. That's your job...an' y'know it." His hands were on his hips. "I brought you down 'ere so we can run the place together. Right? That was it, wasn't it? I go out to work an' you run the house. C'mon, now. Look, 'ere's some dosh, right...should be enough." Becky looked at the notes on the bed.

"I'll need more," she whispered, glancing up at him apologetically. "Honestly. There's barely enough here for food. There's things to get an' there's Maudie, don't forget. She needs her own food now as well, and we've got to find somewhere to put her." She saw his face. "I can't help it, Mike. Look at her. She's sitting up already and she'll be crawling soon…she's growing. And don't look like that," she complained. "I can't help it. She's one of us…we've got to think of her."

Both turned at the sound of feet on the stairs. Mike went to the door and she watched his back as he spoke hurriedly. She could tell that he knew whoever it was and that the visitor was after something. Mike was remonstrating with him. As he spoke, he raised his arms and shrugged but eventually they came to an agreement and the man left. Mike watched him go then shut the door. She heard him click the lock into place. When he turned back she saw his concern. "Who was it?" she asked.

"The boss. Eddie's sent word for me. He wants me, needs me quick."

"But Mike you can't…."

"I know, I know." His hands were raised. "Said he needs me but I told 'em we've bin driving all night and to give me a coupla hours. Rick, that was his man, said he would see," he added. "But he needs me later…*Jeez*." She saw his frustration and watched as he ran his hands through his hair. She moved over to make room for him on the bed but he stayed where he was. "Right then…now listen. Money's tight. OK?" He was scratching his head and frowning. "Just now, that is. We're going to have to go easy fer a while…."

"But we've got to *eat*, Mike…and sleep, for God's sake."

"I know, I *know*," he shouted. "Don't keep on at me, right. Here's three quid look." He picked up the notes on the bed then stood and reached for his wallet. "I can let yer have another two…that's five for Christ's sake. More'n me bleedin' wages." But then he stopped, still holding the notes. Becky's head was in her hands and he watched as her body shook. "Oh, c'mon fer God's sake, don't start on that bleedin' lark."

"I can't help it," she sobbed, leaning towards him for support but he moved away and she fell sideways on to the bed. "Oh God," she wept. "I can't help it…it's awful…I can't."

"C'mon, Becks…c'mon, we'll be all right," he soothed. He had been standing watching, his mind struggling but now he was sitting beside her, one hand rubbing the back of her neck. Eddie Bright wanted him and he had to go but he couldn't just walk out, leaving her and their child like this. Outside the shops and market were opening. The city was coming to life but so was Eddie Bright, and he knew his man.

They thought it would take them an hour but it took them three, and three times Becky had to toil up the steep, dark stairs with heavy bags, twice with Maudie in one arm. After the second time they settled her into the deepest of the drawers from the chipped pine chest in the kitchen. They placed it by the bed and cut pieces from one of the blankets for the mattress and pillow, then folded a sheet to protect her from the sharp edges. Becky fed her then tried to settle her but she began to cry, which turned to screams when they tried to leave. Her mother hesitated, agonising over whether to go or not but Mike pulled her away.

She was asleep on her back when they returned with some groceries but woke when Mike tried to light the range. The chimney was damp and the fire took time to draw, filling the apartment with the heavy, dark smoke of mouldy paper, so they had to open a window. The only one that would move was the one in the bedroom and then only when Mike hammered at it angrily causing Maudie to cry.

He left at midday but before he did he took her to the window and showed her the women who were loitering along Adelaide Place and outside the club in Rendle Street. At first Becky had no idea but, as they watched, a man approached one of the girls near the corner. Now she stared in horror. Never wander about like that, Mike warned her. Always go straight out and back to the shops or wherever and never, ever go out alone after dark. Before he left he told her not to wait up for him. Keep the door locked, he told her. He had his own keys and she should never open it to anyone. Did she understand, he queried time and again. Was she sure she understood? It was different down here, not the same as up in Exford, he explained, kissing her briefly as he left.

3.

"We've *what? Won?*" Becky stared at the man. Ollie Shanks, who had been running his fruit stall in the open at Octagen Circus ever since his shop was bombed, always smiled at the new girl with the shapely figure and bedroom eyes. But today he was beaming and chuckling with delight, his apple-pink cheeks, edged with thick, black sideburns, were positively shining. What little hair he had left was slicked back as usual. As soon as he saw her puzzled frown, he jumped down from his box behind his rows of fruit, rubbing his hands on his striped apron.

"That's right, love. We've won…yeah, won the bleedin' war. Beaten the buggers at last. *Beaten' 'em.* On the wireless it was….special news. It's gen…straight up. *Hey, hey,*" he shouted across to another vendor. "Party tonight, Fred, mate. Everyone'll be there…up the City Centre and on The Hoe. Drinks, dancin', singalong…you name it, pal." Ollie turned back. "Bloody marvellous, eh darlin'." He winked cheekily. "Here you are, luv. Take 'em. Go on…real English apples. Go on…'ave 'em on me." He pressed the paper bag into her hands. "Take care 'o yerself, sweetheart. *Watcha, Jimmy,*" he called out, looking up again. "Bloody marvellous, ain't it, eh?"

All around her people were shouting out the news. It was victory at last…news had come through that the Germans had surrendered. The war in Europe was over and the boys would be coming home. Becky walked slowly back along Union Street. People were pouring out of their homes. Everyone was smiling and laughing. It was barely midday but, already, the pubs and bars were opening. Taxis were sounding their horns; as they went past, people were sitting on car bonnets while others, at least a dozen, were dancing on the back of a lorry.

Even as she watched, bunting and flags were appearing from windows. From the harbour and docks came the sound of ships' sirens whooping and blaring. Somebody grabbed her and kissed her. Whistles were blowing and windows opening: children were running about madly. Everywhere people who had never seen each other were shaking hands and smiling, hugging each other and dancing jigs.

Mike was at work. He had left early, as usual leaving her alone for the day. She had tidied the house and put Maudie down before coming out to do the shopping. Then, suddenly, there was this. It was as if a great heavy lid of gloom and uncertainty had been lifted and everything was bubbling and frothing happily. The cheer she saw now was for real. People, everywhere, were jumping about, grabbing hold of one another and shouting with delight.

*

Later, she felt she had to get out again. She shut the street door of the apartment behind her and looked about. Adelaide Street had quietened but further away, beyond the Octagen and towards the city centre she could hear the sound of music and car horns. The apartment, when she returned earlier with the shopping, had seemed tomblike after the noise and excitement outside. Even when she forced open the bedroom window and leaned out it was strangely quiet, as though she was in a different place. Somewhere beyond the rows of chimneys she could hear a distant buzz but it was nothing.

In fact it was worse than nothing: it made her feel lonely and miserable again. Shut away up there she felt the loneliest person in the world and out of it all. No matter how she tried to bolster her spirits, she remained dull and depressed, just as she had been since arriving in Plymouth. In spite of everything going on today, she felt trapped and melancholy even when she realised it meant that Jack, her brother, would be coming home.

Thinking of Jack turned her thoughts to home and she tried to imagine how the news would be received there. After her cowardly and deceitful departure, her mother and father would be happy at last. She often wondered what they must have thought of her leaving like she did. Every time she saw them in her mind their faces stared back puzzled and angry. And who could blame them for it had all been due to her. But now, today, it would be different. They would be smiling cheerfully. Perhaps they had received a letter from Jack? Perhaps he was home already and they were sitting together in the parlour listening to his adventures. Friends would be calling in to see him, laughing and chatting away and she, at last, would be pushed out of their minds. They would be able to forget about her and the trouble she had caused.

She tried to visualise them all at the village hall. Up there they would have music and dancing just like there used to be but now they would be singing with joy. Everybody would be there – Pat and Mavis, the landgirls and the others from Daddy Warren's garden. The Chuggs and the Thornes and Sam. Yes, he would be there, of course, and she wondered for the hundredth time what he must have thought of her departure. He had been so loyal, so steady, kind and generous, but he had been hurt, deeply hurt by what she had done and she felt the sudden stab of guilt and shame as it drove through her. Everybody would be there, everybody that is except her, and they, too, would have forgotten about her.

Mike had told her never to go out and walk the streets alone. She knew why, but today was different. The city was wild with excitement, even the narrowest and darkest alleyway seemed to be buzzing merrily and held no fears. For once, the tense coldness of where the women carried out their business had gone. It would be safe and it had to be for she was desperate to escape the solitude of the apartment which now, more than ever, had become a prison. It was worse even than St Margaret's. Even if she knew nobody at all, she would be able to borrow a little of their happiness and laughter to help cheer her spirits.

At the bottom of Phoenix Street, just where they had filled in the bomb craters and where they used to queue for water outside the newsagents, she turned into Millbay Road and followed the tramlines. She had planned to go further along to the docks where more crowds had gathered but she turned away instead. She never knew what made her turn up Bath Lane but she did nonetheless, glancing away shyly from the sullen glares of the two women talking together by the lamppost.

Stepping into the cobbled street to go round a pile of rubbish on the pavement, she saw another girl ahead of her and quickened her pace to avoid the curse that would be coming her way. Even from the back she seemed younger than the others and, in spite of her high heels and tight black skirt, she looked short and trim. Her red hair had been cut neatly. Averting her gaze as she drew level, Becky stumbled on the cobbles causing the girl to turn.

Their eyes met and Becky froze. She watched, spellbound and unable to move as the other girl's eyes grew wider before her face broke into a smile. It was the same strange, lopsided smile of the harelip she remembered. Becky threw her arms into the air and whooped with delight. It was Daisy, the same little Daisy Gunn who had helped her to escape.

*

Daisy came round the next morning as she promised she would. Becky had asked Mike if he knew of her but he denied all knowledge. The girls, he told her, were nothing to do with him. His job was to look after Eddie and drive, nothing more.

By now Becky had grown wary and suspicious of this Eddie Bright. She had not yet met the man, seen him even, but she could tell from the way Mike and the others reacted that he had a hard grip on them all. There was something sinister about him that made the others so wary and Mike, she was sure, was not telling her everything. She was certain that there were other things going on that involved Mike but about which he was unwilling to talk.

Daisy loved Maudie. The last time she had seen her was at St Margaret's and for half an hour at least Becky had to watch as she played with the child. It was Daisy who mashed the boiled vegetables together then mixed the powdered milk and waited until it cooled before churning it all up together and feeding her. And it was she who insisted on rocking her to sleep while Becky sat quietly in the darkened room. Once settled, the two crept into the kitchen and closed the door. There was so much to say and the two sat facing one another, one on the only chair, the other on the stool. Their hands were clasped tightly together and every so often they would giggle helplessly trying hard not to make a noise. Or else they would stare silently and sadly at each other when the news or memory was bad.

"But why?" Becky asked yet again. "After all that trouble you took in getting away, what on earth made you come back to this…selling your body?"

"No option," she whispered, coughing again. Becky had noticed the rattling cough earlier and Daisy caught her frown. "Don't worry…only frogs," she grinned and coughed once more. "Police an' the nick were looking fer me up there, weren't they? They an' all that convent lot weren't too happy wiv me neither, so I couldn't get a job in the High Street could I, eh? Couldn't wander about sayin' 'Hi' folks, I'm Daisy Gunn. Got 'nything going?'"

Becky looked down trying to imagine the decision that had to be made. Her head was shaking slowly in wonder. "But *you*, Daisy. You're so young to be doing this. It must have been dreadful going back…there must be something else."

"What tea-leafin'…breakin' and enterin an' that?" she queried. "Nah. Didn't want to know me up there. Got somebody else. Said they were better, but I bet they weren't. Nobody's got fingers like me." Daisy paused, opening and closing her fingers like a pianist. "Not so easy findin' a job like that." She laughed suddenly but broke into another wheezing cough. "An' being on the game? Floggin' meself down here? Nah," she shrugged. "Get used to it after a while…one geezer's the same as the next."

"But isn't it …don't you feel used? Men's dirty, sweaty bodies all over you and pushing themselves onto you…using you and doing things like…I mean, I couldn't…couldn't." Becky shuddered.

"Could if you were starving and freezin', and nowhere to go, I can tell yer. When it's that or snuffin' it in some shop doorway. When you're so bleedin' desp'rate for warmth an' grub that you'd kill fer it…then you'd use yer body. You'd use anything."

Becky's eyes opened and she caught hold of Daisy's hand again. "Sorry," she whispered. "God I'm sorry. Never thought of it like that. I mean, I…most women, we've got no idea, haven't a clue what it must be like."

"Shhh." Daisy put a hand to Becky's face. "Don't worry, love, I'm fine. Honest. It's a job an' that's that, but listen, tell Mike to watch out fer that Swede…the long, skinny bleeder. Doesn't want to cross him. 'E watches all the money…eyes like a snake, 'e has." She paused, running her tongue around her teeth. "Does most of the other jobs as well. Goes out with Eddie."

"What d'you mean, other jobs?"

"Well, you know…*doin'* things, places an' that…shops an' warehouses an' that. Anywhere there's money or goods. Hey, c'mon Becks." Daisy slipped off the stool. "I must go…I'll be late."

"But wait." Becky put a hand on her arm. "Listen Daisy. If they're doing all that as well then why can't you be in there with them…doing what you're best at? Locks an' catches an' things? You're good, we know you are and anything to get away from what you're doing."

"Tried it, love," she shrugged sadly. "Told 'em what I could do, an' y'know what? They said you should never've got nicked. Can't be that good, they said. Getting nicked like that an' getting yerself sent down, you've gotta be bad." She laughed cynically. "Even went straight to Eddie, I did, an' told 'im. Know what 'e did? 'Ad me knickers off there an' then…right there in his office, over his desk.." She saw Becky's face. "Oh aye…'ad his wicked way an' said 'e'd think about it. Think about it, my arse. *Huh,* all 'e thought about was dippin' 'is wick. Watch 'im, too." Daisy turned from putting on her coat and raised a finger. "Right randy sod, 'e is. Good at it though," she laughed mischievously. "Knows how to handle hi'self."

As she opened the door to go, Becky put a finger to her lips. "'*Ere,*" Daisy whispered in her ear. "Let me see her again, just a quick peep," she pleaded. "Make sure she's still there." Becky watched as she tiptoed into the room and over to where the baby was sleeping before kneeling to see better.

"She's an angel, Becks. A real little treasure." Daisy had crept back out of the room. The door to the apartment was open and she was about to go. "Tell her I'll be back," she said softly. "Look after her now….an' you take care, love."

Becky's arms were around her and she felt Daisy's cheek against hers. "Remember what I said, now. Look out fer yerself." A hug and she had gone. Becky stood in the doorway watching and listening below until she heard the front door close.

4.

Money, if ever there was any out there, was like will o' the wisp. At first Mike just put off the things he was going to do or wanted to get. The little dark green Morris tourer he had seen could wait for a start, so could the cot and the pushchair for Maudie, and his new suit. Becky would have to do without her hair being all smart. Who was going to look at it anyway? And that went for her shoes and the make up that had begun to appear in the shops. They would have to wait, all of them.

The food was more difficult. Becky, he told her, would have to see what she could pick up. Search through the rejects and get what she could for free. Her friend Ollie Shanks down at the Octagen would be sure to help. Scrag ends and meat left on the bone were always going at Darwen's the butchers and it didn't matter if it was what they had set aside for the dogs. Use them, he told her. Bring them back and boil them; make a soup or a stew or something. Same with the bakers where there were always bits left over in the bin under the counter or out the back. It wouldn't be long, he promised. Eddie said that things were getting better. It was just for now.

But it led to rows until Becky no longer looked forward to his homecoming which got later and later, until she found herself woken by the sound of his keys in the lock. She became lonelier than she knew possible and began to miss her family and the tidy, neat life in Exford. Instead of the excitement and adventure that life in Plymouth had once promised, she now felt more depressed and frustrated than ever.

The first sinister worms of doubts crept slowly and inexorably into the back of her mind. Doubts about where she was and why, doubts about what she was doing. Yet she banished them, furious and ashamed for having allowed them to steal up on her like that. Mike needed her. The angrier and more quarrelsome he became, the harder she tried. Even when hands were raised in anger, even when she knew he was wrong and even when she saw the long blonde hairs on his collar and sensed the presence of another, she remained compliant and obliging to his ways. She did so because she loved him yet, deep within her and fuelled by these moments of doubt, her free spirit began to pace restlessly, pining for its life back in the wild.

Daisy came when she could and Becky began to count the hours before each visit. She always brought something for Maudie and would sit with the child while she hurried out to the shops, determined to get back to her friend as soon as she could. Shopping became an embarrassment when she put what change she had on the counter and let the person on the other side decide how much she could have. Occasionally she would haggle, watching the frowns and the heads shaking, and sometimes, when she was on her own in the shop, she would beg.

When the money ran out and she had the time, she would walk slowly towards the city centre pausing to gaze into shop windows or stop and watch other people buying the new goods that were beginning to appear. She saw chocolate and eggs, even bananas and oranges. She would look longingly at the nylons and the rayon underwear, the lipsticks, the eye makeup and powder puffs, all things about which she could only dream. But it was particularly hard when she came across things she needed for Maudie or when she saw a tie or a shirt that would suit Mike.

Mostly she and Daisy would sit and talk. In prison, Daisy had learned to knit and she knitted a romper suit for Maudie while Becky darned patches onto holes worn through their clothes. When it was time for Daisy to go, Becky found herself envying her friend's freedom. She would cling to her in the doorway, begging her to come again soon and to try and stay longer. Then, as soon as she heard the front door close with its echoing crash, her tears would come.

5.

The meeting in Eddie's office had gone well. Kenny the Swede would lead, they were told. Lennie Jenks, the safebreaker Eddie had brought down from Bristol especially for the job, would be with him and Mike Daley would drive. The second car with Ricky Hatch would go on ahead and wait. Jake Patterson, the squat little Scot who wore just a vest under his jacket, and two others would be with him.

Eddie would see them in the morning and hear about it then. "No shooters," he had warned, pointing directly at the Scot. It was the first Daley knew for certain that guns were sometimes taken and he breathed a sigh of relief there would be none out tonight. Guns made it all very different. People got scared and if anything went wrong the law came looking, and looking hard. Earlier in the year one of the Plympton gang had gone for the big drop at Winchester and he wanted none of it.

*

"All right then, Mike." Eddie Bright sat back in his chair and drew on his cigar. He had asked Daley to stay behind and they were alone together. Eddie's eyes closed as he let the cigar smoke drift out of his mouth. "Tell me, my son," he commanded quietly. "This little bit o' skirt you're on about…the doll with the nimble fingers. She's been banged up once already, y'know. Made a right mess of things…and now she's got a record as well. Not very clever is it?"

Mike watched him carefully. "Becky swears by her," he replied. Even now he

208

felt uneasy in Eddie Bright's presence. He had not mentioned a word about Daisy Gunn but somehow Eddie had got to hear about what Becky had told him. The man knew everything. It could have come from anywhere; someone who was in the room earlier, or from one of the girls outside, or from talk in one of the bars.

Eddie nodded thoughtfully. "Uh huh." The boss was looking out of the window. "All right," he murmured slowly, still deep in thought. "OK then. But, look. Say we tried her and things went wrong, eh? It'd be *you*, you my son, that I'd be coming to, an' you wouldn't be wanting for that, would you now? That wouldn't do, eh?" He swung back and looked at him. "How does that sound then? If you an' yours reckon that this Daisy Gunn's as sharp as that…an' she's *not*." His finger hit the desk. "Then I'll be coming round an' asking some awkward questions?"

"Fair enough, Eddie. If that's the way you want it…yeah, fair enough." Daley struggled for breath.

"I'm always fair enough, my son. You know me by now. *So*," he swept his hand across the desk. "Let's just say we'll give her a go. As a matter of fact I need an entry boy. Security's tight'ning everywhere. Too many nasty, hungry people out there, all sniffin about looking for easy pickings. I'm after findin' somebody what can get us in…open the place up then scarper. Lose himself…or herself, don't matter which. I'll give it some thought, my boy."

Eddie Bright rose and reached for his finely cut jacket. Daley had seen it earlier behind the door and had found himself admiring the scarlet lining. "Thanks, Mike. Oh, and by the way…that little number of yours you've got tucked away…Becky, ain't it? Yeah?" Eddie Bright cracked his knuckles. "I best come by one day an' say hello. Gotta know everyone down on the patch." He grinned, held the door open and drew heavily on his cigar. "Tell her I look forward to meeting her."

"Will do, Eddie."

✳

The party, as Eddie put it, had gone well, but only just. The keys they had taken to break into the back of the warehouse had not done the job and both Jake Patterson and Ricky Hatch had to force a window. It all took time and it made a noise. And it had been the same inside where the door to the manager's office had jammed. Once in, however, the safe breaker worked quickly and they were away within the hour.

As he drove them away, Daley listened as the Swede and Lennie Jenks went over the night's work. The fact that they were nearly caught trying to get in riled them, but it meant that Eddie would give Daisy Gunn her chance. And if she was good then Eddie would be pleased. It was after they had dropped the safe breaker and were on their way home that the Swede reached into his holdall. By then they were on their own and Mike watched out of the corner of his eye as the money was counted. "Here." The Swede dropped the bundle of notes into his lap.

"What's this, Kenny?" Daley slowed at the cross roads, checked then pulled out into Tavistock road. "Not for me is it?"

"Can use it, can't you?"

"Yeah. Course, but I'm not cut in on this. Eddie said so." Mike Daley glanced across suspiciously. "What's the game then?" He turned his head further to look at the Swede. "Changed his mind, has he?"

"You look too close into the horse's mouth...that's what you Engelish say, yah?"

"It's for me, then?" Daley looked across again.

"Look after it well, yah." The Swede settled back, hunching his shoulders. Soon his head lolled to one side and Daley had to shake him awake when they came to Weymouth Place.

6.

Mike had no idea why he was summoned three days later. When he saw the others in the office, he thought it must have been about the job that had so nearly gone wrong. It was, but not about the job itself. "A little bit of money gone missing, Mike." Eddie Bright sat back with his hands clasped behind his head. "Kenny says he gave you something to look after." Daley glanced round. The two men between him and the door stared back but the Swede, beside Eddie's chair, looked away. "Tell me about it."

"That's right, Eddie." Daley tensed. "Fifty quid it was. Kenny gave it me." He nodded towards the Swede. "Asked him twice if it were for me an' told him I wasn't cut in on the takings." He watched as Eddie looked up at the Swede. "Pressed it on me, 'e did. Dropped it right into me lap."

"Nefer said it were yours...nefer." The Swede's eyes were cold. "Said just to look after it, that was all."

For a moment the room was still but Daley knew he had been framed. He knew, too, that the others in the room were there on business, his business. "*You...said...to me.*" Daley pointed hard and took a step towards the Swede. He could sense those behind him had closed in but he knew he had to prove to Eddie Bright he had kept the money in good faith. "You said to me, 'can you look after it', you said. Yeah? Then, when I still asked yer about it you said not to go looking into the horse's mouth. They were yer very words, Kenny. That's what yer said" He drew in a deep breath. "You *wanted* me to take the dough, didn't yer," he challenged. "And *then,* when I had, you'd come runnin' an' squealing to Eddie that I'd nicked it. Eh? That's what yer did, didn't yer?"

He turned back to Eddie. "That were it, Eddie. Set me up 'e did. Wot would I go nicking fifty measly quid for, an' then hang around here waitin' to get my fingers broke? Eh, tell me that?" He then glared at the Swede. "Go on then, work that one out."

"Take it you did...and you kept it."

Daley's blood surged. It had been a trick and he could see the Swede knew he had been caught. "I know I bleedin' did, an' yer know why I did. Yer schemin' two-faced rat...," he got no further. Even as he began to move, his arms were pinned from behind. "You set me up...set me right up with all that mouthy patter of yours." Daley struggled but he was held. "And against Eddie an' all, at that. I've worked with Eddie for years, 'aven't I Eddie? What'd I want to go an' do something like that for, eh?...an' fer fifty poxy quid? Eh? *Eh? Go on then.* Get yer mealy mouth round that one...answer that." He continued to struggle.

"*Stop.*" Eddie crashed forward in his chair. A hand was raised. "OK...let him go. No nonsense now Mike," he warned, waving away the men who had been holding him. He watched while Daley straightened his clothes.

"Just a little test, my son." He paused, opened his mouth and picked slowly at his teeth while the room waited. "Almost there you were, but not quite...not quite. Like this it was." He raised a hand and fluttered it above the table. "Half an' 'alf, like that. Nearly good but nearly bad as well." Eddie Bright pursed his lips. "That's my money, boy. All of it's mine...right?" He raised an eyebrow enquiringly.

"I know that, Eddie. I wouldn't have touched it less I knew for certain."

Eddie Bright held up a hand. Once again the room fell silent. "Hey, see here, Mike. You're doing a good job. Don't go spoilin' it now. Nobody wants to get hurt. Right?" They looked at one another but only Eddie smiled. "Let's just be sayin' you got it a touch wrong and now you owe me a little somethin'. A little something, somewhere, sometime...right?" He nodded, pointing at the door and dismissing him. "Look after yerself now, my son. Take good care."

Mike heard the door behind him open. As he turned to go he glared hard at the Swede but the man was looking away.

211

Chapter Sixteen

Drew Hawkins stopped by the kitchen door. The top half was open, like a stable, to let a bit of air and autumn sunlight into the house. He took off his cap then brushed his thinning hair back from where it had been flattened against his forehead. It was hot outside, too hot really for driving sheep up to the top of the farm, and his face was sweating.

Midge, Sam's young collie bitch, followed him in and settled gratefully on the sacks that had been folded for her next to the line of boots. The elderly farmer paused, still breathing heavily and inclined his head, listening carefully to where he could hear his wife and son in the parlour. The tone of their distant voices told him they were discussing something. They sounded agitated but at least they were talking again.

He took off his dark grey jacket to hang on one of the metal pegs, then placed his cap on top and smoothed back his hair. Kicking off his wellingtons, he shuffled into his threadbare red slippers. As he washed and sluiced cold water over his face, so his ears confirmed that they were at it again. Her voice, as usual, was raised and he could hear Sam answering her back. His shoulders sagged.

Sam was getting no better and his mother was not helping. For months after Becky Carter had left home he seemed fine, almost as if her sudden departure had ended the uncertainty and taken a load from his mind. That had been back in the spring but latterly his spirits had fallen away. It was the girl; Drew knew instinctively that his son still loved her. In spite of her fall from grace and the flight from home, Sam's devotion had never faltered. But now, just as the days were beginning to draw in, so the life had gone out of the boy. The black dog was back.

At first his mother had not seen it, declaring later that she thought it was just one of his moods: it was not until Dr McKinney had taken them aside that she realised how deep the depression had become. Be tolerant and understanding, he advised. The moods come on unexpectedly and are beyond his control. There's nothing the boy can do about it and the tunnel in which he finds himself is often dark. The dog, with its glistening black coat and its fiery eyes, follows him everywhere and is difficult to shake off. What we don't want is for him to become agitated, the doctor warned, for it will only get worse. If he does then he might find it difficult to climb back.

*

"All right, dear?" Drew sensed the atmosphere as soon as he joined them. "I managed to move they ewes earlier than I thought." He smiled at Sam but saw his son's anxiety. "Us can do the lambs after dinner," he went on but then paused and caught his breath. "'Ere...how's about a bite t'eat then, eh? Just a bit o' bread an' cheese...that'll do fer now."

"Right." Barbara had her hands on her hips. "I'll get it now but…oh *goodness*, do come on, Sam. Try to be sensible. She's gone, gone for good, really she has and I wish you'd stop all this moping around." She looked at her husband. "Honestly, Drew. Try and get him to see it…*please*…it's all *so* depressing."

Drew walked across to his son. He put a hand on his shoulder and was about to say something when Sam rose suddenly. "'Tis all right for you." He was staring at his mother. "There's nort for you to worry over, is there? But I can't *help it*," he cried vehemently. "I can't explain, neither. You'll never understand."

"Shhh…steady lad." His father spoke softly. "Best stay calm." He could feel the tension in the boy: he was shivering. His whole body was taut and strained with the muscles hard and sinewy. He looked at his wife and frowned, raising an eyebrow in warning.

"Oh, all right then." Barbara looked from one to the other and sighed. "Look, I'm sorry…I'll go and fetch lunch." She had seen her husband's concern but Sam now stood with his head bowed. He was leaning on the table with both fists clenched. His eyes were closed. As his father went to pull him towards him his son started to respond but then changed his mind.

"I'm all right," he muttered, easing his father's hand away. "Just had enough fer a while, that's all." He straightened himself, looked at his mother and smiled. "Don't worry, mother. Sorry about that, bain't your fault." Then he filled his lungs, paused and blew, expelling the tension slowly like steam. "You an' Dad carry on. I'll be fine…just walk for a bit an' clear my head." He glanced from one to the other. "Be back in a while."

Leaning back against the shippon wall, he looked up at the sky before screwing his eyes tight shut. Inside his head his mother and Becky seemed to be chasing one another. He found himself somewhere in between trying to catch them but they were too quick. He tried to call out, then he put out a hand in an attempt to stop them but they ran on, their voices ringing loudly as they shouted at each other. It was hopeless, their mad dance continued around him for ages before they faded from view. It was as though he was falling behind them yet their voices went on and on, echoing and reverberating through his head.

Then suddenly his head cleared. He pushed himself away from the wall and stood. The gun, he knew, was in the garage. It was in the cabinet beyond the car and the cartridges were there too. Usually there was a full box at least but he only needed one.

✳

He walked slowly across the field towards the wood at the top of the combe beyond the hay meadow carrying the shotgun, nestling broken in the crook of his arm as his father had taught him. He could feel, somewhere, a strength trying to pull him out of the pit and away from the staring red eyes of the black dog. But it made no odds for there was nowhere to go and, in any case, it was simply not worth the effort. He shrugged and bent forward into the slope. There was no escape and, as he walked on, he felt the deep blackness descending once more.

Sitting astride the gate, he paused to confirm that he was on his own before stepping down. As he did so a pigeon clattered out of the green larches then a second from further away in the dip beyond. Midge, who had followed him, scrambled through the hedge and came up, looking at him quizzically, asking him what they were supposed to be doing. Sam could see where his father had moved the ewes he had mentioned earlier, and smiled, reaching down to reassure her and feeling the wet nose against his hand. Somewhere, out there in the darkness, a face smiled. It was waiting for him and he settled back against the bank.

Slowly, and with care so that it was bound to work, he attached one end of the piece of cord to the trigger and tightened it. He had chosen the choke barrel because it was the one he always used first. Placing the gun down, he bent low to wind the other end of the string around his right boot. Midge moved again, claiming the attention she had sought earlier. The dog had wriggled closer beside him and Sam closed his eyes, gently fondling her head as she nuzzled his cheek. "Sorry old girl...you'll go an' tell 'em, eh? When 'tis done...won't be long."

He coughed quietly then wiped his hands on his breeches before placing the cartridge into the breach. Shifting his weight to his left leg, he lowered the butt of the gun to the ground and gripped the end of the barrel. It seemed strange to be holding a gun like this and stranger still as he bent forward so the cold muzzle pressed upwards and into the soft flesh under his chin. It was a cramped, uncomfortable position, the more so when he raised and lowered his right leg to ensure the cord was short enough for his foot to pull the trigger cleanly. It was.

Once more he bent down, this time to cock the gun by levering back the hammer so it was primed. Then, holding it carefully, he sat back and wiped his mouth. Everything was ready and he nodded to himself as though confirming it. Even as he did so he could hear the voices urging him to be quick. Lifting his right foot to give the twine more room, he placed the muzzle under his chin once again, pushing it hard under the top of his throat, right underneath the jawbone. He had to be sure.

Midge whined before she barked. Wriggling her way forward again as young dogs do when seeking affection, she was at her master's face, this time licking and whining, trying to climb on to him, excited by what was happening yet unable to understand. For a moment Sam hesitated, then he turned and almost overbalanced. The roar of the gun echoed down the valley.

Where the shot went he never found out but in that one, calamitous instant he knew for sure that he had failed, and failed again. He was useless. He was a weak, hopeless creature and already, as if proof were needed, he began to weep, slumped forward with his head in his hands. He should have settled the dog earlier but he hadn't. He had let her remain close knowing that the young-ster would be puzzled by what was going on and would make a fuss of him when he bent down. And she had done just that, exactly as he expected her to do, and had wanted her to do.

He had used her. Midge, the little collie, had been his safety valve because he knew he hadn't the guts to pull the trigger on himself, yet neither had he the courage to stop. He had used the dog and so had failed again. He had failed at everything he had ever tried in life and had failed everyone. Nobody, it seemed, wanted to know him. He had heard them all in the village. He heard the recruiting sergeants behind their desks and he heard Gerry Chugg and the others. And he heard his own mother as he had done on countless occasions. He saw Becky's face staring at him, Mike Daley's and the soldiers at the Edgecott gate. He had failed them all and he knew it.

*

Jack Carter had changed in the four years he had been away. His parents told him so almost as soon as he stepped inside the cottage door. After they embraced, his mother ran her hands proudly across his shoulders and chest before standing back and admiring him. He had grown and there was now a hardness to the slim body. The short naval haircut and his pale grey demob suit made him look younger but the face was lined and the blue eyes had a matu-rity about them.

It was at tea on the first night of his leave that they told him about Becky. They could see by the set of his jaw that he was angry but it was not with his sister. He was angry with the man who had taken her: for her, he was just concerned. It so happened that he was heading that way and his hope was that he might be able to find her.

"Several of us are going," he said, noticing their worried looks. "They're looking for Dockyard Police and've started recruiting. The place's full of ships…Western Docks, up to Sutton Harbour and right out around the Tamar almost up to Saltash." They stared uncomprehending. "Merchantmen, men o' war, oilers…all there an' waiting, mostly to be paid off an' broken up. An' there's still more coming in."

"But Becky won't be there, dear. Not down at the docks."

"I hope not mother. Hope she's nowhere near the place."

"Bad is it?"

"Rough, Dad. All up round there, 'tis nowhere fer a girl like Becks. That's why they're recruiting for the dockyard. They're holding many of the ships offshore but they're starting to bring others in and to break them. Kit an' equipment all over the place. Brings together all manner of rough necks...right bad area it is." The room was silent.

"Be seeing Sam before you go?" Doris glanced at him expectantly.

"Aye, I'll get up there in the morning. Taken it bad, has he?"

"Better now than he were." Ernest looked relieved. "But he's been poorly, mind. Barbara an' Drew had the doctor out last month...'e were very bad then, but better now."

"Poor love." Doris reached down for the oven. "Still thinks the world of her. Doesn't deserve it though, she doesn't. Not many around like Sam Hawkins, and to think she threw him over like that."

"Reckon you'll find her, Jack?" It was his father again. "It's a big enough place down there."

"I'll do me best." Jack nodded thoughtfully. He dare not tell them where he thought they might have gone. If they were down behind the docks then he was going to have to be careful. But he'd have to try. "First things first though and that's to get meself taken on. They'll be having more'n enough to pick from. Most of the fleet'll be out of the service by now an' looking fer work."

※

Jack Carter cut his leave short and went off in search of work but not before calling in at Hayes. Sam was better, even smiling again but his father took him aside and told him of his son's despair. "I'll do my best, Mr Hawkins. Can't do more'n that and nobody wants the lass home more'n meself."

"Aye." Drew Hawkins looked at him. "Reckon us all'd be happy with that. Just depends, doesn't it?"

Jack nodded and took his hand. The walk down to the bus took only a few minutes but he knew he had a problem ahead of him and the longer he took to find her the worse it was likely to be.

2.

Daisy Gunn trotted up the stairs. Eddie Bright had given her a chance and she had taken it. Ten days ago the locks at the Co-op had given easily to her fingers and the team had been away in no time at all. They had been pleased, all of them, even Kenny the Swede, and Eddie had given her another one to think about. The jewellers in Connaught Avenue up on Mutley Plain looked simple enough. She told him she needed three weeks, at least, between her visits or they would remember her. But after her first call she was certain she had found the easiest way in. She had even noted the details of the safe when they left the door open after showing her the pearl earrings.

Becky heard her voice calling out after the knock on the door. She rose from where she had been playing with Maudie and lowered her daughter carefully, steadying her as she sat with a soft bump, then uncurled her tightly gripping fingers from her own. Only two weeks earlier the child had taken her first step, since when tottering about while hanging on to mother's hands for dear life had become wonderful fun. But now, and as if to show her displeasure at the sudden immobility, the whimpering began.

It was her birthday and Daisy had brought some fruit and a sponge cake made by the mother of one of the girls. She played with the child while Becky made tea then picked her up and held her while the two of them talked.

Daisy was worried. "But there's nowt *here*," she observed angrily. "Nowt at all…look, for Heaven's sake, an' you've bin here for what…months now." Becky didn't bother to follow her hand. "What's Mike on about, for mercy's sake?" Becky shrugged and looked down. "Has he been round yet? Eddie, I mean. Says he were coming." She saw Becky's startled look. "Oh, don't go worryin' yerself…he won't bite yer, fer God's sake. Might take a fancy to yer, mind," she chuckled. "An' who can blame him. But so what? If the fella likes yer then he'll maybe do summat about this tip." She tossed her head at the room in general. "Kick yer fella's bum fer a start when 'e sees this place."

"He scares me, Daisy, that Eddie does. Mike an' all the other's are terrified of him." Becky bit at a nail then brushed her hair back. "They say he's real mean and always gets what he wants…from the girls, that is."

"Ah *phoey*. Just the same as the rest of them." Daisy moved herself to cradle the baby against her breast. "Look at her," she whispered. "Tired, eh? Away with the fairies. Cuddlin' up to her Aunty Daisy an' happy as larry…bless her." She paused, picking thoughtfully at the corner of her mouth. "Aye, he can be mean if he wants, I s'pose…an' a right savage if yer don't play the game. Mike's lucky…know about that do yer?"

Daisy told her about the money and the Swede then went on to describe what happened to those that fell foul of the boss. But then she stopped, noticing the worry on her face. "Here, don't go getting' like that, love. If he'd got it in for Mike he would've done summat by now. Yer man's safe enough…knows where his breads buttered," she laughed. "An' does what 'e's told, like the rest of us."

"Aah, he's a proper luv reelly." Becky relaxed. "He always gives me what he can from his earnings…not much though." She smiled affectionately. "Sits with me in the kitchen an opens his wage packet. Splits it between us an' puts a little aside fer Maudie, too. Buys her little things from time to time, bless 'im. Loves 'er he does."

"Oh aye. There's plenty around far worse than your Mike." Daisy assured her. "Always wears a smile, 'e does." The girls in the bars could see that too, she thought. And our Mr Daley was always quick enough to return a compliment or follow a lead if an eye was beckoning. She wondered if Becky had any idea at all.

"Keeps sayin' we're not stopping here for ever, y'know. Wants his own place...back up Pompey way." She grinned at the thought. "Talks about getting' a garridge and puts a little bit by fer that each week an' all. Just a little...whatever he can."

"'Ow d'yer feel about that, then?"

"Crickey." She blew in disgust. "Anything to get out of this hole. Anywhere'd be better than this as long as we're together...an' he wants more. 'e does. More children when we're settled."

"Yeah." Daisy was looking at her, watching her face carefully but her heart was sinking. "That'd be nice," she said slowly. But it wasn't the Mike Daley she knew. Live for today was his way of looking at life and she had a shrewd idea where the money he was putting aside was going. Bella, the redhead over at Legs Eleven could tell her all right and so, too, could that new girl, Kelly, in the Blue Rose. Oh dear, poor Becky, but it was she who changed the subject.

"So what's Eddie coming round here for? Can't be interested in a mess like this. Not him."

"Huh, c'mon, Becks." Daisy looked up from Maudie, now asleep in her arms and with her head lolled to one side. She moved gently, crooking an arm so she could straighten the child. The two looked at one another. "Has to know everything, our Eddie does, 'specially all the women."

"What d'you mean?"

"Oh. Reckons we're all his. You know, king of the castle, top dog...an' takes his pick."

"What?"

Daisy looked at her and shrugged. "Oh aye. Just the way things are down here. Out there, look." She nodded towards the window. "In the clubs an' bars an' that. It's all the same."

"But I'm nothing to do with that." Becky sat back, suddenly horrified. "I didn't come down here for anything like that. I'll not let him near me...him nor nobody else. Here, let me take her now," she said quietly, holding out her arms. They exchanged Maudie in silence taking care not to wake her. "I can't be doing that, Daisy," Becky whispered eventually. "It's not me."

Daisy looked at her. For a moment they held each other's gaze, one looking at the other fearfully, the other working out how she was going to say what was on her mind. "Listen, love." Daisy spoke softly. "'Tis all different down here. The gaffers like Eddie Bright run the whole thing. Mike works for him, I work for him an' life's not bad. 'E does us pretty good, an' all...looks after us. An' if he wants his bit o' fun then so what," she shrugged. "Same as the rest o' them, it's no big deal." She looked at Becky and laughed. "Hey, come on, looks as though you've seen a ghost. Bain't that bad, an' I tell yer what...if Eddie sees this place, 'e won't half get it smarted up for yer. Bet yer anything."

"But...but, I *can't* Daisy. I can't do anything like that. I mean, Mike'd go wild."

"Listen, love." Daisy was on her knees in front of Becky where she had been stroking the baby. "Don't go bleedin' daft an' start shoutin' the odds as to what you like an' what you *don't* like. It's not that sort of place, right? They're big, these geezers. They run it an' what *they* say goes, not what *you* say. I'm not sayin' nuthin's going to happen. Maybe it won't, but if it does then don't go shoutin' an' screaming, sweetheart. Really...you'll be doing yerself bad."

Becky put Maudie down then the two of them talked on in the kitchen but Daisy had to go, promising she would be back before the weekend. For a while Becky sat by the window only half taking in what was going on in the street below; her thoughts were mainly back with what Daisy had said. Fear and revulsion, and images of what it might be like, churned through her mind. Never in her most awful dreams had she considered anything like this. And Daisy had seemed so indifferent about it. Like the other girls down there in the street, it just didn't seem to matter. But then it wouldn't matter to Daisy who'd seen so much of this way of life. A man's a man, she said, and the very thought of it was horrible.

Suddenly, but only for a moment, she thought of taking Maudie and running from it all. But where would she go and how? It was just not possible. She wouldn't get half way round the docks before they came for her, and what then? Perhaps she could go to the police and seek their help. But what was she going to say? That somebody had warned her something might happen to her? Huh, they would laugh in her face and tell her to stop being so silly before packing her off back home again.

Maybe Mike would know. He would be able to come up with something, or would he? But what *could* he do now he was in Eddie's grip? And perhaps he knew about these sort of things. Perhaps he and Eddie had discussed it already and he knew that his boss was going to come round. And what if he simply shrugged his shoulders, unable or too scared to do anything but hadn't dared tell her?

Before she went to bed, she locked the door as usual. Her finger paused on the security catch but she thought better of it. She had done it once and there had been a row when Mike returned late. He had been drinking and had almost hit her so angry had he been. But she lay in bed uneasily, with one hand resting on Maudie where the rise and fall of the tiny chest only served to show how vulnerable they were. By the time Mike came home, she had dropped off but, this time, she awoke with a start as soon as she heard the keys being sorted.

3.

From his back Chief Superintendent Mark Mason reminded everyone of Winston Churchill. He was short, burly and his neck jutted forward underneath a round, balding head. What was more he often stood with his legs astride and with one or both hands on his hips.

And that was exactly as he was standing while Inspector Chris Startin sat waiting to hear his thoughts. But any similarity ended there. Mason was shrewd and ferrety, almost always registering his dislike for whoever he was confronting with a look of disdain. The accent was Yorkshire, south Yorkshire from somewhere like Leeds, Startin guessed. He should have retired years ago but his impressive first war record in the army together with his reputation as a troubleshooter allowed those in authority to waive the rules. And they had. Mark Mason had been sent to shoot straight at the trouble: Startin knew that, and Mason knew he knew.

"Leave the little fish." The Chief Superintendant was staring down from the window across Victoria Park and towards the old Naval Hospital. The temporary wartime police accommodation was cramped and he had been lucky to get the office to himself. For a moment he watched as the gardener, who limped badly anyway, wrestled hopelessly with a pile of leaves caught suddenly by the breeze. "Not worth bothering about and if we begin messing wi' 'em, bell-s'll be ringing all over t'shop. In any roads that's their *wall* an' we've got to get over it, not smash it to pieces. Information, lad...info and intelligence. That's what we're on first up." He turned suddenly, black eyebrows raised inquisitively. "Know the difference?"

"Reckon so, sir." Startin shuffled uncomfortably as Mason's look told him how his reply had been received.

"Aye...information to *build* on, intelligence...to *act* on. We want both and lots of it afore we start rushin' about wi' big sticks. No damn fool heroics though," he warned. "Your team, and we're giving you some o' the best money can buy, they've got to lie doggo an' bring it back to master soon as they know what they're on about. Now then, let's have a luke." Mason sat and pulled the sheaf of papers towards him. "Bit of everyone here," he muttered. "All sorts...CID, Special Branch...including two women. If they're good, mind, then they're gold dust," he remarked drily. "Liaison officer from the docks, naval and military police, Customs and Excise...the whole bloody lot."

"How much time have I got, sir? To knock 'em into shape." Startin sat forward. "I mean they don't know each other and neither do I. Haven't put a name to their faces yet."

"*Time*, lad?" Mason looked incredulous. "*Time?* Not a bleedin' holiday camp, y'know. Yer patch's nowt but a bloody shambles and here you are asking me how much *time* you've got." He pursed his lips. "You're on the job *now*, my son...right now, so get yer arse back up to your place sharpish an' start putting t'show together. Out tonight, right." He tapped the table. "Familiarisation patrols, getting to know the place...and each other. No pussy footing about the canteen, ' 'Ullo, old bean, I'm 'enery,' an' all that crap. Get 'em out there, lad...an' bloody keep 'em there."

*

It took him two days. They were long days, from six in the morning to gone midnight, and it felt like a week. His team was twelve strong and he decided to interview them all twice in between their patrols. The first interview was easy enough, a simple matter of getting to know the faces and what they had been doing with themselves in the past. The second one took longer and here Startin tested himself on what he had gleaned earlier but without using his notes. After that it became more of a discussion between the two of them as to what they had seen, what their copper's instincts were telling them and how they would choose to set about it.

There was a wealth of experience in front of him and he planned to use it all. Everyone of them had good records and he could sense already that a determination to succeed was germinating. Gathering in what was needed was one thing, breaking through Mason's 'wall' and identifying the big fish was another and then, most difficult of all, anticipating what these fish might do next was something else again.

Today it was raining, sheeting down against the briefing room windows which had to be shut tight. A thick, hazy cloud of cigarette and pipe smoke hung above the tables. Coats were off and ties loosened. It was, as the Chief said, a Chinese parliament where everyone put their ideas into the hat. It was also good for team morale, as Startin could see. Furthermore, he was beginning to put names and voices, as well as character, to faces and was starting to see how each of them ticked. "OK, OK." He lifted a hand. "Oi," he shouted. "That's enough...look this way." They had been talking for hours and now it was time to pull it together.

"We'll start with the strip clubs, the ones we know about that is...ten of them we reckon. I'm not interested in the gorillas on the front door nor the blokes behind the bar, or who runs the joint. I want to know who runs him, and that's not so easy." Startin glanced at the faces looking at him. "Then there're the places we don't know about...the clip joints and drinking dens, and the whore houses. Oh aye," he said, looking up at the sudden stir. "The same goes for them." He went on to tell them what and who he wanted to know about. Then came the business of how to set about it.

"What about a couple of matelots, sir." Cummings, one of the naval police, half stood then sat again. "Place's heaving with 'em. Suggest we go in like that."

Startin raised a cautionary finger. "All right to get in," he replied. "The doors're wide open but not too great for chatting up the big chiefs, eh? Not Jolly Jack Tar's scene, is it? Not as far as I know anyway, an' 'specially when he's had one or two," he added to laughter. "And if he's sober then what the heck's he doin' chattin' up the boss, eh? But no, go on, that's all right," he grinned sympathetically. "Keep it coming, no matter how daft it sounds. We're here to squeeze it dry.

"Guns?" The question came from one of the Custom's trio. "What's the score there, sir? We've had a handle on some of these hoods for a while now and we know they've got weapons about 'em somewhere. That lot that was picked up…last…last November." His fingers were waving a pencil. "Two of 'em were armed." The room fell silent.

"Yep." Startin nodded. All eyes were back on him. "That's right. I was going to get the spade work out of the way first…assuming that none of you were going to get a gun shoved under your ear just yet. But yes, we know they're there. Not many but too many for that. We were tipped off a couple of months back." He grimaced. "No idea who, mind you, but they're in there somewhere."

Startin paused. "I'll tell you now, my friends, you're not here just because this place's in a mess." His eyes were moving from one to the other. "That's bad enough but you've been brought together because there're some right bad hats down there…some real nasty bastards."

"Any ideas? Anything at all on who these guys are?"

Again Startin felt the eyes turning back to him. "Yes…but only a couple for certain and we've not got anything on 'em as yet." He sensed the mood changing. "OK, I know…why haven't we told you? Yes?" He saw the nods. "Because, in this instance we've decided we've gotta be going in from the ground up. It's the only way really and we all know it. If we went in the easy way and hit the top first, we'd be all over the ruddy place. We've got to get a line on them. That's a must and we're nowhere near that yet."

"And who's brainwave was that? I say pick up the big guns and the tiddlers'll vanish. End of story."

"Not this time." He could feel the tension. Suddenly some of those in the room had a different angle. "For a start we've got nothing, or very little to go on. The beaks'd chuck out anything we'd hope to pin on them, either that or give 'em no more than a measly slap on the wrist. No," Startin raised a finger. "We've

222

got to piece it all together and there's only one way. Takes longer, I know, and more graft but there we are. Look." He paused. "These guys've been giving us the run around for long enough now and I want them busted...busted once and for all."

4.

It was over a month after Hestor Barclay died that Sam heard the news. He was surprised that his mother had not picked it up but apparently Rose had taken her father back to Dorking to be buried and had then stayed on. When she telephoned Barbara, she had been back at Duxhams for less than a week.

Could Sam, she asked, possibly give her a hand with moving some of her father's things out of the house? She had managed to pack up the smaller bits and pieces but there were others too big for her. Would he be able to come over? At first he objected, telling his mother he still didn't feel up to it. She said she understood and, maybe she had, for it was his father who suggested that it might be a good idea. "There's nobody else, lad," he remarked. "And the maid's on her own."

"But why me? There's all sorts over there...that butler fella, Clements, isn't it? They butlers're s'posed to do all that kinda thing...master's man, an' all that. An' then there's that Mrs Down, an' the gardener an' they lot." Sam made plain his disbelief. "Come on, Dad, what's a fella like me goin' over for when there's all they others?"

"Apparently not." Drew Hawkins got to his feet and tipped back his cap. "Rose told yer mother that she was on her own. Sent the staff an' that Clements fella away for a week or so...soon as she got back. Didn't get on with him so she said. The fella only answered to her father," he chuckled. "An' reckoned he ran the place. An' the others? Well," he pulled a face. "Don't s'pect they come into the house. 'Tis like that in they big houses sometimes. Outside workers never sets foot inside."

Sam looked at him. "Seems daft to me." The two of them were changing the tractor oil in the shed behind the shippon. They were well away from the house yet he still looked round cautiously. "Not mother telling you to ask me, was it? Not getting on at me again is she? I couldn't be having no more o' that business...all this pushin' an' pulling one way or t'other."

"Colonel Ashcroft, as it happens." Drew saw his look and went to push the drip tray further underneath with his foot. "Aye, 't'were him right enough. Saw him in Dulverton yesterday an' he said that the lass were asking after yer. Wondered if you'd give her a hand, like. Just as she said on the phone to mother."

"Then why didn't *he* go an' give a hand then? The Colonel? He'd be far better'n me. Knows her better an' knew her Dad ever so well." He was still doubtful yet found what his father said was interesting him. "What's it about me then? I hardly know the woman."

"Colonel reckoned she, Rose that is, were sorry for him…'bout his wife passing away like 'er did…after she went into that home. Enough's enough, that's what she said to him. And she didn't want the butler to do nort but then she decided to get on with it herself. I dunno." Drew Hawkins scratched under his cap. "Anyhows, she reckoned you'd know what was what. Cuh." He shrugged and laughed suddenly. "Proper old muddle but that's what were said." The two were silent. "Won't take long," he continued but Sam sensed that his father would be pleased if he went and, suddenly, the idea had become more appealing. "Must be difficult enough for the maid…rattlin' around there on her own."

He hadn't seen her for what seemed like months, yet he remembered her clearly as he drove away from the house that day, after going over to see her horses. The way her fingers had caught hold of his hand like that and her laughter as she walked alongside the car. And then, before that, when she came out to see him up in the roots when she asked him to go over. He'd never really understood why she'd done that but then, perhaps she did feel comfortable with him. Perhaps she did like his company after all. But her father had died only a few weeks ago and he began to wonder how he would find her now and how she would be when she opened the door. All weepy perhaps? Or as bold as brass and shrugging it off as they lot often had a mind to do? It was interesting though.

And then, when all was said and done, perhaps she…but no, not Rose Hatton. It couldn't be that. He'd thought about it once before and the very idea had made him laugh. It couldn't be so. He shook his head again but, this time, he smiled to himself and quickened his step.

✳

"His *clothes?*"

"I know," she whispered and looked up at him trying to smile. "I'm sorry, Sam, but I couldn't face it. It was all too close…it was horrid seeing all his little things on the dressing table and his shoes and ties, and the photographs of Mummy with me." Rose shivered and hugged herself. "But I've got everything ready," she said hopefully. "All the boxes and things, even started to lay everything out to sort. But then…oh, I don't know, I just couldn't bear it." She pulled a face and Sam saw the strain. "You wouldn't mind, would you? It's got to be done."

He shifted uneasily. He had come over expecting to move some pieces of household furniture or some of her father's boxes and cases. He had not really given it much thought and had even put his boots in the car in case they would be working outside. But *this.*

Rose had met him almost as soon as he switched off the engine and before he had time to get out: she must have been watching the drive and come straight out. She wasn't weepy, neither did she try to shrug it off but she was quieter than he remembered which wasn't surprising. For a while they talked in the hall and he could see that she seemed a little nervous. She was on her own, she explained, and found it strange so had decided to get on with things. Harry Maidstone, her cousin, was coming down in a week or so and she wanted to get as much as she could out of the way. Try to start again, she said with a shrug and a sudden laugh. It was then that she asked him if he could sort through her father's clothes.

He nodded, noticing her look of relief as she smiled. "Thanks," she murmured. "Come on then, I'll show you where everything is." She turned, holding out a hand as if to show him the way. "Most of it is going to go," she explained. "But I'll keep some of his suits and things back and let Harry take what he wants. He and Daddy were about the same size, but the rest can go."

"Do what I can but who'm I to say what's what." She was leading the way up the bannistered and deeply carpeted stairs and he was following, looking around at the unfamiliar surroundings. He had never been upstairs in such a house before, not with a woman on her own like this and he felt out of place, as though he was entering forbidden territory. And it was as if he was being asked to pry into somebody else's affairs as well, and to do something that was none of his business. It was an awkward, uncomfortable feeling.

There were two rooms, the bedroom and dressing room. He could see where she had started to sort his clothes but there was far more to come out of the wardrobes and chests of drawers. She watched him as he looked around, then hurried across to the curtains which she threw back letting the October sun flood in.

He went from one to the other working out in his mind what he had to put where. "If you could just get everything out of the drawers and lay it all out then I can sort it through later...it's just that everything's where Daddy left them and there's a sort of...I don't know, a sort of spell or something about the place. Once it's all moved and put on the beds then it'll be fine." She was following him trying to explain while he took everything in. "I've put his little things here," she went on. Her voice sounded thin and he watched as she looked at the dressing table. "Just a few things he kept squirreled away. I thought I'd keep them. You know...his little favourites." She turned and he saw her pain.

"Look...I tell 'e what." He stood over her and caught hold of her arm. "I'll do this. It bain't no problem," he assured her. "I'll get everything out and put it all over there look." He nodded towards the dressing room. "Then you can have a look and see what's got to go an' what to keep. Yes? Anything small, like these, I'll put there, up on the side wi' the others." He saw her nod. "Best if I do it now, on me own or you'll be getting' upset. I'll call when ready." He paused. "An' the best thing's for you to get some tea or go out and see to the horses. Right?" He could see that she would never have been able to do it on her own. "Here, c'mon, Rose." He spoke quietly and took her arm again to lead her out of the room.

She stopped and turned towards him, suddenly unsure of herself. One hand was raised as if to catch hold of him. "Thanks," she said, then looked up and smiled. "You're right, I'd be quite hopeless. I'll go and see to the animals…then get some tea. Give me a call."

✳

He worked hard, lifting and carrying the clothes and shoes from where the old man had last put them. He could see what she meant about a spell or a presence in the rooms and concentrated on the job in hand rather than stopping to think about how things would have been were he still alive and pottering about. He tried to banish any sense of intrusion he had from his mind but it was difficult when he came to lift out the shirts and underclothes. The drawers and cupboards had a mustiness about them and a smell of hair oil. The heels of his shoes were worn by the way he walked and there was even some mud on one pair. He felt sure that all this and the feel of his softer clothes were what was upsetting her. As far as she was concerned, he was still there, in the house with her.

When he finished he called her and watched as she looked at where he had laid everything out. "It's so different," she exclaimed, no doubt relieved that the spell had been broken. "Really it is, and it's so much easier to pick and sort. Except that lot." She laughed and pointed to where Sam had put a pile of his under garments on to a sheet. "They're for the ragman."

They went down for tea then came back up again to put what had been sorted into boxes which Sam carried or dragged into different rooms. By the time they finished the light was fading and there remained only the things he had kept back for her. She put on a light and both noticed at once how dark it had become outside. "Here, look." Sam showed her what he had collected together. "Probably too much but I thought it best that way. You can sort through later."

He watched her again as she went to the dressing table. It was not particularly tall yet it made her look tiny when she stood beside it and he wondered how anyone so small would be able to cope on her own in a house this size with all the different rooms and the big pieces of furniture.

Then she called softly, turning and holding something up for him to see. "The name of his ship. Look…HMS Triumph…the one that went down. They were torpedoed you know. A sailor must have given it to him after they'd been rescued. I think it's the band off one of their caps. And look at this," she said excitedly, reaching out for a browned photograph. "Gosh, look…Mummy and Daddy…it must have been just after their wedding. Don't they look *young*.

226

Goodness." Her head was bent forward as she studied the picture in the light.

When she turned, her mouth was drawn tight. She was trying to hold on but he could see her tears. "It's all so sad," she whispered. "So sad." Then she sighed heavily. "Oh I don't know." It was just as she moved towards him that he caught her eye. "You've been marvellous, Sam. Really, you have." As his arms circled her, her head nestled against his chest. He said nothing, for there was nothing to say. All he could do was to stroke her back gently and lower his face to the top of her head.

"Come on," he muttered eventually. "'Tis getting late." He felt her nodding then watched as she stood back and collected her thoughts. "'Tis done now." She nodded again and lifted her head. One arm went behind his neck.

"Thank you, Sam." She pulled back so she could see him better. "You're a dear, dear man," she said softly. "You came to me when I needed you…just in time, and you saved me." He felt her hand pulling him down and he lowered his face obediently until their lips met. At first it was no more than a gentle, tender caress but he felt her mouth relax. She pulled him closer, then more urgently with both hands, and slowly, as their bodies moved together, her lips parted. When he drew back they simply looked at each other. Her eyes had a sleepy happiness about them as if her worries had gone and the storm had passed.

"I'll go," he murmured, gently taking her arms from around him. Then he backed away but she stood there, quite still and smiling, and with her head to one side.

"You'll come back, won't you?" Now she took a step towards him. "Say you will," she demanded quietly. He said nothing but his face broke into a grin. It was a strong, reassuring grin and it made her laugh with delight. "You will, won't you?" she asked breezily, knowing well that he would.

Chapter Seventeen

By one o'clock that afternoon, Colonel Ashcroft realised he had made a bad mistake. By half past three, and with the light starting to go, he knew he must have been mad. He was drenched through, frozen and cursing his stupidity for having even considered hunting on such a day.

The weather had been foul all week, beginning with days of solid rain driving in from the north. Everywhere the ground was sodden and by now even the headwaters of the rivers were barely fordable. On Wednesday it cleared briefly only for it to turn colder when Dunkery was given its first grey muzzle of snow. But then came the rain again, this time from the west, with line after line of heavy-laden clouds sweeping in from the sea determined to drown everything in sight.

In spite of it all hounds met as usual. On seeing that most present were soaked already, the master ordered a quick start to what he thought would be a difficult day. But he was wrong. Once laid on, the pack ran hard across the high moors leaving the field way behind as they struggled through the teeth of the gale and freezing rain. They checked once above Withypool then turned down the Barle valley where they hunted downstream along the left bank unable to cross the floodwaters. Here the river ran straight and wide; swollen high yet strangely silent, carrying with it branches, whole trees even, anything that had been unfortunate enough to stand in its path.

Ashcroft met Rose where the valley widened. It was just above where the river had burst its banks, flooding the fields sometimes for hundreds of yards, and where the original line was no more than a distant ripple of angry turbulence. The wind had eased but the rain continued. Rose and her horse, like all the others, were splattered with mud. The animals themselves were glistening wet and foaming yet still fired up by the chase. Hounds, somebody said, were up to their deer and what riders there were pressed on with the spray, turf and mud flying up and around them all.

Eventually it was the solitary shot, from somewhere ahead, that told them it was over.

*

No more than forty riders were gathered at the edge of the floodwater where two islands, now half submerged, broke up the angry torrent. The stag had been taken at the water's edge but the body had drifted out into the current where it was swept downstream between the islands. Somewhere, out of sight of the riders on the bank, it had been caught up and was held fast. Several had dismounted already to let their horses blow. One or two were talking together, swapping hip flasks and stories of the chase but most were at the water's edge.

Something unusual was holding their attention. There was an excited buzz of expectation. Fingers and hunting crops were being pointed across the water.

Miles Ashcroft and Rose rode up together. Somebody, a local farmer they said, had gone in after the deer, wading across the nearest channel up to his chest and struggling hard against the current. He had made it to the first island and was now searching for the animal. He had taken a knife with him least the marksman had not done his job. Pressing forward to hear more, they heard his name.

"*Sam?*" Rose looked at Ashcroft incredulously. "D'you hear that, Miles? They say it's *Sam...our Sam,* on the island out there...it can't be, can it? Excuse me." She turned anxiously to two farmers. Her voice was raised. "Is it right that it's Sam Hawkins out there? Sam, from Hayes Farm?"

"Aye...mad young beggar."   The second man caught her eye.   "If anyone can do the job then it's him...Sam'll do it."   Another joined in.   "Big enough an' ugly enough."   Rose listened to the voices around her. "Nearly didn't make it though."   "There 'e is look...over by they trees." A fourth man called across to them.   "Cuh...bluidy water's nigh on over his 'ead."   Then a woman shouted shrilly.   " 'Ere he comes look...'e's got him all right."   Somebody else saw who it was.   "'Tis young 'awkins from up Hayes varm."

Everywhere people were watching and pointing. Rose stood in her stirrups to see better and could just make out the figure in the water struggling towards the bank. Suddenly somebody whistled, and then there was a holloa. Clapping and cheering broke out around them. A hound bayed, and another. Then, above the commotion, the horn blew the long plaintive call of the 'mort'.

"My God, Miles, d'you think he's all right? He must be half drowned and so *cold*...poor thing." Ashcroft smiled. He had dismounted and now held Rose's horse so she could join him.

"I'll wager he's all of that but I'll bet he's fine," he drawled, stumbling back as Rose's horse pushed hard against him. As the sweat on its head began to dry the animal had become agitated and was trying desperately to rub. All around them, exhausted horses were doing the same. Some were tossing their heads in the air, others pawed at the ground and shook vigorously. "If that's the Sam I know then he'll shrug it off. Sure as eggs're eggs," he chuckled. "All in a day's work."

"But he'll catch his death." Rose was still in the saddle, looking towards where a small crowd had gathered around the body of the stag. "Oh, heavens, yes...he's *abso-lutely* drenched," she reported. "But, he's fine. Someone's given him a hip flask...and another. Goodness, he'll be all over the place." Ashcroft watched her. Her concern for the man was obvious. He had suspected it for some time, just little pointers here and there and the odd word or gesture but now he could see it plainly. "Gosh, poor thing," she muttered. "And look, they're thanking him…all of 'em."

Ashcroft looked up at the sky and grimaced. What was left of the day was coming to end: it would be dark in less than an hour. He stood on tiptoe to see more easily then moved slightly for a better view. The Master was holding Sam's arm up high and he was standing there like a victorious fighter amidst the applause and cheers. Another of the hunt staff came up and took his other hand. Around them late arrivals were still coming in. Horses were blowing hard, everywhere steam was rising against the rain which had eased to little more than drizzle. Once more the long, thin note of the horn echoed around the valley as the master had ordered his huntsman to blow for 'home'.

*

"All right. *You* see to the horses and I'll go and get things going." Her eyes were shining. "Hot baths, a drink and some food…how about *that?*" It was pitch dark outside but Rose stood in the doorway where the stable light shone on her. "How long d'you think you'll be?"

"Half an hour or so." Sam was rubbing down the grey. Earlier they had argued about it but she had insisted, almost shouting at him, that he was coming back with her. Exford, she proclaimed, was miles away while Duxhams only a short ride. By that time the field was thinning out. The Colonel had gone on and Sam was preparing for his long ride home. You'll die, she almost shouted at him. You're mad, a fool, and at that point she had ridden in front of him, turning her horse and blocking his path. He had given in, admitting to himself that he was indeed cold and his horse almost done in. Their ride home together through the dark had taken half an hour. Exford, on a cooked horse, one which he would have to lead for most of the way, was three hours at least. She was right, and he was glad of it.

"Fine. That'll give me time to find you something to wear." She saw the look on his face. "You're not staying in *that* filthy lot…not in my house anyway," she laughed. "I'll find something…God knows what though. Perhaps Clements's left something, or the gardener. What a hoot."

Sam turned back to the business of settling the horses. The harder he worked the warmer he became and he felt himself beginning to dry. The thought of climbing into somebody else's clothes did not appeal. He'd be dressed like a clown, he'd feel a fool and certainly look like one. All right for her, he thought, wardrobes of the stuff to pick from. But what, he wondered, would she be wearing after her bath? What would she be rustling up for supper, as she put it, and what would drinks by the fire be like? She was going to telephone Hayes and tell them what was happening. And there was a thought: what would they be making of it all?

*

230

Rose put down her champagne. It was her third glass and it had gone straight to her head, but she could not have cared less. This evening was fun, exciting fun and she was going to enjoy herself. Pirouetting as she went and humming the last song, she hurried to the gramophone where the record had finished, leaving the needle to scrape away on its own. He had heard the tune before, one of the bands had played it in the village hall but he couldn't remember the name.

His bath, earlier, had been wonderful but he had insisted in getting back into his own clothes which, except for his socks, had almost dried. She had found a pair of old slippers for him and he had come down for supper in his checked shirt and breeches. At first her laughter had annoyed him, the more so because her red dress, loose and belted like a dressing gown, and the way she had done her hair made her look far too glamorous. She must have seen the look on his face when she brought him his drink because she reached up and kissed him, as if to cheer him up before adjusting one of the buttons on his shirt and brushing at specks of dried mud on his shoulder.

"Carroll Gibbons," she announced quietly, lifting a finger to the new record she had just put on. "Come on, it's *'Dancing in The Dark'*…dance with me, it's fabulous. She swayed rhythmically and twirled around with her arms in the air before coming up to him and taking his hands in hers. "Come on," she whispered.

"Can't…not in all this damned clobber and somebody else's slippers, fer Pete's sake."

"Oh, *Sa-am*. Take them off, silly. Here…I'll join you. Look." She kicked off her own and moved into his arms. "Gosh, you're big…too tall for all this, but it's lovely." She felt his arms go round her, almost lifting her off the ground. He was strong yet surprisingly light on his feet and they moved their bodies in time to the music. They danced in silence until the record ended then danced again to another when she turned off the main lights, leaving just a reading lamp in the corner and the light from the fire which she had asked him to build up.

Swaying gently together, she raised her arms and circled his neck. Feeling him move against her once more, she stood on her toes and kissed him. When the record finished they let it run on until the gramophone ran itself down. They stood looking at each other in the sudden silence. She could see his eyes searching her face.

"Love me, Sam," she whispered almost inaudibly, squeezing his fingers. "I need you…now…please." Her voice was louder. One hand was caressing his cheek. "I want you to take me, now…..here, in front of the fire." Catching hold of his hand, she knelt down, looking up at him and tried to pull him down beside her. "Come on…down here with me."

"D'you mean it?" he murmured, now kneeling beside her. He had loosened her belt and, cradling her head under one arm as she lay back, he slid his other arm underneath and lifted her gently so she could lie beside him. "Come on, then," he urged, trailing a finger across her lips. "Ask me nicely again, will yer. I liked that…and say please this time." He saw her look and his body shook with mirth. "'Tis more polite that way."

"Wait," she cried, sitting suddenly. She pushed him aside and made to wrap her dress around herself. "The rug smells…*stinks*, of dogs or something. *Bugh*." Rose scrambled to her feet and looked round impatiently. "I'll get some cushions and things…hang on We can use that woollen thing from the back of the sofa as well." He half lay, propped on one elbow and watched her, not even moving when she threw the rug on top of him.

"There…now then…*watch*," she commanded, standing at his feet. Her dress had fallen open and for a moment she stood there, quite still, staring first at him then beyond and into the fire. Slowly and theatrically one arm stretched out behind her, then the other. Gradually, as if it was being pulled from behind by some hidden hand, her dress slipped from her thin shoulders. It slithered past her small breasts to her hips where it stopped, leaving her half exposed to his gaze. "Now this," she whispered again then shrugged, wriggling her body seductively to ease the dress down to her feet. Lifting her arms to brush back her hair, she stood in front of him with her legs astride his and her hips thrust forward. She was naked.

Sam still had not moved. He was there, just as he had been, but now staring at the shadows and light from the fire playing over the curves of her body. Then he beckoned to her before falling back onto the cushions as she came to kneel beside him. Reaching out, he took her into his arms, moving only to caress her face as she crept up to him.

"Oh no," she cried. "Come on." Even then she was not satisfied and pulled back suddenly, frowning in mock seriousness. "It's *your* turn now, I've done my bit. Too *right* I have." Her hands went first to his shirt which she pulled from his belt before reaching down again. "Oh God," she squealed in frustration. "They're *dreadful* these things and yours're still damp". But now she was giggling. "What've you been doing down here? We'll have to pull 'em off, both of us…and fast."

She leapt up, stood at his feet once more then turned her back on him before bending low to reach back between her legs. "Come *on*," she cried. "I'm here, look…waiting. Roll them down…all the way," she cried, waving her hands impatiently. "Come *on*. I'll pull, you keep pushing them down."

"Christ that was romantic…and bloody cold, too." Now she was back under the rug. Their bodies were together once more, both naked this time with their arms and legs pushing and feeling their way as they burrowed and snuggled up close. Comfortable at last, she wriggled herself in further, feeling the warmth and hardness of his body enveloping hers.

Slowly, so as not to hurt her, he raised himself over her and paused, looking down. Then he bent lower. Their faces were close: his eyes watching hers, always watching. She sensed his breath against her cheek and waited for him, motionless and expecting, until their mouths met and she felt the roughness of his stubble on her skin. Then her eyes closed. She could feel his tongue, probing and feathering against her lips and teeth before flickering deeper inside to play with her own. His strength and his weight were forcing her down. Now his body was moving over her, slowly and easily.

As they moved together so her hands were at his hair, holding him down and on to her. Without thinking, she parted her legs. Now her body arched up to meet his. She was moaning softly, grimacing with pleasure and clutching urgently at his back. Then, as their bodies began to move rhythmically, slowly and gently at first, she gave herself.

*

Later, when the last of the logs had burned low, they made love again before moving to her bed where they slept until dawn. He left her then, promising he would return as she held onto his hand.

The night sky had cleared. Dawn was cold and the ground still wet but the wind had dropped. As he clattered through the empty streets of Dulverton he brooded, unable either to accept what had happened or to comprehend why. His spirit rejoiced, his heart glowed with the pride of conquest yet, deep within, fear and suspicion lurked together. Surely he had been used, he told himself: plucked from the air with a click of her fingers and used to satisfy her sudden desire, only to be discarded no doubt as soon as she had finished with him. But then he, too, had used her, and he could not deny it. And nor would he either, he vowed, smiling mischievously. The two of them had found each other and they had come together, both finding the solace and comfort they needed.

And there was Becky. She was there, still there, staring at him out of the mist in pained surprise. A sudden surge of guilt tore at him but he laughed out loud at such sensitivity. Why should he feel so? Had he not tried time and again to win her heart, only to be cheated and left to his own misery? Why should he be made to feel remorseful when his homecoming in an hour or two should be a joyful and happy affair. The old Sam; awkward and insecure, despondent and depressed should be banished. In a way it had been, of course, and yet the irritating, niggling doubt was still there and nagging away.

As he rode into Exford and on past the farriers and The White Horse, he looked across to Myrtle Cottage. For him she was still there: he could feel her presence. No matter how hard he tried to shake himself free, that sense of shame kept tight hold. He wanted to look back but dare not, rather he kept his head turned and rode on.

2.

For a moment Daisy Gunn paused, blinking. It was not so much the brightness of the lights for the red-painted bulbs gave off little more than a dull glow. It was the smoke and the fug and the sudden sound of the piano in the far corner. She stepped through the bead curtains and into the bar. Eddie had called for her. Kenny the Swede had sent word and she had come early to see who she might find. It was not yet nine but the Blue Rose was filling already which was usual for a Friday, especially as two ships were in.

The wave from one of the booths beyond the bar caught her eye. She smiled and lifted a hand in reply but she didn't really want to know. Poor Becky, all on her own as usual and here was Mike with that new girl, Kelly Smale. Daisy had seen him with other girls but as soon as Kelly arrived he had made no bones about what he was after. She, the tart, had obliged and now this was their scene. Poor, dear Becky. Daisy lifted her eyebrows and took off her coat, then pulled at the edges of her frock before making her way towards them. "Eddie's upstairs." One of the barmen called over those at the bar.

"Thanks love…give us a bell when he's ready." As she eased her way past the small group standing on the edge of the dance floor, she could feel their eyes. "Oi, you. Wha'd'ya looking at? On yer bike." It was lovely to be able to say that at last and she brightened at his look of surprise. "Sorry darlin'…got better things to do," she scowled. "No, go on, shove off…oh, *piss off*," she shrieked, pulling back from the hand that reached out. "Go on, scram…get back t'yer playpen. Not bloody old enough for this, you're not." She waved the hand away, then turned and lifted her skirt coquettishly, curtseying as she did so.

Then she was there. "Hi Mike…hi Kelly." Reaching down to be kissed by each in turn, she sat quickly where Mike had made room.

"Seen Eddie, have yer?" Daley was cradling his glass. He glanced at her then looked beyond, bending down to scan all those in the club, his eyes moving carefully from point to point.

"No, he'll call," Daisy replied. "But, hey, what's up with you two, then? Eh? Like a coupla novices sitting there scared shitless." She glanced across at Kelly, appraising her cleavage without disguising her opinion. "Behaving himself is he, that Mr Michael Daley? *Him*." She nudged him. "Not keeping him up too late are you, darlin'?" She grinned briefly at Kelly before waving away the waitress that had followed her across the floor. "Needs his shut eye, y'know…hot milk and tucked up with a goodnight kiss. Don't yer, Mikey-boy?" Daisy turned to him, reached up and pinched his cheek. "You just be a good boy and stop all this flapping. No bogeymen out there, y'know an' mummy's not going to come looking for yer, neither."

He glanced back over his shoulder. "No, no, ain't nuthin' like that. Just check-ing out the new faces, that's all. Lot of new faces about, y'know."

"Course there's new bleedin' faces, yer twit. What d'yer think the place is then…a bloody church or summat?"

"No, no." He looked at her again and laughed. "It's just that there's one or two out there…that bloke leaning up against the pillar, look, for one. Beyond the bar, right? Somehow he don't fit in…an' there's another somewhere. Bin here before, ain't they, Kelly? Just not right…not like squaddies nor matelots on a run ashore."

"Don't make no odds to me…all you men're the same." Suddenly she waved towards the bar. "Hey, look guys, I'm off…Uncle Eddie's ready an' waitin' as they say. See yer, then." She put a hand on his arm. "An' you just be a good boy," she whispered.

❋

"An' when's this?" Daisy raised an eyebrow.

"New Year…after the sales they're s'posed to be starting up again." Eddie Bright looked down at his hands. The girl was smart. Everything he had just told her had gone home and he had talked for a good ten minutes about the plan. Maps, photos and sketches, she had taken it all in and the one question she asked had been spot on; they had failed to find out when the security guards changed over. He could have kicked himself and would see the Swede about it. He watched as she nodded thoughtfully.

"End of next month then," she said. "It'll take 'til then. Gotta get meself inside the place, twice at least 'aven't I…to have a good butchers an' that."

"That'll do me. Keep me posted, eh?" The meeting was over and he watched as she got to her feet. Bold as brass, he thought to himself. The girl had balls all right, none of this grovelling and crawling to him, just a straight look and a razor-sharp mind. Mike Daley had done him well. Eddie Bright rose with her. "I called in at Daley's place," he said.

"Nice isn't she." Daisy almost turned in surprise but checked herself.

"A right little cracker." Now her mind was racing. "Said I'd look back," he added.

"Oh aye." That would mean tomorrow and she knew *what* it would mean. It would be difficult to get to Becky before him but there was little she could do anyway. She had warned her already and the girl would have to play it as she saw it. But if Eddie Bright was going to call back on her then it wasn't because he'd left something behind. "Told her so, did yer?"

She watched as he stretched then breathed in and hitched the belt of his trousers over his hips. "Oh yes, indeed I did." Eddie inclined his head appreciatively. "Oh yes…flowers next time, I said. Always flowers when I come calling by, I told her. She's lovely." Eddie Bright put his hands on Daisy's shoulders and smiled. She could feel the strength in his fingers and watched as his face creased into a wide grin. "Clever girl, Daisy," he crooned, bending to kiss her. "She's just the sort of friend Eddie likes to meet."

✳

Mike fumbled with his keys at the door. It was dark on the landing and he had to find the right one by feeling for it. He dropped the bunch twice and cursed loudly before managing to open the door. He knew he had been drinking but had tried to tidy himself after leaving Kelly's flat in Flora Street. His tie was undone and his hair was a bit of a mess but that didn't matter. What surprised him was to see Becky standing there.

"Shhhh," she cautioned. "Not such a noise for God's sake. Maudie's half awake, she wouldn't settle…an' where've yer been at this hour? Eh? Drinking again? Oh, Mike…look at yer."

"Leave me alone." He raised a hand as if to ward her off and went into the kitchen. "I need a drink…cup 'o tea or summat." Becky followed him.

"Eddie Bright called today." She said nonchalantly, folding her arms.

"Oh yeah…good bloke, Eddie. All right was he?" Daley turned and looked at her, watching as she shrugged.

"Not my type, that's fer sure. Fancies his chances an' all, doesn't he. Brought me these look." She nodded towards the chocolates.

"'E's all right, 'e is." Daley screwed the kettle down onto the hot plate, hoping to make it boil faster. "Likes all the pretty girls an' all. And he'll like you." He came up to her and put his arms around her waist. "He'll fancy you, all right."

"*Poof,* your breath…you've bin drinking." Becky sniffed and pulled back. "And what's *that* might I ask?" She sniffed again, closer this time. "Someone got close t'yer didn't she." Suddenly she froze.

"And what's *this*…this here, fer mercy's sake?" Becky tore roughly at his shirt collar. "What the hell's this…a bleedin' great lovebite, ain't it," she cried. "What've you bin up to? Eh?" Her voice had risen. "Eh? Come on then, Mike Daley…out with it. What the devil've you bin playing at…..an' who is she? What little trollop's been chewin' away at your neck then?"

He snatched her hand away, swayed and laughed cynically. He was angry, cross with himself for being caught out like this but furious at her tirade for it was deserved and that only made it worse. "Well that's all right then, isn't it, eh?" He kept his smile but found nothing amusing. "Two can play at that then.

Eddie Bright comes calling round here…chocolates an' all that, an' you've got the bloody neck to start on at me? Just shut yer mouth, right."

"Hey, just steady you." Becky was glaring furiously. "What the hell d'you think I'm doing with that Eddie Bright of yours then, eh? Not got his after shave all over me, have I? And I'm not going to go bitin' nor slobberin' on him like that, am I? Eh? I can tell yer that fer nort."

The first slap when it hit turned her head. The second one, harder, tossed it back again. She tried to reach up to protect herself but he hit her again then held her by her hair, his lividly scarred face screwed tight in anger. "Don't never go messing with me, Becky Carter or I'll have the bloody skin off yer back. Yeah?" He twisted her hair, forcing her down to her knees. Her mouth was open and her face was screwed up in pain. "Just you watch yerself, my girl…just watch it. If you're having your bit o' fun then I'll have mine." He shook her hard to make his point then let her go. Becky collapsed, sitting on the kitchen floor. She was crying quietly and moved only when she heard Maudie's cries after the door slammed.

She had been struck hard and it had hurt but, worse, far worse, she had been cheated and deceived. The man she loved so dearly and trusted, the father of her child had been lusting and writhing with another woman and had then laughed in her face, accusing her of doing the same. Suddenly, horribly, her world and all her hopes had smashed noisily into pieces. Somebody else was better than her. She had failed her man and he had turned away from her, preferring the arms and the love of another. The spell that had bound them together all this time and through so much had been broken. It had been shattered, and it had been done by him, the man she thought had come back for her, and who had taken her away from home with all his promises.

Just where he had gone to now, she neither knew nor cared.

3.

Twelve of them started the course. Four soon dropped by the wayside but the remainder, Jack Carter included, saw it through. He found the first week dull but later, when the police came to talk to them, he sat up. However, it was the lectures on crime in the city that decided him.

He would go and talk to them himself. They would be getting a week off for Christmas so he had to be quick; just walking into the station and stating his case should be enough.

✳

Detective Constable Brock sat back and looked at the man in front of him. He had explained already that the police were not a missing persons' bureau but the visitor had insisted on having his say. Dave Brock, his black and grey-flecked beard matching his eyebrows, frowned impatiently, suspecting the persistence was due to his search for sister and niece.

"Look." Brock held his gaze and signalled for Jack to be quiet. "We'll do what we can, obviously, but it's going to be difficult. We haven't got a starting point have we? Now if she were a Plymouth girl…or there was a family, an address even. But there's not is there? Mm?" He could see the man understood, and he looked down at his hands. "And there's another thing," he explained. "We really can't be devoting police time to this. It's…it's…well there're other more important things."

"True." Jack sat forward with his elbows on his knees. It seemed as though he really was wasting their time. "Her man'd be your best lead, y'know. They never took to him at home…nasty bit of work so they reckon. And he'd be easy enough to see, wounded like he was," he added hopefully.

"Trouble is, m'lad, we've got no *reason* to be looking for him, have we? I mean we don't want him for anything and there's no record we know about. Far as we know, he's an innocent man and we never go chasing after people like that…unless we want them. And why should we?" He paused, thinking how best to put it. "Look, your sister's hardly a child, is she? She's a woman of her own mind and if they've decided to go off and set up home, well…." he shrugged and smiled kindly.

Jack nodded. "Aye. It was just a thought that's been on my mind. Him, that is. Reckon I had to try everything. Thanks anyway." He rose and took the detective's hand. "If you do by chance come across him, Daley that is, then I'd love to know."

"We'll see. Can't be promising anything but we know where you are. And thanks for coming in." He waited until Jack had gone, then sat again drumming his fingers idly before reaching for the notes in front of him. It must be hard losing a sister like that. The man was fond of her, he could see it clearly, and it must have hurt the family when she disappeared like she did. Brock turned the page. He was a heavily built man and shuffled in his chair to sit more comfortably. The man Carter named looked interesting though. Daley, Michael Daley, the wounded soldier from Portsmouth. Badly burned face who could have been involved in the Black Market. Driver or mechanic.

There was not much to go on but it was worth a try. He would get on to Portsmouth and ask Records there to have a look. Might just be something and if there was, then Inspector Startin would want to know. He would want to know everything about anybody coming this way who even sniffed of a record. It would be easy enough to get hold of Carter for an interview, even borrow him from the Dockyard for a while if needs be.

Brock glanced at his watch. Half past three. He had less than an hour before he had to brief one of the new teams. Chris Startin had been right. There were

238

guns about the place; two gangs, at least, were believed to be armed. Life in 'A' Division was looking up.

4.

By now much of the rubble in war-torn Plymouth had been cleared. Pavements and alleyways that had been blocked or avoided became usable again. The rows of houses in Union Street resembled mouthfuls of bad teeth. Some, not many, were in good shape, most others were broken or blackened, or patched up, then there were the gaps. And as with any mouthful of bad teeth, when a ill wind blew it got very uncomfortable.

For Becky life had been uncomfortable since she could remember but now, with Mike doing what he wanted, it was worse. He claimed to be giving her what he could but it was never enough. She was still having to beg for food and clothing but the friendly open market at the Octagen had closed, however, and the street traders had gone. Everyone was hanging on to their ration cards: nobody dug up public places to grow vegetables anymore. During the war years everyone shared, making sure that nobody went without but now there was less food about and less still to be discarded or given away. Each looked after his own and with winter approaching, there was little to spare. A week ago she had been chased away from looking through the rubbish boxes at the back of Hammonds, the shoe shop, in the hope of finding a discarded pair that would fit her. Maudie was growing fast and toddling everywhere; she needed clothes and shoes now, not shawls.

Daisy had taught her to knit. She had also promised to spend Christmas with them as well, insisting that the apartment would be decorated and that the meal, somehow, would be fit for good King George himself. The very thought of Daisy warmed her. The naughty, bubbly little character brought happiness and laughter to the cheerless apartment. Becky always waited impatiently for her visits, treasuring every minute of her company and would beseech her to stay on for as long as she could. As soon as the front door closed behind her, the place became empty and soulless once more.

The days themselves, when Daisy might come round, were not so bad. There was always something to do and people to meet. But the evenings were different. As the light faded so a silence came with it and when Maudie was down Becky's loneliness turned to worry about Mike coming home. She never knew when he would be coming nor how she would find him. Would it be drink and the shouting with Maudie awake and crying, or perfume and lipstick on his face with that guilty smirk or would there be just a sullen silence at the end of a bad day? She longed for the time when her stomach would no longer turn at the sound of his keys. She longed for a little more money which she knew he earned. More than anything, though, she yearned for a comforting arm around her shoulder, one that would pull her close and which would be followed by a tender kiss.

✳

She fairly leapt at the cough behind her, dropping the saucepan and gasping with shock as she turned. Eddie Bright must have let himself in with his own set of keys.

He was grinning his usual cat-like grin, where his lips peeled themselves back over his teeth. A finger was raised in warning for her not to cry out. Maudie, he suggested by pointing at her room, was asleep and he did not want her woken. Becky's heart was already beating faster.

He caught her looking past him towards the door and grinned again, this time holding up his keys. "Don't worry, sweetheart," he whispered. "It's locked…I locked it behind me so nobody's coming…an' nobody'd going." He saw the sudden look of panic. "No problem," he insisted. "Honest, there's nothing to worry about…got my men down by the door. We're safe…and all on our own."

"Didn't know you'd be back so soon, Eddie." Becky's hands were behind her back where she had pressed herself up against the stone sink to face him.

"Aha, a surprise then, eh? Well, here's another one…here look. Not much this time o' the year. Christmas Daisies the fella said, or summat like that." He peeled the wrapping off the flowers with a flourish. "Smart, eh? Brighten the place for a bit."

"That's kind, Eddie…they're loverly," she nodded. "Thank you." Becky had not moved and she watched him closely as he put the flowers down.

" 'Ere, c'mon then…aren't you goin' to say 'ullo." He threw his leather jacket onto the table. "C'mon, darling, give us a kiss…make us feel welcome then." He had come right up close and placed one hand heavily on either side of her, trapping her against the sink. "Here, c'mon." Becky saw him lean forward and turned her head.

"No Eddie…please." Now she felt the first chill of fear.

"Come 'ere." He caught hold of her chin and forced her face back to him, hurting her as he did so. "Don't be like that, darlin…makes Eddie cross. 'Ere." He crushed his mouth against hers, holding her head firmly by her neck. She tried to move but it was useless then she tried to call out but his mouth was against hers. She could smell the tobacco on his stubbly flesh and as he forced her mouth open she tasted the bitter nicotine and felt the slippery warmth of his tongue. Suddenly his other hand was feeling high between her legs. She buckled and tried to gasp, then tried to force him away with her knee. But, again, he was too strong.

"Goin' to show me a bit more of that, eh? Felt nice it did…all soft an' warm."

"Eddie, please," she gasped breathlessly, leaning as far back as she could. She was trying to push him away. "No," she whimpered, pushing still harder against his chest. "*Please* Eddie...the baby. You'll wake her and Mike's due back." She stopped and looked at him. Now fear had taken its firm hold. Her mouth was dry and she wiped it quickly: her eyes were wide with alarm.

He was grinning again, his same cheesy grin with his eyebrows raised in surprise. And he was shaking his head slowly from side to side as if to tell her that it was no good at all making excuses like that, for nobody was coming and nothing was going to stop him. She flinched as a hand went to her blouse. She could feel his fingers kneading and squeezing the softness of her flesh. "No," she pleaded again, feeling him trying to undo the buttons. "Stop it, Eddie...*stop it.*" Her voice had risen in panic as she struggled to take his hand away.

"Oi, you. Listen to me, sweetheart, an' listen good." Suddenly his face had clouded into a scowl. "I've not come round here to waste me time. Right? I've come to see you, to see you proper like. Mike's not coming back...he knows what's good for him, 'e does. Off out for the evening. So it's just you an' me, see." He paused to catch his breath. "So...in *there.*" His head jerked back towards the bedroom.

"I can't...the baby. She'll wake and...and...Eddie, please don't. I don't want to." He had her by the arm and was pulling her from the sink. His fingers dug into her flesh. "No," she cried. "No." He was too strong for her and pulled her across the kitchen after him.

"In there." The order came as a hiss. "We're going in an' if there's any noise, I'll make it bleedin' hurt for the pair of yer. So in there...*now.*"

He stood watching her with his back against the bedroom door. Both heard the baby whimper and turn in the cot but the child slept on and he motioned her to remove her dress. Next he pointed at her brassiere. She did as she was told then stood in the half-light with one leg pressed in front of the other and her hands across her breasts. While she was undressing in front of him, his eyes drooled over her and now she stood helpless and terrified. Terrified at the thought of this brutal, evil-smelling giant who had begun to remove his own clothes and terrified that her child would wake crying, causing his anger to flare up. What he would do to them she had no idea but when he made his threat she believed him.

The light from the street lamps lit the room enough for her to see his powerful hair-covered shoulders and chest, and the fleshy bulge of his stomach. She watched, in revulsion, as his body moved about jerkily until, finally, he was naked. In the sudden stillness that followed, even from where she stood, she smelt the warm, bitter body sweat and the staleness of his breath. "Here," he whispered, moving towards her and pulling her roughly to his body. He was reaching behind her, pressing hard against her with his body while bending her back as his hands pushed her pants down beyond her buttocks. As he lifted her he gasped, surprised no doubt at her weight for she had let her body go limp and she lay supine on the bed as he pulled the last remnants of her clothing from her feet.

His sex, although grunting and urgent when it came, was less violent than she feared. It was so because she let him have his way, too terrified to try and fight him off. Her mind and eyes were closed to what was happening and her fists were balled tightly to keep herself from crying out. She let him take hold of her as he wished, to turn and lift her, to grope and feel with hands and tongue and to thrust and push his body whichever way his lust dictated. All she ever did was to blow the sweat from her mouth when it dripped from his face. She let him do what he wanted because she had no choice and she lay there, drenched and used, as he dressed and left her.

When he had gone she rolled from the bed and staggered to the kitchen where she threw up, retching violently time and again into the sink. After she had rinsed the bile from her mouth she filled a pan of cold water and squatted down over it to sluice him from her body with her fingers. Only then and after she had stumbled weakly back to her room, and after she had torn back the bedspread in disgust; only then did she finally break.

Chapter Eighteen

Of the two he had interviewed so far, Perkins the ex-army sergeant looked the better. The man had worked for years in an Officers' Mess and appeared to have just the right approach. Stevens, the scented and effeminate second butler from Knightshayes, thought too much of himself and Harry had seen his cousin bridle at the man's attitude. He was bogus Harry thought. There was one other applicant to see tomorrow but Perkins looked the man.

Captain Harry Maidstone turned sideways to the full-length mirror and looked at himself before the knock on the door made him pause. His uncle's clothes fitted to a tee, even the tails and morning coat. "Wow...very smart for the middle of the day." Rose laughed at the sight of her cousin in her father's evening dress. "Time for one more dance, perhaps?"

"They're marvellous, Rose...and it's all here. Studs, cuff links...everything. D'you really mean it? Isn't there anybody else?"

"Nope. And the sooner you take them the better...the whole lot." She waved airily at the wardrobe. "And don't forget there're the boxes next door. Honestly, have whatever you want."

"Goodness, there's masses. I'll need a van or something." Harry took off the jacket. "But who on earth sorted them all...I mean Clements has gone, hasn't he...weeks ago?" He straightened his tie and was about to take a suit from its coat hanger. "Oh, by the way, that reminds me. Perkins, the first fellow I saw this morning. He's the one for Clements's job...looks just the ticket."

"Uh huh." Rose sat on the edge of the spare room bed. She had thought so too and was hoping Harry would choose him. Four had applied for the post of butler and her cousin had insisted on her waiting until he came down before making any decisions.

"You didn't do all this yourself did you? Surely not?" Harry walked across to her.

"Sam Hawkins helped me. Remember him?" she queried. "From Exford. You met him out hunting...about a year ago...when Spiffy Foxley was down, and Miles Ashcroft came over to dinner."

"Him?" Harry sat next to her. "Gosh, yes, I remember. A big fellow, farmer chappie." He bit his lip and nodded slowly. "So he's around is he?" Rose looked down. "See much of him?"

"Now and then." She was studying her engagement and wedding rings, turning them slowly. "I asked him over to look at the horses, really, but then got him to give me a hand as well. Clements had gone, I'd had enough of him by then and I thought Sam would be able to do it. And he did." She glanced up briefly but avoided his eyes. "You remember him don't you?" she asked again.

"Yes, yes." His reply came quickly. "We talked about him at dinner, that evening. A nice fellow. We all thought that but...well, nice enough and good company."

"Oh, yes, I know," she sighed. "A good chap and all that but not good enough. God, yes, you lot made your point." Rose got up. She had been waiting for Harry to bring up the subject of who she had met down here and who she was seeing. There had been occasion enough yesterday when they had ridden out together and later lunched in Taunton but, somehow, the opportunity hadn't arisen. Until now.

Harry had been meaning to find out. Everybody had asked him to let them know what his cousin was getting up to down there on her own. 'Don't come back without the answer,' Archie Wallace had instructed. Spiffy and the others had suggested that something like this might be going on. 'Bounced on to a right old bit of rough and now she's stuck with him.' The words had stung and Harry had almost rounded on him, but that was just their way of putting it and it was true enough, he had to admit. He, too, had been wary of Rose's softness for the farmer but it was difficult. Harry Maidstone was very fond of his cousin. He was the closest to her now and a wrong word from him would be met head on: she would see it as the official family line. Anything he said like that would be bound to hurt but he felt he had to make his point.

"Rose, listen. I never said there was *anything* wrong with him and there's not...not as far as I know, but everyone at home misses you and're worried that you're simply disappearing. Don't get yourself too tied down, will you. Not yet anyway."

"Oh Harry, for Heaven's sake. I'm not getting tied to anything or anyone. Honestly, you lot must think I'm a born idiot or something. I'm not rushing around throwing myself at the locals...give me some kudos." She could feel his eyes on her and knew by his silence that he was weighing her words. "It's just that Sam's a good friend, that's all, and is somebody I can trust. Don't worry...I wasn't going to let any old person into the house...to come up here and sort through Daddy's things." She knew already she had said too much. He would be wondering why she was getting so touchy but it was too late. "No...he happened to be free that day and that was that. Come on...*lunch*. You can finish all this later. We've got tea with the Smarts, over at Combe Head. Remember?" She turned at the door. "And stop prying," she laughed, wagging a finger. "Your little cousin's fine; she can look after herself."

"Yes, ma'am," he saluted her jokingly, laughing in relief that she had not made more of it. "I'll be right with you." He watched as she went down the stairs then pulled a face. Not good: she had reacted exactly as he expected her to do, just a little bit too quickly and the others would grill him.

✴

Barbara listened to the logs thumping into place where Sam was still stacking them. Drew had been determined to get the wood in and to deal with it all before the New Year. The two of them had been at it for days. With Christmas only two weeks away, they had first brought in the long beech poles from the fields where they had been stacked since last winter, drying in neat lines against the hedgerows. All day yesterday they had been sawing and now, today, Sam had the task of getting the logs under cover. The recess in the hall next to the stairs was always the last to be filled.

His mother could see the change. He had brightened, of that there was no doubt, and there was a spring in his step rather than that awful, lugubrious plod with his chin down on his chest. Yet he seemed to have distanced himself from them as though he was wary of being drawn on something. When he told them about his night in Dulverton, his father had been indifferent to the story he told but she had watched him carefully, alert as to how he told his tale and eager to know more. At first she found it difficult to believe he might still be seeing her but he was off again this afternoon.

"What time're you away, dear?" Barbara waited until the figure bending over the wheelbarrow straightened. "I've got a couple of things that need collecting."

" 'Bout an hour or so." Sam looked round. His face was flushed with effort. There was sawdust in his hair and all over his jersey. He was breathing heavily and stopped, seemingly glad of the excuse. "Soon as I've done 'ere." He wiped the back of his hand across his brow.

"Well there's no need to rush with this." Barbara dried her hands on the dishcloth. "Why don't you leave it for now…go and get yourself ready. I must say it's nice of her to ask you over like this."

"She needs a hand, that's all. Seems to reckon I know my horses…got another one in to look at, a grey from Morebath way."

"Another? Gracious she must have a whole yard full over there."

"More or less." He brushed at the sawdust on his jersey. "Keeps two or three up for her friends an' that. Says it saves them having to hire."

"Oh that's kind. She's *such* a sweet girl and I'm so glad you're friends."

"Bain't nort there, mother," he laughed. "Honest there's not. Rose's got her own sorts, come down from London, mainly, at weekends."

"Oh, come on, dear." Her son had his back to her but she studied him closely. "Don't go running yourself down like that. In many ways you're both well suited…horses and Exmoor and so on. And you're good company for each other, I can see that when you're riding together."

"Hey, c'mon now, mother. That's as far as it goes." He stepped back from the alcove. "I keep tellin' yer, there's nuthin' in it. Mustn't go reading things into it."

"Well it's very nice anyway. Father and I are delighted."

"*Father?* What's 'e been sayin' then?"

"Oh, this and that," she blustered hurriedly. We've talked about it, of course, and he thinks she's charming." She watched as he turned the wheelbarrow towards the door.

"Can't see that. Not like father to go on like that." It was the first he knew his parents had been talking about them.

"Well of course we do. We're both very happy for you, dear. It's high time you had somebody in your life. Somebody, well…well suited."

Sam upended the barrow against the shippon wall. Mother was at it again but this time she must have sensed something. He smiled to himself and rubbed the back of his neck where the sweat was drying. Rose Hatton was a lovely, lovely girl but never in a day was she for him. He kept telling himself that but still hadn't worked out the other night and what must have been on her mind. But then she had enjoyed herself, that was for sure, so he couldn't be that bad. No matter what Becky and the others thought of him, Rose Hatton hadn't turned him down. Oh no. In fact it was her who had made the running, sparked up on champagne or not. She hadn't mentioned it since and he was certain by now that it had been no more than one of those moments. Never mind, he was seeing her again and he took a kick at a pebble in the yard, then at another.

Becky Carter had gone and was slipping from his mind. From time to time he thought of her, wondering how life must be, tucked up somewhere with her soldier boy and their child. Once, just once, there had been a sudden moment of longing. There was something about her he missed but it had gone and he would no longer get himself into a state about it. As he came into the kitchen he was humming one of those tunes the band used to play in the village hall, the same one that Rose had played on her gramophone that evening.

∗

"Can't say I likes the idea, Ern." It had been on Drew Hawkins' mind to catch Ernest Carter on his own and to ask for news. Several times he had tried but there were always people hanging around the forge and he wanted to talk quietly. But today he had caught him. He had seen him making his way across the green and had called out; now the two of them stood together.

Jack, so Drew heard, had found himself a job but then Ernest asked about Sam and he told him what he and Barbara had been thinking. "Rose Hatton's a fine young lady...very fine, a luverly maid but not for our Sam. An' I told the missus," he added quickly. "Told her straight, I did, but her didn't want to hear none of it."

"'Twouldn't do to see the lad getting upset no more." Ernest toed the ground with his boot. "'Tis hard to forgive Becky fer walking out on the boy like 'er did."

"Cuh, 'tis all over an' done with, Ern." Drew put a hand on his friends shoulder. "Don't 'e go worrying now. 'Twas one of they things and once's done, 'tis over. Nort you an' Doris could have done different." He checked himself. "But you've heard, I s'pose...heard from the maid, like?" Ernest shook his head. "Didn't like to ask straight out," Drew went on. "But I 'ave bin wonderin'.'"

"Not a word, but s'pose that's to say that nuthin's amiss neither...not too bad anyways." Drew could sense the worry in his friend. "Doris an' I can't help but wonder sometimes. 'Tis a bit hard though, not knowing like." The two men looked at each other.

"Aye...dare say." Drew Hawkins squeezed the other's shoulder. "I'll be glad enough when you're telling us one day that the maid's on her way back home. Maybe it'll bring young Sam to 'is senses...instead of all this chasin' off after the fancy ladies like he is. I don't like it, Ern...and nor do you neither, I can see that. Bain't right." They walked slowly, talking quietly together until they came to Myrtle Cottage where Drew took his leave. Ernest watched him go, noticing how the large frame rolled gently as he made his way. Drew wasn't happy these days either. It didn't help to know that but it was a comfort of sorts, something that made his own worries a mite less painful.

2.

It was Kenny the Swede who told her. One of the barman in the Blue Rose had sent for him earlier and broken the news immediately after the police left. A Royal Naval shore patrol had taken Mike straight to the naval hospital where he had been stabilised before being moved on to the City Hospital. It all started, they learnt later, with a fight between some Italian and Maltese sailors in East Street which had spilled over into George Place and from there into the bar. Mike, like the others, had been caught up in it and it was he who had been hurt.

Daisy ran as fast as she could. At first she got no reply but she saw a light and knocked again, this time calling urgently. When Becky came to the door, the two stood looking at each other in amazement. Both were stunned.

It was almost two in the morning yet Becky was dressed. Daisy saw at once that she had been crying but before she could get over her shock, she started again, this time shivering uncontrollably as she sobbed on her shoulder. For a moment they stood there before Daisy began easing her back into the apartment where she noticed that Maudie was dressed and awake, while Becky's suitcases were packed and ready.

She was going, she sobbed. She didn't know where or how but she was getting out. When she began to tell her about what Eddie had done earlier in the week her cries got louder. Mike, she told her, didn't really seem to care. He had come home early last night and they had rowed but tonight he had gone off as usual, leaving her on her own and it had all been too much. It was then that Daisy told her the news.

"Honest, love, they say he's bad...living like, but they've taken him in to operate. In the stomach it was...one of they bleedin' spicks from Italy or summat. Kenny an' Rick're up there now. Reckon we'll know by morning."

"Know what?" Becky looked at her. The sobbing had stopped but now she sat wide-eyed with worry, clinging to the hankie in her lap. "Know *what*, Daisy," she whispered.

"If he's goin' to...how he'll be getting on." She watched as Becky's eyes filled with tears again before she lowered her head and began to weep, this time silently like a child. Daisy took her into her arms. "Now look, you're going nowhere tonight. We're stoppin' right here, Becks. You an' me. C'mon now." She waited, looking around the kitchen and thinking quickly. "You're going nowhere, sweetheart...nowhere 'cept to bed...an' I'll be there with yer, after we've had a cuppa tea." She waited again. "C'mon now, you see to Maudie, put her back down. Poor little soul...wonders what the bleedin' heck we're all doing at this hour. "C'mon, Becks." Daisy was on her feet. "Get yer coat off an' look t'yerself."

Daisy stayed the night. She lent Becky some money and made her promise to stay while she went and found out what had happened. Mike would be needing her, she said. At first Becky just shrugged but Daisy told her again. "Don't do nuthin' 'til I'm back," she ordered. "That there's fer food an' that, not fer a bleedin' bus fare." She stabbed at the coins on the table. "Stay 'ere, right. I'm away out to see what's what an' if I'm goin' to do that for yer, yer may at least stay an 'ear the news. Right?" She bent down to look up at Becky's face. *"Right Becks?* I'm not talkin' to me bleedin' self now, am I?" Daisy watched as she shook her head.

✳

Becky didn't know how long she had been on her own but she looked up at the sound of the keys in the door. For a moment she waited to see who it was but it couldn't be Mike and it couldn't be Daisy. She frowned and started to rise but stopped suddenly, then gasped in fright as the door opened. "Eddie," she whispered. "What're you doing? Why've you come back...you haven't come for more? No please...I couldn't." Her voice was raised. "No Eddie." But then she stopped. The door was still open and he was standing there with both hands half raised as if to calm her. As he moved slowly towards her, he shook his head reassuringly.

"Nuthin like that, sweet'art." His grin revealed his teeth. "I've come to tell yer that Mike's goin' to be OK. He were lucky."

"*Lucky?*" Becky's eyes were raised in surprise.

"That's what they reckon. Ricky knows one of the porters an' they reckon he got away wiv it lightly. Missed everything it did...a whole lotta blood an' that but the boy was in luck. A very lucky man is our Mr Daley."

Becky sat weakly and Eddie Bright with her. "Na then...here's a surprise. We're goin' to move yer. Move yer off outa here."

"Move me, Eddie? But why? An' now, just before Christmas an' that?" Eddie Bright looked down. He was toying with his heavy gold chain bracelet and for a moment Becky sat watching him. The shock of seeing him in the doorway had gone and she was more curious than afraid, especially when he began to chuckle. By the time he looked up he was laughing and reached out a finger to touch the end of her nose, but she swayed back just in time.

"Your little Daisy...*our* little Daisy was what done it."

"*Daisy?* But she was here just now, an hour or so. What's she done, Eddie? She's all right isn't she? Don't tell me that she's...."

"Steady, steady steady." His hands were raised again. "Bad as one another, you are. *No*...Daisy, Daisy Gunn gave me a right roastin', so she did. Didn't know whether to laugh or cry. Told me I'd been a big, bad boy down here." He pointed at the table. "An' I were, Becky, I know that. Wrong I were the other night but then she said to me to get back down 'ere an' have a look at the place. A festerin' tip, she called it, and that when Mike's home again it'll be no place for him, she said." He was still laughing. "A right bollockin' it was. An' you know what...she were right an' all."

"This is true, Eddie, is it?" Becky was looking at him. She felt helpless. All her strength had gone and she could scarcely take it all in. He, Eddie sitting there like he was, Mike coming home from hospital, Daisy and her stamping feet, and now the move. " I just dunno. What about Mike, what's he got to say?"

"Mike ain't sayin' nuthin, darling. He's away with the fairies right now." Eddie paused then grinned his wide, greasy grin as he reached out to take her hand. Feeling her flinch, made his grin all the wider. "No, straight up...honest as I'm standin' here. There's a little ground floor place up in Victoria Street. Not far, half a mile or so. Ricky an' the lads'll be here this afternoon." He squeezed her hand. "Get it over an' done with right away." He paused. "Hey, an' now then." He pulled her hand towards him. She didn't try to resist him; there was no point. She simply let him cup it in his. "Not thinkin' of doin' a runner any more, are we? Eh? Not with Mike comin' back an' a nice new place an' that…an a pay rise as well."

Becky watched as he reached into his inside pocket then looked at the big white notes in his hand. "No, I couldn't, Eddie." She saw his smile fade. "Couldn't do that. It wouldn't be right."

"Don't be so bleedin' daft. *'Ere you.*" He moved quickly and she froze as a hand gently stroked her hair. "You've bin a good girl, Becky, an' Daisy says I've bin a naughty boy…so that makes it all fair, dun it?" He pinched her cheek softly then stood, standing in front of her and looking down. "You've bin a good un, sweet'art, so don't go spoilin' it now. I'll be looking after yer, right." He caught her by the chin, lifting her face so she could see him. "So take care o' yerself, darlin'."

Becky watched as he left the apartment, then sat alone with her thoughts until Maudie disturbed her.

3.

It was an interesting idea and, while they considered the options, the two policemen sat in silence. Daley, the man who had been injured in the fight, was undoubtedly the one they had been warned about. And now there was somebody out there hell bent on tracking him down. They, the police, held all the cards but they had to be careful or there would be trouble. On the other hand, if they played their hand well, Daley could lead them straight to one of the gangs.

"I reckon we let him run, sir." Detective Constable Brock pulled on his beard. "Portsmouth had very little on him…the usual juvenile nonsense but nothing more than that. Small fry is our Daley, in spite of the wartime heroics. He's recovering well we're told, and's due out in a couple of days…we can put a tail on him."

"Agreed." Inspector Startin sat back. "Yep…that's it. Makes sense And keep that fellow who told us about him, Carter wasn't it, keep him well out of it. We don't want him and his mates from the Dockyard muscling in on the act.

"That might not be so easy." Brock leant forward and clasped his hands together. "Even if we don't say a word to him about Daley, we can't really stop him sniffing around. That scrap the other night'll be talk of the town round Union Street and he'd have to be deaf not to hear something. My guess is that Jack Carter and his chums are down there anyway."

"Unless we pull him in and warn him off?" Startin's eyebrows were raised and he watched as Brock's head moved from side to side while he weighed the odds.

"Trouble there is that he would have wound up his mates by now, wouldn't he? Probably started poking around already and if we put the skates under him they'll wonder what it's all about...they'll sniff summats up and get keener than ever. Try to get to him before we do, so to speak. We want Daley to run smoothly, not ducking and weaving with half the Dockyard Police on his tail."

"Reckon he could lead us in, then?"

"Could do, sir. There were some pretty interesting faces sussing out the hospital the other day. Here look." Brock turned the file towards Startin and opened it. "Special Branch got quite excited."

The inspector nodded, glanced briefly at what he had seen earlier before pushing it aside. Then he yawned and glanced at his watch. "Jeez, half-eleven. And what about this woman that's tangled up with Daley...Carter's sister? How does she fit in?"

Brock rubbed his nose then shook his head. "Got to take her chance, I reckon, sir. We need her there...Daley'll make for her and hole up for a while to lick his wounds. Once they're tucked up together we can think about staking the place out."

"You're sure about all this, Dave? Certain that this Daley's got something to show us...that he's working for somebody and's not just some unlucky sod who found himself in the wrong place at the wrong time? I mean, staking a place out takes time and manpower...it's one hell of a performance. You're sure, are you?"

"As sure as we can be." Brock looked at him. "Everything points to it...the clubs, the area, the faces that have been seen. Daley's in there all right. Up to something or other."

"He better be." Startin grinned. "If he's not then the guv'nor's going to go right up the wall." He paused, pursing his lips. "All right," he said slowly. "I'll go for it. We've got a bit of time, not much mind you. And we'll say nothing to that other crowd. Best leave them to their own devices. If they get bitten then...well." Startin shrugged and rose wearily. "That's their look out."

4.

It had been a good lunch and Rose stood in the hall doorway, watching those still at the table. There were only six of them but the noise was dreadful and she looked on admiringly as Perkins cleared the last remnants of the meal from around them.

He had been marvellous, she thought, insisting on returning on Boxing Day to prepare for the house party. Rose always knew she would like the trim, sandy haired Londoner with his sad eyes and clipped moustache but he had been everything she had hoped for and more. Most important of all though, he seemed to be getting on with Mrs Down and the two housemaids. The only problem was that he knew nothing about Sam. She was determined to keep it that way but had no idea how she was going to arrange things. He would find out eventually, she was sure. Just watching him move quietly between the chairs, she could see he missed nothing.

Sam had come over briefly on Christmas Eve, just before she went off to stay with Miles Ashcroft. As usual he helped with the horses but then they had two wonderful hours together, sober this time, and he had been much more relaxed. She saw him now for exactly what he was, a simple, easy-going west countryman with his slow Devon burr and gentle smile. There was a strong, powerful earthiness about him also as she had seen when he dealt with the horses. But there was a gentleness, too, and she couldn't imagine him ever shouting or throwing his weight around. There was something deliciously different about him which calmed and steadied her in return; none of the hassle and drama that came with the others. The thought that he had been deeply hurt and forced to his knees only endeared him to her the more.

When they were together, he talked about the things she loved hearing about, real country things like the pair of herons they had seen on the Barle, or about the way stags fought for their hinds in October when the leaves were coming down. Or about lambing in the Spring, when he got such joy at watching a new born lamb struggling to its feet, tottering and shaking, only minutes after being born. She smiled at the thought, hugging herself briefly at the memories.

"Come on, Rose." It was Archie Wallace. Louder even than Spiffy Foxley, he was fun for a short time but then set one's teeth on edge. "Over here, darling." He reached behind him for one of the chairs against the wall but Perkins had already put it in place. Rose saw his look of surprise. "I want to hear all about tomorrow…where we're going. Molland isn't it…one of those estate shoots?"

"You're pissed, Wallace." Spiffy Foxley turned back from the window. "Can't take you anywhere…God knows what Daphers sees in you. Where is the girl anyway?" He turned further and raised his cigar in acknowledgement to the wave from the table. Daphne Manners, blonde and painted, and dressed, as always, in black, had swapped places with Harry Maidstone. She and Ella Summerfield were discussing something, leaning towards one another and frowning in concentration. Her wave of acknowledgement was more one of dismissal than anything else. Harry was talking with Annabel Smith-Wyse, a woman brave enough or mad enough to have held onto Spiffy for more than a year. And they were all yelling their heads off.

Perkins was by her side. "I'll leave the port, madam. Brandy and liqueurs in the drawing room?" He raised his eyebrows inquiringly and waited. "Thank you, ma'am and I'll have the coffee ready."

"Thank you, Perkins...oh, who's out there today? Lily isn't it? Let her go as soon as you've finished. And you as well. No, go on...I insist." Rose had seen his look. "No, that's it now until dinner." She acknowledged his bow. "Come on everyone, next door." She clapped her hands but with little effect. "Harry, bring the decanter, would you."

"Are we going to see this chum of yours?" It was Spiffy Foxley again. "The hunting fella you've taken such a shine to?"

"Don't be so *silly*, Spiffy. You and Archie are like a couple of spies." Rose saw him about to protest. "Oh, yes you are. And I know who sent you...the Downwards, I'll be bound. They and Tubby Hayes."

"*And* the Crossleys...*and* the Bentleys...and, and simply *hordes* of them. All pressing for the gen on this big-booted heavyweight you've got your claws into."

Archie Wallace had joined them. "Oh yes. Quite a splash, you are, my love...news has even reached the locker room at the golf club, for Heaven's sake.."

"What piffle." Rose had reached the drink tray. "But look," she warned. "Just watch what you're saying, all right. Sam's a dear and I don't want any of your humming and hawing...or getting on your high horse, Archie. You can be jolly mean, both of you, and I don't want it. *Seriously*." She wagged a finger. "Now then...what d'you want? Archie, call the others would you then Perkins can clear away."

＊

As Webber, the groom, was ill, Sam had come over. He had promised to help but arrived earlier than arranged so he could be home again before dark. Jerry Chugg and Greg Thorne were coming over to Hayes and the three of them were going on to the Hunt Dance at The Crown. Five horses were enough for anyone to bed down and the bran mash was a messy business if you had guests about the place.

He paused by the saddle room door listening to the sounds coming from the house before glancing at the five heads watching him impatiently. He knew them all well but, of the five, he had to admit that 'Windsora', the dapple grey mare was his favourite. While the mash was cooling he mucked out what was necessary and made down the beds.

Only then, when he was on his way back to the feed room did he notice the front door of the house was open. There were voices as well, footsteps on the gravel and they were coming his way. One of them laughed, then the other who had seen him called out. "I say, you there…hang on a minute." Sam paused again, waiting for the two figures to come up through the gloom. "You're Sam, aren't you? Sam, Sam the ladies' man, what?" His companion laughed again.

"Sam Hawkins's the name." He could see them in the light and knew instantly that they had been drinking. One had his tie undone and, even from where he was, he could smell their breath. And drinking since noon or earlier, he surmised. Behind them he could see two more figures. He knew Rose was one for he could hear her voice.

"Oh, I say, it's like that is it…*Hawkins is the name*. How very grand."

"That's right. Now look, I must get on so if you'll pardon me….."

"*Pardon* you? I don't *pardon* anyone unless they've done something wrong…dropped a bollock or something. D'you ask anybody to *pardon* you, Spiffy? Hey, Spiffy, I say, *pardon old chap*." Sam paused, frowning to look at the man in the light before turning to go into the nearest box.

"Oi, don't slide away like that." Spiffy Foxley sounded angry. "Listen, you're the chap we met last time, aren't you?" Sam ignored him. "*Hey*, don't bloody well turn your back like that. And you really do fancy your chances, don't you? Oh yes." He could see the man better now. "You're the one who's been sucking up to Mrs Hatton. A right lusty romeo, so they say."

"Rose'll not take kindly to that." Sam turned to pull the door shut behind him.

"Oh, so it's Rose is it? That's a bit of cheek for starters…too bloody familiar I'd say. An' who said you could get all pally like that. Rose, I suppose. Well…*well*."

Archie Wallace had come up to the stable door. "You want to remember your place in this world, my friend. Remember where you come from. Just because you're out hunting together doesn't mean…."

Sam spun round. "I know my place", he cut in, pointing at them with a brush in his hand. "And it don't need nobody like you and your friend there to tell me that."

"Hey, watch it you. Don't you damned well start talking like that…how bloody well dare you." Archie Wallace was fumbling with the latch of the stable door.

"*Archie?…Spiffy?*…what's going on?" Rose had run the last few yards. "What on earth's happening?" She saw Sam standing there. "Oh, God, what's happened?"

"This ruddy great thing was pushing his luck…damned ill-mannered," he muttered. "Bloody chawbacon."

"*Stop it*, Archie...stop it at once. *Shut up*," she cried seeing him about to continue. "Oh God, Sam I'm so sorry. They've been drinking and have had far too much. It's my fault."

"No it's not...it's *his*, the bloody oik."

"*Archie!*"

"Hang on, Archie." It was Harry. "Come on, leave him be...come on." He pulled him away from the door.

"Oh Harry, this is simply ghastly. Take him away. Go on, get him to bed or something. And you Spiffy, go on...please. *Please*," she screamed. "*Now!*"

✳

Sam comforted her when they had gone. Her tears were bitter. She was ashamed of her friends. She felt dreadful at the things they had said. They didn't mean it, she told him. They would feel awful in the morning and she would get them to apologise. She wanted to help him clean up but he took her to the front door and saw her inside before returning to finish the job on his own.

He worked in silence with his anger burning on. He had met that sort before. Bad enough sometimes when sober, it all came out with the drink. Some, like Harry Maidstone were fine. They seemed to know but they others were something else. Right arrogant swanks, they were. And there was more from where they came from; heaps more, he'd seen them here. And they were her friends. How could *they* be her friends and *he* be a friend also? They were so different, totally and utterly. They were smart, toffee-nosed townies who knew nothing of the countryside and its ways, and who just came down to play around. They were privileged and rich and threw themselves about the place. He could never be easy when there were people like that about the place, and this lot were always going to be around. She would always be having them down and they would never accept him, never.

He stopped on his way home and pulled in to the side at the top of Winsford Hill. He switched off and wound down the window where he sat, listening to the tick of the engine as it cooled and the wind buffeting the car. He knew then that he would never be able to live up to her. She was one of them and that made it impossible: difficult enough for her but impossible for him. He had been shamed in front of her, humiliated, but this time he had stood his ground and now he was defiant. The anger lingered, a deep, smouldering resentment where once there had been just helpless dejection.

Chapter Nineteen

Eddie Bright had made up his mind. It was Kenny Maelmo, the Swede, who suggested operating further afield where pickings were richer and the chances of being caught grew less as the distance from Plymouth increased. He saw it at once.

When the years changed, there should have been much to celebrate. The old year, still weary and war-torn, ought to have been discarded with a flourish like some tattered piece of clothing. But it was not: victory jubilation had long since evaporated. People simply concentrated on what mattered most, namely survival and, where possible, making some sort of slow headway. Nobody knew quite what lay ahead; there was no bright new dawn, rather the old struggle seemed interminable.

With the New Year came the cold. First it was the wind which chilled the bone. For those who had to brave the elements, eyes watered and flesh stung with the bite from the north-east. Rubbish and tin cans blew noisily along the streets. Coats and scarves were swept into the air as their owners leant back, grabbing hold of their clothes as best they could. Then came the snow. Not much but enough to crunch underfoot until the pavements and roads became hazardous. And there it stayed, thawing occasionally before freezing again. Next day more snow would fall and the process would begin all over again until the landscape became a grey-brown, frozen mush.

But, in spite of such dull cheerlessness, life did go on. The bars and clubs stayed open. Big bands and concerts filled the dancehalls, while in hotels and country clubs such as Bowden Court the ballrooms were packed. And it was here, the Swede declared, that the richest pickings of all were for the taking.

*

Daisy Gunn was sent to look. The dark blue tyrolean-style hat, with its pink cord and feather, perfectly matched her three-quarter length herringbone. Her dark almost black wig, swept back into a bun and the clever make up, made her resemble just the sort of person who might apply for the post of assistant housekeeper. She had been selected for interview because her application form and letters of reference caught the eye. Her twelve years of domestic service could be verified either in writing or by telephone, so her covering letter explained.

Just one call had been made by the manager of Bowden Court. The letterhead address said 'Metropole Hotel', but it was to a tobacconist's office in Plympton that the call went where an associate of Eddie Bright's verified the good Mrs Hamer's credentials. Her husband had indeed been killed in Normandy, he confirmed, while serving with the Westminster Dragoons: a military unit about

256

which Daisy knew nothing but about whom Mike Daley briefed her carefully. The good Mrs Hamer, as Daisy was masquerading, was plumper than usual in her padded-out clothes, while the high heels on her lace-up boots, hidden by her long tweed skirt, made her look taller than she was.

Mike was not to drive her. Instead, one of the others took her to the taxi stand in nearby Totnes, exactly where a lady on such a mission would alight from the Plymouth train. Mike and Ricky were in other cars, sent out by day and night to check the grounds and the security of Bowden Court. It was here, on the third Saturday of the month, that the grand Ides of March charity ball was to be held.

Daisy enjoyed her day. She lunched with the senior staff and only once did she almost forget her name when Mrs Hamer was asked for the salt. In addition to the usual requirements, the assistant housekeeper at Bowden Court shared responsibilities with the day manager for security and accounts, matters about which she was questioned closely. Mrs Hamer's replies were convincing, in particular when she asked for the actual housekeeping ledgers and cashbooks to be produced in order to demonstrate her knowledge. Her understanding of household security, including matters concerning alarm systems and keys, impressed also.

Later, Mrs Hamer was shown around her proposed domain where, already, preparations were in hand for the forthcoming ball. The chambermaid who escorted her forgot nothing, and neither did she. Rooms were opened, attics were visited, cellars were checked and routes retraced. When she returned to the office to say farewell, her host had been called away but Mrs Hamer managed to entertain herself gainfully until her taxi returned. She then departed, for ever.

✳

"You're sure, Daisy, sure as that?" Eddie Bright glanced at the others around the table. He could tell that they, too, were uncertain about what she claimed. "It's a big place, plenty of money an' nice things there. Security's gotta be tighter than that."

"Well, I couldn't see it. An' remember I had time to do it proper." She tapped the table in frustration. "Twice most of it," she added. "Once when they were making a fuss of me. Thought I'd been given the job fer a minute," she quipped. "And then when I'd had a good butchers after I reckoned I'd worked out me plan...I had another look all on me own. But don't ask *me* why," she shrugged. "Must reckon they're safe, all tucked away out there in the sticks, I s'pose. But I could hardly believe it meself."

"And the grounds...bad there too?" Kenny the Swede leaned forward. He was sitting next to her, too close, and Daisy leaned back. She hated the cold, thin man with his yellowy skin and she knew he had little time for her. Nobody had ever seen him with a woman and Daisy, like the others, thought it spooky the way he crept about. Always a step behind Eddie with something clever to say, the Swede was ever present, his eyes covering anybody he thought was watching.

"Too many bleedin' trees an' that. Christ alive, you could hide half the army out there, an' no lights nor nuthin, just a couple of old bods dodderin' about with a torch, so they said. Yeah, reelly," she saw the Swede's doubt. "Go an' bloody ask 'em yerself then...an' don't think I wouldn't have had a ruddy good look if I'm going to be workin' there. Bloody hell, man." Her eyes glared angrily until he looked away.

"OK." Eddie held up his hand. "Let's move on...tell us how we do it, then. How do we get in and out?" All eyes were on her.

"Well, we've got the tickets, right?" She waited for Ricky to nod. "I need a partner, somebody what looks the part, like a geezer or a toff with plenty of dough, an' what can speak proper...somebody the guys on the door'll stand up for. An' I don't mean anyone here. Sorry, Eddie, but if I don't get the right face wiv me at the door, we're done for. Right...so, in we go. Whoever it is, has my little bag with him. Once in, he hands it to me and gets himself lost. Don't wanna see 'im again." She waved a hand, now aware that she had centre stage.

"Then off I goes up to my bedroom. Huh...how I *wish*." She grinned at the faces looking at her. "No, it's a gungy little hole alongside the linen cupboard and furniture store. God knows what they keep it for, sort of a junk tip but I can tuck myself away in there easy enough. Lock meself in an' get changed out o'me glad rags and into workin' clothes. An' that's where I stay." She tapped the table again. "Saturday night an' Sunday mornin'. Then all day Sunday an' Sunday night 'til you want the doors open. Simple as that."

Eddie's office was very quiet. "That's a long time. More'n twenty-four hours. What about food an' drink an' that."

"Simple," she shrugged, impatient at the question. "Come on, give me a chance. Got the run o' the place, ain't I? After all that lot have gone an' they've shut the place down I can go where I like, when I like...place's me own, so long as the geezers outside don't get curious."

"And timings?" It was the Swede again but the question was direct. He, like everybody else, was listening hard.

"OK." Daisy blew and looked down. "We'll say that they'll be back in on Sunday morning...to clean the place up an' that, an' also to clear the tills and sort the cash...that's the ticket money, all the charity an' raffle takings an' all the staff wages. A whole truck load o' bleedin' dosh," she emphasised. "Say they work late...to get it all ready for the bank run first thing Monday. Say they work until ten...give 'em an hour or so longer...say to midnight. Reckon I come out me hidey-hole then and get things ready. So...say one o'clock.

Reckon the place'll be dead by then.

"And the safe, lass?" Lennie Jenks, short, thin and nearly bald had been brought down from Bristol again. His features were grizzled and grey like the world in which he lived and worked.

"Mayworth an' Chubb." Daisy looked at him. "Double lever and cross-wheel spin. It were in the back office an' I 'ad a good look when it were opened."

"D'ya get the registered number?"

"Here, both of them." She pushed the slip of paper across the table. All eyes turned to the Scottish cracksman.

"Wheee," he whistled quietly. "That's nay problem…ah knows them, done 'em before." Having crumpled the piece of paper tightly in his hand, he put it into his mouth and began to chew. "Half an' hour," he mumbled. "That's all, but what about the windows? Light an' that?"

"Bit of a risk here." Daisy pulled a face. You can see straight in from the outside, through the office frosted glass an' all. I'll have to get down there an' draw the office curtains. Do them a wee bit at a time after everyone's gone. Should be all right but…" She shrugged. "What d'ya reckon, Eddie?"

Eddie Bright lifted his head and stroked his chin. Suddenly he looked brooding and swarthy, like a picture of one of those negro singers Daisy had seen. "Can yer do it blind, Lennie? No lights?"

"Aye." The cracksman never hesitated. "It'll take a wee bit longer though…say an hour."

Eddie looked round the table with one eyebrow raised. "I'm buying it," he muttered. "Buying it reel good. So, wheels roll on Saturday, March the fifteenth then…good old Julius Caesar, eh?"

2.

The weather cleared slowly yet snow still clung to the gullies and the north-facing high ground which the sun failed to reach. Spring staghunting had begun and the master, determined that days would not be lost, ordered the location of meets to be changed until the ground softened. Hayes Farm was high but not as high as Alderman's Barrow, the scheduled venue. The Hawkins family, Martin Trumper surmised, would look after them well.

Barbara was thrilled. There was ample room for parking, plenty of room in the front meadow for the field to gather and Desmond, the huntsman, could kennel the pack at the farm if they wished. Then, suddenly, less than two days beforehand the wind changed, swinging right round to the south-west and bringing with it rain that cleared the snow. For a moment she panicked, terrified that the meet would be moved again but it was too late. What was more, on the morning itself, the weather brightened; as the first riders came up the drive soon after ten o'clock, a watery sun broke through.

*

Archie Wallace was banished, Rose had decreed, until he was no longer an embarrassment. But the decision, sent by letter from Duxhams, irked his friend. They had been chums for years and Spiffy Foxley relished their expeditions into the darkest wilds of Exmoor. However, Spiffy knew when he was beaten. He himself had apologised. Champagne and flowers had followed his missive and his return to Dulverton had been sanctioned, albeit on probationary terms. There was an occasion when he had been tempted to plead his case but the presence of Miles Ashcroft dampened his resolve.

Nonetheless, last night had been a merry affair and the four set out for the meet in good heart. Spiffy Foxley, in what he took to be a further gesture of goodwill from his hostess, had been allotted the magnificent 'Windsora.' As they topped Mounsey Hill, the sun forced its way through there as well. Everything, as far as they could tell, was just as it should be

*

"Pat, listen will you. Take six of each…six port, six dry sherry and six whisky. On the big tray, and go carefully." Barbara Hawkins had decided to begin serving the stirrup cup. "Mavis, here's the cake. Rich plum on the left and linseed on the right. *One* slice each, until I say…there're some greedy tummies out there. Nancy…here's your tray. Both hands now. And Terry…where's *Terry?*" She looked round anxiously. "Where's Terry…somebody fetch him will you."

The kitchen was alive. Almost two hundred glasses had been gathered for the occasion. Bottles lay open. Cakes, some still warm, sat waiting on baking trays while the small army of helpers came and went. "Ah, Sam, dear." Barbara was taking off her apron. "Good…look, I'll do the hunt staff." She paused for breath. "Can you take a tray around to those at the back. Colonel Miles'll be there, and the Hatton party…and a number of others. Look after them, could you."

As soon as he came out of the front door, he began to search. The pack was at the top end of the yard. He recognised the huntsman and the two whippers-in, one of whom moved suddenly on his horse to head back a stray hound. Martin Trumper was there talking to a group from the village. His wife was there also and, as far as he could see, the rest of the hunt committee. Seventy, eighty, ninety riders had gathered in the yard already, more were in the meadow beyond and still more arriving, coming up the lane in a steady cavalcade.

More cars than they had seen for years were parked on either side of the drive almost all the way back to the road. A number of cattle lorries and horseboxes had been shown into the far field and he could see horses being unloaded. Foot followers were everywhere, many had climbed onto the banks and some, without bye or leave, were using the two trailers up against the shippon wall as grandstands. The rich, tangy smell of fresh horse dung hung heavily. Everywhere there was chatter and laughter, the sound of hooves swivelling on cobbles and the occasional shout above the hubbub. The farm dogs in the shed next to the hen house were going mad. Getting anywhere with a tray of drinks was going to be difficult.

Rose was talking to the Colonel near the gate leading into the field, while the rest of her party were a few yards away. One of them Sam recognised immediately: he could hardly forget the fellow and there he was, mounted on his own great favourite, Windsora, the dapple grey.

Just as he was approaching with the drinks, half the party moved away and it was then that he saw the grey was nodding a bit: she seemed to be favouring her near fore. It wasn't much, probably no more than a tweak in the tendon but the mare shouldn't be hunted today.

"Good morning, sah." Miles Ashcroft beamed as he doffed his bowler. "Very good to see you Sam, dear boy, and my congratulations," he drawled. "The whole place's looking in splendid shape, apple pie order, even now with this lot. And what luck with the weather, too." He reined back to allow Sam through.

"Hi...Sam. What's this, though? Not hunting today?" It was a happy, cheerful greeting but she pulled a sad face. "Oh, dear. And from here as well, Sam...from home."

"Be out later," he replied. Rose had taken a dry sherry and he had half turned towards Miles Ashcroft. "I'll come on later with the pack," he added. "They're kennelling them here and I'll give a hand bringing them on." He paused while the Colonel took a glass. "But listen, Rose...take a look at Windsora, will yer. She's slightly lame, I reckon. Over there look." He nodded his head in the direction of the others. "Near fore, I think. Not much but she should never be out like that."

"Really? Can't be." She stood in the stirrups trying to see. "Where...I can't see from here. Does Spiffy know? We'd better tell him."

"I'll go, just get rid of these first. And what's he called? The fella on him?"

"Foxley. Spiffy Foxley, but Spiffy'll do. Your chum." She was smiling but cautiously. "And, Sam..." Rose held out a hand. "Shush now," she soothed. Still smiling she put a finger to her lips. He nodded and pulled a face. "He's on his very best behaviour today," she added.

"Oh aye."

Foxley, he could see, was watching him as he made his way towards them. Sam noticed him turn to the others in the party and nod back over his shoulder towards him when the others looked his way. One laughed and the three drew closer together.

"Morning." Sam watched their brief acknowledgement. One of the riders he had not met before muttered something but they were all watching him, waiting for him to announce his business. "Mr Foxley, isn't it?" Sam, free now of his tray of drinks, stroked Windsora who lowered her head expectantly. "Look, I hate to tell you this but I reckon the mare's going short. I saw her from over there, when you moved just now. Her near fore."

"Rubbish, she's fine." Sam noticed the defiance but it was less than it might have been.

"And who're you? The groom?" The heavily built man in the riding mac, on Tempest, urged the animal forward.

Sam looked at him. "No, we own the place. You're on our land, actually…in case you didn't know it." He watched the man look away then turned back to Foxley. "It's true enough about the mare, I'm afraid and you shouldn't be out today…not with something like this."

"Oh, come on for goodness sake. It's nothing…can't be. Look, I've paid my cap and as far as I'm concerned I'm hunting today and that's that."

"What's all this? Argy bargy at this hour?" Humphrey Gervaise, the last of the party, had joined them. "What's up, Spiffy?" Sam glanced at the newcomer but ignored him.

"I know the mare well enough, Mr Foxley, and she's not right, not right at all…you could do lasting damage out today, y'know. Seriously. What I suggest is we take her back over there and have a look. Jump off an' we'll walk her up and down a bit. Just to check. I could be wrong but it didn't look good." He had Windsora by her noseband and the grey pushed against him. "Steady gal." Sam stroked her gently. "I'll get Rose if you like…she'll need to see one way or the other anyway."

❋

Sam saw at once. He was walking backwards, leading the mare. Foxley had dismounted and stood disconsolately. Rose could see it too: she was not right. Something had happened on the way over. "Oh dear, poor you, Spiffy. "She is favouring that leg and I'm afraid that's it. You couldn't possibly hunt like that." She sounded dejected. "Now…what're we going to do?" She looked at Sam. "Get a lorry or something? What d'you think?"

"We'll get you back." Sam nodded at them both. "Won't be fer a while, I'm afraid, not 'til they've moved off but one of us'll drop you back to Duxhams. And it'd be best for the mare to stop here fer a while...day or two anyway. Eh, gal". He was slackening the girth and let her reach down to snuffle at some hay that had been put out for the sheep.

It was later, when everything and everybody, except for a few lorries and cars had gone, that Spiffy Foxley tried to make his peace. He had been standing about looking out of place and feeling strangely vulnerable in his hunting clothes. Eventually he and Sam were alone together. "Look...Mr Hawkins, er...Sam. I think I owe you an apology."

"Oh aye." They were by themselves in the yard and Sam was standing with Windsora's saddle in the crook of his arm. The horse was in a loose box. Restless and curious she was taking mouthfuls of hay from the net and coming to the door to look about expectantly. "I wouldn't worry yerself. It bain't no problem, she'll be fine here."

"No, no. About when we met last. As soon as I saw you this morning I remembered...it all came back. Rose told me where we were coming to but I didn't realise it was you, your farm I mean." Sam could see the man's discomfort. What had prompted this sudden confession he had no idea but, once on their own, these sort were never quite so sure of themselves. And standing there in his breeches and bowler, with his gloves and his whip in his hand he looked truly out of sorts, quaint almost. And felt it, too, probably. He could see the man in front of him knew he was being appraised.

"Forget it. Bain't worth worryin' about."

"No, but look...I really do apologise." Spiffy was now walking with him towards the saddle room. He was a chubby little man and, somehow, reminded Sam of a small boy who had been caught at something and was trying to talk his way out of it.

"Best forget it Mr Foxley, as I said." Sam looked down at him. "If you'm concerned about it then 'tis up to you. But fer me...'tis finished, dead." The man had tried, he had to give him that. Whether or not he would have done so elsewhere, with his friends about him, he was not able to say.

He lifted the saddle onto a saddle tree, ran up the stirrups and folded the girth. When he turned the man's hand was out. Sam wiped his own on his breeches and took it, feeling the pudgy softness. His smile might have looked friendly enough because the fellow smiled back, but it wasn't. He could never be friendly with any of them for he had seen the man for what he was and nothing was going to change him.

"Hang on then. I'll get the keys...an' we'll run you back to Dulverton." Sam saw the look on his face. It was a mixture of relief and gratitude, but mainly relief and it made him feel good. And why did he feel so good about it? Was it not perhaps for his deed well done? Oh no, it was something much, much better, that made him feel like he did and he took one of his kicks at a stone.

3.

Life for Becky was easier, but there was little time to think about it. As soon as she had settled in the new apartment, Mike was home. For three days he was bedridden but then the doctor came and changed the dressings. The black stitching had pulled his stomach wound together and the flesh either side looked yellow and bruised, but he was satisfied and showed her what to do. Maudie helped also, learning to wait by her father's bedside with her arms outstretched until he helped her scramble up beside him. When Dada got up and dressed himself carefully, it was she who held out her hand to steady him and it was she who showed him the new cooker and fridge and the smart kitchen floor. All these she pointed out with wet fingers straight from her mouth, and a look of studied concern.

Becky was happy too. Mike bought her a new dress. He paid for her to have her hair done and got Daisy to babysit while they went to the cinema. She knew she was happier; she could feel it. Daisy told her she looked better, too, and Mike started to talk about their future again. The day after she walked with him to the surgery to have his plasters changed for the last time, he went in to work, then he drove again. Then Eddie Bright came home with him to tell Becky he was giving her man a better job. He put the first week's wages on the table in front of them and they gasped. A day later and he was back to work full time.

It was two days after that, Saturday evening, when she was waiting for Mike to come home, that she found the gun.

The semi-automatic fell from the shirt where he had hidden it, clattering heavily into the drawer she was tidying. It was black and shiny and there were bullets in a little cardboard box. It was heavy and Becky's hands flew back in horror. She gasped, staring at it mesmerised, then backed away, leaving it exactly where it was. She hurried to Maudie and picked her up before leaving the room and shutting the door behind her.

❋

"But *why*? In God's name why? What's the bloody thing for?" She had her back to the kitchen sink. She was angry and very frightened. But she was depressed also for here they were, arguing again as noisily and angrily as ever. This time, however, she was not going to back down. Sheer fear was tearing at her and had been ever since she found it. "D'you realise what this *means*? If you use the thing and somebody gets hurt...killed? D'you *realise* what'll happen t'you, Mike? Fer Christ's sake think, man...*think* and get rid of it right now."

"Listen, Becks." As he came towards her he held out his arms. "I told yer before, it's not there for real...it's only just in case we have to frighten 'em off.

Eddie's asked me to look after 'im an' there's some nasty people out there. It's just for when he's about his business, that's all. That's it, nothin' more'n that. Just to scare them off."

"*Rubbish...to hell!*" Becky spat the words "That's crap, absolute crap an' y'know it. Get a wooden one or a toy one or summat, but that thing's *real*...I've seen it, held it in me hands an' seen the bullets. You're bloody mad an' you ain't fooling me."

"Look, *listen*, will yer...bloody *listen*," he shouted catching hold of her and shaking her. For a moment they stood glaring at one another. He could see her defiance but he was angry, too, furious with himself for letting her find it. Now she would know why the extra money was coming in. Yes, they were going for high stakes now and they were having to play hard. But now she knew. "Listen, Becks." His voice had softened. "I'll get rid of it. Right? Honest I will, love. You'll never see it again. Honest to God, but listen. Not a word. OK?" She had relaxed and he had taken into his arms. "Not a word, darling. Promise me? Promise Mike not a word, eh?" He bent to kiss her but she pulled back.

"Just get rid of it," she muttered, looking away. "But, Mike." Now she was staring at him again. "For God's sake don't use it...don't even *think* of taking it out with you. Honest...if you'd got it with you, you might just...oh, fer God's sake." Her head was buried in her hands. "*Don't*," she pleaded. "Please don't."

"Don't say a word, will yer love? Not to Daisy, not to no one...I'll get it out of here. Promise."

"No...get *rid* of it." Becky looked at him. Her voice had risen again. "Lose the thing, chuck it away."

He nodded meekly. "Yeah, OK." But that was it. There was no promise. He didn't say how he would get rid of it and he didn't say when. He had stopped short of giving her the promise she wanted to hear.

"You will, won't you?" She pulled him into her and put her arms around his neck. "Please, Mike."

"Yeah...promise." He nodded and looked down before easing himself away.

4.

Daisy slipped into Legs Eleven. She preferred it to the other bars. The Blue Rose was dingy and Eddie had his offices on the floor above. The Naked Angel was all right, good for a laugh, but the Legs was the one she liked. 'Meet me when the legs's open', was a cry she and the others gave the boys and it never failed. Legs Eleven was brighter, too, and some of the girls there were her friends. Tomorrow night she was off to the big dance but tonight, Friday, she was on her own.

She went over to the bar, swung herself onto a stool and looked around. Sandra was there, talking to a couple of sailors, and Cherie, a new girl she barely knew, was with somebody else in one of the booths. It was quiet, still early she reckoned, so she ordered a drink and lit up. Only one of the other tables was occupied. The three men had been watching her since she came in and she caught them looking her way. They were expecting her to join them and one of them smiled invitingly. She lifted a foot in reply and smiled back, then waited as he made his way over. "Like to join us, luv."

Daisy looked him up and down. She always did that: it was an old trick that Gypsy Meg from Taunton taught her. Always let them know you're pickin' an' choosin'. Take yer time, it puts them back a bit an' gives you time to think. Let's them know there's nuthin special about them. Then they'll be chuffed if you give 'em the nod...pay up easy, then.

"What?" she replied, frowning at his impertinence. "All three of yer, at once?" She smiled and blew smoke in his face. "One at a time, darlin', that's me but not tonight. Time's out." He was a tall lad. He stood up straight and the short, neat cut of his fair hair gave him away.

"Mind if I talk?" Daisy shrugged and looked away as he pulled up a stool. They always asked that. "Been here long, have you?"

"Oh, give over, ducks. Blimey, it's the oldest line in the book." She watched as he shuffled uneasily on to his seat. He didn't look new to the game but there was a first time for everyone. "Can't you do better'n that? What're you after then, eh?"

"No, no. It's not that. Don't worry, I'm not that green. Been around a bit too, y'know."

"Oh yeah, big deal...so, what's yer game then? Wa'dya want to talk for?"

"I'll tell yer." He beckoned, getting off the stool and pointing to a corner table. "C'mon." As he took hold of her arm, one of his companions called out but he brushed the remark away. "There's summat I want to know, an' maybe yer can help." Daisy followed and sat, mildly curious at the strong Devon accent yet alert to what he was after.

"I'm 'ere looking for someone, a young woman. As a matter of fact, it's my own sister." Daisy studied his face. "Here...look." She watched as he opened his wallet and took out an old photograph. "Here." He turned it round and pushed it towards her so she could see the four figures standing by the haywain. "That's her...not very good I'm afraid." He flattened it on the table and sat back so she could see it better in the light. "That's her...over six years ago now. Becky's her name. Becky Carter and I'm her brother, Jack."

Daisy froze, still staring at the fulsome country girl, kneeling down and holding the dog. It was Becky, without a doubt. Those eyes and the mouth, and the way she held her head. She started to speak but stopped. Her heart was pounding. "Go on," she said quietly without looking up. "Tell me more."

"That were taken up on Exmoor. Where us grew up. The man who Dad worked for, an old army man…a colonel, he took it and gave us a copy. Well then." He paused and took back the photo. "After I left and war broke out there was a spot of trouble. A soldier came along…" He stopped again, knowing at once by the look on her face that she knew. She was staring at him: her eyes were wide, not with fear but they were bright with curiosity. "You know her, don't you? I can see it all over yer face. Hey, that's great…wunnerful." He was smiling. "Is she here, down hereabouts? She is, isn't she? I can see you know. She's all right, isn't she…and the baby? She had a child with the soldier."

"Look." Daisy had a hand on his arm. "Yes, I know her. She's OK. Honest she is, but she's done a runner, y'know. Run away from the family an' that. Doesn't want to know 'em. I know you're her bruvver. Told me a lot about you. Thinks the world of you, she does but…."

"Then where is she?" Jack was leaning forward. "I've got to find her, for God's sake. I've come all this way. Can't you tell me…or take me there?"

Daisy sat back. Once again her eyes looked him over. She knew he was her brother; of course she did. She could see it a mile off but she had to be careful. What about her family? Maybe she didn't want to know them any more, even him. And what about Mike? It didn't sound as though he and Jack were exactly friends. "Look." She was picking her words. "I'll tell her. No, don't worry." She patted his hand. "I'll tell her we've met and I'll get back to yer. Honest to God, I will. I've known her since the convent days; helped her to get out of it an' all. I know her as well as anyone. Here, look, tell yer what…gimme your phone number. Once I've spoken to her, I'll call you. Go on, write it down an' yer address as well." She watched as he got up to go to the bar then waited while he wrote.

"I tell yer what, though. Jack, isn't it? Don't go asking no questions down here, Jack. People don't like it. It's not that sort o' place. But Becky's all right and the baby, I can tell yer that. She don't work here nor nuthin' like that. Not on the game nor nuthin'. But keep yer nose out of it, right, an' I'll get back to yer, soon as we've spoke."

She patted his hand reassuringly. "Now then, off yer go, darlin'. Back t'yer pals." She got up and left him sitting there. Even after she had returned to her bar stool he was still there but then he looked up and grinned, flicking her a mock salute as he rose to join his companions. She tossed her head and raised her cigarette in reply then turned to the barman with her empty glass.

5.

She looked at her watch and rolled off the bed, then turned to stub out her cigarette. No matter how many times she looked at the dress hanging from the wardrobe, the sight of it still thrilled. It was a bit old fashioned, to be sure, but the lady from Clifford's in Exeter said the style suited her, made her look a bit taller and it was very, very elegant she had assured her.

It was a full length evening gown of pale green lace decorated with bands of silver lame. The shoulder straps were sequined as was the big bow at the back that fell away. The shoes and handbag matched exactly and her hair looked lovely as well. Somehow the extra bits they had given her blended perfectly with her own deep auburn curls. Daisy stood, all five feet three inches of her, and looked at herself in the mirror.

But, before anything else, she had to pack the holdall. It was a new one, far too smart for what was going inside, but then there were the blokes on the door to impress. First there was the black balaclava, then the dark green army shirt and socks, and the brown slacks. The black army PT shoes were almost new and she had been wearing them during the week. Then came the surgical gloves, then the string, the knife and her tiny blue torch with the shade. Next were the dental probes and plastic strips plus her own set of master keys for the locks. And finally, last of all, there were her goodies: the nuts and chocolates and her bottle of water. Over it all she packed her nightie with some undies and a few girlie things just in case they opened the bag to check.

She glanced at her watch again and flexed her fingers as if preparing herself for the locks and catches that were waiting for her. There was exactly an hour before the car came so, slowly, so as not to disturb her carefully set hair, she undressed and went to run the bath.

Chapter Twenty

"So what's he up for?" Chief Superintendent Mason frowned and smoothed back his hair. There was precious little on his polished dome to tidy but it had become a habit, in particular when he was frustrated. Their footsteps, brisk and together, rang out down the dimly lit corridor.

"Receiving stolen goods, sir. That and he's a pimp…one of that nasty new crowd on the other side of Millbay." Inspector Startin hurried to keep pace with his Chief. The man they were holding had decided to talk and it looked as though it could be the breakthrough they had been waiting for.

"What's his game then? Why's he offering to sing?" Mason glanced at Startin with one eyebrow raised.

"Not sure exactly, sir, and we didn't push him. Seeing as he wanted to talk to you on your own, I thought we'd leave that sort of thing…give you a chance to break the ice."

"Hmmph…this it?" They stopped at the interview room door and Mason hung back to allow Startin to go ahead. It was the usual, cell-size, almost window-less chamber with the regulation sea green walls and dark blue stripe, plus the attendant spartan furniture. Detective Constable Brock stood as they came in. Mason nodded and raised a finger as the uniformed constable in the corner came to attention. "That him?" Mason ignored the man in the chair and held out a hand for Brock's file.

"Kenway, sir. Thomas Walter Kenway, currently on remand."

The Chief wrinkled his noise. "And what does he want, fer cryin' out loud?" He still had not acknowledged the existence of the prisoner.

"Says he wants to talk…but only to you, sir. Says he's got something we've been looking for."

Mason half turned then suddenly crouched low and rounded on their visitor. "Yer, what? What, might I ask have you got for me…that makes my visit here so worthwhile? Eh? Fell out with Eddie Bright and his lot did you…is that it, Kenway?" Mason rose and leant over the man. "Didn't want to know yer, did they, eh? Come on then, don't be shy." He watched as the prisoner nodded. "Can't say I ruddy blame 'em, either." He pulled up the chair vacated by Brock, spun it so that it faced him then sat, all the while glaring at the man in front of him.

"Right then." Mason looked up and at the others. "All right Inspector…that's all, thank you. But you, DC Brock, you hang on and you, too." He glanced at the uniformed man. "OK, Kenway." Mason leant forward once more. "Before you start, let me just whisper a few sweet nothings in that grubby little ear of yours. Eh? Let me just remind you that we've got yer cold, my son...dead in the water. Just like that." He let the flat of his hand fall silently on to the table. "Stolen goods and prostitution...for the third time...all adds up nicely fer a good stretch." He paused.

"So, hear this, you." Now he was talking quietly. "If you're having us on, wasting my time, lad, then I'll throw the bloody book at you." He tapped the file on the table. "Nah, on second thoughts...better'n that, we'll take you back to Bright's patch. We'll tell 'em all just what you've bin up to, calling in on us here...and then we'll let you loose in the middle of one his joints when they're all ready an' waitin'. Blue Rose or Dusty's Bar...summat like that. Eh? Just imagine it, a nasty, squealin' little grass served up for dinner...."

Kenway, a swarthy man with shoulder length hair and piggy eyes, was biting his lip. "I'll be straight with yer...dead straight, and no messin'." He glanced at Mason then away quickly. "No need fer that guv', honest."

"Well, that's very considerate of you, my friend." Mason's words came slowly as he motioned to Brock to start writing. "All right, then ...out with it, but take yer time," he advised. "Take just as long as you like."

"Don't know much mind but what I do know's gen...dead gen." Kenway looked from one to the other. He drew in his breath, looked at his fingers and exhaled slowly. "It's gonna be a place called Bowden Court, up near Totnes." Mason met his glance. "Some posh joint. March the sixteenth, I heard, the night after some big do up there. And they're going to take shooters in with them...gonna be armed this time." Kenway paused and wiped his mouth. "That's it...just that. Don't know nuthin' more."

"And who gave you this juicy little tit-bit?" Mason sat back. "C'mon Kenway...that's more than yer life's worth to tell me this. If word ever gets out ...you're as good as dead. Yeah? Next week, next year, it won't matter. If they ever find out they'll be waiting for you." Mason watched, letting the words sink in.

"So let's start all over again, shall we...and this time we'll fill in the gaps, and you'll be telling me just why you've come running. Won't you Kenway. Don't s'pose you fancy a little trip down Union Street way. Not with that Eddie Bright an' his crowd waiting to welcome yer." Mason cracked his knuckles. "All right, my sunshine. Let's be having it. Everything...and I mean everything."

※

Time was against them but, with the Chief himself in charge, the police moved fast. Suspecting Bright had been given information from inside he decided not to bring the management of the country club in on his plan. It would have to be done cold, from the outside and they would have to hit them while they were on the job.

It was going to be difficult but, at that point, the gang would be relatively immobile and their resources split. On the other hand they would be at their most alert. Against that again, once the police moved in the gang would be trapped, bottled up, and the law could take its time. It was a fine balance but a stake-out it would have to be. An ambush with all routes covered. Applications for the use of firearms would have to be submitted also. Mason wasn't going to start taking chances: he wanted them alive if possible but he wanted them any way they chose to come.

"And it's the big'uns we want. OK?" Mason looked round the table. "Kenway's running...we've got him released on bail, on pain of a slow and horrible death if he makes a cock of it, I might add. His girl, the one Bright took from them, is doing what she can. Works from the Blue Rose but the heathen savage raped her stupid an' she's turned King's evidence...singing like crazy." Mason paused. "Our pal, Bright, overdid it this time. And *so*...a woman scorned, eh?" He grinned back at the smirks.

"No, seriously, we know some of Bright's top men are going on this and they're the ones I'm after. Right, *Chris*." Mason turned to Startin. "Let's have a look at what you're proposing." The inspector got up and went to the blackboard where he pulled the cord on the drop, revealing the layout of Bowden Court and the approaches.

"Hang on...before you start." Mason held up his hand. "Now look...all of you. It's a tricky one this...aren't they all, but I've laid down certain principles for Chris Startin and his team to build on. Right...*one*." Mason held up his left hand and took hold of his index finger. "We hit them *on* site...while they're there an' their heads're buried in it. *Two*...maximum force to contain them. I don't want any running battles all over the bloody countryside. I want to surround them there and keep them there. And *three*...weapons will be taken but used only where life's been threatened and there's no other way of stopping them. It's the usual green card procedure but we all need to be clear on that. Right, Chris, away you go." Mason sat back. "When you're through we'll take a break an' then tear you to bits. Off yer go, lad." He half turned his chair towards the board and loosened his tie.

*

Daisy was ready by ten. The last of the hotel staff had gone ages ago but she waited to ensure none of them returned, to tidy or collect something they had forgotten before Monday morning. As she sat waiting, she listened to the wind in the eaves around her. For a time it rained, the brushing and swishing against the roof making her hideaway feel snug and secure. But it cleared and the clouds passed, allowing a glimmer of light to enter what had been an inky blackness. Sometimes the lights of passing cars filtered through the trees and in through the skylight, playing along the low ceiling above her. Other than that there was nothing and she sat on alone with her thoughts, just waiting. Then, at eleven, she moved.

She pulled the office curtains, just as she promised, one piece at a time, keeping herself beneath the level of the outside windows. Lennie Jenks was set to approach the tradesmen's door from the bushes behind the dustbins. She would have to be ready for him but she trusted nobody and set about organising herself to a plan she made on her earlier visit. One o'clock came and she was ready for the cracksman. At ten past he was there, exactly as planned and she led him in.

*

"Higher." His ear had been pressed against the lock but now he sat back looking at it. Daisy moved the torch as he asked and waited while he stared at the lock and thought. "Nope." He spun the wheel gently. "It's the third tumble," he whispered. "Thirty-two...eighty-one...nineteen...twenty-six it has to be...c'mon yer bitch." He moved forward again, placing his ear against the lock once more.

Daisy's eyes moved from his fingers to his lips and back again. Each time he breathed a number, his fingers turned the dial. Sometimes he grimaced or shook his head. Once he lowered his hand then rolled his shoulder to ease the cramp. But, suddenly, he looked up. Then slowly, as if hardly daring to move, he eased himself back, pulling open the door of the safe behind him. "There," he breathed. "There we are, my bonny wee bairn...quick now. The first holdall...*here*, and hold the torch." Most of the money was in canvas bags. Eddie had told them to go for that first, then grab whatever they could.

Daisy reached for the holdall but stopped. She turned, froze for a second then clapped him on the shoulder. He sat back and listened. Then it came again. Whistles, police whistles and there were several of them. Then they heard the shouts. "*Get out,*" he hissed. "*Quick, get out*...follow me. Back the way we came in. C'mon...*run.*" He had gone but Daisy let him go. She stopped where she was, listening and testing the air, waiting until she knew for certain which way to go.

*

"*Shit...look.*" Mike Daley reached for the gear stick and gunned up the big V8. He and Jake Patterson had been waiting for Daisy and Jenks. One of the police cars had come round to the rear of the building from the far side and a second had stopped short. Another they could see had pulled up close to the front door. There were men running and one, no two, were coming their way. "Here...take the sodding thing an' use it if we have to." He passed the gun to Patterson. "Hold tight...we're getting out." With a powerful roar, the big car leapt forward, pressing both men back into their seats.

But there, half way across the drive was another car. *"Down."* Daley accelerated. The heavy girder behind the bumper of the Pilot took the splintering crunch but the police Rover spun crazily behind them.

"Step on it man...there's another behind us." Patterson was leaning out of the window. Daley heard the gun firing.

"Keep it, man. Keep it for later. Hang on we're going left." Daley swung the wheel, then back again as the car slewed wildly. Once through the wide entrance, he changed down and accelerated hard once more. "Hey, hey...now we're away," he yelled. "See how she flies now, Jake me lad."

"Jeez...look out!" It was Patterson who saw the next car. It was parked half across the road in a blocking position further down the hill, just on the bend and above the deep drop down to the railway line. "Shit," he cried, shrinking back. *"Look out!"*

"Christ." Daley's eyes were wide. "Hold *on."* The Ford Pilot almost managed to clear the car. Just after the two policemen with torches had leapt aside, it crashed head on into the police car's side, half rolled it then rose up and on to it before hitting the roadside barrier. The cutting down to the railway line was steep, almost vertical and the big car seemed to pause before plunging the sheer forty or so feet to the first rocky ledge. Those in the road saw the bright flash of the explosion but the car tumbled on until it hit the track where it came to a rest upside down and still burning fiercely.

Just there, at the bottom of the cutting, the railway line bent sharply to the right before falling away, exactly where the drivers liked to pick up speed. The nine twenty-two from Penzance would never have had a chance of stopping in time even if the driver had seen what had fallen directly in his path. When he did manage to bring the express to a halt, he was several hundred yards further down the line. By then, what was left of the car and its occupants had all but vanished.

✳

When Daisy moved, it was towards the cellars. Each door she passed through she locked behind her, jamming the key. Once down the cellar steps it was black but she knew where she was going. Even so, and although she had been there before, the heat in the boiler room surprised her. Once again, she locked the door behind her and ran quickly through to the coke hole, locking that too. Scrambling over the mountain of coke she reached the bottom of the chute and began to climb, pressing her plimsolls against the sides to stop herself from slipping back.

At the top she inched up the heavy, wooden trap door that lay flat to the ground. She had checked it earlier and now fixed it open with the wedge she had left there. The lid of the door was raised no more than an inch or so above the ground but it was enough for her to look and listen. And there she waited. Later, much later, but still well before dawn she eased it higher and wriggled out, then ran swiftly to where Mike Daley had left the bicycle for her.

2.

"Aaah...*look*. Sam, how *sweet*. What ever's it doing, like that?" Sam chuckled quietly at her question and watched as the orphaned lamb struggled after the ewe. It was dressed in the skin of another lamb which had been smeared with blood and it was calling plaintively. The sheep, with one lamb behind her, turned and butted the smaller lamb, knocking it flat. It rose to its feet gamely, still calling, only to be butted again. "*No*...stop her, Sam. I can't bear it...she'll kill the poor little thing."

"Nope." Sam shook his head. He was talking to himself rather than her. "She's not taking it...I'll get the dogs." He bent down and lifted the lamb from the pen, placing it by her feet where it stood, shivering and confused. "'Tis our only chance," he muttered. "Won't be a sec."

Rose had come over to ask Barbara about the new blacksmith in Dulverton and was not to know that lambing at Hayes was in full swing. Drew, after being up most of the night, had gone to bed and she had come across Barbara in the kitchen feeding tame lambs in a box near the oven. Another, smaller and seemingly lifeless, lay close to the lower oven door which was open. For once Barbara looked tired. She had forgotten her make up and her hair was tied untidily. In answer to Rose's questions, she told her that reports were good and that the man, son of the North Molton farrier, was already making a name for himself. But Sam would know more. He was, she explained, out in the lambing shed behind the shippon.

And it was there that she found him, unshaven and dishevelled, having worked with his father until breakfast, then gone on by himself. Now, almost noon, he looked ready to drop. His hands and clothes were filthy: everything everywhere, and he in particular, stank of sheep. But seeing her there cheered him and they talked briefly until he asked if she would like to come round with him. It was then that they saw the ewe with the two lambs.

*

The dogs came first, rushing excitedly from their confinement, delighted at their sudden freedom and eager for whatever was afoot. "Tell me what you're doing." Almost without thinking she had slipped an arm through his. "Come on." She squeezed his arm between hers and her body. "Little townie here wants an explanation from the master himself." He smiled and looked at her, then patted her hand.

"'Tis an old trick we'll try...well, parts of several, reely. This littl'un here, look...the one in the skin. She lost her mother...died at birth an' we took the

274

lamb in, bottle fed her for a few days. Then here." Sam nodded at the ewe and lamb behind the hurdle. "The old ewe lost one of hers last night after the rain. But there's milk enough there fer two so I skinned the dead lamb and put it on this'un here. Smeared it with blood, too, to give her the right scent. Don't always work, mind," he warned. "Either her takes it straightaway or…well, her doesn't want to know…like we've just seen."

Rose nodded, enthralled by what he was saying and found herself drawn comfortably close to her shepherd by this deep love he had for his flock. As he finished, she hugged his arm tightly. "But why the dogs? What're you going to do?"

"Here, I'll show 'e." He eased himself away from her and opened the pen, placing the orphan lamb close to the ewe. The lamb began to call and Sam picked her up and placed her closer still. Then, before the ewe had time to think, he called in the dogs. "*Gid on in there,*" he commanded. "*Gid on, gid on.* Here…Midge, Midge, Midge, Shep, Shep…*gid on, gid on*…Ksssss…ksssss."

Rose watched horrified as the dogs leapt at the ewe who backed away and stood defensively over her lamb. Both dogs barked furiously, feinting attack after attack but kept dodging back from the horns as the ewe charged and butted, bravely defending her young. Sam picked up the orphan which had been knocked over and, once again, placed it close to the ewe. Again it struggled forward but now she allowed it to seek shelter behind her while she kept the dogs at bay. Once Shep fell. The ewe was quick and charged, and it was Sam who stood in her way.

He called them off before they tired, telling them to lie which they did, panting heavily while their master waited patiently. The ewe moved forward out of the corner and they watched as, first her own lamb, then the orphan began to feed from her, wriggling their tails contentedly. The mother stood quietly, suckling the lambs while watching and waiting lest the dogs should return, her eyes glaring fiercely at where they lay. All fear had gone; once she stamped in anger and snorted challengingly but the dogs never moved. "There we are. Looks as though her might take 'er." Sam took Rose's arm and stepped back, pulling her with him. "Leave 'em be fer a while."

"You love it, don't you?", she asked, looking at him enquiringly. She now saw him more clearly than ever in his own distinctive light and it was as if she was trying to measure him, weigh him against the other men she had known. "It's your life, isn't it, Sam, your whole life?"

It was such a different world here on the farm, in springtime, when nature brought in new life and where men, men such as Sam, played their part. There was a strength and goodness about those who communed with nature like this, as if nature herself had allowed them to enter her own great world, where some vast, mysterious force reigned supreme. Most men, almost everyone she had ever known, would be useless and helpless in such a situation, quite unable to offer anything, yet here was one who seemed at peace with what was happening. He was part of it.

"Not just right now," he quipped. "But aye, 'tis a way of life...you'm born to it. Here...Midge." His dog had barked. Then they, too, heard the call.

*

"Hullo, Barbara." It was Rose who spoke first. "You're looking very cheerful. What's all this?" Sam's mother had come upon them suddenly, accompanied by two strangers. That was bad enough but she was grinning triumphantly, looking as though she had just stumbled across something that amused her. "You're looking very pleased about something. Go on...what is it?" Rose pressed, smiling enquiringly.

"Nothing you could ever imagine, either of you," she assured them, still smiling. "No, not in a thousand years," she went on. "But, *now then*...well, no. I'll let them introduce themselves but they reckon you've met before."

"*Me?*" Sam saw her look. "When's that then?" He stepped forward, frowning uncertainly and wiping his hands."

"Near on three years ago, now." The taller and fairer of the two men, dressed in corduroy slacks and a polo-necked sweater, was nodding. "Yep...it's you all right. You're the one." He stopped in front of Sam looking at him expectantly. "Remember me?"

Eventually Sam broke the silence. "*Cuh...aye*. The plane crash...up to Larkbro'." He looked at the other, an older, darker and shorter man dressed in a brown, fleece-lined jacket. "Cuh...yes, I remember the pair of yer. I helped you out, didn't I? Sitting in the doorway, you were. You an' one of they others." He was shaking his head for he could see them now, sitting or half lying there waiting for him. Suddenly it all came back: the sharp stench of fuel, the black smoke and the pinging of hot metal. "Just the two of yer, weren't it?"

"That's right...Jerry Duckworth was the other one...the Flight Engineer. But he's gone, poor lad. Killed. Bought it over the Ruhr...almost two years ago, now. I'm Sandy Holmes, the wireless op."

"And I'm Jimmy Bond, mate." The dark, older one came closer. "Listen, it's bloody great to see yer again, pal...I can tell yer. Came right inside fer me, so yer did. Hell of a state I was in. Bloody marvellous...saved my skin." Sam flinched as the man threw his arms around him. "No, honest, straight up...bin meaning to do this fer a long time now...streuth." Rose had joined Barbara.

"And they others...what of them?" Sam stood back.

"Chris Amebury, the Canadian, never flew again, poor sod. Op after op he's had but his back had gone. An' poor wee Billy Higgins, our front gunner, the littl'un with his hair all over the place? Killed on his way back from Hamburg. Just got caught…a coupla months more and he would have made it."

"Skipper's all right though. Jammy bastard." It was the cockney, Bond, again. "Wing Commander now, scrambled egg everywhere and buckets of gongs. And that's the lot, mate…just the six of us, there was, an' we all got out. Thanks to you lot. But here…hang on a mo." He looked from one to the other. "There was a girl, wasn't there? Up there with her dad. Where's she then?" Bloody lovely she was…didn't half look after us. Loved her to death, we did. Ain't around, is she?" Bond glanced at the faces.

"Moved on." It was Sam's shrug that told them, and the way he said it. The two visitors were silent. Everyone was for a moment, until Barbara broke in.

"They wanted to go up and see the spot," she announced. "See where they came down but they've only got a car and I said I thought the track'd be too bad just now. And there're all those warning signs and things up there."

"Aye." It was Sam again. "I could take yer up d'rectly if yer want but you'd best wait awhile yet…'tis awful wet up there. We've taken the grass keep again an' we'll be putting the ewes and lambs up there d'rectly. May, June time's best. Dry underfoot an' you can walk right up to where t'was."

"Doesn't matter for now." Sandy Holmes pushed himself away from the beam he had been leaning against. "It was you we came to see…you, my friend. We asked in the village and they said you're up hereabouts. We're only down at Chivenor, so we can hang on a bit…come back when it's warmer, as yer say. An' we'll try to get the skipper along as well…he'd like to see you again. Make a day of it, all of us…all that're left, anyway."

"Aye, daresay. Cuh…'tis still hard to believe." Sam was shaking his head. "Often wondered what'd become of yer all."

"Come on now…tea." Barbara broke in. "We can talk on inside. I knew you'd be thrilled, Sam. And so was I…daresay I gave myself away just now, but we had to come and get you or you would never have come. Well you wouldn't, would you?" she laughed, stepping round the mud.

✳

Sam had never really given much thought to what he had done that day. Rose could see it by the way he dismissed it, and so could the airmen. They talked on about the war and what they'd done but Sam never mentioned he had tried to join up. They would have thought him a right bloody fool, he said later. Men like them would never understand why anybody would ever be turned down and told to stay at home like that. Only once was Becky mentioned again but there was another sudden silence and the matter was dropped.

The airmen had to leave and Sam had to get on, so they parted, the airmen promising to return. To see all the sheep they'd missed when they crashed, Jimmy Bond vowed. Barbara went too, rushing as usual, this time to get to the chemist's before they closed.

For a while the two of them were silent. "You never told me anything about that." Rose had moved round the table and now came up to him. "Why not?" she whispered, reaching up to stroke back a lock of his hair. He shrugged. "Mmm? What else have you been up to? Who else's going to come around the corner…or drive up the lane here, and start telling tales about you? Mmm?"

"There's nort else," he laughed. "Bain't done nuthin else, that's fer sure." He shrugged as she watched, then looked away. He was desperately tired; that she could see. Yet he was about to go out again. The good shepherd that he was had no option but to push himself on. But he wouldn't have wanted it any other way. He would pick up his crook from the wall, let out the dogs and then, with that slow, steady stride of his, he would be around the flock until it was too dark to see.

And the man never, for a moment, knew what a man he was. Nothing, not even the grateful thanks of the aircrew, could make him see it. Suddenly she longed for him, for the silent strength of his presence, his warmth and his humility. They walked together to her car where he held the door for her. But then, just there, with the door half between them, she threw her arms around his neck. She pulled him close, and he her until she felt his hands on her back. As she got into the car, her eyes filled and she dared not look at him, and it was not until she had lost sight of him in her mirror that she wiped at the tears.

3.

Mike had told her that he might be a way for a night or two and that she was not to worry. Nor did she. Maudie loved her new pushchair which Daisy and her mother had found at the Octagen church bazaar. She had her rag doll and the old crochet blanket as well, and was never happier than when she and her mother walked to Victoria Park in the afternoon to feed the ducks. So, while she waited, Becky just walked a little further and dawdled a little longer.

She never bought a paper so she would not have read the article about the fatal accident on the main London line. Even if she had she would have thought it quite usual to read that the police were not releasing any further information until their enquiries were complete. But then, after two days of silence she did begin to wonder. It was the longest he had been away and it was strange that nobody had told her anything. She never went near Union Street but now she forced herself. As far as she could tell it looked the same. She even walked past her old apartment and asked one of the girls outside Dusty's Bar but nobody seemed to know. The girl just shrugged and turned her back.

She knew Daisy would come sooner or later but, when she did and they heard what each other had to say, they could do little other than stare at one another. "You *sure* he's not back?" Daisy asked again, turning to take off her coat. Now, suddenly, it was different: Becky knew that something must be badly wrong. "He should 'ave been by now…coupla days ago at least."

"Oh, c'mon, Daisy…I were goin' to ask *you* that. Course I'm sure. I'd've told yer straight, else." Daisy could see she was telling the truth. "Summat's happened, hasn't it?" Becky's voice was urgent. "Why's he not come back, then…an' where've yer all been? What's up, Daisy…c'mon, tell me." Now her voice had risen.

"I dunno." For once Daisy seemed vague and lifted a hand to her cheek. "He's not down the clubs nor nuthin. Bain't nowhere down there. I've looked. I just dunno," she muttered. "Strange, isn't it." She didn't mention that for the last twenty-four hours, she and the other girls had been asking around. Something must have happened: had Mike and Jake Patterson been caught, the police would have been round. On that point they had all agreed, but there had been no sign of them.

"Daisy, *tell me*…fer God's sake let me know." Becky had her by the shoulders. She shook her then took her face in her hands. "Something's wrong isn't it…summat awful…please Daisy. What've you all been up to? What's been going on? " she pleaded. It was then that Daisy told her all she knew. Only later, after they had been asking each other the same questions over and over again without getting anywhere, did she remember Jack. Becky was thrilled, over the moon.

"Oh, my *God*…Daisy why didn't you tell me? *Why*…oh, never mind, it doesn't matter but yes. Yes please, *please* tell him where I am. Oh, Jesus…*Jack*…how wunnerful. I've got to see him. Perhaps he might know…but no of course not," she gabbled. Suddenly she laughed and wiped at a tear. A moment ago she had been worried stiff, now she was baffled and confused yet beside herself with joy, and all at the same time. "No, he wouldn't know nuthin, would he?"

Daisy settled her, promising to come back as soon as she had made contact or as soon as she had heard anything about Mike. But then, not long after she left, everything changed, and changed for the worse.

✳

She contacted Jack just as she promised she would. But by now she was certain that something dreadful must have happened and she knew also that Becky and Maudie would need her help.

She rang his number twice then ran to the dockyard gates where she had to wait until he came back in from patrol. Watching his face as she told him made her smile, but she had to struggle in his arms when he lifted her up and swung her round with delight. His hat fell off when he swung her again and he was still laughing as he grabbed hold of her after he had taken his sister's address. Tell her, he urged, that he would be around as soon as he could after work that very night, probably about seven.

It was when Daisy got to Legs Eleven and met the girls that she heard. As her mouth went dry and the cold chill of fear coursed through her, Cherie had to tell her again. She sat for a moment, calming herself as her mind raced. "The Swede," she whispered. "God, no...*him?*"

Cherie nodded. "True as I'm sitting here, luv. Eddie an' he never went on the job last weekend but Eddie went last night, late it was but he just took off. Tried to get Kenny to go with him but he wouldn't move. Mickey, down the Blue Rose warned us...came all the way up to see us, he did. Said the Swede told him he had some things to do...some tidyin' up."

"What did he mean... *'tidying things up'?*" Daisy was still thinking fast, but it was a needless question. She knew all right: she just wanted to be sure.

"Close down those what he reckons knows too much. B'lieve me, Daisy, he's after you...wants you out of the way...you an' Mike's girl. Do yer in, he will 'cos you're the ones what know. The fellas bad...evil and he's out there now somewhere already."

"Sure...sure." Daisy was nodding. "Yeah...sure." She paused, still thinking then suddenly she got up. "Look, thanks love. I'll go now...I'll warn Becky, tell her to get out quick. But listen, if yer hear anything about Mike, *anything*, let me know. OK? Thanks, sweetheart." She bent and kissed the top of the girl's head.

*

She ran as fast as she could. She was fitter than most but a lot of the way was uphill, so every so often, she had to slow to a walk. The second time she stopped. She was gulping for air, leaning back against a wall and panting heavily. Her chest hurt but she dare not lose any more time so she pressed on as best she could.

Becky *had* to be in. So she knocked again, harder this time and bent down to listen. A cough behind her made her jump but it was only a passer-by on the pavement and she turned back again. This time she bent down and pushed open the letter-box, shouting loudly before turning her head to listen. She rattled the door knob as hard as she could then banged on the front window, but still there was nothing.

And she *had* to reach Jack as well. She had to catch him and tell him so he could warn his sister. She half ran down to the telephone box in Cambridge Street but it was out of order. The line was dead. She swore, opened the door to leave and glanced about, this time fearful that somebody might be watching. There were still people about but the light was failing and, by now, the man who wanted to kill her was out there. It had become a race, a terrible, desperate race.

She knew that time was against her so she started running again, this time further down the hill for the telephone box in Rendle Street. It worked and she pushed the pennies in then waited with her finger on the button. Jack's number rang…and it rang until she knew there could be no reply.

Exhausted and despondent, she barely had the energy to replace the receiver before falling back against the inside of the telephone box. There was nothing she could do, nothing more at all other than go back to Victoria Street and wait for Becky. She shook her head in despair and wiped the tiredness from her eyes before half rolling out of the door. Not until it had swung shut behind her and she stood did she look up. And there he was.

Although he was some way off, the moment she saw him, she knew the Swede had spotted her. By now it was almost dark but it was the way he moved and how he started forward that alerted her. As soon as he began to move, she knew instinctively that he was coming for her. The hunter had found his quarry. Once more she began to run. This time she was desperate, running with her head thrown back and her arms pumping. She ran as fast as she could, sheer terror driving her on, but she knew he was gaining. He was a big, gangling man and she knew she could never outpace him.

She tore across Manor Road and into Adelaide Street, pausing briefly to throw off her coat so she could run faster. She had no idea where she was going but she could hear him behind her and it drove her on, even when she lost a shoe. Wild panic took hold and without even thinking she turned and crashed into the one doorway she knew. It was Number 27 and it was open. She fled up the stairs, onwards and upwards into the darkness, her lungs bursting as she pulled herself up on the iron stair rail.

She hammered frantically with the flat of her hand. But no, the door to Number 27B was locked. No matter how hard she tried it, the locks held. Then she remembered how Eddie was looking for new tenants. "Jesus Christ help me", she gasped rattling the door again in some last, desperate effort. As the door downstairs slammed shut, she spun round, panic stricken then turned back and tried again, for one last time.

The swish of his mac made her turn. Trapped and helpless, she flattened herself against the door. His face was the same cold, expressionless mask. Only a lank strand of fair hair on the top of his head flopped down as he came for her. She put up her arms to protect herself so she never saw the knife. Her scream was half muzzled by his hand before she choked, but it didn't matter for the apartment was empty.

He held her against the door with his thigh and sliced her throat again, deeper this time, cutting urgently into the flesh like a butcher filleting his meat. Then he stood back, satisfied, and moved his leg, allowing her to slide to the ground. But he had to jump suddenly to avoid the spout of blood from the wound as it sprayed over the concrete floor. To help her bleed, he held her head back with his foot until the flow eased and her body lay still. Then he bent down to examine the deep, crimson gash just to make sure. Only then did he smile.

✳

Jack changed as fast as he could then caught a taxi, stopping at the flower seller in Market Avenue. There was no sign of his sister so he left a note telling her he would be back in the morning, early before he went on shift when he knew he would catch her. But again there was nothing. He could see little from the window and nothing at all that he recognised as hers. The back door was locked as well. Puzzled, he decided to try the other address he had been given.

Leading Seaman Jack Carter knew the smell of blood: the creamy richness of it could never be forgotten. He smelt it first in the Dulverton slaughterhouse before the war. And he had smelt it again when they had had to go in and cut out the pieces of human remains from the twisted metal after the shells had torn into the side of his ship. He had seen most things in life by now so he used to tell himself, and perhaps he had, but when he saw the girl who had made him dance with delight just a short while ago it stopped him in his tracks. He could see she was dead but it was that same smell of blood, the smell of death, that hit him first.

Chapter Twenty One

Jack Carter rang his Dockyard Superintendent from the Central Police Station. He had been advised to make the call in order to explain his whereabouts and the reason for his absence.

Immediately after finding the body of Daisy Gunn, he had run into Union Street where he found two police constables who returned to the flat with him. Once the body had been secured he accompanied them back to the Central for questioning, and it was Dair McNally, the duty inspector, who sanctioned his call. Later, when McNally was satisfied that there was no case for him to answer, a second call was made, this time to Chief Superintendent Mason's operational headquarters in Stonehouse.

There, Inspector Chris Startin saw at once that this was the next piece to their jigsaw. Only last night they had been alerted by the Salvation Army hostel in Bakers Lane that a young woman and her child had sought refuge there after threats to her life. Her name was Becky Carter, the same name as had been given to them some time ago by a dockyard policeman claiming to be her brother. But it was not the family reunion that interested Startin, rather the link between her and the petty criminal Daley. Even now, one of his WPC's was down at the hostel taking her statement.

Furthermore, it was this same brother of hers who had now come across the body of one of Eddie Bright's bar girls. Startin smiled wryly. Detective Constable Brock had been right: Carter and his chums had indeed been down there poking around and getting in the way.

The secret in any jigsaw is that both curves and colours of each adjacent piece have to match perfectly. Startin was almost certain that the badly mangled and burned body of the Ford Pilot's driver was that of Daley but he had to make sure. All evidence to date had suggested that this was the case but it was the matching of the prints from the two complete fingers left on corpse that put it beyond doubt. Daley it was, and now the mother of his child had to be told.

*

The WPC began to stand as Startin came into the hostel dayroom. Becky turned in her chair but the inspector waved them both to remain seated. "How're you feeling?" he asked kindly.

"Not too bad," she murmured. Her smile, however, failed to hide the strain. Last night they had told her what they suspected but she had not yet received final confirmation. "It's still a shock though." Becky watched as he drew up a chair beside the WPC. "He's had more'n enough of his share of bad luck."

Startin nodded and smiled sympathetically. "Look, I'll come straight to the point." He lifted his chair a bit closer. "You've been very brave about it all...and a great help, too, but I'm afraid to say that we now know for certain the body we've been talking about is that of Mike Daley." He nodded slowly as they looked at each other. "They managed to take some fingerprints which matched perfectly with what we found in the apartment. They were all over the place...on his hairbrush and comb, on two pairs of his shoes and...on the little girl's cot." He watched her face as she sagged back in her chair. "It's him I'm afraid and we're looking no further.

"The blood grouping gave us a very good indicator," he went on. "But no more than that. Maudie's blood...'A' rhesus positive was a *possible* match of a combination of your 'O' positive and his, but that took us only so far." He paused, not wanting to rush her. "You see, as I said earlier, it only suggested rather than proving anything."

Becky nodded. "So there's no doubt at all then?"

"No...none at all." Startin shook his head. "Everything else fits...your identification of his watch and the shoe, plus what we've learned already. It's all there." He watched as she lowered her eyes. "I'm sorry," he said quietly. "No matter the circumstances, it's a cruel blow, I know." As WPC Farmer rose to comfort her, Startin quietly placed the keys of her apartment on the table.

"But listen, Becky...your brother, Jack. We mentioned him earlier. Remember?"

"Yes why?" She started suddenly. "He's not in all this is he?"

"Well, no...not exactly but he's here, in Plymouth, and I've sent a car for him. You haven't seen him for quite some time, I believe?" Startin didn't wait for her answer. "He's been looking everywhere for you."

"Jack? Yes, yes of course...oh, my goodness." Becky's hands were to her mouth. "Yes, Daisy told me. She told me she'd seen him and that he were asking for me. But no...I haven't seen him for ages." She shook her head, unable to recall the last occasion but then dropped her hands and beamed, suddenly cheerful once more. "Oh aye, Daisy'd said that he'd be along...get on well, they do. An' she thinks he's smashin'." Then she stopped. "But why's he with you lot?" she frowned. "That don't seem right."

Startin had been watching her closely. They knew that she and the Gunn woman had been close. All through the earlier questioning she had referred to her and it was obvious that a strong friendship had developed. One of the reasons he had asked McNally for her brother to be sent across was so that he, Carter, might be able to break the news of this other death. It might come easier from him. But now he had second thoughts. Better perhaps for her to hear right now rather than have the joy of her reunion ruined. The news, whenever it came, would shatter her, but her brother walking through the door would be the tonic she needed. She should know now.

"All right, I'll tell you." Startin glanced at WPC Farmer. "Your brother, Jack's done nothing at all wrong. Far from it…he's got himself a good job with security down here at the docks but a few weeks back he came in to see us about tracking you down. He knew that you and Daley were here somewhere, and it was through what he told us at the time that we were able to start putting a picture of Daley together. But he's been looking around for you himself as well, and I'm afraid that when he went back to your old apartment yesterday evening he came a cross a body.

"*What? A body?*"

"A friend of yours, I'm sorry to say…it was this Miss Gunn, Daisy Gunn." Becky clutched at her throat and blanched, then stared uncomprehending, first at Startin then at the policewoman.

"Oh, God help us," she murmured. "Dear God alive…Daisy…*Daisy*…." She looked at him incredulously. "*Dead?*" Startin nodded sagely. "*Killed….done in?*" He nodded again. "Who in God's name'd want to harm Daisy. She was luverly girl, a real true, luverly friend…reelly she was. And now she's gone." Becky still stared, looking at them helplessly.

✳

Inspector Startin's intuition had been right: the news broke the woman. Within minutes Becky had collapsed, weeping hysterically on the policewoman's shoulders. He got up quietly and left the room.

As soon as he got out of the car at Chief Superintendent Mason's headquarters, Jack ran up the steps. He had been told to ask for Inspector Startin but found himself in the Operations' Room before somebody directed him to the right office. His sister and her child, he was told, were safe and well but the news of the two deaths had shocked her badly. He should go straight to the Salvation Army hostel and ask for WPC Farmer who had been told to expect him. The police car had gone so he walked, rather he ran and walked as fast as he could.

✳

"But I came looking for you as soon as I could and you'd gone…..the place was locked, back and front." Jack and Becky were alone. The message from Inspector Startin was that they were free to go but they sat on in the dayroom together. Maudie was still with the day nurse. Becky simply nodded tiredly. The sofa on which they were sitting was soft and lumpy but she had clung to her brother with one arm around his neck. Eventually, long after WPC Farmer had gone, she calmed and they talked. "What made yer run like that, Becks?" he asked. "Summat must have made yer get out like that."

She nodded again. "One of the girls," she mumbled trying hard to hold back her tears. "Kelly Smale her's called." She pushed herself away, sat up and wiped her face. "One of the girls at the Blue Rose. Knew Mike, she did...said she an' him were good friends. Said they all liked 'im, she did. But then, other night when things went wrong, she an' the others heard that the bosses were coming fer us...after me an' Daisy, 'cos we knew too much." Jack nodded. "Said she had to come and tell me quick, like." He nodded again.

"Said they were goin' to stop us and that the Swedish fella were goin' to do it. Kelly said fer me to get out...to run quick, just like I was, she said. An' if I were to see Daisy, then to tell her as well. But I didn't, did I, eh?" She looked at her brother tearfully. "Didn't see her, Jack, an' they got to 'er first, didn't they?"

"The police know all this?" Becky nodded. For a moment she sat in silence with her head bowed, gulping back her tears. Jack put his hand on hers. "'Tis all right now, love...'tis all right. Good job yer went when yer did." And a damned good job it was, too, he told himself. He looked at his sister and saw, instead of Daisy Gunn, another figure lying on the concrete floor just like he found her, lying in her blood with her head forced back and her eyes staring emptily. It was her, Becky. His sister had become Daisy, just as it might so easily have been. "You did the right thing," he whispered. "No doubt about it, Becks. But you're safe enough now...safe from all o' that."

"But I can't stay 'ere." She stared at him helplessly. Her eyes were still wide with fear. "I couldn't, Jack...couldn't stay. Not me an' Maudie. Not now...not after all this."

"No...you're going home." His reply was immediate. He had been thinking of it himself and had not hesitated for a moment. "Back home, Becks...that's where."

"*Exford?*" she whispered. "*Mum an' Dad?*" She saw him nod. It was what she thought he said but she stared at him in disbelief. "Home?" It was said quietly, as if she really could not take it all in. "But they...they." She stopped, unable to describe how she imagined they would react. Their shock and their anger: she could see it on their faces and hear the cries of outrage coming from the kitchen. It had happened before but they had taken her in...and then she had run from them. She tried to envisage what they would do when they saw her on the doorstep again, this time with Maudie on her feet. And what it might be like back in Myrtle Cottage with all of them together once more. "I couldn't, Jack...*couldn't*. They'd...." Again words failed her and she shook her head.

"Oh aye, home it is, yer know," he said quietly. "Home an' no mistake. We'll go...together. I'll tell 'em...tell 'em you're safe an' well...both you an' Maudie. I'll telegram them d'rectly. Police may have bin round already, mind. Then I'll write...tell 'em things are fine but they've changed, an' that you're coming home again."

Becky's head fell against his shoulder. "Home," she muttered, the thought of it still beyond her.

"Aye…c'mon now." He sat her up and pulled himself off the sofa. " 'Tis the best place of all an' you'll be long gone from all o' this. Think of it, Becks…think of it back there, up at Exford. Think of all yer friends…Pat an' Mavis an' they. I'll tell them…let 'em know an' they'll be fine, you'll see."

2.

Sam parked the car in the small lay-by just beyond the front gates and walked up the long, steep drive. He never really knew what made him do it this way, it just seemed a better way to approach her. There was something less assertive about walking in like this, rather than sweeping up to the front door in a car, especially when he had to break such news.

He was glad he did so because he saw her before she saw him. She was making use of the sudden fine spell and was in the garden, doing something with the rose bed on the terrace, it seemed. It gave him a final few moments to think, so he paused behind the scarlet azalea, well hidden from both her and the house.

He was quite clear in his mind about his decision, in fact he was surprised at how calm and detached he had become about it. It was nothing she had ever said or done, rather it was the other way round in that he had had his doubts for some time. There were a number of reasons but basically it was her friends who had demonstrated that she and they hailed from a completely different world to his. In those early, heady days it made little difference and he thought he would be able to live with it. But, after a while, the constant snipes and jibes began to hurt, then the brutal, head-on confrontations convinced him it would never work. What was more, she had been pulled both ways by it all; he had seen it, and saw how it upset her. At first it used to upset him too, and it got him down, once badly. Perhaps he had been imagining some kind of life for them both where these sort of things didn't matter. But they did: they always had and they always would. They mattered to everybody and it would ever be thus.

But she had not seen it or, if she had, she had not allowed it to get in the way and her heart had simply run away with her. He could sense it, as clear as day. There had been too many indications: how she always took his arm and smoothed his hair. How, whenever she saw him, she would always run up and make a fuss of him, and how she was always chatting and prattling away so excitedly about this and that. It was all there and it had become unsettling, embarrassing almost. If it had somehow been able to continue quietly, as it had begun, then all well and good but it hadn't. She, Rose Hatton, was in love with him. He was trapped and it was getting worse. He had to tell her now that it wouldn't work, that it couldn't, possibly, ever work.

She was a lovely, lovely person who he would always admire and there were memories he would cherish forever. But he had to put an end to it before it was too late. Only a few days ago she had asked him what he was going to do with himself and he had shrugged it off. He felt fine about the future and had not been worrying about any such thing. It had simply not crossed his mind. Life had been difficult, for sure, and there had been those hard, black moments but they were behind him. It was how she might react, and what she might do with herself that worried him. Sam took a deep breath. He had still not worked out what he was going to say but he couldn't hang around any longer.

It was not until he was half way across the lawn that she saw him and when she did, she made clear her delight as usual. "Well, well, well...what a *lovely* surprise. Where's the car? You haven't walked, have you?" she joked.

"No, thought I'd surprise yer, that's all." He could see how pleased she was. "Left it in the road and crept up on yer...all the way from Exford." It was difficult to banter like this.

"And boo to you, too." She reached up and kissed him lightly. "There...now, tea or something a little stronger?" She glanced at her watch. "It's early enough but so what?" she chortled. He watched as she took off her gardening gloves. "What's it to be?" she asked.

"I'm fine. Reelly...I can't stop long but, seeing as I were passing, thought I'd just look in."

"Yes, all right...well, that still means a drink or something, doesn't it?" She cocked her head on one side. "So why not? And why're you looking so serious...you're all right aren't you? We're not the gloomy, down trodden purveyor of dismal news about something are we?"

"No, no...nort like that." He paused but she was too quick.

"Well, what is it? Something's up...I can see it. Is that why you've come over?" He knew he could delay no longer. No matter how much he might try to put it off, she would see through him. She had already: he could see it in her face.

"It's us, Rose." The words had been on his mind but they tumbled out before he could think of anything better. "I thought it'd be best fer us to talk."

"Go...on." Her words came slowly but her eyes were steady enough. "What d'you mean, us?" Her little laugh was uncertain. He knew she would ask him that but he had no idea how to reply.

"Well...you an' me, Rose...us keepin' on like this, as we are...I mean...." Her sudden, quick glances from eye to eye told him that she knew.

"What d'you mean...what're you trying to say, Sam?" She raised a hand as though to take hold of him but let it fall. Then her eyes dropped away from his. He wanted to go on but he couldn't; he just had to wait and hear her out.

"D'you mean…are you thinking…oh, yes you are, aren't you?" Still looking away she reached for his hand. "I think…look, come and sit, over here by the terrace." They walked together in silence then sat. He put his hand down and gripped the edge of the garden seat in the gap she had left between them. "Why is this…and right out of the blue?" As her eyes searched his for an answer, her head was moving slowly from side to side as though she couldn't believe what she was hearing. "But tell me." She cleared her throat. "Is there somebody else? Has somebody…has she come back to you?" Rose's eyebrows lifted expectantly.

"No." He looked down and shook his head. "No, there's nobody else," he whispered. For a moment she, Becky, was there, looking at him like she did in the trap that day when he asked her to come back. She was looking at him just as he remembered but then she faded. "Nobody at all."

"Promise?" Her eyes told him she was hurt. Suddenly she looked tiny and forlorn, and vulnerable. Her pale brown slacks with the belt and her open, checked shirt gave her a boyish look and she was looking at him, pleading with him like a child that had been hurt and who couldn't understand why.

"Yes," he nodded, clearing his throat. "Yes…there's nobody else, I promise."

"Then why, Sam?" She shrugged as if to emphasise the strength of her question. "We're doing no wrong…we're two free people who enjoy…who love one another. Well, don't we?" As she asked him again, she took his hand. "So what's so wrong about it that you've to come all the way over like this?" He looked down at his feet then up and beyond the garden, screwing his eyes as if staring into the far distance. He knew she was watching him, waiting for his answer. "*Well?*" He swallowed then moistened his mouth, now nervous and confused. Once again, he found it too difficult to explain.

"'Tis the way we are, Rose." He was looking directly at her. "We're *so* different…such different people. I've told yer time an' again that it'd never work out…not if us were to go on. You know that. Said so yerself, several times but then said it don't matter." He paused. "But it *do* yer know." His voice had fallen. "You an' I know that it'd never work." She had turned away from him. He could see she was hurt again but he could tell also, by her silence, that she knew it to be true. "'Tis best this way," he whispered. "Better all round." As his arm went round her shoulder, she leaned against him. Then slowly, as his fingers caressed her, she nodded.

"Oh, Sam." She sighed heavily then sighed again. "In a way you're right. But there're other ways, too, you know." Her head was resting on his chest. "And you've done so much for me…you were so good to me, when daddy died. You meant so much." She moved herself closer. "You were you know, and we've had such fun. I thought it might…I thought it *could* work, but it would have to have been the two of us, wouldn't it? And if…well," she shrugged. "If there's not two, then it never will, will it?"

"No...that's right. So I... I just thought it best to leave things as they be." Even though she was looking down, he could see the pain in her face. "Wouldn't be fair, would it?" She was silent. There was little to say because they both knew he was right.

Then suddenly she sat up, smiling bravely again through her tears. She wiped her eyes then gave a little laugh at herself. "Yes...I know, I know...and we've tried haven't we." She paused, looking at the button undone on his shirt before reaching out with both hands to do it up. "But listen...we can still be...we can still see each other, can't we. Oh dear," she finished fiddling and patted the button, then looked down again. "It sounds pathetic, doesn't it...like a couple of little teenagers...but we can can't we? Nothing like that need change, need it? Mmm?"

"No." His silly, mournful look as he shook his head made them both smile. "No need fer any of that...least ways, I hope not."

"No, please don't let it. I couldn't bear it. Let's just...let's just sort of stay as we are...*please.*" He had got to his feet but she held on to his arm. "Please, Sam." He nodded then reached down and pulled her up. She rose quickly, not looking at him but putting her arms around him. They stood together, swaying gently, rocking slowly from side to side until she broke away. "Go," she sobbed. "Just go...I'll be fine. Really I will." It was little more than a whisper but he knew by the way she was shaking that she was weeping.

Slowly, so she would not feel he was hurrying, he eased himself back. She turned for the door, not daring to look round and moved away until only their fingers were touching. He let her go, dropping his hand as she did hers. Then he watched. She walked slowly, still did not looking back but continued on and into the house with both hands up to her face.

3.

A young boy, barely into his teens and wearing a black waistcoat and cloth cap, held two enormous farm horses. Several hunt horses were there also. It was a usual group that gathered outside the forge most days but, for Becky, the sight brought memories flooding back. Maudie noticed them, too, even before the car stopped. She scrambled to her feet in her mother's lap, turned and pointed, her hand brushing Becky's face. Her mother flinched and caught hold of her hurriedly but it made no odds. Maudie considered what she had seen was important and that everybody should know about it. She continued to point, demanding their attention but they let her chatter on excitedly.

Becky looked out from under her scarf. She barely moved but her eyes were taking it all in, watching carefully least anybody she knew might recognise her. Her brother had parked next to the green and she could actually see Myrtle Cottage. She said nothing, just glanced around suspiciously. They had planned to go in together but she didn't move, preferring the security of the car.

"Right then?" Jack looked across at her. "Want me to take her ladyship?"

Becky remained still. "I'm feared, Jack. Whatever d'you think they're goin' to say?" It was a question she had asked him a hundred times. She was afraid of the expressions she would see on their faces, or how they might react. Yet, at the same time, she felt a strange cosiness about the homecoming. Exford really did look like the home she remembered. She looked round half in fear, half out of curiosity but it was all too much and still she could not bring herself to move. "Don't know what to do."

"I'll go then." He patted her knee. "You stop here an' I'll take Maudie. Father'll love her, you wait…an' mother as well." He reached for the driver's door.

"No wait." She grabbed his arm but then stopped. Her nerve had failed yet again. "No…don't matter. You go on then, I'll stop 'ere."

She watched as he walked slowly, bending down every now and then to tell Maudie what it was she kept pointing at. Once, when she stopped for a conversation with a little black cat, he paused and squatted beside her. The two of them had got to know each other well during the week she remained in the hostel. Jack had had to attend the coroner's court but it had been adjourned and he had been given a week's leave. He took to the little girl as if she were his own, and she to him. As they reached the front door, Becky leaned forward to see better. Somebody must have opened it for they went in, her brother helping his niece up and over the problem of the front steps.

As soon as Jack and her father came out, she knew it was all right. She never realised how much taller her brother was and he was striding out, making her father hurry along beside him. But they were laughing about something and when Jack pointed to the car her father nodded eagerly. Maudie was not with them, though. Her mother must have kept her inside with her and she tried to imagine the scene.

But there was no time. They had reached the car already and she could hear hem talking. Then the door opened and her father looked in. He was bending own with both hands reaching out. Becky swung her legs, then pulled herself ut and stood. For a moment they looked at one another, then her father opened his arms.

✳

Jack stayed for three days. It was the first time all four of them had been together for years. Perhaps it was that which had made it all so much easier than any of them had expected. But then Maudie became the centre of attention and it was not long before she had taken over the cottage. So perhaps they all found it easier to communicate with each other through her. If that was the case then she loved it, and used it shamelessly to her own advantage.

They said little about what had happened. Becky suspected that her father and brother talked about it when they were together. Maudie's father was not mentioned at all, it was as though he had never existed. And it wasn't as though Exford did not know about Maudie already. Whatever had been said about the manner of her arrival had been said a long time ago. The little girl, with her long dark curls and dark brown eyes, was accepted as though she had been born there.

Jack had no idea when he would be back. They were all sad when he bade farewell but Maudie clung to him making it difficult for him to get into his car. It would be as soon as he could, he promised, and they would be together again. But it was her grandfather who won the little girl's heart. As soon as he pulled up at the door with the pony and trap she would be there, standing by the front gate and holding out her arms impatiently to be lifted up.

Becky went with them, sometimes sitting beside her father with her arm through his. On other occasions she would drive while her father took Maudie on to his lap. Sheep became important to her: sheep with their lambs and the swallows who dived and wheeled above the cart or skimmed across the village green. Maudie would point them out to her grandfather, turning to explain what she had seen before turning back again. But by then they had gone; a matter that would puzzle her momentarily before something else took her attention.

Once Becky drove past Edgecott alone. It was strange, almost ghostly, to see the house and the stables, now quiet but which once had been the centre of so much. On her way back she slowed the pony to a walk, giving herself time to remember the sights and sounds that had attracted her. The open space where the lorries were parked was still empty. The beech tree by the gate, where the sentries stood and where she and the other girls used to meet, was just coming into leaf. She was sure she could hear their laughter and their loud shouts, and the sound of their boots on the gravel; always the constant noise of talking and laughter, of doors slamming and engines starting up.

And there was one today also; there, right now. But it was a car coming out of the garage by the house and she flicked at the pony's reins.

4.

"There you are then." Doris Carter did up the last of the buttons on Maudie's coat and stood, using the edge of the kitchen table to pull herself up. "There look…proper little maid." Maudie looked up in disgust, first at her then at her mother before snatching off her woollen bobble-hat and throwing it down. "Oh, *dear*…that's not very nice."

"Don't worry, mother. Leave it…I'll put it on if 'tis breezy up there but not to worry fer now." Becky bent to retrieve it. "Dad'll be here soon…leave her be or her'll only get frazzled." After checking the wicker basket her mother had prepared, she adjusted her headscarf in the mirror. *"Oh, scissors,"* she cried, suddenly remembering. "Daresay there'll be some flowers about."

Doris watched the preparations, now a mite wary of frustrating her grandaughter any more but it was Ernest's shout that settled the matter and she took Maudie's hand. The trap had arrived and, as far as the little girl was concerned, nothing else mattered.

✳

The long, winding track up to Larkbarrow from the road rose sharply before levelling out and it was only from that first crest that the countryside opened out. To see the old farmhouse meant going a little further on, up even higher to the next crest. But Becky was in no hurry. It was warm, very warm for late April, so she took off her scarf and tossed her hair free, smoothing it back and lifting her face to the breeze.

Above her the larks were singing, some so high she could not even see them. Almost every few yards more rose up from the sedge to flutter away gracefully before alighting further on, or else climbing high to join the choir. And it was then that the chorus would begin. Everyone, it seemed, was singing to each other, filling the air with their own joyful music. With them were the curlews, her favourites. Only then, when she heard them again, did Becky realise how much she had missed the haunting, bubbling cry of these beautiful birds. And then there was the flash of golden plovers and the mewing of the wheeling and plunging lapwings, and the little wheatears bobbing by the side of the track in their smart pink coats and white rumps. Everybody was there and Becky stood, looking skywards with one hand shielding her eyes, turning this way and that as she listened. It was as if they had all come to serenade her, to welcome her home, surprised and delighted at seeing her again.

hen, at the next crest, she pulled up. There, in the distance, half hidden by the ng of beeches that were now in their apple-green first leaf, was Larkbarrow. 1e dropped the reins, allowing the pony to pick at the grass, and stared. It was ill there, all of it, but it looked forlorn and unloved. And there, beyond the rm, was where their cottage used to be. But it had gone, or most of it had. One all was still standing, as far as she could see, but not much else. Curious at hat had taken place yet saddened, she drove on.

)nly some of the trees were left. She thought she had seen more earlier, but nany were broken, torn apart as if some mad giant had ripped off the branches. Those that were left were trying bravely to come into leaf as was the blackthorn with its smudge of white flowers in the hedge by the barn. She could see where their lorries had parked when they came to take down the fences. Somebody had built a fire, somebody else had dug a large round hole, scattering the spoil about the place. But there were several of these, too many for that, and she realised with a shock that these were where the shells had exploded. They had told her what had happened up here and now she could

293

see it. Larkbarrow and her home had been beaten savagely and the cruel blows had hurt, some terribly.

She tied the pony near the spot where they used to pen sheep, then lifted Maudie down and began to walk. She walked slowly, looking about warily and stopping frequently to ponder. The poor, dear house had been smashed and broken leaving the windows and doors to gape back at her, open and empty. Half the roof had gone also, and one of the chimneys. She walked up through the yard. Most of the shippons were damaged badly as were the stables where the Colonel used to keep his hunters. It was so sad, such a mad, brutal waste and now they had gone on their way, all of them, leaving their waste and destruction behind.

She stole along carefully, stepping over the rubble and keeping tight hold of Maudie's hand. She peered into the stables, pulling open one of the broken doors and starting back as a nesting swallow flashed out past her head. The smell of old, musty hay was still there. Then she scrambled awkwardly over a pile of rubble to peep into the kitchen where she saw the old sink and plate rack still in place. It was a terrible, mournful sight but it was only the house and the buildings and a few of the trees that had been destroyed. Outside, in the spring sunshine, nature was living again.

She hurried through to the garden and went straight to her roses. They were there, all of them, and she clapped her hands in delight. The swelling buds and young, purple shoots were making their way up from the old stems that had lasted so long on their own. All around her, in the hedgerows, she could see the flowers she used to pick. The primroses and the purple orchids were still there along with the tiny violets and the taller, delicate bluebells. Somewhere there would have been great spreads of daffodils as well but they were over by now. Looking over the hedge into the orchard she saw the apple blossom and, on the banks, the first of the red campion.

Slowly, as if to savour the moment, she turned back to face the sun and close her eyes, breathing deeply. Up above them she could hear the birds. But th swallows were there also, lots of them, all the way back from so far away. Li' her, the little birds had returned as well. On top of the thorn bushes and t fruit trees, and high up in the beeches, the yellow hammers and chaffinche and the tiny warblers were singing away. They had all come back. Man ha gone, thank goodness, but nature had returned.

Maudie watched as her mother showed her how to pick primroses then busie herself, squatting low to see better and grunting with effort. It was only after she had reached the flowerbed under the front window that Becky saw the collie The dog was hot; she could see it had been working but it was a friendly dog and came up to introduce itself, licking Becky's hand hurriedly before dashing off from whence it came. Alert to the presence of another, she waited quietly, listening and watching, for she knew the shepherd must be there somewhere.

※

By the time Sam had ridden out of the valley below Larkbarrow, Becky had long since left the pony and trap, yet he saw it at once. It puzzled him for it was not the sort of carriage he would expect to see so far from the road. A horse and cart perhaps, but not a light trap like that right out here at Larkbarrow where he and his father had taken the grazing.

Becky saw him as he came around the corner of the old stables and knew, at once, who he was. He was riding slowly, stopping every so often to check before kicking on again. She stood very still and thought he might have missed her. But he stopped again and looked her way. He stared, slowly lifting his cap to wipe his brow, then turned his horse. Maudie had seen him and stood pointing, frowning at this strange new sight.

Becky hurried to her least the dogs should frighten her, then stood and watched as he rode through the gap where the garden gate once was. She could feel her heart beating faster. That and the nervous apprehension that had taken hold of her, made her breath come more quickly and her mouth dry. Sam, for his part, sat still as a stone not ten paces from her. Then, without saying anything, he dismounted, threw the reins over his horse's head and walked up to her.

"Becky." His eyes were searching her face. "'Tis true, then. You're home."

"Hullo, Sam." She moistened her lips. "Yes, bin a week or so now." She smiled, but only fleetingly, not knowing how he might take what she said. Perhaps he might have expected her to have called him at home.

"That's good then. Daresay you've come up 'ere fer old times' sake?" He paused, choosing his words. "Terrible isn't it…all the mess an' that." He felt he should have said something more but he hesitated, wondering what she might say next.

"Yes, but there're the flowers, look." She held out the primroses. "They're all back now. An' Maudie an' me…oh sorry, Sam. This is Maudie, look." She pulled the little girl forward but the toddler shrank back, catching hold of her mother's skirts to hide from the sudden attention. "I've…we've come up to see what's that." She shrugged expansively. She, too, was lost for words but she wanted show that there was no other reason for her intrusion. She glanced away shyly, then back at him. But then, seeing he was looking at her affectionately, she averted her gaze once more, this time confused and suddenly self-conscious.

"Back fer good then?" She nodded, still looking away but glanced up sharply as he drew closer. "I'm glad you're back, Becks." His voice was soft, more or less as she remembered it. "It's bin a long time, hasn't it." She nodded, fiddling with the posy in her hand. "I've missed yer, y'know. Bin thinkin' of yer ever since I heard you was back."

Now she stared at him. She was frowning slightly as if she had misunderstood.

295

"*Missed* me, Sam? An' bin *thinking* of me? *Cuh*...I dunno. Don't deserve nuthin like that. Not after what's gone on." She was searching his face, anxious to hear more and anxious to see how he felt about what she had just said.

"What's done's done, maid...can't do nort about that." He smiled dismissively and shrugged. "Can yer now? Eh?" He watched as she turned away, shaking her head. "'Twould never do fer all of us to keep worryin' about the past, would it now?"

"*Hmm.*" It was Becky's turn to shrug. "When yer past's like mine...when you've thrown yerself away an' made a right damn mess of yerself, like I have. When yer've come home on bended knee then turned round an' run off again...then yer needs to worry."

"Ah, phooey." He reached out and took her hand. It was to reassure her, no more than that, but she flinched nonetheless. "Don't be like that, Becks. What's done's over an' done with." He still had hold of her hand and held on to it until he could feel her relaxing. "All of us make damned fools of ourselves...I do...all of us do. Here...come on." He took her gently by the shoulder and turned her towards him. "Don't be getting like that, maid," he whispered. There's no need...honest."

She pulled a face, a long, sad face, then looked at him appealingly. "D'you think people'll ever forget...forget all that I did...Maudie an' that." They both looked down at the child who glanced up enquiringly at hearing her name. "Runnin' off an' that? D'you think they will, Sam?" She sighed heavily. "Bain't easy, y'know." Her voice sounded plaintive.

"*I* have, Becks." Sam pulled her gently towards him. " I've forgotten all of it and I'm glad you're back," he said quietly. "Ever so glad."

"Yes," she whispered. "So am I."

THE END

296